The Delving

OVERTHROWN – THE CHRONICLES OF DENORIL

AARON BUNCE

AUTUMN ARCH PUBLISHING
Iowa
www.AutumnArchPublishing.com

PUBLISHER'S NOTE

This is a work of fiction. All names, places, characters, and incidences are either the product of the author's imagination, or are used fictitiously, and any resemblance to actual people, alive or dead, events or locations, is completely coincidental.

A product of AUTUMN ARCH PUBLISHING
Cover design: Christian Bentulan
Interior design: Aaron Bunce
Map Design: Francesca Baerald
Proofed by: Yvonne Bunce

TRADE PAPERBACK ISBN: 978-0-9992026-9-2
Amazon Kindle: B07MCW3X35

1st Edition 2019

-The Overthrown Series-

Volume 1

The Winter of Swords (Available Now)

Volume 2

Before the Crow (Available Now)

Volume 3

A March of Woe (Available Now)

Volume 4

The Prince of Orphans (Coming Soon)

Volume 5

Blade of Ashes (Coming Soon)

Volume 6

A Song of Bones (Coming Soon)

-Overthrown - The Chronicles of Denoril-

(An all-new supplementary series)

The Delving (Out Now!)

Acknowledgments

I want to take a moment to consider my awesome group of Beta readers. You guys and gals helped make this book into what it is today. Thank you for your dedication and honesty! Behind every author is a fantastic and equally talented group of developmental readers, and mine are:

Adrienne Gilmere, Dennis Green, Kara Nordberg, Leah Gough, Lyric Kali, Sara Vogt, Sarah Ockershausen Delp, Colton Peyton, and Seth Douglas.

For Gary B and Gary S – your examples have helped me become the man and father I am today.

DENORIL
Black Moors
Ban Turin
King's Fall
Laniel
Sunset Brine
Tidesburg
Barden's Pass
Nordson Bay
Dagger's Point
Trader's Way
Long Boat Bay
Lakeside
Bardstown
Red Fish R.
Queen's Rise R.
Bargeron
Broken Tooth R.
Bear Claw R.
Ogre Springs
New Dilith
Burned Sand Bay
The Crystal Waters
Freedom's Point
Dagger Coast
N
W
E
S

By Decree
No Delving

Delving is hereby declared a heinous crime, deserving of judgment and punishment, to include enslavement, the lash, and a hot brand upon one's flesh. If any man or woman, high born or low, be caught entering sealed crypts or burial chambers, with the intent of plunder, theft, desecration, or dark magical crafts, they will be punished immediately, and severely. That punishment shall extend to the end of their days.

Professed on this day, the first moon of Autumn, in the first Thaw of the Council's rule.

The voice of the Council, Gladeus DuChamp

Chapter One

For a Family

...Tenth winter thaw of the Council's rule, pre-harvest.

THORBEN PAULSON scanned the wall of wooden racks, using the candle's gentle glow to pierce the deep shadows. He lifted a bag of grain, only to find a dead mouse underneath. He cursed, and swept the dead vermin onto the ground, before carefully pulling the sack free.

"Idle mouths and empty bellies," he groused, looking around the dark room. Boot prints covered the dirt floor, tracing the circuitous route the Earl's men had woven to empty the small space.

"Thieves! And they spit on me for not having the coin to fill the Earl's coffers. They fill their bellies with our food...grown in our land...and tended by our hand. Ah, I hope they choke on a turnip," Thorben yelled as he pulled himself free of the root cellar. He stomped his boot and slammed the rickety doors behind him.

He stuffed the swollen pin back into the latch and gave the doors an exploratory tug, confirming they were locked before dropping to a knee. He gathered up his findings – a handful of brown potatoes, dried garlic, greens, and onions, but they were all well past their season.

His wife was a wizard in the kitchen. She had regularly filled their bellies when times were lean, concocting savory meals out of odds and ends mixed with meat scraps, but this was well beyond anything she'd had to work with before.

Thorben's anger turned cold, twisting at his heart as he looked down at the armful of pathetic food. Somehow, he needed to keep his family fed – six boys and a growing girl, whose appetite rivaled every man in the house. But how would he do it? The woods around the house provided no immediate reply. Not that he expected one. *He* had to do something, or the people he loved would starve.

Tromping around the house, Thorben threw his body up against the wall as a girl appeared suddenly, her head down and in a full sprint.

"Gracious, girl!" he yelled, but she laughed breathlessly and bounded into the tree line.

He made it around the house, his youngest son, Kenrick, almost bowling him over, too.

"Father!" Kenrick yelled, his five older brothers stacking up behind him and almost knocking him to the ground. "Where did she go?"

"And why..." Thorben started to ask, but his question devolved into a barely-suppressed chuckle. The six young men were a mess, but more than usual. A clump of mud broke loose from Kenrick's shirt and landed with a *plop* on the ground. He looked between each of his sons, taking note of their dirty faces and soiled clothes.

"You boys are right filthy! Wait until your ma sees you. She'll have at your rears with that wooden spoon of hers," he said.

"Not our fault, Pa! She crawled up into a tree overlooking the fishing hole and threw dirt clods at us while we was swimming. Then, we get out of the water to tell her to stop and find she put worms in our boots. If you ain't gonna punish her, then we're gonna pound the stuffing out of her, Pa!"

Thorben coughed to hide his mirth, and after a moment of contemplation, said, "She went that way, boys," and pointed in the vague direction of the outhouse. She actually ran south, towards the town square, but he wouldn't tell them that. "And don't hurt her. She's smaller than all of you!" he hollered at the boy's retreating backs.

The rich smell of baking sweet rolls drifted past him as he approached the kitchen. The top half of the door was pinned open, while the bottom remained latched. Thorben stopped short and leaned into the doorway, resting his weight on the lower door.

Dennica finished kneading some bread dough, slapped it with some flour, gave it a twist, and slid it into their open, clay oven. Then she used the flat spatula to pull a hot loaf out and drop it on the wide cutting table.

"Nothing smells like your bread, love," he said, hanging his head further into the room.

Dennica jumped, her hand jumping to her breast. "Curse you, husband. You startled a ghost out of me," she cried.

"Sorry. I just love watching you work. It's truly magic of the most delicious nature," he said, unlatching the door and stepping inside. He walked over and unloaded the armful of food onto the table, where it came to rest next to the steaming loaf of bread.

"Is that it?" she started to ask, her gaze lifting to his. His face felt tight, matching the despair swirling inside of him. He tried to smile, to show her that it would be all right, even if he didn't believe it himself. He could tell immediately that she didn't buy it.

"They cleaned it out," Thorben said, flatly.

"All of it?"

"Mostly," he said, pulling the vegetables into a tighter pile.

"Damn, blithering, tongue-biters," Dennica growled, her flour-covered hands balling up into fists.

"At least we have your bread. That fills bellies as good as anything else!" he said, trying to lighten the conversation. "And we can sell a loaf here and there for some extra coin."

Dennica started shaking her head before he finished speaking. "What am I to bake with? I have enough flour to make bread this day, but you know how the boys eat. We should have just given them the coin and hoped they left our cellar be."

"Shhh," he hissed, jamming a finger to his lips and turning to look out the open door. "We told the Earl's men that we hadn't any coin. That is why they took our food. If they find out that we stashed it away, they'll lock us up in a hole in the ground, and our children will never see us again. If we'd given them that coin, they would have just taken our food anyway."

"But what are we to eat? Yes, harvest is coming, but our garden and field stake is small. That won't fill our cellar. You've got six hungry boys to feed, Thorben. And Dennah eats almost as much as the lot of them combined. How many cold days do you think we'll manage through before they're eating each other?"

"I could use the saved coin to buy smoked sausages, salted pork, and dried garlic. That would help us get by–"

"And then what do we buy our seed for next season with? If we don't have grain seed, we don't have wheat and a field share to take to the mill to grind, and then we have no bread. We talked about this, husband. Mayhaps our garden flourishes, and if Mani is shining her blessings down, the south field doesn't flood next year and we can finally grow a proper crop of our own...have food goods to sell at market beyond what we need. If we can, we might be able to dig ourselves out of this hole."

Thorben reached up and rubbed his weary eyes. He tired of the struggle, the fight just to safeguard his family another season of meals.

"I thought the Council was to make things easier...not harder. Their tax is no better than that damned mad fool, Algast king, Djaron."

"Shhh. Don't spit that name in this house, husband!" Dennica snapped.

"I'm sorry, love. The drearies have me bad now. We've been all throughout these parts, at least the parts safe enough for folk to travel in, and what did we find – some mushrooms, a few rabbits, and some wild rhubarb? Folks've foraged these parts clean. Can't earn a wage mending fences or roofs, as most folk don't have the coin to spare. We're in a bad way, and I can't think of a–"

Dennica came forward suddenly and pulled him into a hug, cutting off his despair.

"We'll make due, like we always do. You just can't see that yet," she said, quietly, squeezing him with a strength born from a life of hard labor. She pushed him out to arm's length after a moment. "Why don't you take your pipe, have a nice little smoke, and take a quiet walk. The best ideas always come when you're not looking for them."

A loud commotion sounded outside, and the bottom half of the kitchen door flung open with a *bang.* A girl darted into the kitchen, a crowd of red-faced and cursing boys at her heels.

"Wow, and what is this?" Dennica yelled, as Dennah leapt behind her, hiding under her apron.

The six brothers all tried talking as one, shaking their fists and pointing to the crusty splotches of mud dried to their clothes. Thorben turned on his sons, his patience exhausted.

"Enough!" he bellowed, stomping his foot and silencing them.

"But, father!" Reginald, the second youngest complained. "She–"

"No!" Thorben interrupted, and then pointed at the door and yelled, "Out!"

The group of boys grumbled but filed back out of the kitchen.

"You best avoid them for a time, girl," Thorben said, addressing the little girl hiding under wife's apron. Dennah appeared from her hiding spot, looking quickly from the door to his face. She flashed him a mischievous smile, jumped up to kiss her mother's cheek, and took off at a run, disappearing out into the sunshine.

"That girl..." Dennica said, shaking her head.

"I'm not sure her brothers are made of strong enough stuff to handle her."

"Her brothers?" Dennica laughed, "The darkest wilds of Denoril don't stand a chance!" They laughed together for a few moments, the levity a welcomed change, but then the weight of their circumstances floated back in, hanging over them like a dark cloud.

"I'll take that walk. I have some thinking to do. Thank you," Thorben said, leaning over and kissing Dennica on the cheek. Their eyes met, her strength and resolve shining through. Thorben managed a weak smile and walked out of the kitchen, leaving his wife to make sense of their soon-to-be empty bellies.

Chapter Two

Surety

Once outside, Thorben knocked his pipe clean against the side of the house, stuffed it with fresh leaf, and stopped at a lantern hanging from the edge of the roadway to light it. He puffed on the pipe and walked, letting the sweet smoke drift lazily over his face, intermittently thinking and letting his mind go blank.

He skipped around some road apples and turned, tracking the sound of a girl laughing. Dennah jumped and ran in a field to his left, scattering and chasing a swarm of brightly colored butterflies. Thorben watched her play for a few moments, marveling at her energy and fearless nature.

He'd silently cursed the notion of having a daughter those seasons back, wondering how a lone girl would fare growing up in a household of rowdy boys. It didn't take Dennah long to prove his concerns false. She was fierce.

Thorben's thoughts inevitably slid back to their empty cellar and he started to worry anew. He took a long drag on the pipe, and methodically started working through the problem. It always boiled down to coin, as there was no food shortage, only the ability to buy it. Boats floated in from Pinehall and Freedom's Point regularly, carrying salted thrasher fish and smoked crab. But those merchants listened only to the song of jingling gold and silver. They wouldn't parlay or trade, and they surely weren't plied with sob stories or the promise of repayment.

His meanderings took him down the road, the brisk, fall wind whistling gently through the canopy overhead. Occasionally a leaf would drift down from above, so he would stop and watch its lonely journey all the way to the ground.

Of course, there were always jobs available to men and women of select trades and skills, if they knew who to ask or where to look. Thorben took another drag on the pipe and tried to shake away the thought. He'd lived a very different life when he was a younger man – been a different person, done things that clashed with his ideals now. That life paid handsomely, but could just as easily reward a man with death, or worse, a life sentence spent breaking rocks in the Council's mine.

Thorben considered something he'd heard around the common hall fire a few moons before, about a wealthy merchant in town providing loans of gold and silver coin to folks hard up for food. Word was he was asking interest paid along with coin in repayment.

If it could get a person by for a time, a handful of copper might be well spent to keep a man's family from starving, the old grey-haired man had said, telling Thorben as much as rationalizing his own dilemma out loud. He'd stubbornly argued the point, based squarely off his own closely-guarded principles. But who was he to tell someone they had to suffer through the pangs of an empty stomach, when he would turn around and do the same, or more, to keep his own children from suffering a similar fate?

The idea of borrowing coin from a stranger sounded as odd a concept as a fish walking across the road or a bird swimming through the water. And yet, if it kept his family fed until his fortunes changed, how could he consider that a bad thing? The seasons changed whether he wanted them to or not, but each brought new risks and opportunities. Perhaps that was the key, biding time until new chances could arise.

Thorben picked up his pace and turned left at the next road, making his way across one of the many rope and timber footbridges. Frogs and other animals chittered and croaked beneath him as he crossed the small gorge, calling out to him from the brown-tinged reeds.

The idea felt less strange with every step forward. He would secure his family's immediate future, and not have to watch his children lick their fingers hungrily, or scrape at empty bowls. He would see their bellies full and eyes bright, no matter the sacrifice. It was a risk, yes, but it would see him forward just long enough to search out the next prospect. It was time Dennica didn't have to scrape meals together out of old vegetables and weevil-infested grain. Yes. He just needed more time.

The next bridge brought him into Yarborough, the large town so embedded in the borough's thick forests that many travelers wandered into its midst without even realizing it.

A mule cart rumbled by, the wagon filled with the body of an enormous beast. A mass of legs hung over the side rails, the beast's hooves twice the size of his fists. Thorben couldn't see the creature's head, although he could see its blood-red fur, and mane-like frill of branching antlers. A single, thick arrow shaft stuck out of the beast's side, the striped fletching as long as half his arm.

"A successful hunt, it appears!" Thorben said to the older man perched on the wagon seat.

The man pulled his straw hat off, scratched his head, and chuckled, but there was no mirth to the sound.

"Damn buck appeared in the night. Knocked down two trees and killed my prize bull...never seen a rootstag this large or aggressive before. Beast would have killed me and mine, too," the old man said, slapping lightly at the reins.

Thorben grunted, pulling on the pipe as the wagon rumbled away. Rootstags weren't uncommon in the boroughs, but they normally weren't so large.

Thorben had seen the beasts from a distance on several occasions, and often mistook them for an elk or large deer. After all, their fur was normally brown. Normally timid, rootstags kept to groves of dense trees, occasionally wandering down streams in search of food. And yet, for those that stumbled across the red-furred beasts, that mistake could prove deadly. Once a season, male rootstags would travel far and wide in search of rare pauper trees.

He'd heard stories about them, and how they would savage the trees, breaking branches and tearing away bark, until finally bringing down the whole tree. The stories told that the rootstag would then burry themselves in the roots, the thick, blood-like sap staining their fur red. The beasts changed, the poisonous sap driving them into a mating craze. They became wildly unpredictable, killing and consuming anything in their path, beast and plant alike. That madness continued until they finally mated – or died.

Thorben puffed on his pipe, contemplating the rootstag's fate until the cart followed a curve in the path and disappeared from sight. He continued forward, silently wondering what it would be like to have a singular desire burn so strongly that it washed away all other thoughts and needs – to be fully consumed by it. And then he silently decided that he didn't ever want to.

A building appeared to his right, the bluish green block and mortar covered in thick, curling trails of moss. Another building appeared to his left, this structure smaller and even more expertly blended into the surrounding forest. Yarborough materialized out of the rolling hills and lush forest before him, the roads and buildings nestled into the forest like budding clumps of stony mushrooms.

Townsfolk clustered on corners or the steps of buildings, sharing in casual conversation, while a bard pontificated from a small pedestal at the very center of Merchant's Way. The colorfully dressed man pointed at passersby from the base of the Bough – the colossal Stonewood tree looming above him, its thick branches climbing high above every other tree. The strange tree may have died ages before his ancestors settled there, but to Thorben, it was the town's heart, a symbol of steadfast strength.

He passed the bard, the young man's falsetto voice spinning a tale he'd heard many times, but never truly fancied.

"Peasant and pauper, merchant and fool, did bow to the shadow of Denoril's king. A storm of madness and cruelty did reap, for fell the people from ocean to ocean in grief. Virtuous and true, for his heart truly knew – sired by the ram, good Gladeus saw what the gods deemed just..." the bard started anew, dancing out from under the stone tree and around Thorben.

The young man sang and danced, hooking one lady by the arm and pulling her into a spin before skipping between two men. Thorben picked up his pace and veered towards the buildings on the right, desperately seeking to put distance between himself and the bard. He didn't hate song, far from it. In fact, he'd been known to entertain a room from time to time with a passage or two of old Fanorian tunes, but he'd just watched the Council's tax collectors pick through his cellar, claiming their food in the name of Gladeus and the other wealthy Council lords. He just wasn't in the mood to revel in their "goodness" or just leadership.

Thorben passed down several lanes, the bard's song still audible behind him when another appeared down a wide road to his left. The other man, dressed in similar brightly colored clothing, danced and sung, pulling people into a group and encouraging them to join in. Although the group clogged the middle of the lane, Thorben could just make out a long line of wagons further down the road. A host of soldiers clustered protectively around them.

Stopping involuntarily, a stab of anger clouded his thoughts. He knew what sat in the back of those wagons, and it felt no less like theft than if someone walked up to him at that very moment and took his coin purse. Not that anything would be in it, but that wasn't his fault. Not this time.

"Greedy bastards!" Thorben spat, and set off again. He struggled forward, the weight on his shoulders increasing with every step. The idea of bowing to a wealthy man for a handful of coin, after a council of wealthy men just plundered his cellar, was almost more than he could take...until he considered turning around, and returning home. What if the harvest wasn't bountiful? How long before they were all hungry? How could he watch his children slowly starve?

A sign hung above a doorway to a large, stone building across the lane to his left. "Lamtrop Woolery" was carved out of the rich, dark wood, the raised letters covered in gold filigree.

The door pushed open easily, the barrel hinges turning with only a whisper of noise. He closed the door quietly behind him and looked around, exquisitely aware of every noise. Glimmering glass lanterns hung from the ceiling, suspended from heavy loops of some shiny metal he'd never seen before. Wide pools of yellow light fell over highly polished tables, exceptionally tailored clothing displayed on top of them. His gaze crept outward, where dark shelves stretched up to the high ceiling. Thick blankets, rugs, and tapestries filled the many cubbies.

A young woman worked to his left, quietly and diligently sweeping, while a boy no older than his Dennah polished the dark, wood tables to his right. He watched them for a moment, before clearing his throat, hoping to catch their attention. Neither looked up, however.

Taking a deep breath, Thorben walked forward under the glimmering lanterns and between the fancy clothes. He approached a long, high counter stretching across the back of the shop, shelves filling the wall behind it. Jars of exotic foods from every corner of Denoril filled the lower shelves, while candles, expensive oils, and rare herbs sat higher up.

Thorben couldn't recall the last time he'd seen so many fineries in one place. A floorboard creaked to his right, snapping his attention from the shiny jars and gilded boxes to find an incredibly short man standing at the end of the counter. A small door hung open behind him, an unusually burly figure wedged between the jambs.

The small man paced quietly forward, almost disappearing behind the counter, before elevating suddenly, his feet thumping against some unseen stair or stool. Thorben watched the substantial, muscular figure untangle himself from the doorway and clear the counter to come and stand just to his side and slightly behind him. A silver-clad scabbard hung from his hip, catching the lantern light with a gleam.

The small man cleared his throat impatiently, pulling Thorben's attention reluctantly forward and away from the fighter. Thorben's gaze drifted up the merchant's silk and wool vest, the buttons and baubles each gleaming as if recently polished. The merchant had a long face, despite his short stature, dark eyes, and severe, almost angry slant to his bushy eyebrows.

"Uh, greetings, sir. Might you be Lamtrop?" Thorben asked, stumbling as the big man shifted behind him.

"I am Vernon Lamtrop, purveyor of the finest mercantile from every corner of Denoril. Are you here to buy...sir, my time is very limited," the merchant replied, pausing to consider Thorben up and down.

Thorben swallowed, biting back a sudden spike of anger. For such a small man, Lamtrop seemed surprisingly well versed at looking down his nose at people.

Calm yourself! The man won't lend you any coin if you lose your temper! he thought, sucking in a cleansing breath.

"Well, no. I heard from other folk that you are in the habit of loaning a man coin, if he finds himself in need." Thorben struggled to spit out the words, his mouth horribly dry.

Lamtrop gave an abrupt nod, ducked down behind the counter, and reappeared a heartbeat later. The small man slapped a sizable leather-bound ledger down, peeled it open, and lifted a black feather quill before tapping it into an inkwell. He pulled a small coin sack out of his vest and plopped it down next to the ledger.

"What is your name?" Lamtrop asked, his hand floating back over the parchment.

"Thorben, sir. Thorben, son of Paul."

Lamtrop mumbled, the quill scratching loudly against the parchment.

"Very well, I require interest paid on all loans - at the rate of two copper for each silver borrowed. Agreed?" the merchant asked, not looking up as he scratched away.

"Yes, sir." Thorben felt the anxiety lift a bit, the sum far lower than he feared.

"And you understand that if you accept my coin, then you will be indebted to me, and will be required to pay back the sum borrowed along with the interest I demand, by say...the end of the first freeze next. Agreed?"

Thorben nodded eagerly. That left him plenty of time to collect the coin needed.

"We are agreeable. There is only one last step before I put coin into your hand. Please show me both of your wrists," Lamtrop said, finally looking up from the ledger.

"Huh?" Thorben stammered, his hand frozen in mid-reach for the sack of coin.

"I like to know the character of those in my debt. It is a formality, I'm afraid. Just a quick glance and the coins are yours."

"I just need it to get by, through the cold season and to spring, when our fortunes can change. Maybe the field won't flood next..." Thorben said, speaking faster, desperate to change the subject.

Lamtrop nodded and Thorben felt the floor sag behind him, the fighter's bulk crowding in. Strong hands snapped in before he could pull away and locked onto his wrists. His shirt's old buttons put up almost no resistance as his sleeves pulled back. Thorben looked away as the pale, raised flesh of his brand appeared.

"A branded man...you're a brigand, sir," Lamtrop said with a sneer, eyeing the mark of shame.

"No sir," he said, desperately shaking his head, "I never hurt anyone, you must understand–"

"I think I understand well enough," the merchant cut him off, his tone now clipped and cold. "But I am not without mercy. The coin can still be yours, with the proper surety."

"I don't understand," Thorben said, glancing quickly back at the bulky fighter. The man's hands hung ready, as if prepared to grab him once again and pull off his arms.

"A branded man is a brigand and without honor, and therefore, cannot be trusted. If you wish me to even consider putting *my* coin in your hands, then you need provide some surety that you will not simply take to foot and run. So, if you seek this," Lamtrop said, nudging the coin bag, "you need to offer me more surety than your fool's word. Interest paid is my reason for loaning you the coin, and the surety is your reason to repay."

"I have no livestock, sir, save for a few goats and sheep, but we need them for milk and wool, and they're small and haven't much meat on them. The Council's taxmen have already stripped our cupboards bare, and so you see, I just need this coin to bolster the fall harvest and stock our cellar for the winter...to keep my young ones fed."

"I have watched the tax caravans weave their circuit of the provinces through the rule of two kings and the early thaws of our Council, but their burden of gold and food has grown in recent seasons. There is nobility in your plight, sir, I understand that. Others have brought me similar stories of need, on this very day, no less. But you must understand, I cannot simply give away my coin to dishonored men. The risk is too high." Lamtrop's features softened just a bit, his eyebrows losing their severe angle for a moment.

"I could sign a note of promise," Thorben offered, remembering the old man's story.

Lamtrop nodded, lifting the pen over the parchment once again. "Your home as surety, then? Or perhaps, a child? Say, the purse of fifty silver, with interest of ten silver paid by first freeze next? That will keep your family fed through the cold months and give you all spring next to earn it back."

"Ten silver? I thought you said two copper? Wait...my home? A child? And what, you would take them?" Thorben asked, taking an involuntary step back. The idea cut into him like a knife. He'd helped his father toil for thaws, clearing the timber and building the house. No, it wasn't just a house...it was their home, the product of more than just his blood, sweat, and tears. It was all they had – the roof over their heads, but it was still just four walls and a roof. The idea of handing over one of his children to the merchant made his stomach lurch and the room spin. It was appalling, sickening.

Then it struck him. He turned back to his left, and the young woman sweeping the floor, and back to his right, where the boy polished the fancy tables. Had she been someone's wife, the boy someone's child? He'd assumed that they were either the merchantman's family, or perhaps in his employ, but now he found it far more likely that they were the child or lover of someone just like him.

He spun back to the counter, his eyes dropping to the sack on the counter. The silver tributes bulged teasingly against the leather. It just sat there in the open, enough coin to alleviate most of their concerns. His hands involuntarily twitched forward.

Lamtrop dropped a small hand onto the coin sack and pulled it back, before slowly pressing it against his chest. The fighter shifted, moving in behind Thorben. He could smell the man – a heavy combination of leather and musk.

"I have had Rance here," he said, pointing behind Thorben, "run down countless fools over the seasons. He dragged some back, beaten and bloodied, while he had to break others, and some, kill. Before you call me a monster, know that it is rightful, as decreed by the Council. According to our laws, if you are dishonored and fall into *my* debt, I can claim ownership of you, your wife, children, or home, as I see fit. It is surety after all. I don't like tearing a child from their parents, or throwing a family out of their home, but these are the ugly necessities of life."

Thorben looked up to Vernon Lamtrop, his eyebrows once again severe, his scowl dark and ominous. The small man clutched the coin purse to his chest, the skin pulled tight around the bulging silver. This was the man's true face. It was ugly – greed wearing a man's skin.

"No man ought lose a lover or child because of coin, nor should he lose his honor or freedom for doing what any other reasonable man would. Coin is just metal, while we are flesh and blood. This is wrong. All of it. Wrong," he said, his voice rising.

"And yet you shadowed *my* door, desperate for *my* coin. I deal with two kinds of people – those who seek fineries, and those with none. One is welcome, the other is not, especially branded fools," Lamtrop spit back.

"You take advantage of people when they are at their most desperate! Take from them what is not yours to claim," Thorben retorted. "What kind of man are you?"

"What kind of man am I?" Lamtrop asked, taken aback by the question. "I can trace my lineage back to the boats from Fanfir, the merchant trade running in our blood almost as long. Lamtrop is a noble name, my kin living with distinction and honor...not a branded fool in the whole lot. I cannot say any of that for you, pauper of a peasant's son."

Thorben felt his neck grow hot, his hands clenching painfully into fists at his side. His family wasn't wealthy...far from it, but they'd maintained a reputable name for generations, serving their kin and family in a respectable manner.

"Better to be an honest pauper than a corrupt and soulless wretch, spitting fanciful tales to people on hard times. A false coin-counter trying to steal away a man's own children...a...slave trader!" Thorben yelled, and when words couldn't adequately convey his anger, he swept his hand over the counter next to the merchant, scattering the displayed goods onto the floor.

"Remove this...fool from my shop, Rance. Beat him from my sight, and if he ever shows his fool-face on my property again, kill him!" Lamtrop spat, slamming the ledger closed and sweeping it off the counter.

"Aye. I'll be leaving, me lord," Thorben said, half-bowing in mocking fashion. He swiveled and kicked the scattered goods at his feet for good measure before turning for the door, but a muscled arm dropped around his neck and pulled him into a suffocating embrace.

"Get yer hands off of me!" he howled, punching and wrenching against Rance's hold, but the larger man snapped around, driving an impossibly hard fist into his stomach.

The world spun as Thorben's breath was violently knocked away. He swung around and tried to hit his attacker, but Rance twisted out of reach, wrenching him over like a limp doll, and picking his feet completely off the ground.

Thorben caught sight of the dark tables, the floor, and then a child's face – locked in an expression somewhere between fear and shock. Then the door swung open. Rance wrenched him through the doorway, his knees and shins banging painfully in the process.

Everything tilted, and then he tumbled, sprawling painfully to the ground. Bright lights burst before his eyes and he rolled just as a boot swung in, catching him in the hip. Rance grunted and swung in again and again, his foot smashing Thorben in the stomach, and then his chest. He lifted his arms to protect his face, just as the boot swung in again, snapping his hands and head violently backwards.

"Don't come back here ever again, or next time, I start cutting," Rance growled, dropping a foot on Thorben's chest and pushing him over.

Before he could collect himself and respond the hulking man walked back into the shop, the heavy door slamming shut behind him. Thorben grunted and wheezed, rolling over and pushing off the ground. He managed up and into a seated position, sharp pain flaring seemingly everywhere at once.

With a glance back towards the door, Thorben stood and staggered down the road. He stopped and leaned against the building, sipping down shallow breaths, the pain still throbbing in his side. A horse nickered nearby. He didn't need to look up to know that the street traffic had stopped, that the busy bodies were all watching him.

Enjoy the show? he thought, bitterly. Thorben understood how the boroughs worked. The tale of how he was physically thrown out of Lamtrop's Mercantile and soundly beaten in the lane would find its way to every table and fire, painting him as a would-be thief or drunken brigand. The stories would grow and change, building him into a fire-breathing beast, consuming children and wreaking havoc on farms and towns alike...that is, until the next scandal caught the town's attention.

"You can think what you like," he said, grimacing and pushing away from the wall. "I know what and who I am."

Thorben cleared Lamtrop's shop, the dark alley between buildings filled with a small twisting, curling tree. He'd barely made it two steps past the alley when someone spoke from the darkness. He wheeled about, just as a figure materialized from the shadow.

"What they would say if they knew what you *used* to be, old friend. Oh, how they would admire you," the man said.

Chapter Three

An Unexpected Proposal

Thorben limped along, his sense of pride propping up his aching body. It would be a moon or longer before his pain was gone, but he didn't need everyone in the boroughs to know that, too.

"I believe you should sit for a while," the man said, quietly keeping pace. Thorben ignored him, maintaining as much focus as he could muster on walking in a straight line.

"At least slow your pace, Owl. You appear ready to keel over at any moment."

Thorben skidded to a stop and spun, a sudden stab of anger rising up inside. "Don't call me that, Iona, you bastard!" he fumed, quickly scanning around them. There wasn't anyone close by, however. Just him and the man he'd hoped to never see again.

Iona took a half step back, lifting his hands up in surrender. The man looked exactly as he remembered him, save for a slight peppering of white hair in his dark beard. His hair was neatly trimmed and combed to the side, while his usual brown, cotton shirt and leather vest appeared clean and well maintained. The fact that the past ten seasons seemingly hadn't aged or changed Iona much angered him even more.

"Apologies," Iona bowed, and when he straightened back up, wore his usual, jovial smile. The man's large, brown eyes drooped, until they were barely open. It was a casual and irritatingly disarming expression, used to great effect on men and women alike. Thorben could see through it, however, unlike all those thaws ago.

"When I set out to locate you, Thorben, I never thought I would find you lying in the dirt, being kicked like a dog. For a man of your abilities, I anticipated a large home, wealth, women – all the imaginable comforts," Iona said, his smile disappearing. His accent was fainter than Thorben remembered it, but still there – a poetic quality of south islanders, emphasized by a subtle lilt favoring the end of each word.

"Why are you here, Iona?"

"There is the Owl I know...as blunt as a club and straight to business," Iona said, walking forward and flicking something off his shirt.

"I said, don't call me–"

"Oh, yes, I heard you. But a name like that, a reputation like yours, should never be forgotten or ignored. It is always there, whether you want it or not, like a second skin. Wear it with pride."

"Owl, fox, and mule? You and I remember those days very differently, Iona. You took impressionable young men and convinced them...me, to steal – to break into honest folks' homes and take their livelihood, to violate the edicts of kings and councils, raid tombs and defile the sacred. I wasn't Owl before I met you. I was Thorben, son of Paul, as honest a man as any."

"Honest, but poor. I lifted you up and showed you the way to support your family. I showed you how to balance the scales, when less deserving men stood above you and deemed to call themselves your betters," Iona said, calmly, "and why...because of the contents of their coin purses and not their character?"

Thorben sputtered, his anger faltering for a moment. It was the same argument, the same recruitment line Iona had used on him, and so many other young men, for a long time.

"And in all that time, you never harmed a single person. We never poached from the poor or needy. Your marks were well-to-do merchants and nobility, resting easily on the fat of lesser people's labors. We turned around and sold their treasures to others just like them. Did your father ever question you about where your coin was coming from? The coin that helped build the roof that he, and now you, call home?" Iona continued, moving closer, his hands weaving wide, almost gentle circles in the air.

Thorben felt a flush of guilt as those memories came washing back – of the lies he fed to his father all those thaws, and how he justified it all.

"You made me into a thief, Iona – a deceitful and dishonest louse preying on the living and the dead. I took what wasn't mine, from folk who worked and earned honestly. Owl died thaws ago. I buried him in the dark, stinking depths of the Council's prison mine. You closed the shackles around my wrists as surely as those guards when you brought me into that life. Had I never met you, I never would have spent those thaws breaking my back swinging a pickaxe. I have a family to consider. Now, goodbye," Thorben said, and abruptly turned and walked away.

"I am truly sorry that you feel that way, but it was a stroke of ill luck, Thorben. You picked up your family from the slums, provided them with food, clothing, firewood in the winter, and coin for healers when your father was infirm and unable to work, and your mother with child. That sounds honest to me, no, it sounds heroic. Were your intentions not honest and good?" Iona said, catching up and falling into step, but remained a respectful distance away on the other side of the road.

Thorben clenched his fists, before wrapping his arms around his body, the chilly wind suddenly a bit more harsh. His anger, like his warmth, was bleeding away, and he knew it. He wanted to scream at Iona, unloading every moment of resentment and frustration from the past thaws – the hardship in the prison mine, the struggle of starting over and raising a family, but mostly, hiding the ugly truth of his past from his own children.

"I lined your pockets with gold and silver. Don't make yourself out to be some sort of saint," he said, finally, his voice lacking its previous conviction.

"Yes you did," Iona agreed, but continued on in silence.

Thorben continued to walk, until the sprawling maple trees to his left opened up, revealing a clearing and a sweeping hill. A mill sat midway up the incline, its fabric-covered sail rotating slowly in the breeze. He'd walked right past the turn to his house and not known it. Thorben limped to a stop in the middle of the road, his side on fire and his chest aching.

He looked up the heavily shadowed road, and back in the other direction. How could he go home now, with nothing to show for his efforts, save the cuts and bruises of a beating? They just added to the shame and defeat, and there was no way he would be able to hide them from Dennica and the kids. He'd left the house with no coin and an empty cellar, and would return with the same.

I am a failure, he thought, and glanced back up the road. Klydesborough laid a few days walk ahead. He'd find passage on a riverboat there, either downstream to the lakes, or upstream to Pinehall. Maybe Dennica and the kids would be better off without him.

"I know what you are thinking," Iona said, softly, from the other side of the road.

"You know? You know...how could you possibly know what I am thinking?" Thorben spun on the spot, now more hurt than angry.

"You are hurting, old friend. I can see the pain written plainly on your face."

Thorben frowned. "I'll heal," he snapped, and started back towards home. He just needed to lie down and rest, and then he would be able to decide what he would do next.

"That isn't what I meant, and you know it, Thorben. I followed the tax caravan down from Klydesborough...watched it settle in. I watched one wagon rumble down this very road...just back there," Iona said, pointing down the road towards his home. "I watched them burden their wagon with your food. I admire your strength. The rage must have filled you, watching them strip away everything you have worked so hard to acquire. I know it angered me, and it was neither my home nor my food."

"Enough!" Thorben yelled, and panicked. He tried to run away from Iona, from the humiliation and powerlessness of it all, but only made it a few steps before his side cramped up and he fell to his knees.

"Please, don't hurt yourself trying to run away from me. I did not come here to pour salt into your wounds," Iona said, hovering above him.

"You may not wish it...but that is how it feels. Even now, the weight of your shadow feels like a mountain of stone pressing down upon me. Cannot you simply leave me be? I have nothing. I am bloodied, beaten, and broken. I am nothing."

"You of all people should know that a man is never truly broken, nor is he ever nothing. Not when he has love and kin looking up to him. Do you remember what I told you all those thaws ago?"

Thorben knew. How could he forget? And despite his resentment towards Iona, he remembered how hearing it lifted his spirit and gave him hope. A small, strangled portion of him yearned to hear it again, although he couldn't stand the thought of admitting it out loud.

"Dusk loses its battle to the night, and at its blackest, only the stars exist as distant reminders of brighter times. It is when we believe that night cannot get darker that the dawn is born, breaking through as a whole new day – new possibilities."

Thorben was trapped in the darkness, with only the memories of good times to remind him that they existed at all. They would come again; he just had to believe they would, and keep from giving in.

Iona grabbed him under the arms, and with surprisingly little resistance, pulled him to his feet.

"I am sorry that you suffered, Thorben. I truly am. I have wanted to check in on you for many thaws, to make sure that you have been okay, but things have been...complicated. But now that I am here–" Iona said, brushing his hands together, as if brushing away the excuses that kept them apart for all that time.

"Please...I can't," Thorben breathed, interrupting him before he could get going. He didn't want to deal with the temptation...the struggle he knew would undoubtedly come with Iona's next words.

"You are an honest man, with a wife, and family, Thorben. You have built an honest life for yourself. But the odds are stacked against you. The brand you hide under your sleeve gives the Council's tax collectors the power to take more from you than any other person. Allow me to do what I can to make you whole, to repay some of the debt...no, the sacrifice you endured for us. I ask only that you hear me out and take time to consider my offer, as a courtesy to an old fool."

Thorben tried desperately to hold onto his anger, to let his resentment and bile rise up so that he might rebuke Iona once and for all. His left hand slipped to his right forearm, his fingers easily finding the raised flesh of that terrible scar. He remembered the bite of chains, the jailer's horrible stench, but most keenly, the smell as the red-hot brand bit into his flesh, marking him forever. It all flooded back to him, the painful memories making him feel older than he should.

He grudgingly looked into Iona's warm, dark eyes. Dennica looked at him the same way –unquestionable compassion and empathy. He felt the last of his anger slip away, like a leaden blanket sliding off his shoulders.

"I am going home, to be with my family," he said, and started walking.

Iona fell into step quietly beside him. It was as much what he didn't say, than what he did. He'd give the man some time to speak his piece, at least until he got to his lane. After a short time, Iona took a deep breath, as if collecting and putting his thoughts in order. Thorben didn't stop him.

"Do you remember the kongelig blöd mounds?"

Thorben nodded. Of course, he did. They were some of the first dalan burial crypts discovered in Denoril. To his knowledge, no one had ever managed to find a way in.

"What if I was to tell you that I have learned of an entrance to the crypts - one that no one else knows about? And more, I hold a map detailing its location."

Thorben chuckled, but it was without mirth, and when Iona didn't join in, he coughed. "I have seen the mounds. The crypts are on the cliffs, the south side of the hill. The stone covering the entrance is enormous. No man, or army of men for that matter, would be able to roll it aside to get in," Thorben said, after a moment of silence.

"For several thaws, a group of Denil monks studied the mounds, picking over every stone, blade of grass, and finger breadth of rock. One monk, addled by wine, stumbled off the road and became lost in the hills. He wandered for a time, before discovering a narrow river. Thinking that the waterway would at the very least lead him to help, the monk followed it. He stumbled upon a cave set just off the river. That cave led him to a tunnel, and then to–"

"This monk sounds like a very fortunate individual. He could just as easily ended up in some beast's belly. But how did you learn of this?" Thorben interrupted, not looking up. He didn't want to appear interested, but struggled to deny his curiosity.

"I have my ways. Needless to say, a fair amount of coin passed between hands," Iona admitted.

"Surely if you know of this tunnel, then a host of others do as well. The seal of that crypt is as good as broken and its contents looted by now."

"Oh, I assure you, it is still quite secret. The monk detailed an intricate shape carved into a pedestal just inside the tunnel's entrance." Iona gave him a sidelong glance, and although Thorben didn't take the bait, he swore the man wore the subtlest hint of a smile.

"But how can...?" Thorben started to ask after a moment, but paused. What shape did the monk find? Did he confirm that the tunnel led to the crypts? Was it sealed when he found it?

Iona stopped walking and slipped a hand into his vest, before removing a folded piece of parchment. The lane to his house stood just two dozen paces ahead and up on the next hill. But despite himself, Thorben stopped walking, his attention pulled to Iona's hand.

"I have several buyers that will pay a king's ransom for the most exotic artifacts recovered from that tomb. They pay in gold and gems," Iona said.

"There are no guarantees, as you know. Death and dust might be all you find in that tomb. The dalan were smart. They built hundreds of burial mounds all over this land, the vast majority empty...like that site we found in the woods north of Ogre Springs, or the one near the Red Fish."

"I don't think so, Thorben. This is the largest, most securely sealed crypt south of the Bear Claw. Compared to the others, this site is practically royal. This is the treasure that will not just change our immediate futures, but our long-term fortunes for good!"

"You're touched!" Thorben laughed, and resumed his walk home. He felt the fool for even hearing him out.

Iona appeared next to him suddenly, and slapped a palm against his chest. Thorben stopped and swatted the hand, only to have his finger close around a crinkly sheet of yellowed parchment.

"What is this?" he asked.

Iona stepped away, his hands clasped lightly together. "Just look," he said, "you'll know."

Thorben held the parchment out, turning it over to inspect it. The corners were bent and soiled, numerous stains and wrinkles marring the once pristine sheaf.

"Go on, it won't bite you," Iona urged, when he didn't immediately unfold it. Thorben watched the older man, the excitement practically radiating off of him - just like his kids sitting before unwrapped winter festival gifts.

Thorben glanced back down the road. He could see the path to his house now, the large quaking aspen trees marking the spot, their leaves shimmering and shifting in the breeze. He could just drop the parchment and walk home, hug Dennica, and forget anything happened - the woolery, Iona. All of it.

His fingers moved before he could consciously decide, pulling the corners apart and unfolding the sheaf lengthwise. He unfolded it again and was rewarded with...nothing. Thorben hastily turned it over, only to find a mass of dark scribblings.

"It's just a bunch of..." he started to argue, but then saw it. They weren't just scribblings. It was a rubbing. A relief image appeared in the middle of the sheet, the charcoal filling out its outline perfectly. It was a round eye, its pupil the shape of a star, carvings of what looked like lightning extending where eyelashes should be. He had seen the eye before, many thaws ago.

Impossible, he thought, his heart starting to race. Thorben fought to keep his face expressionless, but failed, and could tell that Iona saw it, too.

"Do you see it now? Tell me that you see it!" he prodded, gesturing towards the parchment in Thorben's hand.

He nodded, letting go of the parchment. The sheaf floated lazily to the ground, drifting towards Iona, only to curl back towards him before settling in the grass.

"The dalan eye marks this crypt. The same one that marked the tomb outside Lake Madus, where you found the Mask of the Ancients," Iona said, his smile now fully formed.

"I've never called it that," Thorben said, but didn't need the reminder, he'd dreamt about that day off and on ever since. That small tomb, simple and relatively unadorned, had been tucked away, forgotten by the world. It wasn't laden with gold coins and gems, just a single sarcophagus, and resting on the stone lid, a weathered, metal mask.

"You know how society, noblemen, and merchants are. They will pay twice the sum when an artifact has a name. Hells, they are seeking out dalan artifacts more than ever, willing to drop considerable wealth to acquire the most rare and exotic relics to add to their collections. Rumors abide of a number of magical swords crafted by the dwarves and enchanted by the dalan that may still lay in one of those undisturbed crypts. If we could procure one of those–" Iona said, excitedly, his voice rising in volume and pitch.

"Death and dust," Thorben repeated, cutting in.

"We find a relic of that quality, and you move your family out of this quaint hole in the woods and into a castle, Thorben. Your children and wife will never see another lean winter, half-empty plate, or have to fear the tax collector's visit again!"

Thorben chuckled, watching him and struggling to hide his excitement at the prospect. "That would be nice," he replied, sheepishly, although he knew it was just as likely he'd end up in chains.

Iona moved a little closer, his voice low and fast. "A few days walk, a day of exploration, and a world of possibility, Thorben. I've already hired a group of mules...strongbacks, but I need an owl – someone wise to lead them, that's breathed old tunnel air, and knows the difference between broken pottery and a priceless relic...something we can give a name. I need you, Thorben. Out of all my delvers, you were my most trusted owl. And now, with this," he said, scooping the parchment off the ground and pointing to the ghostly outline of the eye, "you know what likely waits within that crypt; have the experience, the hands and eyes, and the savvy I need on this delving. You and you alone."

"I...I," Thorben stuttered, struggling to form an argument to Iona's unexpected plea. He remembered the thaws by the man's side, first sneaking through the shadows and slipping into richer men's estates, and then later, after they'd discovered that rare and alien relics were a far more profitable commodity. A wave of nostalgia washed over him as a cool breeze whistled through the trees. He swore that he caught an earthy, dusty scent on the wind – a musty, stale odor of damp and decay.

Thorben's memories turned dark, however. He remembered feeling the sun splash across his face as he pulled himself out of the tunnel they'd dug into what turned out to be an empty burial chamber, only to find gleaming spear points and angry faces waiting for him. His nostalgia turned to anger, the thaws old whip scars on his back and legs twinging in response.

"You are here now... in my town, after all these thaws. I paid the price back then, but it is my wife and children who pay it now. Where were you?" he asked.

"I don't carry whip marks, broken hands from the pickaxe, or the Council's brand upon my flesh. I won't tell you that I suffered alongside you, Thorben, or that I completely understand what you went through. That would be an offense to your sacrifices. All I can do is make you and your family whole again. *This* delving *will* be the one to change fortunes, Thorben. And by fortunes, I don't just mean coin in your hand. I know a healer, an outcast from the Manite order, blessed with powers beyond any other. You delve this one last time for me, and I will have her remove your brand. You will be a new man, free from the burdens of the past and able to move your family anywhere in the provinces you choose. I am offering you the power to claim the life you deserve."

Iona held out the sheaf of parchment. Thorben hesitated, but finally accepted it. He felt the brand twinge on his forearm, or it could have been in his head. He hated the mark, and longed for a day when he no longer had to hide it from his children.

"I am staying at the River's Mouth Inn, in the green room, until sunrise after morrow. If you want to pull yourself up and stare your tormentors in the eye, that is where I will be. If not...well, it has done my heart good to see you again, and I hope you and your family Mani's blessings."

Thorben held the sheaf of parchment out, but Iona shook his head.

"Keep it," he said, and promptly turned and walked away.

Thorben watched the man move quickly down the road, disappearing into the canopy's heavy shadow. And just like that, he was gone.

Chapter Four
Hard to Swallow

Thorben took his time to walk the rest of the way home, intermittently stopping to look at the folded parchment. He tried to crumple it up, to throw it away, but his hands refused him. The image mocked him, reminding him of those young thaws when he lived recklessly, but easily, the coin plentiful and regular. He'd enjoyed those thaws, despite all the risk. Now, life just felt hard.

"I can't take those risks anymore...not with the kids," he said, suddenly, taking the picture and stuffing it into his shirt and out of sight. He decided to burn the parchment when he got home. "Stoke the fire, kiss the woman, and have a glass of mead," he said, rubbing his belly. It made more sense to focus on what he had, than fill his head with fanciful tales and dream about what he did not. And if he was out of mead, then he would simply enjoy the other things.

The Thorben homestead came into view, the tall gables appearing through the thick curtain of papery birch trees. He walked by the gardens, the late season vegetables clustered in the warm sunshine. Beyond that, rows of tartberry, blackberry, and snowberry bushes stretched around to the back of the home, the fat fruit waiting patiently to be picked. He visualized spreading some of his wife's jam onto a slice of hot, freshly baked bread, and his stomach rumbled. He stopped for a moment and shook the fence circling it all, the thick timber stakes and prickly weavers hardly moving under his weight.

His gaze swept up from the fence and sprawling gardens to the house, each of the thick timbers and shingles lovingly crafted. He'd helped his father hammer every pin, nail, and stud into place, infusing the large home with equal parts blood, sweat, and blisters. The thought that someone would readily stake ownership over everything they had worked so hard to build for a measly handful of coins incited another wave of anger.

Fists clenched, Thorben stomped over to the splitting stump and wrenched the axe handle free. He grabbed a thick piece of dry elm, stood it on end, and drove the axe down, splitting it violently into two uneven pieces. He grabbed another piece, and then another, allowing his anger to flow into something constructive. The piles of split wood grew until, finally, he sagged against the axe, the pain in his side too much to ignore.

"What ya doin', pa?" someone asked. The voice was small and feminine, but infused with a strength and resilience he immediately recognized.

Thorben turned to find Dennah seated on a massive log, his saw leaned against the tree just to her left. Her legs and arms were dirty and bruised, while green stains and burrs covered her dress.

"Just cutting some firewood, pebble. You look fresh from an adventure!"

Dennah nodded enthusiastically, her smile stretching from ear to ear.

"You want to help?" he asked, gesturing to the axe.

The girl nodded and jumped off the log, stumbled, and caught her balance, covering the distance between them in a heartbeat. She latched onto the axe and yanked it free, and before Thorben could stop her, leaned back, lifting the iron blade into the air.

"Easy, girl," he laughed, wrapping an arm around Dennah as the weight tipped her backwards. "First, before you even lift the axe off the ground, you need a firm base. Set your feet. Just...like...that." Thorben helped the girl widen her stance a bit.

"Now, straighten your back, don't slouch, and pull your shoulders back. Here," he said, and helped her heft the axe up, letting the weight come to rest gently on her shoulder. "Now slide one hand up here closer to the blade, and keep the other down here." Thorben moved Dennah's hands into position and stepped back. She teetered for a moment, but set her jaw determinedly, and fought the weight.

"Like this, pa?" she asked, trying to maintain the posture.

Thorben laughed, and moved in to help her hold the weight. He lifted a ratty piece of firewood onto the stump and made sure it wouldn't fall.

"Are you ready, pebble?"

Dennah wobbled under the weight, nodded, and promptly scrunched up her face.

"All right. Now let me teach you a little secret about chopping firewood," he said, pinching her cheek. "The trick is to let the axe do the hard work. You just make sure you hang on."

With a monumental effort, Dennah brought the axe head off of her shoulder and let it swing forward. The iron blade hit the dry piece of elm with a *crack,* the wood splitting partially from the weight of the strike.

"See, you're a natural!" Thorben exclaimed, patting his daughter on the back.

"You think? You think?!" Dennah exclaimed, releasing her hold on the axe to wrap him in a hug.

Thorben winced as she squeezed, but wrapped his arms around her and pushed painfully to stand, lifting her into the air.

"I can chop more, daddy, lots more!" Dennah offered, but he shook his head and planted a kiss on her cheek.

"Not now, pebble. Later. You can help me stack it up, too," he said, and headed for the kitchen. Thorben smelled food before rounding the corner and by the time he passed through the open kitchen door his mouth was watering.

Dennica was bent over the clay oven as he entered, the flour-plastered, threadbare fabric of her apron the only part of her visible.

"I caught a scrawny jack rabbit on my walk home. I don't think it has much meat on it, but its bones should make a tasty broth," he said, lifting Dennah up and snuffling playfully on her belly.

"Rabbit would be tasty, for sure, husband. And surely tastier than the hedge rats that have been feasting in our garden," Dennica said, turning from the oven and hastily dropping a dark loaf of bread on the table.

Dennah roared and pretended to chomp on his shoulder, but Thorben's humor had already bled away. He let the girl drop to the floor, the pain in his side and leg flaring from the effort. His wife's eyebrow ticked a little higher, her large, brown eyes watching him.

"But I...I built that new fear totem, and the fence. The fence should be more than enough to keep them out. My aviary has kept the birds out, and I planted that fence base deep into the soil. That garden is almost as secure as the keep wall in Klydesborough," he said, but trailed off as Dennica's hands dropped to her hips, the lines around her mouth deepening. "How bad is it?"

"It's like I telled you last thaw, it's not enough. We should have traded one of the goats for a pair of pups out of old lady McCreavy's litter. Those dogs would be a full thaw old by now and could keep those hells sent, thieving hedge rats out of our garden. They got into the squash, the gourds, and my onions...probably the garlic, too. We can eat some of it, but it'll spoil fast for sure. The rest isn't ready for picking, and is just sitting out there, waiting for them to come back."

It never gets any easier. J'ohaven, banish me now! he thought, withering under her gaze. He'd worked with all six of his boys to build the fence around the garden. Hells, it took them nearly a fortnight to construct, and the damned rats found another way in. No...he drew out the plans for that fence. It was strong, tight, and true. Thorben thought for a moment, trying to put together a plan before speaking. It wouldn't do him any good to add fuel to his wife's fire.

"We harvest from the garden early...have your cousins help us gather what we can, and move that food to the cellar for safe keeping? I can go out and inspect the fence...make it good enough for now," he proposed.

"Aye, that sounds wise, husband. But you see, the boys an' I already went through it while you were out walking. We picked and picked, saving what we could. I moved the food I could save to the cellar, and will jar it morrow. Then I can roast the dodgy stuff, dry the herbs, and if Mani hasn't abandoned us completely, lay the rest out for seeds. But those vermin have the taste of our freshly growns in their belly now. Ain't nothing to stop them from creepin' in during the wee hours and eating what's left."

"I could–"

"What? Sit out there and guard it all in the black of night, like some armor-clad knight?" Dennica cut in. Her face was flushed, a few strands of stray hair drifting over her eyes.

"If need be, aye," he said, more firmly this time. "The boys and I could keep them out...if it's what needs being done. What is a little lost sleep compared to food for the cold, dark season ahead? I–" Thorben said, passionately, buying into his own words the longer he went, but Dennica cut him off again.

"It's just so much to ponder on, husband, so very much lately – the food, the money, the Council's taxmen, and the children. I don't want to talk on it anymore for now. Let's sit down and enjoy some pottage and bread, and maybe, after we've filled our bellies and put our young ones to bed, we can look onto our troubles with honest eyes."

Thorben nodded, reaching out to tuck his wife's flyaway hair behind her ear. She threw her arms around his midsection and pulled him into a hug. He sucked in a strangled breath as the pain flared in his side, and despite his great desire not to, he groaned.

"What is it?" Dennica asked, swatting his arms out wide, and before he could stop her, she pulled up his shirt. "Mani's mercy! Did a tree fall on you?" A dark silhouette marred his side, the sizable bruise already a horrible looking blemish, and he feared, just a mere taste of what it would become.

Thorben hissed and pulled away, favoring his side. He told himself that he'd experienced worse, and lived. But there was more at stake now, and Dennica had an irritating habit of seeing through to the true heart of a matter. He'd never be able to convincingly lie about it, for that matter.

"I..." he started to say, his mind whirling. What should he say? How much should he say? A hundred possibilities flooded his mind at once. Finally, he decided on the narrowest and straightest path before him. "I went to Lamtrop's Woolery, as I heard tell that he was lending coin to those in need." Dennica started to shake her head, her eyes narrowing as they so often did when she soured on a topic.

"Thorben Paulson–" she said, trying to cut him off, but he knew that if she got her ire up again he wouldn't get another chance to speak, or she'd set her spoon against his backside.

"I just went to inquire, that is all, but I didn't like his terms, so I refused to sign the note. When I refused, well, he had his brute throw me from the shop."

"He had you thrown out, just like that?" she asked, her lips drawing thin. He'd only ever seen Dennica spitting mad once, and she was close. He suddenly feared for Lamtrop's wellbeing.

"Aye. Right into the dirt. Then his man savaged me. I picked myself off the ground and limped home. Has not been my day, wife."

"What business does a man of means have employing a brute like that? And what does a man like you," she said, narrowing her eyes, "have shadowing a man like that's doorstep? You just stay away from town for a while. The last thing we need is you running into that man again."

"As wise as ever," Thorben said, nodding, hoping he could leave it at that. His wife eyed him for a long moment, the right side of her bottom lip pulled between her teeth. She tapped her fingernails against the table, and after a weighted moment, brushed both hands against her apron.

"Well, if you can manage it, go round up the children for some supper. Then I want you to take ease after, to get some rest and heal up. You're no good to anyone under this roof a cripple."

Dennica turned back to the fireplace and worked to lift the heavy pot from the hook. "...out sniffing for trouble, if you ask me. A man with a history is best served avoiding those airy, coin-grubbing merchant folk. I ought pay that stuffy little man a visit and teach him how to treat folk. Kick a man when he's down...I'll show him my rolling pin," she huffed, mumbling under her breath as she dropped the iron pot smartly onto the small table next to the fire.

Thorben limped quickly out of the kitchen and breathed a sigh of relief, fully aware that his wife needed time to vent, and he very likely dodged the worst of it. At least, for now.

He limped around the house and almost immediately stumbled onto two of boys – Paul, the eldest, and Tymon, one of the middle boys. They sat with their backs to the house, their feet propped up on thick pieces of firewood. Paul whittled on a stick, while Tymon watched.

"Boys, would you run and fetch your brothers and sister? Bring some fresh water up from the well and get washed up for some supper," he said.

"Right away, father," Paul said, putting his knife away and springing up from his perch. Tymon fell over awkwardly, rolled to his feet, and sprinted to catch up with his more athletic, older brother.

He watched Paul disappear around the house, pride swelling in his chest at the thought of his firstborn so close to manhood. He turned and made his way back towards the kitchen, just as a gust of wind rolled through the trees, the chilly air damp with the promise of rain. He could remember a time when he longed for the first snow, but now...now winter loomed before them like a savage and faceless beast.

Dennica wasn't in the kitchen as he walked inside, so he stomped out of his boots, and closed the bottom and top doors. He found his wife in the dining hall, laying out bowls and goblets onto the long table. He lit candles as the troop entered noisily into the kitchen and banged around with washbasins and a bucket of water. They laid out bread and started to fill bowls with pottage, Dennah first appearing through the door, followed closely by her older brothers.

Dennica stood at the head of the table, her back straight and body motionless, perched like a mighty, war totem. The six boys filed around the table, moving slowly and respectfully under their mother's hawk-like gaze. Dennah skipped, humming a quiet tune, seemingly oblivious to it all.

They sat together and only started eating once Thorben lifted his spoon and tapped it on his bowl. The calm disintegrated then, boys eating and talking, and Dennah shouting her responses, often with food falling out of her mouth. Thorben ate his pottage quietly and simply listened, enjoying the barely constrained chaos that was his family. The six boys - Kenrick, Reginald, Darro, Tymon, Henrick, and Paul, from youngest to eldest, chewed through several loaves of bread, sopping up their bowls, before returning to the pot for seconds.

"What news from Klydesborough, Paul?" Thorben asked during a rare lull in the conversations.

"The road was quiet, father. The city was full of people...loads of wagons and boats at the market. I saw a horde of dwarves in from Braakdell–" Paul said.

"We don't call them a horde, son, they're not animals. Maybe a group, or party," Thorben interrupted, chuckling quietly. Dennica snorted into her goblet.

"Yes, father. Sorry, father," Paul said, gulped down a drink, cleared his throat, and continued. "I met with the Earl's Clerk of Service. After my sixteenth name day, I can commission for a post with the River Watch!

They post on the Bear Claw, the Snake, and all the way down to the Broken Tooth River, darn near Ogre Springs! I would train with bow and spear! Just another moon and I can commission!"

"Will you be able to visit often? You must say yes," Dennica said, leaning over the table and fussing with his hair.

"Of course, mother!" Paul said, and leaned away, trying to escape her attention and grab more bread. He scooped up the second to last slice, just as Darro jumped from his chair to secure the rest.

"Are there trials?" Thorben asked.

Paul ripped off a mouthful of bread and nodded, chewing loudly. When he spoke, crumbs rained down his shirt. "Marksmanship, boatmanship, and wilderness travel. But if I pass all three, then I become an apprentice River Watchman," he said, wiping his mouth on his sleeve.

"And become an honest servant of the earl! I'm so proud of you, son!" Thorben beamed.

"Why do you want to watch the river, Paul?" Dennah asked, pushing up onto her knees so she could speak at the boy's level. "It's just a bunch of muddy water going on and on and on."

Paul replied as Thorben pushed out of his chair and carried his bowl over to the sidebar. He picked up the ladle, but aside from a few bits of carrot, the pot was empty.

The conversation moved from Dennah to his other sons, their enthusiasm ignited by Paul's impending name day. Thorben dropped the ladle into the pot and caught his wife's gaze as he turned. She took a measured bite and chewed thoughtfully, before pointing to her own bowl. She was offering him her modest serving of food, once again willingly sacrificing what little she had for him or their children.

Thorben waved her off and rubbed his belly, sticking it out to indicate he wasn't hungry anymore. Her frown was gone, but the worry lines around her eyes remained. He waved her back, indicating that she should eat – Mani knew she'd earned the time to sit and take ease for a while. Dennica nodded and took another small bite, her attention drawn back to the ongoing conversation. She rarely chimed in, instead choosing to sit back, listen, and simply enjoy.

Dennah clawed at Henrick's arm, trying to pry her way into the conversation about the Knights of Silver, but the boys were too riled up now. Thorben dropped his bowl into the pot, gathered up the empty dishes, and carried the load to the kitchen. He listened to the children talk and shout, spinning wistful and fanciful tales of their future adventures, of honor and prestige. It emboldened him that they still believed, that his hardships hadn't broken them. Occasionally Dennah's voice would ring out, challenging something one of her brothers said, or just fighting to be heard.

He quietly washed the dishes with clean water, wiped off the chopping table, and swept the floor, before lighting a lantern and heading outside. He closed the door behind him, the crisp night air washing over him. A gentle breeze blew in from the river valley, carrying the song of timber crickets up from the trees. The whimsical tune filled the silence like a gang of out-of-tune minstrels.

Thorben stacked the firewood he and Dennah split, before making his way down into the cellar. The warm lantern light filled the dark space, splitting the shadows and revealing his wife's earlier labors. Several of the previously empty shelves were filled with food, cheesecloth draped over them to keep flies and other vermin away. He lifted the cloth and inspected the haul, his heart sinking. At first glance it appeared roughly half of what they usually had this time of year. Could hedge rats have eaten that much without them knowing? It didn't feel possible, not with the enclosure he'd built for the garden.

Tromping back up the stairs, Thorben grabbed a pitchfork leaning against the wall and closed the cellar doors. He made his way to the garden and walked around the perimeter, holding the lantern low to inspect every stake and finger-length of thorny weave.

The warm light glistened off the locust wood he'd used to weave the fence, the long, dark thorns sticking out like a phalanx's spears. He involuntarily rubbed his hands against his pants, the sores from working with the thorny wood healed and yet still fresh in his mind.

Thorben completed his walk around and surprisingly found no breaks or gaps in the fence's thorny weave. He turned and made his way back around in the opposite direction, now inspecting the aviary he'd designed to keep the birds out. Long poles extended up from the fence, specifically cut and bracketed to lean in toward the garden's center. Even now, with the aid of a single lantern, Thorben could see that all the posts were still in place. The tightly woven fishing net appeared to be intact, too.

Strange. So how are they getting in? Hedge rats don't dig, he thought, unhooking the gate and swinging it open so he could enter. He walked down the well-maintained rows between plants, their efforts to keep the space weeded evident even in the dark.

He walked past a half dozen plants before seeing the first sign of damage. A row of cabbage sat at his feet, fresh holes marked where mature heads had been cut away, but many others were left in place. Thorben leaned in, cursing under his breath as the light exposed teeth marks in some, while several others were chewed down to the stem.

"Little bastards," Thorben growled, his chest growing tighter as he continued his inspection. It was more of the same, their food...ruined.

A plant rustled somewhere to his left, followed quickly by the telltale sound of teeth cutting into a fibrous stem. Thorben spun toward the sound, his left hand thrusting the lantern out before him, while his right readied the pitchfork. He glanced back and confirmed that he had closed and latched the gate behind him. Nothing had followed him in. Had they followed Dennica in earlier? Surely she would have seen or heard them.

Slowly, he crept forward, moving silently on the balls of his feet. Thorben stopped and listened, then redirected to his right. The lantern shone down a row of green beans, the knee-high plants swaying gently in the night breeze. A crunch sounded directly ahead and one of the plants twitched violently. A cat-sized, dark form moved between the plants, and then another.

"Not my beans!" Thorben growled and jammed the pitchfork towards the closest hedge rat. The tines bit into the soil, a handful of dark, furry shapes scattering.

He chased one of the fat creatures down the row, only to have another appear from the plants and scurry to the left. Thorben followed, jabbing the pitchfork at the ground, but the wind and the rocking lantern made the shadows dance and jump, and he missed again. He pulled the tines free, his rage building.

"You eat our food...then we'll eat you...roasted hedge rat!" Thorben grunted and danced between rows of vegetables, stabbing the pitchfork down repeatedly, attacking anything that moved.

A hedge rat ran right between his feet and he spun to follow, desperate to enact his anger on at least one of the guilty beasts. The creature waddled in a straight line down a row of peas, its belly fat with his food.

Thorben pursued and pushed off the fence as the fat animal veered right, the wood groaning under his weight. The hedge rat ran right into a small blueberry bush, its bulk making the entire shrub dance and shake. He pounced, jabbing the pitchfork at the base of the bush again and again, the tines biting with a satisfying *plop.*

Chapter Five

Witt's End

Thorben pulled back, his side and leg aching from the chase. He let the pitchfork fall to the ground and dropped to his knees. He pulled the branches aside, fat blueberries shaking loose and peppering the dirt, and reached in to pull the dead animal out. His fingers sunk into...dirt. Scrambling, Thorben pulled more of the branches out of the way and leaned in, holding the lantern close.

There was no blood, or dead hedge rat, only a scattered pile of berries, and a dark hole burrowed next to the plant's base. Realization swept over him and he pushed up from the ground, moving quickly with the lantern held just over the ground.

It took him a few bushes, but Thorben found another small burrow hidden under a raspberry bush. After just a few moments of searching, he'd found more burrows than he cared to count.

"But...hedge rats don't dig," he muttered, spinning on the spot and taking in his cleverly constructed fence and roof.

Despair filled him like ice-cold water, his muscles trembling as he slapped the gate open and exited the garden. He'd spent moons harvesting the right kind of timber. It had taken him and his boys another moon to dig the stakes, and strip the thorny, locust branches, before soaking and weaving them into what he'd believed to be an impenetrable fence.

And yet, despite all of his labors, the hedge rats – animals he'd never seen dig – simply burrowed under and into the garden, gorging on what should have been their winter stores. His despair turned to hopelessness, tears bubbling up and running down his cheeks.

"There is no reward, is there? I put the thievery behind me and accept you... start living a good life, and now...now," he sputtered, lifting his head skyward, where the moon hung like a large, silver disc. "We praise you...offer up what we can. Cannot you spare just a meager blessing? Must you kick me while I'm in the mud, too? Hedge rats don't dig...did you teach them just so they could torment me?" He didn't expect a response – no lightning strike from the heavens, or a ghostly apparition that would instantly and magically ease all of his woes. He was a believer ironically enough, and knew that wasn't how gods worked. Their hands worked far more subtle deeds. Part of him was glad Dennica hadn't heard him, just then. She was the practical one, after all.

Thorben tromped back into the house, dropped the lantern onto the kitchen prep table, and fell into a chair. He sat brooding on the day's ill fortune, struggling with whom or what he was angrier with – Lamtrop, and his burly thug, the Earl and his sticky-fingered taxmen, or the hedge rats. They all felt like villains, in their own way. One at least acted out of an understandable impulse to survive.

Death and dust. I can pick a lock, disarm a bear trap, and build a sturdy house, but I cannot manage to keep insufferable beasts from eating our food.

The ceiling creaked and groaned above him as his children walked around, no doubt preparing to lie down for the night. He wondered what it would feel like to no longer have the roof over their heads, watching as they struggled to stay warm in the cold season or dry when the spring's monsoon rains turned the sky dark and the ground soft. What would they say when their coin purse emptied and there wasn't enough food to fill bellies?

Life was about balancing each and every risk versus the potential reward. His thoughts spun back to Lamtrop's Woolery, and he started to doubt. Did he overreact? Yes, he did. The man had no right to claim ownership over people's homes...their kin, or lovers, and all for coin. Regardless, he shouldn't have let his temper get the best of him.

Should I have agreed to his terms? he wondered, imagining the look on Dennica's face if he'd walked through the door, arms laden with food and a bulging sack of silver to boot. And for what? He might have worked harder throughout the fall and winter - split firewood, mended fences, swollen doors, leaky roofs, and broken windows, to pay it back. But that was only if he could find those jobs, those people willing to pay someone like him, to pay a branded man.

Thorben silently debated himself on the topic, tipping one way, and then the other, spiraling deeper into doubt and remorse. He sat indecisively in the sturdy chair, his legs fidgeting, an uncomfortable, crawling sensation prickling his skin and muscles.

Struggling to find direction and answers to his pressing questions, Thorben moved to stand, but in a horrific moment, his body denied him. The house sat still and dark, the occasional creak of a timber beam or gust of wind the only reminder that anything existed beyond his own thoughts. Thorben sat and listened, his mind racing, suddenly a prisoner without ropes or chains.

He turned and looked at the door to his left. It led to the rest of the house, and his family - the people that relied on him. His gaze swept across the dark room and fell on the split door that would take him outside. A horrible thought swept through him, and he nearly became sick considering it. He could walk out the door and leave. He could run. He considered the fact that his family might be better off without him.

Thorben balled up a fist and pounded his leg. It felt like he was trapped in a maze, every twist or turn leading him to either a dead end, a hulking man with a sword, or a swarming pit of hedge rats. The kitchen shrunk around him, the walls creeping in until his heart hammered in his chest and sweat broke out on his face and arms. The air became unbearably heavy and close.

"I cannot," Thorben whispered, struggling to catch his breath. It was too much to take...too many problems crushing down on him at the same time. They were strangling...choking him. Had his pride doomed his family? Had Dennica doomed their children by picking him over other suitors?

Thorben rocked forward in the chair and dropped his face into his hands, forcing his eyes closed. He took a deep breath and visualized the empty cellar, hungry children, Lamtrop and his burly thug, and the hedge rats. He hated all of them.

He was up and out of the chair without conscious thought, the door wrenched open and banging against the wall behind him. Thorben stumbled after a few steps and fell to his knees. He gasped down a breath of cool, fresh air. Wind roared in the trees and insects buzzed.

Thorben took another deep, shuddering breath, and opened his eyes. The crushing walls and inky-dark shadows, the oppressive burdens surrounding him, were gone, at least for the moment. He could breathe again. The button of his left sleeve had come undone, the tattered fabric falling back to his elbow. White moonlight fell upon the raised flesh of his forearm, the brand he'd spent every waking hour for half his life trying to hide now exposed and in the open. He hated it most of all.

Pushing away from the ground, Thorben stood. He took another breath and felt his heart slow, even though his legs continued to shake. He held his arm up before him, the stars twinkling overhead. A shooting star streaked across the night sky.

Branded like an animal, he thought, his gaze darting to the dark, swaying trees. His grandfather's voice rang out suddenly in his mind, the old man's wheezy voice breaking through his despair.

A man is flesh and bone, like the beasts of the fields and forest. But a man can think, speak, and reason. Beasts cannot. We claim ownership of animals, for food, wool, and hides, marking them so others know they belong to us. When one man marks another, he tells that person they are lower than he, that he is a beast, and is owned. This is sickness. One man should never own another.

He'd heard his grandfather give the speech many times before the fire. It was the same speech he gave from the town square as well, and the reason why many folk in the borough called him crazy. He was the old man that ranted about the uncomfortable things - the things most preferred to ignore.

Thorben now understood what he meant. He'd broken the Council's edict and was punished, but the punishment hadn't ended with his release from the mine. Their brand marked him, like a beast, as something less than everyone else, someone to be ridiculed and feared. It meant that merchants could charge him more for their wares or services, that people would pull their children to the other side of the lane if they saw him coming, but mostly, that the Earl's caravan could collect more from him in tax than other folk. He couldn't hide it from the taxmen, like he did everyone else. They knew. They always knew.

Thorben collected himself, wiped his cheeks, and stood, pulling his sleeve down and fastening the button. There were many reasons to keep it covered and hidden, but what if he didn't have to?

Coin was central to all of his struggles, and inexplicably tied to the brand. If he had coin, he could buy the food they needed for the winter, seed to plant in the spring, build a proper stone wall around their property, and a pair of dogs to keep the hedge rats at bay. If he had coin, all of his problems would simply go away.

He patted his chest, abruptly, a shaking hand sliding into his vest and pulling the folded parchment free. Thorben unfolded the rubbing and held it out, the sheaf glowing bluish-white in the moonlight.

Was it so horrible to delve one last time, if it meant his family stayed warm and well fed all winter? If it meant that they wouldn't have to risk their home, or worse, losing one of their children? If Iona was good to his word, and his healer could remove the brand, then Thorben's life would become much easier.

"No, I would do whatever it took," he whispered in response to the silent questions, and despite the bitter taste the words left in his mouth, he knew it was the truth. He couldn't stand the thought of Dennica or his children sweeping floors or polishing tables for men like Lamtrop...living as a slave, as property.

"I hope you understand," he whispered to the heavens and stowed the parchment back inside his vest. He could reconcile with the goddess afterwards, but had a feeling that she knew and understood better than anyone else. The goddess approves of selflessness above all other traits, or so the priests always told him. He wouldn't delve for him. It would be for his family, and their family when he was gone.

Thorben walked back into the house, closing the door quietly behind him. Every step forward felt a little easier, the weight bending his back lifting just a little. One task for another, *a delve for a brand.*

He picked up the lantern off the table and made his way through the dining hall and to the small, crude desk against the far wall. Pulling a wrinkled sheaf of paper from the cubby, Thorben lifted the lid off the inkwell, tapped the quill into the ink, and started to write.

Thorben wrote the runes slowly, stopping frequently to dip the quill into the ink as he decided what to say. He stopped and stared at the lantern, the flame flicking and arcing behind panes of soot-stained glass. Guilt stabbed into his heart as he dropped the quill back down to the parchment and quickly scribbled out the rest of the lie. He dropped a large pinch of sand onto the sheaf and gently blew on the wet ink. Once he was satisfied it wouldn't run he tapped the sand onto the floor, and read his message–

Dearest wife,

It is I that is to blame for our difficulties as of late. As you know, I am an honest man, if nothing else, and feel compelled to right this wrong – for you and the children. I met a merchant while in town that offered employ escorting a wagon of valuables down the Broken Tooth road and through the swamp country to Ogre Springs. He asked that I tend his wagons and gear if anything should break. You know how rough the road is. He has provided assurance of further work after, if my services are to his liking, and guaranteed passage on the return journey. I will return to you and our children within a fortnight with coin in hand. I pray that Mani keeps you safely in her keeping.

You devoted husband,

Thorben

Thorben read the note out loud, and before he could second-guess the decision, pushed away from the desk and strode back into the kitchen. He set the letter down on the table where he knew she would see it.

He carried the lantern over to the far wall, dropped to a knee, and pried up a loose floorboard. A small cotton pouch sat in the void beyond, the sparse collection of coins jingling together as he lifted it free.

Thorben opened the bag and dumped the contents into his palm – half a dozen dull, silver tributes and double that in copper. Hardly the fortune he'd expected after breaking his back almost all hot season, but honest men won't pay an honest wage to a branded man. Dennica accepted him, why couldn't they?

"I'm sorry, my love. I'll make this right. I promise," he said, dumping half the coins back into the bag, and stuffed it into his pocket. He dropped the remaining coin on top of the note and left the kitchen, his gaze lingering. *A guilty man leaves in the night*, he thought, struggling with his parting deception, and that he wouldn't be able to hug or kiss them goodbye.

Moving as quietly as he could, Thorben moved upstairs. Dennica slumbered quietly in their bed, the sound of her breathing almost lost amidst the noise of the increasing wind. A storm was building outside.

He gathered up a satchel, stuffing a change of clothes, a traveling cloak, and a handful of candles inside. A flash of lightning flared outside, the sudden burst of light filling the room. His wife grunted and shifted. Thorben's breath caught and he froze, but a moment later Dennica rolled over, pulling the lion's share of the blankets with her. Had he been in bed, he would have likely woken and found himself uncovered and chilled. He wished to be in bed with her in that moment, her body warm against his.

"Sleep well, my love," he whispered, and tiptoed out of the room.

Thorben stopped by the first door to his left. Four beds were crammed against each wall, a boy slumbering soundly in each, random arms, legs, or blankets hanging precariously.

His two eldest sons slept in the room across the hall, their door closed as usual. Paul, especially, was a stickler for privacy. He moved quietly to the bedroom at the end, stopping in the doorway.

Dennah lay backwards on her bed, her feet propped up on her pillow, a cloth doll trapped in a stranglehold. Thorben moved forward quietly. He scooped the blanket off the floor and gently covered her, snugging the knitted bedspread right up to the girl's chin.

He skipped over the creaky stair pads, and around the soft spots in the floor, finally leaving the dark house behind. Thorben trekked out into the night, thick clouds sweeping in to cover the formerly clear skies. Lightning flashed overhead as he reached the end of the lane. He turned, bidding his family a final, silent farewell, just as the storm covered the last of the star-covered sky.

A piercing cry sounded somewhere in the distance, the wind warping the eerie call in its blustery grasp. It was a rootstag, prowling for a mate. Thorben very much wanted to avoid the beast, so he set off at a determinedly fast walk.

The rain threatened for a while, large, fat drops of water hitting the ground around him sporadically. He heard the storm hit, however, moving like a mountain of water through the forest ahead. Thorben barely had time to pull his traveling cloak free and pull it on before the rain and wind fell over him.

Thorben slogged his way into town, resolutely marching forward, while second-guessing himself every other step. And yet, he continued forward. He had no other choice.

He walked into Yarborough, the town shrouded in the dark fury of the storm. The only light came from the street lanterns, their wide, metal hats protecting the flame from the deluge. He found the River's Mouth

Inn after circling the town twice, having walked right by the two-story wooden structure without knowing it.

The interior of the building was cold and dark. Thorben stood in the entryway, sizing up the space, the rainwater running off of his oiled traveling cloak and pooling by his feet. The innkeeper, Jarvis Gaslight, lay sprawled across the counter just inside the front door, his breathing ragged and loud. He knew him only by reputation – the kind that preceded a man and not for goodly reasons.

Jarvis was a particularly unpleasant looking man, his narrow head capped with a wreath of greasy-looking dark hair, framed in by oversized ears, and punctuated by a crooked, pointed nose. He looked disagreeable, even in slumber, and Thorben couldn't imagine him any more enjoyable awake.

He watched the man sleep for a few moments, contemplating a jab in the ribs to rouse him. After all, it was bad form to enter a man's home without announcement, but thought better of it and made his way quietly up the stairs.

The stairwell was narrow and dark, leading him to equally dark and narrow hallways. The first door he came across was painted black, long, irregular cracks running through the wood. Bars and rivets bridged the breaks, where someone had clearly kicked the door in. Thorben passed a blue door, and then a red one. The end of the hallway stood in deep shadow, the lantern opposite the furthest door missing.

"Still living in shadow, I see," he whispered, and rapped lightly on the dark door.

He held his breath as something moved in the space beyond. It was a quiet sound, muffled. Most wouldn't have heard it, but Thorben had learned long ago to pay attention to the small things. An impatient person would have knocked again, but not Thorben. A second knock in a place like the River's Mouth Inn could just as likely reward you with a blade in the gut.

After a rather lengthy wait, the lock clicked, and the door swung in a fist-breadth. Half of Iona's face appeared in the opening, light from the room glimmering off a short, but very sharp looking knife.

"Step into the light, or be gone from my door," he hissed, all of the previous warmth and compassion gone from his voice.

The darkness reveals the real man, Thorben thought, and stepped forward into the light shining from the room. "I think maybe you should lower that knife and show me the map you spoke of...to the kongelig blöd mounds. But first, I want your word that your offer is on the level...that your healer can remove this," Thorben said, and wrenched up his sleeve, exposing the heat-scarred skin of his brand.

A smile spread on Iona's face as he pulled open the door.

"Welcome back, Owl. Here, please come in!" Iona said, sliding the knife into his vest and motioning him inside.

Chapter Six

Mules and a Mouse

Iona was packed and they departed the River's Mouth Inn before the rooster's first crow. The rain thankfully stopped, but a thick fog moved in, blanketing the trees in a dense murk. It didn't bother him; in fact, it felt preferable to walking openly out of town with Iona at his side, who appeared eager, almost desperate to put the boroughs behind him.

They walked in silence until Yarborough was well behind them, passing hastily through the smaller Clivesborough, before stopping in Laneborough. Thorben bought a stuffed bread loaf from a street vendor. He savored each bite, the flavor triggering many memories of his younger days in the boroughs. Iona watched him as he licked the remnants from the paper after taking the last bite.

"You still eat like a starving man. Is this woman, the one you took for a wife, not a good cook? The Thorben I remember spoke often about finding a woman who 'has an appreciation for good food'."

Thorben crumbled up the parchment wrapper and stuffed it in his pocket, and stopped at another merchant's wagon.

"Dennica can work miracles with a knife and spoon...but we've seven hungry mouths to feed now. So..." he said, picking through the merchant's wares. He set aside two bundles of rope, a pair of leather gloves, and a small stone hammer. Thorben hefted the hammer, testing its make and balance, before ensuring the bladed head was properly affixed to the handle. Finally satisfied, he dropped it onto the pile. He couldn't afford to have his most important tool fall apart opening a cairn or trying to dislodge a door seal.

"Seven children! Mani truly blessed your loins! " Iona said, loudly. The merchant coughed uncomfortably and quickly glanced around. "That must make you jealous of the younger, unwed men, who fill their bellies with second and third and fourth portions." His smaller counterpart bounced on his heels, his eyes flitting down the lane.

Thorben gave the merchant an apologetic smile as he counted out the coin from their meager savings and dropped it into his outstretched hand. A pang of guilt stabbed into his gut as he stuffed the few remaining coins back into his pocket.

Mani, tell me I am making the right decision!

"...well!" he turned and laughed, his voice breaking in an effort to sound upbeat, "with the way my young ones eat, I am lucky to get a portion at all."

With his new gear stowed, Iona set off north out of Laneborough once again, Thorben struggling to keep pace. The late summer sun rose lazily, gilding the thick layer of fog, before finally burning it off close to midday. Thorben's side burned a little as they walked, but it didn't prove detrimental. In fact, the longer he walked the stronger he felt. Iona, however, struggled to keep his fast pace and began to labor, his stiff-legged movements and regular stops speaking of a man more suited to long-distance carriage travel.

"I've not seen a man walk at such a pace...at least one not chasing a girl or a hot meal," Thorben joked as Iona stopped and sagged against his knees, huffing to catch his breath.

"I'm just eager...this could be the find that...changes things for us both, Thorben," he said, and without another word, set off up the road.

A sign appeared on the right side of the road a short time later. The post looked new, the horizontal crossbeam on top holding four arrows, two pointing north, one east, and another south. Hillborough and Klydesborough lay to the north, Darimar to the East, and home, to their backs.

"And here is where we venture from the beaten path," Iona said, and immediately moved into the field to the left.

Thorben paused on the edge of the road, the long, reedy grass grown wild and almost up to his knees. A thick tree line sat a league ahead, the horizon lost in the rolling, covered hills. He stood on the threshold of the wilderness for the first time in many thaws – the first time leaving his family behind...the first time delving. His hands started to shake, and when he clutched them together, the shiver passed down his arms to the rest of his body.

He gave a final glance at the road sign pointing towards Yarborough, and set off after Iona's receding form. They trekked overland for a while before Thorben caught sight of smoke in the trees, the telltale scent of a campfire carrying on the wind. After cresting another few hills, a camp came into view.

A fire sat in the middle of the clearing, round rocks laid out in a protective ring. Four simple tents sat clustered around the fire, their thick fabric bowing crude, stick frames. Three men stood around the fire, the two facing them looking up as they approached.

"Iona, we were expecting you moons from now!" the shortest of the three men said, almost jumping over the fire in his haste to greet them. He fit the bill of every mule Thorben had ever worked with, short, stalky, and powerfully built.

"We made far better time than I originally expected, and we're all better for it," Iona said, hesitantly slapping the short man on the shoulder.

Iona hooked an arm around Thorben's shoulder and pulled him forward to stand before the three men.

"Thorben, these are three of my most trusted strongbacks – Renlo, Hun, and Gor," Iona said, gesturing to the shortest man first, then a man of medium height with short-cropped hair, a severely crooked nose, and muddy brown eyes. The last man, Gor, was massive. His shoulders were wider than his hips, his chest broad with long and well-muscled arms, all supported by legs that looked more like tree trunks. Thorben eyed him up and down, instantly wondering if the man was too large. Tombs were so often confined spaces, and well, size was everything.

"Aye, we're strongbacks alright!" the small man, Renlo, said, and laughed loudly.

"Fellows, this is Thorben. He and I go back ages, and is the most gifted delver I know. He singlehandedly retrieved some of the rarest artifacts I have ever seen–"

"...and sold for a pretty profit!" Gor cut in, smiling broadly. More teeth were missing than were left in the man's mouth, and his breath smelled of rotten cabbage.

"You *will* follow his lead on this quest. Consider *his* word *my* word," Iona said, ignoring Gor's interruption, but as he spoke a fourth individual, almost child-sized, appeared from the far tent. Thorben turned his gaze to the young woman as she approached, a bit of unease turning his stomach.

"Is that to mean you're not delving with us?" she asked, joining the group.

"Thorben this is Jez. She will be your mouse," Iona offered, gesturing to the young woman. Iona dropped his gaze for a moment, his dark eyes clouding over as he refused to meet the young woman's eyes. "And no. That is why I have an owl, like Thorben here. He knows his way around the crypts, and has an eye for valuable trinkets. Alas, my skills lie with parting wealthy men from coin and making them believe they cannot live without my goods. But I will make the march with you, and once we are within proximity of the mounds we will set up camp...and there I will await your return."

To watch the entrance of the tomb and safeguard your investment from walking away, Thorben wanted to add, but smartly kept his mouth shut. He'd learned his lesson at Lamtrop's. Everything rode on this delving. The last thing he wanted to do now was offend Iona, especially after spending a goodly portion of their savings.

Iona scattered the group then, the mules and their small, surprisingly young mouse breaking down camp and stowing their goods with evident familiarity and speed. Thorben watched Gor and his two bulky counterparts argue over who would stow and carry the heaviest of gear.

"To chance, as with all things in life," Gor declared loudly, and pulled out a large, flat, copper coin. He flipped the shiny coin between his fingers for a moment, the movements deft and obviously practiced, and then laid it flat on his large thumb. A flick sent the coin flipping high into the air, before dropping into his massive palm. Gor slapped it against the top of his other hand and held it out. "A ram's head it is...better than a thatcher's bundle. I win," he said, his voice deep and guttural.

Renlo went to work, but Hun groused, stopping to pick and then scratch his horribly crooked nose. Thorben turned as Hun's gaze turned his way, and promptly walked away. He watched the mules finish packing from the edge of camp, keeping tabs on the sword belts, and long, boar spears they hoisted last. The bladed spear points caught the sunlight streaming in from the trees above. They looked freshly smithed and sharp.

They were marching west again in short order, the three mules, with spear and sword, leading the way. Thorben followed Iona, while Jez drifted almost aimlessly behind. After a time, Thorben held up a bit, slowing his pace and letting Iona gain a bit of distance. Jez tromped by, ducking nimbly under a low-hanging tree branch before jumping and crawling over a fallen tree. He clambered over the tree, struggling to match the young woman's grace, but managed to clear the sizable trunk without falling on his face.

"How many times have you delved?" he asked, appraising the girl with a sidelong glance. Her black hair was cut short, sticking up in unkempt tufts. She had relatively close set, brown eyes, thin eyebrows, and a narrow nose. Although she was small, Thorben had difficulty guessing her age. Yes, she looked young, her features delicate and skin unblemished, but there was an age, a weathered quality about her that he couldn't deny. She was either older than she looked, or was young, and had already lived some hard thaws. He could relate.

"Never before," Jez said, simply.

Thorben continued forward in silence for a few long moments, unsure whether he should speed up, slow down, or kindle the conversation.

"Jez, is that short for something?" he asked, finally making up his mind.

"Yes," the girl said and nodded in response, her eyes never leaving the forest floor. Thorben waited for a follow up or an explanation, but it never came. The silence stretched between them, until he cleared his throat and cut sideways and gave her some distance.

It troubled him that Jez was likely the same age as one of his middle sons. He couldn't fathom ever allowing them to delve, and here she was, tromping through the same woods as him, prepared to violate the same Council edicts that earned him his brand, and with unsavory men, to boot.

And I was younger than her when I first delved, and probably just a few thaws older when they caught and branded me, he thought, trying to justify her presence, and thus, comfort his disquiet. But it didn't work. If anything, it made him more uncomfortable.

Thorben pushed around a scraggly pine tree, the skirt of scratchy branches brown and dry, needles peppering the ground. He took a deep breath, fighting the urge to pull her aside and tell her his story, to beg her to turn and run away. What if she wouldn't listen? Or what if she did?

Gor and the other mules marched along ahead of them, making surprisingly little noise despite their size and burden. He didn't doubt the keenness of their ears, either, nor where their loyalties lay. His gaze caught on their gleaming sword pommels and moved to the long spears held loosely at their sides. They weren't so unlike Lamtrop's thug, and Thorben didn't suffer any delusions. If Iona wished it, the three men wouldn't hesitate to turn those spears and swords on him.

Thorben took a step forward, the ground slanting down and away from him into a large, sweeping valley, what looked like a creek at its center. The trees thinned out, the sprawling pines giving way to smaller spindly trees. A breeze blew up through the valley and over him, an earthy, ripe smell tainting the wind. But there was something there, beneath the odor of damp underbrush and silty creek bed, something the previous day's rain had not washed away.

Thorben stopped, smelled the air again, and finally recognized it. Rot. Something was rotting in the valley ahead. Although not an unusual thing in the forest, he knew better, his grandmother's old singsong adage popping to mind - *Run the lane, dance the field, but wary cross the stream.*

Gor and the other mules lumbered down the valley ahead, their packs bobbing along like oversized turtle shells. The men continuously scanned the forest around them, their long spears held ready. Thorben's eyes snapped up to the tall and narrow trees standing creek side. Sunlight streamed down, dancing from the shifting branches. Something sparkled in the shifting light between the trees, like the glint off a diamond, just for a heartbeat, and then it was gone.

"Wait!" he gasped in horror, kicking forward into a run. His boots bit and slid treacherously on the eroded slope. "Don't approach the water!" Thorben hollered, moving as quickly as the footing would allow, but Gor and the mules were approaching the creek, and worse, lowering their spears and sloughing off their packs.

Iona turned towards him, his face scrunching up in alarm. Thorben shoved by him and jumped over a large puddle. He jumped onto a rotten log, the crumbling wood and fungus collapsing as he kicked off. Thorben landed awkwardly in the broad-leafed plants, teetered, and just managed to keep his balance.

Thorben reached the mules just as Renlo pulled the stopper from a water skin and took a step towards the creek. He bounced off Gor's considerable frame and snagged his fingers inside the neckline of the short man's shirt, both falling and pulling with all of his might. Renlo gave a startled, strangled cry and fell backwards, his weight dropping squarely on Thorben.

There was a commotion, a scuffle, the ache flaring in his side and leg. Renlo rolled free, but a boot swung down and caught Thorben on his shoulder, knocking him back down and pinning him to the ground. A bladed spear point swung in a heartbeat later and hovered just below his Adam's apple.

"What kind of man attacks when another's back is turned? I ought to give you a new wind hole!" Gor snarled, towering above him.

"You don't understand...I was just trying to help..."

Gor leaned forward, shifting even more of his considerable weight onto Thorben, cutting him off. Renlo stood next to the big man, rubbing his neck where the collar left a red imprint.

"Hold...Gor, please lower that spear!" Iona hissed, pushing past the two smaller men.

"No hold," Gor snarled, his fleshy cheeks scarlet and his eyes wide. The shiny, copper coin sat perched between two of his meaty fingers.

"A coward, he is a bleedin' thug," Renlo said, trying to push past Iona, "Cowards attack a man's back...when he ain't looking. Cowards can't be trusted. You said he was good, but it appears you are wrong. This one's a coward."

Something shifted in the tall trees above them, a small cloud of leaves drifting down around them. Thorben seemed to be the only one that noticed. He tried to lift his arm to point, to tell them, but Gor smashed him down again.

"Gor, let the man up and speak his defense. There has to be a reason, let's hear his piece–"

The big man's massive knuckles popped, the spear shaking in his grip. Thorben's gaze flitted from his hands past the big man's face and wide eyes, to the dark recesses of the trees. Something was moving in the shadows, uncoiling, too many legs unfurling and wrapping around the largest branch.

"Gor!" Iona said, all subtlety and gentleness gone from his voice. He stepped forward into the big man's shadow, a child in comparison to the spear wielder.

Gor's attention wavered, his dark eyes sliding to Iona. "You don't decide these matters...fate does!" the big man said, and without hesitation flipped the wide coin into the air and caught it. He looked down, snorted, and rocked back, the bulk of his weight falling away from Thorben's chest.

With the weight gone, Thorben rolled away and pushed up to his knees. He stabbed a finger up to the nearest tree, the dark branches creaking and swaying.

"Get back! I was...trying to...warn you," he gasped, heaving, his ribs protesting every movement.

The group moved as one, their eyes lifting towards the tree, and then they all fell back, stumbling and shoving past one another to get clear. Thorben lumbered forward, staggering into Iona and knocking Jez aside. He turned just as two long, dark legs extended out of the tree's shadowy foliage, extending just enough into the narrow band of sunlight to be seen.

Gor, Renlo, and Hun fumbled their spears up defensively.

"A death fisher! Good eye, Owl! Where there is one, there may be more. You just saved us all from a painful end," Iona said, slapping him on the shoulder.

"Wha...what is that? And why couldn't I get a drink of water if it's way up there? I'm fast like..." Renlo asked, his mouth agape.

To answer his question, Thorben scooped up a handful of leaves from the ground at his feet, carefully stepped forward, and tossed them into the seemingly clear space between trees Renlo would have passed through. The leaves scattered in the air, but only a few hit the ground, the rest catching on and sticking to an almost invisible web.

"It wouldn't matter how fast or strong you are. Once snared by a death fisher, there is little hope. They spin their sticky webs along spots like this, and once you become caught–"

"I'm strong. I'd break out of any web. No matter the beast," Renlo interrupted, slapping his fist against his chest, although his eyes didn't drop from the shadowy branches.

"Have a look for yourself," Thorben argued, and gestured to another gap in the trees, just down the creek.

Renlo begrudgingly turned to look, leaned, and approached cautiously. The narrow trees were bent, their lower branches broken and hanging. Thick gouges marred the bark, the ground churned for a stone's throw, as if turned by a horse and plow.

Thorben pointed to where the tree's branches came together, forming a wide canopy. A considerable shadow hung in the mass of branches and leaves, the bottom of two reddish legs and hooves just visible in the light. Renlo recognized it and immediately jumped away, his spear jabbing the air above him.

"That rootstag put up one hell of a fight; and if it's a female, I wager it outweighed you by at least what, ten stones, maybe twelve? Do you still think you'd be able to break free?"

Renlo looked back down to the mud, to the deep furrows, and then to the trees, where the beast's antlers scored deep into heartwood. He swallowed and shook his head, reluctantly meeting Thorben's gaze.

"Run the lane, dance the field, but wary cross the stream."

Gor led them back up the valley, where they traveled parallel to the creek for a while before finally working up the bravery to pass down through the valley. The mules led, waving their spears before them to detect invisible traps and snares.

They traveled in silence after that, Renlo grumbling quietly and refusing to meet Thorben's gaze. Iona walked just ahead of him and behind the three mules, a map held out before him, studying the details with great interest.

"Murderers…the three of 'em," Jez whispered, appearing next to him without warning, and nodded towards Gor and the others.

"Murderers?" Thorben asked. She slapped a finger to her lips, shushing him.

"Murderers," she repeated, simply, her eyes telling a story he didn't understand.

"Tell me."

"You don't know who they really are. It is in their eyes, the way they talk and move. Look for yourself. Decide for yourself. You're not safe," Jez said, her voice low. A shiver coursed through his body.

"Sometimes people kill others to defend themselves," Thorben said. He understood the power of stigma better than anyone.

Jez shook her head, and stopped suddenly as an animal screamed somewhere off in the distance. Thorben watched her scan the forest. Then he spotted Iona standing a fair distance ahead, the map clutched tightly against his chest. He was watching them, his dark eyes unreadable.

"You don't seem to be like the others. You look nice, so I just thought you should know. You shouldn't be here," Jez whispered, her eyes not leaving Gor and the other mules, and then abruptly moved off, slipping almost silently through the trees.

Thorben suddenly wondered what kind of people he was traveling with. He turned and quickly cast an eye over the woods behind him, before following the others.

Chapter Seven
Not What You Think

Using the map, Iona led them through the forest for the better part of the day. The sunlight filtering in through the trees dimmed, and by the time they cleared the woods, dusk was upon them.

"We're clear of the woods and should camp here for the night. The Klydesborough River Guard patrol just north of here, so we should be relatively safe," Iona said, inspecting a patch of flat, dry ground.

Thorben stayed out of the way as Gor and the mules set up the camp, and reluctantly joined Iona and Jez around the fire once they were done.

"You needn't worry, my old friend. Let the mules do the work. That is how they earn their share of our reward. Soon enough, you will earn yours," Iona said, noting his indecision. "We all contribute in our own ways."

"Another day's travel?" Thorben asked.

In response, Iona held out the folded map, Renlo ducking around him to hang a kettle over the fire. He accepted the parchment and unfolded it, turning to use the fire's warm light.

He immediately recognized the Snake River, the oft-traveled road running north through the boroughs, and the Bear Claw River's run west. A stretch of forest extended north and west of Yarborough, and just beyond that stood the immense, sloping bluffs of the kongelig blöd mounds. A river sat just beyond the bluffs, extending from the Bear Claw and running southwest, before disappearing into a scribbled clump of trees and blocky hills.

"What is this river here?" Thorben asked, pointing to the strange waterway, "your map shows no name."

"Keen as ever, Owl," Iona said, unpacking a sack of rolls. "It is the 'unchartered river', and our destination."

"It doesn't appear to be a small river. How could it have gone all this time without being charted? With river merchants traveling up and down the Bear Claw, and the River Guard out of Klydesborough, surely someone would have named it by now," Thorben offered.

Iona shrugged his shoulders, "All good questions, but I'm afraid that I am not the one to answer them, Owl. I do know that it is to our benefit. The river shallows out just north of the mounds, separating into a small delta and some dozen or so smaller waterways. Our entrance is just off that delta. The Council built a bridge, and a fairly rough road from the Shale approach. We have to watch for patrols along that route, as well as around here, and here," he said, coming forward and pointing to the edge of a forest bordering the southwestern edge of the mounds.

"Patrols?" Thorben asked, the idea of sneaking around trained soldiers spiking his worry. A twinge suddenly pinched his wrists as he considered the idea of men shackling him once again. They wouldn't just brand his other arm, but would throw him back into that stinking, dark mine. He wouldn't breathe free air, lay with his wife, or see his kids ever again. He'd die there this time.

Iona waved him off. "Don't worry yourself; it is a nuisance at best. They're sellswords working for the Council's copper. The bulk of their force is stationed here, at the crypt's main entrance," he said, circling the southern bluff, "which is far from where we will be. Our path is well hidden, trust me, they'll never be the wiser."

"There is risk in all deeds," Jez added, quietly, from her lounging perch on the far side of the fire.

"Including speaking out of turn," Iona scolded, turning his dark eyes on the young woman. Jez dropped her gaze to the fire, her mouth screwing up in a sour frown.

"Don't listen to her, Owl. You will be like a shadow before the sun. Treasures lay within those crypts unlike any other delved before. Wealthy men will gaze upon their treasures and whisper our names as legends for thaws to come. I just know it!"

"Or not, and we risk everything for nothing," Jez whispered harshly, leaning towards them. "What makes him the 'delver of legend'? He isn't the smallest or largest of men, the youngest or oldest." She shifted her gaze from Iona to Thorben, adding, "I mean no offense, but there is more at risk here than copper, silver, and gold. You appear to be a particularly ordinary man. I see nothing exceptional about you. You don't even understand what you've stepped into..."

"Silence!" Iona hissed, throwing the girl a simmering glare. Thorben flinched back from the smaller man. There was something in his expression that went beyond anger, deeper.

"Ignore her, Thor–" the broker started to say, but Thorben cut him off and sat up. The girl's words sounded strange in his ears, ringing oddly out of tune with Iona's initial promises. He hadn't delved for half a lifetime, and surely hadn't grown stronger, faster, or smarter in that time. Something continued to feel off, and for once, it was nice to hear someone else say it.

"She's right. And yes, Jez. I've never been the biggest, the strongest, or the nimblest. But..." he trailed off, his thoughts and memories sliding back to his younger thaws. He struck on the thrill of near capture, but also the way the darkness wrapped around his body when first stepping into a crypt. It was truly horrible, the smell of damp and decay lingering with him for so many thaws. He remembered the thrill of stepping back into the sunlight the first time after. It was being born all over again.

Iona cleared his throat, and gazed nervously around the camp. Thorben jarred loose from the drifting memories. He took a breath and continued.

"...from a young age, I just seemed to understand how things worked. I stole iron shavings from my uncle's forge and taught myself how to pick the lock to his tool shed. I tapped the barrel hinges out of the cupboard door to eat the sweets my mother locked up, then put the door back on and replaced the hinges. She was convinced a wraith plagued her kitchen. Later I learned how to mortise and tenon beams together, and helped my father and grandfather build our house. When I was twelve winter thaws old, my father took me to Klydesborough so I could help the armorer repair the River Guard's crossbows. Those little, moving pieces always made sense to me, in some ways more than people ever did. I could look at them, puzzle them, and make them work."

Jez nodded, the faintest ghost of a smile pulling on Iona's lips.

"A man with such skill could live like a king – with such skill he could have secured the patronage of every merchant and skilled craftsman in all the boroughs, built trinkets for the wealthy, or serve the Earl himself," Jez said, her gaze dropping from his eyes and crawling over his old, tattered shirt and plain trousers. Her eyes said what her words didn't...*if blessed with a rare skill, why do you dress like a pauper?*

Without thinking, Thorben's hand dropped to the cuff of his shirt.

"No, you don't have to..." Iona said, shaking his head vigorously, but Thorben ignore him and pulled the sleeve up, the scarred brand almost glowing in the fire's warm light.

"I was a fool and careless, and have spent every sunrise and sunset since paying for it," he said, and let the sleeve fall back down, not bothering to refasten the button.

*Learn from my stupidity, girl. If you can be anywhere else, go. Don't make it any harder than it has to be...*he thought, imagining what it would feel like to run his fingers over the smooth and unblemished skin of his forearm once again.

Thorben returned his gaze to the map, studying the lay of the land – the unchartered river and its rocky gorge, the hills and sweeping valleys, and hoped beyond all hope that the drawn likeness was exact. He didn't want to see the shock or pity in the young woman's eyes, whichever one it was. He only hoped that she would take his warning seriously. Most of all, Thorben hoped that he could capture just a little bit of luck and delve without losing his life, or his freedom, return home to hold his wife, watch Paul realize his dream of becoming a river watchman, and hold the rest of them.

Thorben traced a finger over the map, troubling over the approach to the river. If they committed to an approach and it didn't provide cover or access to the river near the hidden cave, then their delving was doomed before it ever began. He was glad Iona seemed to understand the route.

That evening they ate a cold meal of salted meat and pickled carrots, washing it all down with a cup of bitter, odd-smelling tea. Thorben took a bedroll and set up as far from the three mules as possible without losing all of the fire's warmth. He lay on his back, catching brief glimpses of the stars through the clouds.

Iona sat by the fire for a long time, muttering quietly to himself, studying the map and scratching in a rough, leather journal. Thorben watched him for a time, even after everyone else had turned in. Iona's demeanor changed then. He would be sitting, staring at the map one moment, and stand up in the next, staring into the darkness before pacing back towards the fire. There was an anxiousness about his movements, a restless quality that Thorben knew all too well. He'd spent enough sleepless nights lately thinking and praying for something good, while at the same time dreading the bad that usually came instead, to recognize the signs.

Iona had practically pushed him out of the River's Mouth Inn, and then set a walking pace that even Thorben struggled to maintain. Now he was awake in the black of night, watching the darkness as if something or someone might appear.

But what was following him? It was a question Thorben wasn't sure he wanted answered.

* * * *

Exhaustion and anxiety swirled together, tying Thorben's belly into knots and at the same time, playing tricks with his mind. Dreams fell over him, but he wasn't entirely sure he was asleep. The backlit clouds slipped in front of the moon, the wind rustling the long grass and trees all around their camp, but it was quiet – too quiet.

He was at home in the next moment, walking in through the gate to find Dennah and the boys playing in the yard. Dennica greeted him at the open kitchen door, her embrace warm and soft, her hair clinging to the aroma of lavender oil and freshly baked bread.

"You know that we want you just as you are, I hope you know that," she said, pulling him into a kiss. The kids groaned at the display of affection but rushed over and swarmed them over, smashing together in a massive hug.

"I thought you were like them, a scoundrel...a killer, but I can see now that you're humble...you're good, in your heart...I can tell," she whispered, her soft lips grazing his ear. Someone reached in and shook him, the tangle of arms and bodies suddenly gone.

"It doesn't matter what everyone else thinks of you, husband. It doesn't. Your family loves you, and we will make it together." He heard her voice and longed to pull her close, for a bit of warmth.

"Wake up!" Thorben felt a jolt again, and his mind snapped out of that pleasant place, all the comfort and familiarity of home pulled away in an instant.

He opened his eyes, the air cool and damp against his exposed skin. A pain stabbed in his back and side, a lump poking through the bedroll's worthless padding.

"Did you hear me," someone hissed, a bony finger poking into his arm.

Thorben started, his mind finally detaching from the dream. Jez hovered next to him, her face so close he could have counted her eyelashes.

"Wha…?" he asked, still muddled by sleep. He tried to roll over and get up, but she shoved him back down.

Jez glanced up, looking around the camp, fear drawing her eyebrows up.

"They're murderers…the lot of them. I thought you were like them, too at first, like the others. But I can see that you're different now…can see it in your eyes. I don't know what Iona told you, but it isn't the truth. He has forbidden me from talking to you. Please, he isn't what you remember…not your friend. None of them are. Iona doesn't want you to know that you aren't the first he's asked on this quest. There were others before you, but they couldn't do it. They couldn't open the door. If you can't get them what they want, then they'll…they'll…hurt us," she sputtered, her voice low and fast.

Footsteps sounded beyond their camp, and Thorben turned to see Hun appear from the early morning fog. The wide-shouldered man stopped just inside the camp, facing him, the fire casting his face in a devilish glow. Thorben turned back to Jez, but the girl was gone, the bushes a few paces away still shaking.

Thorben pushed painfully up to an elbow, grimacing as the stiffness pulled his shoulder tight. He rubbed his eyes and turned back to the fire. What did she mean by, "He isn't what you remember? He's not a friend"? Thorben tried to make sense of the girl's warning, but his mind was still addled by sleep and the fading dream.

A shiver rolled up his spine as he laid back down on the bedroll. The last fragments of his dream rolled around in his mind, but like wisps of cloud they were already breaking up and drifting away. The warmth, the last bits of comfort, faded with them.

Hun settled into the camp, letting his long spear fall quietly into the long grass as he sat next to the fire, adding wood and stirring the glowing embers. Thorben felt the mule's eyes on him, but rolled over, pretending to sleep. The sky was still dark, but the birds in the nearby trees were already singing to rouse the sun. He decided not to go back to sleep. There was something about Hun and the other mules that gave him pause, but he couldn't put his finger on why.

They would break camp before the sun rose, and he wanted time to think.

Chapter Eight
The Unchartered River

They ate a hot breakfast of eggs and bacon and broke camp quietly, the three mules having stowed most of their gear before he'd even risen for the day. Thorben ate the meat, a few mouthfuls of egg, and some toasted rolls, wondering why they'd been chewing on jerky and hardtack up till now, when far more appetizing food was available. Unable to finish the substantial portion heaped onto his place, Thorben subtly dumped the rest into the long grass and cleaned up.

They set off shortly after sunrise, Renlo and Gor leading, while Hun stomped out the last of the fire. Thorben interested himself in the clouds as he passed the large man, desperate not to let his gaze linger on the obvious droplets of blood on the mule's hide breeches. Hun quietly fell into step half a dozen paces behind him, his quiet mutterings unintelligible.

He didn't see Jez again until they were well away from the camp. She appeared from the woods to their left, Iona keeping pace just behind. They settled into the group just ahead of Thorben. He watched the young woman walk for a while, taking note in the changes to her gait and posture. Her head hung towards the ground, shoulders tense, and her arms, which swung purposefully at her sides before, clutched tightly to her body now.

They crested a hill midmorning, a small handcart appearing just ahead. The landscape sloped down beyond that, the kongelig blöd mounds appearing off to their distant left, and a sprawling forest to their right.

Renlo and Gor led them past the seemingly abandoned cart, neither of the strong men giving it a second glance. Thorben slowed as he approached, however. Burlap sacks covered the ground, some ripped and snagged on the cart's rough side rails, while a few crates had been upended, and their contents spilled over the ground.

"Who would travel through this country, when there are roads...?" he started to ask but paused. His gaze fell on bits of hard bread scattered amongst the grass, a potato and canvas sack lying not far away. Thorben sucked in a quick breath, swallowing back a curse as the wind flattened a clump of long grass, exposing a worn boot.

Thorben passed the cart and stopped. The remnants of a small fire stood just outside the wagon's shadow, heat and smoke still drifting into the chilly, morning air. The long grass was trampled down in a wide swath, his mind racing to recreate the events that would have caused such a hectic scene. His eyes caught on something just under the cart, the sunrise's long shadows having shielded it just a moment before.

A pair of legs sat behind the wheel, one of their boots missing. The bare foot was pale, like freshly picked cotton, and smudged with dirt. Just beyond, and tucked further into the shadows was another smaller form, and another.

"Let's keep moving, Owl," Hun said, his huge hands curling around Thorben's arms as the man swept him forward.

"Should we at least bury them...and ask Mani to take them into her keeping?"

"These folk lived and died in the wilds, ain't a care you can give them now, and no guarantee they worshipped your goddess. Best keep pace, now move!" Hun said and pushed him forward, the blood spatters on his clothes darker and more apparent in the morning sun.

"Don't push me!" Thorben spat, spinning around on the large man. He connected it all together in his mind – Hun tromping back into the camp in the dead of night, fresh food for their breakfast, the blood on his clothes, and now these travelers murdered and their belongings ransacked.

*They are murderers...*Jez's words echoed in his mind, the food filling his belly suddenly turning uncomfortably. The big man loomed above him, his thick fingers rolling the dark wood spear shaft over and over. Hun's scraggly beard split, and for the first time in the past few moons, he smiled.

"You got spirit, Owl, I'll grant ye that. And you saved Renlo from that beast back in the woods. That'll give you this one pass, but now it's all used up. Turn and walk, or I start cuttin' parts off until you do."

Thorben turned, reluctantly putting his back to Hun, and set off. He walked in silence from then on, listening to the mule's footsteps behind him and wondering if he could outrun him. If he could get back to the woods, he was confident that his smaller frame would allow him to lose the mules in the trees. And yet, now he had the open, rolling hills standing between him and cover, the long, reedy grass perfectly suited to snaring feet and ankles. Plus, he'd never been a strong runner. The big man would likely outrun him through the grass, and use the spear's long reach to cripple him, or if he was practiced, bring him down with one good throw. Thorben's guts quivered as he thought about the spear piercing his flesh, and kicked forward into a slightly faster walk. His small knife and hammer felt paltry on his belt. Hells, he'd never get close enough to the big men to use them.

They made quick and quiet travel through the hills north of the mounds, a small herd of rootstags crossing their path before disappearing into the woods further up the valley. Iona gathered them together behind a cluster of large rocks a short time later.

Thorben climbed up the smooth rock face and laid flat. The ground fell away on the other side, round, smooth stones jutting up and covering the surprisingly steep river gorge on the other side. A narrow, but deep-looking river rushed by at its center, the water crashing over exposed rocks and spouting a misty spray into the air. A thick, misty fog hung a man's height above the water as far as he could see, the air heavily perfumed by damp and silt.

Thorben took it all in, understanding why the river likely had never been charted. The waterway was too deep and the current far too strong, and that wasn't considering the rocks, which would likely smash a sturdy riverboat to kindling in short order.

He spotted a path worn into the long grass on the other side of the gorge, the trail barely visible above the thick layer of fog. A man appeared from a bend in the path further up river, his brown, leather armor and dark green cloak making him difficult to spot against the rocks, trees, and foliage. The soldier carried a pike, the long, bladed weapon serving as his walking stick as well.

"They patrol this path, and there, down by those rocks," Iona said, next to him. Thorben scrambled in surprise, almost sliding off his perch. He hadn't even heard the man climb the rock, let alone settle next to him.

"I didn't mean to startle you, Owl. But there, down by the rocks. Do you see the bridge? When this soldier reaches that bridge, another will pass him moving north. Watch," Iona said, extending his arm out and pointing down the gorge.

Thorben squinted, willing his eyes to pierce the mist, and finally made out the bridge. He watched the man pick his way down the path, disappearing and reappearing through low spots in the trail. The mist seemed to pool heavier there, floating up the river valley before curling up like massive fingers and drifting back towards the water.

The bridge loomed in the mist, a shadow of bulky timber and taught rope, spanning the rocky gorge. The dark silhouette of another soldier appeared on the far end of the bridge, the two forms converging briefly in the middle, before continuing in opposite directions.

"They patrol from sunup to sunset, and during the night, with torches," Iona said, answering his unspoken question.

"How much time passes between patrols? How much time do we have to cross the bridge?"

Iona chuckled, but Thorben's sidelong glance confirmed that the man was not smiling.

"Our route will not take us across the bridge," Iona said, flatly.

Thorben searched his face for a moment, his gaze snapping down to the treacherous rocks jutting out at the water's edge, and across to the western bank, where a small, but dry-looking sandbar hugged the gentler slope.

"According to your map, the cave entrance is on the western side of the river, and the rocks on the eastern side look–"

"Yes…I know your mind, Owl. But it is far more complicated than you realize. Also, I did not say we wouldn't be crossing the river here. I just said we wouldn't be crossing the bridge. The river valley becomes much steeper south of the bridge…an almost sheer cliff with a life-crushing drop into the rocky water below. That, I would suppose, is why they chose this spot for their river crossing. The trail our soldier friends patrol to the north and west is too close to the water's edge, so we cannot cross further upstream and use the sand bars and shallows. They would see us, even in the mist. You see, their patrols are expertly planned, leaving very little time for us to break from cover and cross the river before being spotted. We have to cross the water there," he explained, pointing directly under the bridge, "where the shadow is darkest, and the mist thickest."

"That is madness!" Thorben spat, and immediately slid backwards to move off the rock, except something barred his way. He turned to find Gor immediately behind and below him, his massive frame perched half on and half off the rock.

"It is!" Iona laughed, quietly. "You've lost a bit of your old touch, Owl. On most occasions it was you concocting the most extraordinary solutions to our problems…like that tomb we discovered east of the Snake River. Do you remember?"

Thorben nodded. Of course he remembered, he had blisters on his hands for several moons after that delving to show for his efforts.

"You couldn't get into the crypt, as a massive stone had been wedged into the opening, so you dug through the dirt on the hill above for two sunrises, before finally lowering yourself down with a rope. None would enter that space but you. This situation is no different. Put some trust in me, old friend."

"It will take more than trust to cross that water, Iona. That water looks deep and the current wild. We'll be swept downriver and drowned by the undercurrent, or better, bludgeoned against the rocks."

Iona's expression remained flat, and this time Gor chuckled, the sound raspy and ominous. Thorben knew what it meant. The river would only kill him if Gor allowed it to. The big man's spear hung at his side...more a promise than anything.

"Like I said, Owl. Trust in me. Preparations have been made," Iona said, and promptly slid back off the rock. Gor raised an eyebrow and turned, allowing Thorben to follow.

"If trust is what must move us forward, then I guess you have it. My job starts at the crypt's entrance, not here in the wilds."

"Good," Iona said, Gor and Renlo pushing past to lead. Then he hooked a hand around Thorben's arm and gently, but firmly, directed him to follow. Hun chewed on an apple and fell into step just behind them, his spear tapping a quiet cadence against the rock.

The mules led them downriver, picking their way slowly through the tall, jutting rocks. Thorben followed, narrowly avoiding a deep fissure in the rock. He waited on the other side of the dark opening and helped Jez cross, then Iona. He tried to settle in towards the back of the group once they were moving again, to talk with Jez, but Iona and Hun were there, watching and pushing him forward.

The mist became thicker as they approached the bridge, the rocks shielding them from the patrols growing shorter. Thorben pushed by a shrub to follow Gor, something within the plant jabbing through his trousers and into his leg. He hissed, dropping back against the rock, and managed to pull free, the plant breaking loudly.

Thorben's fingers trembled as he pulled a disturbingly long thorn out of the meat of his thigh. He lifted it up to his face, examining the barb in the mist. Long and viciously sharp, the thorn was covered in barbs from stem to tip, bits of fabric and his skin still stuck in place.

"Hunter's snare. They grow all over this valley," Iona whispered, appearing from the mist, "incredibly aggressive plant...best to watch where you step, and cover your manhood. Hate to catch one of those barbs in the..."

"Aggressive plant?" Thorben muttered, picking his way forward once again, giving the bush a wide birth. As he inched past, the hunter's snare started to shiver and shake, its thorny branches lashing towards him. He instinctively dropped a hand over his genitals and moved into the clear, favoring the throbbing cut in his thigh. Blood already formed a small, coin-sized stain on his trousers.

Thorben lifted himself up and crawled between two rocks, and almost dropped onto another of the horrible plants on the other side. He landed, danced awkwardly to his right, and just managed to lift his legs out of the way as the thorns snapped out. A stab of pain stabbed into his bruised ribs and he keeled over, his breath momentarily rejecting him.

"Give me my chair and my fireplace...I'm too old for this," he muttered a few painful moments later, when he was finally able to choke down a breath. "You tangle with a thug...and he pummels you, so you decide to trek out into the wilds and what? Get attacked by thorny plants. You fool; you should have stayed home..."

Thorben stumbled around the plant and came upon Renlo just ahead. The mules waited behind a cluster of rocks. A massive timber loomed above them, a copper brazier burning brightly, the mist swirling angrily around the dancing flames.

The mules led them quietly along the rocks to their right, the bridge spanning the dark river, while the ground dropped precariously below them. He slipped and slid down several rocks, the slimy, moss-covered slope like ice under his boots. He slid, caught his balance, and almost pitched forward into Renlo's back, just managing to reclaim his balance.

Thorben picked his way down one careful step at a time, thick strands of cobwebs dragging across his face in the blinding mist. He sputtered and almost swiped at his face, but knew that if he took his hands off the rocks, he would fall. It would only take one of them to lose their footing and knock the rest of their group tumbling down the slope. If that happened, he could only hope that the fall against the rocks killed him, and he wouldn't have to wait to bleed out, or for some hungry creature to happen upon him.

The mules clambered ahead and below him, somehow moving sure-footed down the lethal rocks. How were they so confident climbing down the rocks? He couldn't see more than a pace or two ahead of him, and they moved as if they'd trekked down this slope before.

Thorben swallowed down the panic and took a step, and then another. He dropped his foot and found a hold, and miraculously, the mist lifted. The water rushed by noisily, the sound previously blocked by the thick mist. He took another dozen steps and found himself standing at the narrow river's edge.

Renlo and Hun stood to his right, the water rushing by their feet in a sweeping torrent. Thorben looked up the river, and then down, astounded by the sight. The thick layer of mist hung above his head like a thick, wool blanket, and yet everything beneath it was perfectly clear. He couldn't see the sky, or the sloping riverbank, the bridge supports disappearing in the mist above. The patrolling soldiers were somewhere above them, too, marching along, the heavy *tromp...tromp...tromp* of their boots loud against the planks. He hoped that he was as invisible to them, as they were to him.

Jez appeared suddenly out of the mist and slid, losing her footing. Thorben reacted on instinct and swung around, hooking the young woman around the waist and pulling her back, so they fell together to the steep bank, before momentum could carry her into the water.

"Thank you, Owl. I see you've found a bit of your old reflexes," Iona said, appearing from the mist, huffing and struggling to catch his breath. Thorben grunted as the young woman pushed off to stand, his thigh now throbbing in time with his aching side.

"Are you...okay?" he asked her. She nodded hastily, tucking a few strands of loose hair behind her ear. She hastily turned away as Gor appeared down the slope, the massive man moving down the treacherous rocks with more grace than Thorben thought possible.

Iona looped an arm around Jez and pulled her towards the water's edge. "Let us cross quickly, we are so close to the cave now. I can feel it," he said, and promptly reached up into the mist.

"I still don't understand. How are we supposed to cross? Just look...the water is far too deep. We cannot swim it; the current will push us down..." Iona cut Thorben off by promptly kicking his legs out, his body miraculously hanging just below the mist.

Thorben watched in horror as Renlo reached up into the mist as well, his added body weight pulling a rope down into view. Iona stepped back and let the mule take his place. The stout man then dropped his boots into the water, and hand over hand, started making his way across the river.

This is madness...I can't, he thought, and moved to back away. He couldn't pull his gaze away from the dark, rushing water, its violent, swirling current straight out of a nightmare.

Hun followed Renlo, and then Iona gestured Thorben forward. When he didn't immediately respond, Gor moved up behind him and muscled him forward. Thorben picked his way over the rocks, his boots just clear of the churning water.

"Still afraid of water, Owl?" Iona asked, turning to watch the two mules disappear into the mist. "Come. Take it slowly, and you will be fine. After all, wasn't it you that once told me, 'the only thing that separates a successful man from a fool is preparation'? The ropes are expertly strung. This is as safe a crossing as we could manage."

Thorben finally tore his gaze away from the water and met Iona's gaze. The man used his weight to pull the rope down, and grasped his right hand, forcing it up and onto the line. "Now, over you go. I wouldn't dawdle in the water...best to be quick."

Thorben resisted his nudge forward, trying to swallow past the hard lump now perched in his throat. Safe? How could he consider such a crossing safe? Gor moved behind him and a hard, sharp point came to rest against his lower back. He inched forward until the water lapped up and over the toes of his boots.

His suspicions solidified. Iona and the mules had already walked their path, and very likely new what lay before them. If Jez was to be believed, Thorben wasn't the first delver either. What other surprises were waiting for him? What else hadn't Iona told him?

Iona has already crossed the river, Thorben told himself. *He has. It is safe. I am safe.*

The spear jabbed hard into his back, forcing Thorben to step out into the water. His aching side protested the sudden strain of body weight, his throat closing from fear. He fished around for a few moments, until the sole of his boot snagged on something just under the surface. Thorben relaxed just a bit and let the rope suspended in the water carry his weight.

It is simple. Just put one hand in front of the other...and then one foot, and so on, he thought, walking his hands forward, before blindly stepping out to find the rope with his other foot. *Don't look down, you fool. Just focus on the rope.*

The rope sagged under his weight a little with each step forward. The churning water rose up over his ankles, his knees, and then his thighs, until he was waist-deep in the dark water, the strange blanket of mist hanging just above his hands. The damp rope jumped and squirmed in his grasp as someone made their way behind him.

Thorben's heart pounded away in his chest as he clumsily inched forward. His boots started to feel heavy, the cold water sapping the feeling away from his legs.

"I should have stayed home, I should have stayed home," he gasped in a mantra, his teeth chattering together. Thorben thought of home, Dennica, and the children – anything to keep his mind off the cold and dark water churning around him. The pain, the sacrifice...he was doing it for them. A fish jumped out of the water a short distance away, the brightly color creature thrashing its fins as if trying to fly. He flinched as another leapt not far away.

Thorben hooked his hand forward, taking another step as another of the fish burst out of the water somewhere behind him. The rope under his feet moved suddenly, his entire body sagging deeper into the water. The current swirled around him, pulling his whole body sideways. A sucking noise filled the air as the water worked to pull him down. The rope jerked again, and in response his body rose a moment later.

Oh, gods. Mani, see me to dry land!

He held his breath, waiting for strangled cries and splashing – but only silence ensued. A heartbeat later the rope shook as the others started to move. A bird shrieked above him, the odd squawk quickly answered by another. A dark form streaked through the mist above him, another swooping down to skim the water to his right.

The rope jerked again, just as debris rained down from above, peppering his head. The water came alive around him, the surface bubbling with dozens of the brightly colored fish, each flopping and leaping above the surface.

Black feathers beat the air next to his head as one of the large birds swooped down, scooping a fish cleanly out of the air. With the fish latched in its talons, the winged creature hovered for a moment. It wasn't a bird, at all, Thorben realized. It had a scaly body, with small, reptilian arms tucked tightly to its body. It had no beak, either, but a smashed, flat face, with massive, cup-shaped ears, and a mouth filled with pointy teeth. The beast had no eyes, or if it did they were too small for him to see.

Iona's words echoed back in his head – *be quick. Best not to dawdle.* The reality of that warning sunk in as a large, dark form moved through the water to his right. In response, a school of the brightly colored fish bubbled to the surface, flopping and jumping into the air.

Thrasher fish, he thought, just as another of the winged creatures swooped down towards the churning water. It dropped its talons into the water, snared a small fish, and flew right by him, careening off into the mist.

Wobbling on the rope, Thorben swung forward a step, and then another, his movement clumsy through the water. His eyes darted upriver, and then down, searching the dark surface for signs of movement...but he couldn't make anything out in the turbulent water.

His mother told him stories of thrasher fish growing up – how the beasts could grow to the length of a man and double their weight. She drew pictures of them in the dirt outside their shack...finger-length teeth sticking out of a long, snapping maw, razor sharp barbs covering their fins, and massive, unblinking eyes.

She'd told her story, toothless, and drunk on bread liquor.

"I was a girl when I first saw them...the thrashing beasts. Big, monsters they were, but not fish. Our people say they are the spirits of dead mothers, driven mad by the memory of their dead children. They haunt the water, always looking for children to pull in, to pull down into the depths and drown, a child to hold for all time."

Thorben remembered the story. He'd peed himself, his gran immediately throwing a spoon at him. He hadn't gone swimming since, the fear of being pulled into the water and eaten like the children in her stories growing into such a debilitating terror that he refused to even approach the water's edge. Now he was waist deep in it, surrounded by the very monsters of her stories.

He managed another half dozen paces forward, the rocks of the western shore materializing out of the fog. Thorben cleared his throat, and tried to swing his right arm forward again, his fingers catching the slimy rope and promptly sliding off. The sudden shift in weight spun him, and before he could grab the rope again, his boots slid free.

"Nnno...!" Thorben hissed frantically as the entirety of his weight fell on his left hand, his body sliding chest-deep into the water. He managed one terrified jab for the overhead rope, before his fingers broke loose.

Thorben's head plunged beneath the surface, his arms going rigid with panic. He dropped like a stone in the cold water, until something hard snagged his arms, his weight forcing them out straight. It hit him, and he clutched just in time, the submerged rope almost sliding completely out of his grasp. Thorben hung in the water for a moment, the strong current pulling his body out and away from the rope. Pain stabbed into his chest as panic fought to unravel him.

Lungs burning, Thorben pulled forward and tucked the taught rope against his body, and gave a mighty push. His face broke the surface and he gulped down a quick breath, and then another, but the current quickly pulled him under once again. He fought forward again, but the strain was too great, and his body too heavy. This was it. This was his end.

Thorben forced his eyes open and gave a strangled cry as something moved in the water before him. He felt it more than anything, but now that he was surrounded by the water, everything appeared in a strange, blue-tinged clarity.

A massive form approached, its body undulating smoothly, propelling it against the current. The thrasher fish moved through a column of dim light shining from above. Long, sharp teeth curved over its elongated mouth, the scales covering its body shimmering like blue-green gems in the diffuse glow.

The fish approached, easily as long as he, if not longer. Colorful ridges and spines covered its fins, driving it easily towards him. Thorben tried to scream, his voice lost in a flurry of rising bubbles. He flinched, anticipating the bite, his eyes locked on the animal's toothy grin. Only the thrasher fish didn't attack. It tilted in the water, its massive, silver eye studying him.

Thorben pulled his legs up as the creature flicked forward in a surprising burst of speed. He turned, choking a bit as the urge to draw breath grew in intensity. The fish circled twice, its unblinking silver eyes appraising him, and then without warning, the water denizen flicked its large tail and disappeared into the depths.

Water slipped into his mouth as Thorben's body almost forced him to draw a breath. He pulled on the rope, but there was no more strength in his arms. He'd never be able to pull himself up for another breath; so instead, he pulled his body along the rope. Hand over shaking hand Thorben went, a dark fuzziness creeping over his mind.

Bright flashes of light started to fill his vision, but he could see rocks ahead. They jutted up from below, slanting away from him. He managed another pull, and then another. The rocks were right under him, growing in size and rising towards the surface. Thorben hooked a boot on the closest rock, pushed off and caught another.

The rope slid out of his hands as water rushed into his mouth. The urge to draw breath intensified, but a horrible, cold pressure bit at his chest. He clawed at the rocks ahead and above him, pulling his body forward, the current pushing him stream at the same time. He reached for the next rock, but missed. The fuzziness closed in as dark objects splashed into the water to his side.

Chapter Nine

The Real Reason

Thorben's body felt heavy, and in an instant, became buoyant again. He was rising, the dark water getting lighter, until his head broke the surface, the unruly water gushing around and spattering his face. And yet his arms and legs felt dead. Lifeless.

He floated forward before dropping heavily onto the sandy rocks, the heavy, icy pressure in his chest strangling him. Thorben tried desperately to draw breath, but couldn't seem to find any air. Strong hands released their hold on his arms, the sharp rocks stabbing into him as he rolled over onto his side.

A blow struck him in the back, between his shoulder blades, and the tightness in his chest intensified. Thorben slipped a little further into the darkness, silently yearning for a release from the pain. A second blow rocked him, and then a third. A dull roar filled his ears, distant shrieks and calls barely piercing the blanket of sound.

Water bubbled up his throat and out his mouth, his entire body starting to shake. Thorben gagged, and coughed. Air, blessed air, entered his lungs. Another sharp blow snapped him forward, the strike causing him to cough up another mouthful of warm water. His guts contracted, water and vomit flowing up and out of his body. He retched into the darkness, his eyes still unseeing.

Gritty sand forced its way between his fingers as Thorben finished, curling his numb limbs into his body, his chest and side aching with every violent cough. He blinked over and over, but everything remained dark and blurry. Finally, after an untold amount of time, he rocked onto his back and managed to sit. Thorben swiped at his face, dislodging sand, mucus, and rock.

He took a deep, shuddering breath, a raspy rumble sounding inside his chest. This time when he blinked, his surroundings started to come into focus.

"W...h...a...t?" he croaked, trying and failing to form a simple question. In response, the darkness above him shifted, and strong hands pulled him off the ground.

Renlo held him a moment as his legs shook and threatened to fail. His gaze fell to the spear at the man's feet, his eyes snapping back to the stout man's dark eyes.

"The others are on ahead. Let's catch up," the mule said, and firmly urged him forward.

Thorben wanted to tell him no, to demand more time to collect his wits, but stumbled forward instead, mostly blind, doubling over and waving his hands before him. He tripped on a rock, stumbled over a shrub, and almost walked into a tree. No, not a tree. The hewn pine log jutted up into the fog, supporting the stout bridge somewhere above them.

Yes, the bridge, the fog...the river, Thorben thought, finally putting things back together in his mind. He leaned against the thick support, took another deep breath, coughed, and wiped his face. He looked back to the river and its violent, dark water. He'd managed it...made it across, if only just.

Renlo moved behind him, but it wasn't the poke of a spear point in his back to motivate him forward, but the gentle grasp of strong hands. Thorben pushed away from the log and moved to walk, but the strong man held him back.

"You should have said...about the water," Renlo said, his flat, crooked nose and broad forehead appearing less severe in the fog, his dark eyes less menacing.

"Would it have mattered?" Thorben asked, his voice still hoarse.

The mule considered his words for a moment. "You helped me back there...in the trees, with that beast. I...I..."

"It's not something a man easily admits...that he is afraid of the water...that he cannot swim," he said, interrupting the shorter man.

"All men fear something. Death, beasts, blades," Renlo whispered, his dark eyes searching Thorben's face.

"True," he said, choking a wet cough into his hand. His chest didn't ache quite so bad this time, the pain throbbing in his side less acute. "But is that something your fellows will admit or accept from a man like me? I think they would sooner laugh in my face and mock my weakness."

Renlo looked to his left and down the river valley, where his counterparts moved somewhere in the mist. His forehead scrunched up for a moment, and then he silently shook his head.

"Why did you come? You're not like the others," the mule said after Thorben coughed and wrung out his shirt. "You don't belong out here."

Chuckling quietly, Thorben unbuckled his satchel and poured out the water trapped inside. "Thaws ago I was that person. I spent more time in the wilds than at home and lived for each delving, but now..." he said, his thoughts sliding effortlessly to Dennica and the kids. He envisioned them grasping shrunken bellies and shivering from the cold...suffering. "...now, I have no other choice. I am here, because if I am not, my family will not survive."

Renlo hovered next to him for a moment, his thoughts playing out through his changing facial expressions. Finally, after shifting his weight between feet several times, he said, "Let's go. It is just down the river for a time. We shouldn't keep Gor waiting."

They moved off together, the big man draping a wide hand on Thorben's shoulder, guiding him onto a sandy strip of bank where the rocks weren't quite so treacherous. The river bubbled and rushed by just a few paces to his left, and its angry current entirely too close for comfort.

Thorben fought to keep his gaze locked on the ground before him, fighting the urge to turn toward the dark, turbulent surface.

The heavy fog cleared after a time, the oppressive smell of silty water lifting with it. A short while later Thorben came around a bend and spotted Iona and the rest of the group waiting.

"Owl, I am so relieved to see you up and well. When you dropped into that water, we all feared you lost," Iona said, but it was Jez that leapt off of her rocky seat. She ran forward and grasped his arm, her eyes wide and glassy. For a moment, he thought she might cry, or hug him. Thorben saw something in her eyes...a message she couldn't convey with words. Was she happy to see him? Or...sad?

I can't return empty handed, he thought. He wished that he could make her understand. There were stakes that involved more than just him.

Clearing his throat, Iona stood and moved over behind Jez. She sniffed, quickly looked away and walked off, their brief connection broken. They fell into line and moved down the river, the wind picking up gradually.

Thorben looked longingly at the sun's diffuse light kissing the opposite side of the valley, where the rocks left no room for shade trees. He shivered, wishing only to stand in the light and let the warmth dry his damp clothes, but that wish would not come true.

They moved around a tight bend in the river, the jagged rocks no longer gently sloping up, but now creating an almost sheer wall of solid stone. A wide shelf extended from the cliff and hung out over the water, supported on both sides by what looked like natural columns of stone. A dense curtain of ivy hung from the shelf, draping onto the ground and looping in massive, green vines and purple leaves, before disappearing into the water.

"The very spot where our fortunate monk found himself lost," Iona said, sweeping a hand towards the vines. Thorben turned around, surveying the somewhat sheltered cove. His eyes crawled over the stone, catching on every drawn shadow and large gap, and yet none looked large enough for a person to enter. And more strangely still, he struggled to identify a spot where a person might crawl down into the valley.

"I don't understand. You said there was a cave?" Thorben said, picking his way forward and pulling the curtain of ivy aside. A shallow cove hung behind the wall of vegetation, a small pool of mossy water covering the ground, but no cave.

"Your eyes have been too long from delving, Owl. You know, as well as I, that the dalan hid their secrets well," Iona said, but there was no mirth, no warmth, in his voice anymore. His eyes flitted quickly between Gor and Hun before returning to Thorben. A look haunted Iona's eyes, one eerily similar to what he saw in Jez. Did they both know something?

Thorben involuntarily turned and looked behind him, his gaze flitting up the river, across the bank to the stone, and then back down the valley. A thought nagged him, hovering at the back of his mind. He was missing something...*but what?*

"Follow me," Iona said, and picked his way past the ivy curtain, moving down river. He passed the end of the shelf and turned right, disappearing into a shadow.

Thorben abruptly stopped and looked to Jez. She gave him a sidelong glance, before Gor prodded her forward, and she too stepped into the shadow.

"Now you," Gor said, the three mules hovering just behind him, their bulk spaced out like a wall of muscle and spear.

Reluctantly, Thorben walked toward the shadowy corner, his hands reaching out for what his eyes told him was solid stone. And yet, his fingers passed into the darkness and found only air.

"A trick of the shadow...an illusion of stone?" he whispered, and stepped forward. Thorben passed into dark and back into light in the span of a heartbeat, a shoulder-width passage curving around to his immediate left. He turned and marveled at the hidden entrance, his eyes crawling up the jagged stone. A number of thick, rocky outcroppings hung above, stepped one above the other and splayed like barely separated fingers. With the layer of mist gone, he looked straight up to the sky, where the sun hung high overhead.

"Of course...to catch the sunlight and keep the entrance in shadow, even as the sun moves across the sky," he breathed in awe.

Gor stepped through the entrance to the passage then and forced him forward. The massive man had to turn sideways, his shoulders too wide to fit down the narrow passage.

Thorben moved along the path. He turned as the maze-like passage curved sharply to his right. Gor, Hun, and Renlo filled the passage behind him, cutting him off. For the first time since meeting up with the group in the woods, he was trapped, boxed in by stone and sharp spears. Running was no longer an option.

Thorben followed the path as it wove serpent-like through the rock, until finally, it turned right once again and opened up into a wider alley. A stone slab door sat straight ahead. The thick stone was cracked and broken, almost a third of its bulk lying on the ground to his left.

He walked up to tomb door, a single relief carving decorating its smooth surface. It was a round eye, its pupil the shape of a star, the telltale carvings of lightning extending as eyelashes.

"The monk found this? This is where he made the rubbing?" Thorben asked, and reached into his bag. He pulled the parchment free, but it was a pulpy mess, the river water destroying its captured image.

"In," Gor grumbled, and prodded him forward with the spear shaft, the ruined sheaf of parchment falling to the ground.

"Someone has already...no, you've already broken into the crypt," he said, pointing to the fractured portion of the slab.

"In!" Gor repeated and smacked him harder with the spear shaft, pushing him hard towards the opening. Thorben staggered forward, the force jarring his bones and reigniting the pain in his side. He dropped awkwardly to his knees, and crawled into the gap in the stone slab.

"You could have asked," he muttered, crawling forward on his hands and knees.

The air was stale on the other side of the door, and very dark. Thorben stood, immediately aware of the dampness of his clothes, the stagnant air closing around him like a tight, icy blanket. He drew in another deep breath, the achy rattle still buzzing in his chest. There was an odor on the air that he couldn't quite identify, beyond the heavy aroma of mold and damp.

Sparks ignited in the shadows, and a moment later a torch flared to life. One burning torch became two, and then three. Thorben stood shivering just inside the shattered slab door, his arms wrapped protectively around his body, trying and failing not to shiver visibly.

"I...I...If you've already broken through the door, what do you need me for?" he asked, shivering and looking around, his voice echoing between walls.

Hun walked around the outside of the circular chamber, stopping every dozen paces to dip his torch into a stone brazier. The stout man skipped over several braziers on the left side of the room, leaving half the space in heavy shadow.

Thorben stepped forward, taking in every detail as the light blossomed, revealing reliefs carved into the walls around him - ivy branching and trees crawling, while strange and fantastical creatures leapt or soared on massive wings. The carvings branched all the way up to the smooth, domed ceiling, where a chandelier of silver rings and crystals hung. The crystals caught the firelight, redirecting it in long splashes of rainbow color. He watched the chandelier rotate ever so slowly, the reflections moving in a slow arc around the circular chamber.

A waist-high column stood immediately to his right and inside the broken door, the stone so finely polished that it almost glowed in the firelight. Thorben ran his hand over it, taking in every detail, before leaning in closer and blowing a fine layer of dust off the top. A small, round hole had been cut into the flat surface. He ran a finger around the stone's rounded edges and moved forward.

"Not the crypt, but the doorway to one," he surmised, as Iona approached. The man crossed his arms over his chest and watched Thorben, a peculiar expression haunting his eyes.

"I thought we were going to make camp, and you were going to wait there?" he asked. Iona swallowed, and moved forward silently, his dark eyes flitting over Thorben's shoulder. He turned his head to follow the gaze, only to find Gor standing just inside the gap of the broken door, his spear held ready.

"I am truly sorry, old friend. And I do mean that. At one point, I considered you more than just an associate, but a friend...maybe even family. That is why I didn't want to bring you...tried everything in my power to prevent dragging you back into this life, but you must understand, I'm a desperate man," Iona said, walking up to a circular platform located directly in the room's center. Intricate patterns had been carved into the stone, a podium branching out of its back edge. A number of strange, barrel shaped contraptions stood on end atop the podium, spun or carved out of some rich, dark wood. A heavy gate broke the solid stone of the far wall, the stout metal still gleaming after untold thaws of damp and darkness.

"Desperate? I don't understand? What is going on?" Thorben asked, stepping towards the podium and its odd decorations. A warning bell rang in his mind, all of the strange glances, comments, and behaviors spinning together. But he couldn't put them together. Thorben absently reached towards the podium.

"Don't step on the symbol! Don't touch the keys!" Jez shouted, running in from behind them.

The girl slapped Thorben's arm down and pulled him violently away, tearing his shirtsleeve. Before he could react, Hun moved forward and pulled Jez back, lifting her feet clear of the ground in the process.

"Let her go!" Thorben shouted, and moved to help the struggling girl, but Gor surged forward, the spear snapping up and leveling at his belly.

"Okay, Owl. No making camp, no more talking...we're here, and 'tis time for you to do yer work. Do what we brought you here for, and get us into that crypt!" the big man said, his eyes wide as he moved forward.

"What is your man about, Iona? What is going on? Tell him to let go of her!" Thorben demanded, backing away, his eyes dropping to the spear point. He turned to Iona, who stood just to his right and back a few steps.

"Please don't hurt her. You promised you wouldn't hurt her if I did everything you said! I did it all didn't I? I got Thorben, he is here now," Iona said, his voice breaking, and took a halting step towards the mules.

"I only said I wouldn't kill her," Gor snarled, Hun's arm tightening around Jez's neck in response. "She lives if you get me what's promised! You...?" The big man's words died off in a threatening chuckle.

Iona faltered, and spun, his eyes swiveling rapidly between Thorben and Jez, as she struggled in Hun's arms. Thorben watched the two mules, something moving in the corner of his eye. Renlo stood just beyond the other two, his face scrunched up in an almost pained expression.

"It was all a lie..." Thorben muttered, putting the pieces together finally. "Was any of it true?" he asked, pulling his ripped sleeve up and exposing the brand.

"I'm sorry, Owl. You never would have come if I'd told you the truth. And I would not have blamed you...especially considering the stakes," Iona said, unwillingly meeting Thorben's gaze. "But you see...you're my last shot to get into that crypt. There is more at stake here than wealth and brands…I needed you to come. I need you."

Thorben looked from Iona, to Jez, and up to Gor's ruddy face. It clicked into place, and he instantly felt the fool. The girl had Iona's dark hair and eyes, his height and build. Damn, he'd let his mind get slow…let his family and troubles bog down his thoughts. Why hadn't he seen any of it sooner?

"Jez is your daughter?" Thorben whispered the words, but Iona heard, and nodded, his gaze dropping to the floor.

"Enough talk. We've played our part long enough…waited long enough…now get to it! Gor said, his eyes flashing Thorben and the podium.

"Play your part?" he echoed.

Gor nodded. "Yup…we played the dim, bowing and scraping, willing little mule servants. Did it good, too. All cause Iona didn't trust that you'd make it all the way here. He feared you'd get scared and run off into the woods and leave him alone, and we weren't for chasing any more of you tricky little bastards down, neither. But now you're here, so do your part. Simple."

"You want me to open up that gate…for you?" Thorben asked, watching the big man's mouth move, his remaining teeth gleaming in the torchlight.

"Yes, clever man. You said it yourself, remember? You understand how things work. Now be clever, and open that gate! The River Guild will have the treasure Iona promised, or the blood debt will come due," the big man said, holding out a torch. "Open the gate, or my spear starts letting blood."

"Wait, I don't know…" Thorben said, accepting the torch, but swallowed his own words, realizing in horror the consequences of that admission. If he couldn't do what they wanted, then he had no value to them. "Alright! Just give me a little time! Let me take a look around...no one needs to get hurt." He eased away from the spear, his hands held up defensively.

Turning, Thorben moved towards the raised pad, unwillingly putting the big men and their spears to his back. He held the torch out before him, the flickering light illuminating the carved pattern covering the raised platform. The shadows drew, stretching as if trying to get away from the light, but the glow couldn't seem to penetrate the darkness pooling inside the carvings. And then Thorben realized why. He saw a dark spot on the stone, and then another. A bloody smear stretched off the left side of the pad, down onto the floor, and disappeared in the dark side of the chamber.

The carvings etched into the platform were filled with blood.

Chapter Ten

A Key to Survive

Recoiling from the sight, Thorben circled the pad, his eyes crawling over the rock. Now that he'd noticed the blood, he saw it everywhere – pooled in the cracks and carvings, smeared on the ground, and dark spatters on the podium and its strange contraptions.

He knew he wasn't the first man to try and open the crypt – all indications told him that Iona had likely talked several into the task before him. His desperation was proof enough of that fact. And yet, from the look of the platform, none of those men walked back out of the chamber again. Maybe carried…or dragged.

"This controls the gate?" he asked, gesturing towards the podium. *Jez called them keys,* he thought, leaning in to study the three wooden barrels. Each was covered in multiple carvings, the runes separated by inlays of rich, gold filigree. A sliver of crystal sat embedded in the podium just before each key, evidently serving as a marker. The first shone like emerald, the second ruby, and the third clear, like a diamond.

Iona nodded, moving around the opposite side of the pedestal. "Gadric surmised quickly that they are keys, and must be turned in the correct order and combination. He was like you, Owl…clever. Given enough time, I believe he would have figured it out. Unfortunately…"

"Given enough time?" Thorben echoed, cutting him off. In response, Iona's gaze drifted towards the shadowy side of the chamber. Gor and Hun shuffled in behind them, the spears held level with the ground, a silent and effective reminder. *Be clever. Open the gate, or…*

"The keys can only be turned once a person is standing on the platform, and if they aren't turned in the correct order, they…they die. You have three chances."

Thorben swallowed hard, his chest going tight. He circled back around the platform in the other direction, holding the torch close to study the runes etched into the keys. He recognized several of them from tombs he'd delved before. *Think, you fool. The answer is usually simpler, no it's always simpler, than most people think…step back, relax, and watch. You can figure this out!*

Taking a deep breath, Thorben cleared his head, willing away the cluttered, frantic thoughts jumbling his mind. He turned and walked towards the gate. His gaze snapped to the ground and crawled up the wall, using torch light to soak in every detail.

"The dalan were thorough records keepers. I found bits and pieces of their stories carved into each crypt I delved. Sometimes it was their legends - tales of gods and battles, but others honored their fallen, detailing their deeds in life," he said, studying the stone all the way around the gate.

He pulled his rock hammer and a chisel out of his bag and tested several spots. The hardened steel bounced off the stone, rebounding with an echoing *ting,* but didn't leave any noticeable mark. Thorben leaned in closer, holding the torch right up to the stone. Small symbols were etched into the rock, the foreign runes glowing in the fire's heat. He traced them all the way up and around the gated entrance.

"A spell perhaps…to harden the stone?" Thorben mumbled and dropped the chisel into his bag. He reluctantly slid the hammer back into his belt.

"A spell? Men already tried to break through. None could even scratch that gate, or crumble the rock. You can read their runes, then?" Gor asked, his voice right over his left shoulder. Thorben jumped, but tried to play it off.

"No, not their runes. Not read it, like I would scrolls or tomes, at least. But yes, to an extent. You see the dalan used symbols and pictures as part of their language. They decorated their homes, tombs, and meeting areas with them. You see them enough, and start to understand their significance. I believe the dalan were, well, are storytellers…just like us.

We sit in fest halls and share mead, ale, or wine, but more importantly, memories and stories. We want others to carry parts of our lives with them. Scribes and monks write them in scrolls. It's a tradition. The dalan did the same thing, only they left their tales behind in a different language...and not in scrolls, but etched into Denoril herself," Thorben said, his old confidence slowly coming back.

"So...you can open the gate," Gor said, impatience oozing with every word. The copper coin rolled between the large man's fingers. Waiting.

He met Iona's gaze and looked back to Jez. Hun sniggered and leaned in to sniff her hair. She fought and thrashed, but it was all in vain. Thorben knew there was only one answer Gor and his associates would accept. He could tell them no, but that would only bring Iona and his daughter more pain.

"Yes," he said, the lie echoing uncomfortably in his ears. He lifted the torch again and made his way left, stepped around a brazier, and resumed studying the carvings on the wall. This etching depicted a burly, horned creature, perched atop a jagged rock, the trees and plants barren of flowers or leaves. He'd never seen an animal like it before.

Thorben continued, moved around one of the broken braziers and abruptly stopped. Shiny, unblinking orbs reflected back the light of his torch. He inched forward, the light revealing twisted limbs, stained clothing, and rumpled hair, all hidden in the shadows of Hun's unlit braziers.

"Mani...no!" he whispered involuntarily, his light revealing at least half a dozen bodies. The men were tossed haphazardly together, brown trousers, heavy twill shirts, and leather bags tangled and smeared with blood. He looked down at his outfit and cringed. They looked just like him, save for one small difference. He hadn't yet been added to the pile.

"I weren't asking ya," Gor said, moving up right behind him. A sharpened spear tip came to rest against Thorben's back. "I were telling ya. Unless," Gor said, and pulled him around and held the large, copper coin out between them. "...unless you'd rather not. Then I can flip here to see if it's the girl or her father who turns the keys first."

Thorben swallowed and turned, the pesky lump still sitting awkwardly in his throat. The torch light shifted, the pile of bodies falling back into darkness. His mind raced, a multitude of details spinning forth at once. The blood under their bodies was still glossy. It hadn't dried. The air smelled of death, but not of decomposition. Surely, if the men had not all died together, some had lain there longer than others. And stranger still, there were no flies, no signs of larva. That he could see, at least.

Gor prodded him back towards the middle of the chamber. Hun and Renlo crowded in closer, prodding Jez and Iona towards the platform. Thorben stopped just short, his eyes darting from Jez's face to Iona and back to the podium and its odd, barrel-shaped contraptions.

"Don't do it. You'll die," Jez whispered, before Hun silenced her with a choking arm. If he refused, then she'd die first, and he would have to watch. The thought was unbearable.

"Turn the keys, clever man, and unlock the gate!" Gor growled.

"I'm not ready. I need to continue studying the chamber...looking for clues...figuring out the order in which to turn the..." Thorben argued, but the spear point bit deeper. He arched his back to avoid the weapon, but the big man maintained the pressure, until he staggered forward, his right foot landing in the middle of the platform.

"No!" Jez cried out, her voice small and strangled.

Gor prodded Thorben forward again, jabbing the spear into the back of his left leg, forcing him to step fully onto the inscribed stone.

"Three chances," Iona whispered. His voice was almost as strangled as Jez's, only he didn't have an arm around his throat.

Thorben looked at the small man, cowering beneath Renlo and Hun's bulk, his mind twirling in a frantic dance. He looked to Renlo, trying to catch a glimpse or sign in the man's eyes, but he quickly looked away.

Death and dust, Thorben. Open your eyes and think!

Turning slowly to face the podium, Thorben closed his eyes and took a deep breath. The room stopped spinning, although not for its lack of effort. His hands and legs shook, the impulse to turn and stare at the pile of dead delvers almost overriding his sensibilities. They weren't just other delvers, but they were owls, like him - all intelligent, crafty men. Most likely had more experience than he.

"Don't think about them. Think about the keys," he whispered suddenly, and forced in a quick breath and pushed it back out again. They were gone, and could only serve to distract him. There was too much at stake for Thorben to allow that to happen.

Opening his eyes, Thorben leaned forward, and using the torchlight, inspected the wood keys. He reached for the one on the left, but paused, his finger hovering just above the highly polished surface.

"Will I know...if they are turned in the wrong order?" he asked, pulling his hand back.

"I believe so," Iona said, his voice thick with something. Pain, fear?

I believe so, Thorben thought, echoing the strange reply. He turned, a question faltering on his lips. Iona's dark eyes were hooded, their usual sparkle gone. Yes, he would know.

Thorben turned back to the gate, Iona's words echoing in his mind. *I'm his last chance to get into the crypt,* he thought. If he failed, it wouldn't just be his body added to the pile. He tried to believe that the three men wouldn't harm Jez, but Hun whispered something a heartbeat later, and he realized that hope was folly. With the weight of three lives pressing down on his shoulders, Thorben leaned forward and considered the first key.

Three keys...that means I have one chance in three to get the first one right. Those aren't horrible odds, he thought, but then remembered that he only had three chances period. The first carving depicted a branching tree, star-like flowers blooming within its foliage. The next showed a skeletal, barren tree set amongst a starry sky, and the last, which he had to lean forward on his tiptoes to see, depicted a small plant, budding to life, a blazing sun behind it. He checked all three keys, confirming each contained the same carvings.

"A budding plant, a full grown tree, and a dead one," he said, rationalizing the progression in the three carvings. *From seed to ash...birth to death. The cycle.* Confident in his discovery, Thorben took the first key and turned it. The wooden barrel rotated slowly, a sharp clicking noise punctuating the halting movement. The key clicked a final time, the carving of the budding plant catching the torchlight as it stopped beneath the emerald marker.

Thorben excitedly moved towards the second key, but a deep hum sounded at his feet, the stone platform vibrating beneath him. A tingle formed in his feet, and trickled up his legs. Thorben tried to shift his feet, to shake away the uncomfortable sensation, but discovered in horror that he couldn't move his legs.

"Wait! I can't move," he cried out in alarm. He twisted about, the tingling sensation burning all the way into his thighs. Jez sobbed, her face already streaked with tears. Iona met his gaze, his mouth turned down in a pitiful, sour mask. He'd told him. Once he turned the keys, he could not step off the platform. And unless he discovered the correct order, he never would.

Thorben turned back to the three keys, a silent prayer forming on his lips. He reached up and started turning the second key. The wood was cool in his hand, the surface so finely polished it almost felt like crystal.

Hold Dennica in your keeping, watch over Dennah, and help her become a strong woman, like her mother. Allow my boys to become good men, this world needs them, he thought, the key clicking and stopping, the ruby marker pointing to the carving of the fully-grown tree .

Thorben reached over to the third key, and before he could stop himself, turned it to the last carving, the skeletal, dead tree and sparkling stars glimmering in the torchlight beneath the diamond. As soon as the key clicked into place, the platform beneath his feet started to buzz. He could feel it in his feet and ankles, accompanied by a hum so low he could barely make it out.

His gaze snapped up to the gate, but it hung unmoving, silently mocking his desperation. Thorben waited another lengthy moment, hoping that some noise would split the chamber's horrible silence, and the gate would start to open.

"Birth to death...several of the others surmised that as well," Iona said, suddenly, appearing next to him without warning.

"Could you not have shared that bit of helpfulness before I started?" Thorben groused, eyeing the keys before looking back to the small man.

"Apologies!" Iona whispered, hovering next to him.

"I need all the information I can get, otherwise I'm just poking about in the dark...hoping for a prayer."

Iona nodded and then promptly shook his head, his shoulders sagging. Thorben watched him for a moment. This wasn't the man he remembered – a cutthroat, strong willed, brash, and yet, decidedly compassionate merchant – a crook, maybe even a villain in the right people's eyes, but not evil or uncaring. He'd picked up on some early signs, but now it was apparent. Iona looked changed, worn down, perhaps even broken. Thorben looked up to Gor and his cronies, Jez trapped in their midst, and wondered what had happened to him in the thaws since they parted ways.

Gor mentioned the River Guild, which Thorben had only ever heard about in stories. They were a small group of merchants and boatmen, organized out of desperation. He'd heard whispers that they were honest men once, coming together to fight against the Council's oppressive taxes on the river folk.

Their influence and strength grew quickly, winning them more than a reprieve from the burdensome taxes, but affording leverage over the very men lording over them before. Corruption and darkness seeped in, and the men who once sought only fairness, became the very thing they once cursed and despised.

His thoughts immediately flooded back to Lamtrop's Woolery, and considered that Iona and Jez's story likely wasn't too dissimilar to his own – Iona needed money, and the River Guild stepped forward. Part of him wondered what the crooked river men demanded in return.

Thorben reached down and gently rubbed his side, the skin and muscles beneath the damp fabric still sore to the touch. Gor and Rance were the same monster, just shrouded in different skin. Their leashes were held by different masters, true, but the motivations were one and the same. Whoever Gor's masters were, they wanted the treasure locked away behind the gate in front of him.

A weapon, Thorben suddenly thought, remembering something Iona said. He'd mentioned that swords of incredible power were rumored to be locked away in one of the dalan crypts. He'd heard stories of ancient weapons, powerful enough to kill men and beasts by the droves. His skin instantly turned clammy at the thought, as he imagined Gor turning such a weapon on him.

Turning back to the keys, Thorben cleared his throat and cracked his knuckles. He refused to be added to a pile of corpses. He would figure out the key to open the crypts, and then maybe, he would figure out a way to prize them all away from men like Gor and Lamtrop. And if a weapon lay within the crypt, keep it out of their grasp.

"Did they try death to birth?" he asked.

"Yes," Iona said with a nod, his eyes locked on the keys.

"And?" he pressed, his anxiousness building.

"...we have tried every combination."

Thorben's spirits plummeted, his knees going weak. He turned on the smaller man, "you brought me here, knowing that you've tried every combination? I don't want to die, Iona. I want to see my wife again, hold my children. See my sons become men, pass their trials, and serve, maybe even one day put grandchildren on my knee." A wave of despair accompanied his words, and had his legs not been frozen in place, he would have crumpled to the ground.

"I...I...I'm sorry," Iona stammered, "I know how you work. You used to thrive in the moment, seemingly coming up with answers when none existed. I...I thought that if I didn't...If we didn't overload you with all of our failures, you'd be able to see something we missed...to the truth of things."

"Or more likely, you didn't want to mention that those dead bodies over there," he growled, and pointed towards the pile of dead men shrouded by darkness, "had already tried every practical combination of these three keys. And...and what? I'd pull a miracle out of the air? That I'd manage something they couldn't? Or was it more likely that I would say no, and fight, or run, and leave you alone with these men?" Thorben glared at Iona, and then back to Gor and the others. He knew the answer, even if none of them...well, save for Jez, would have admitted it. Had they told him, he never would have set foot on the platform, knowing he'd be staring his own death right in the face. A spear in the back while trying to escape seemed wholly preferable, considering he might have at least died on his own terms.

"My death is on your hands," he hissed, so only Iona could hear, and turned back to the keys. Hands trembling, Thorben reached up and grasped the second key. The barrel spun, stopping only when the fully-grown tree met the ruby marker. He flinched, but nothing happened.

Dennica forgive me, I am a fool, he thought, and reached up and started to turn the third and final key. The wood barrel moved, the unseen mechanism providing more resistance than the first two. It ground and clicked, his arms shaking from the effort, until the bare tree appeared, the carved stars and crescent moon meeting the diamond.

As soon as the key clicked into place, the air around him started to buzz, as if a horde of flies had suddenly taken to flight. The darkness pooling between the braziers grew deeper, the chamber falling into gloom as the light lost a bit of its life. His stomach lurched, and the pressure on his legs grew even more intense. He wanted to curse, to cry out in anger, but even that small task felt monumental.

One, he thought, his heart hiccupping in his chest. Thorben dropped his hands onto the podium, his body sagging from the pressure. It felt like he was in the river again, the invisible, dark water working to crush him into dark oblivion.

Think, you fool. The answer is somewhere, likely hidden in plain sight. You have to find it...you must find it! Thorben took a deep breath, and intentionally avoiding Iona's gaze, picked his head up and looked around the room. The gate glimmered straight ahead, shining like a prize just out of reach.

His eyes dropped to the keys, the podium, and then to the ground. The deep carvings in the platform beneath his feet were ornate and fantastic, but he couldn't immediately discern any images trapped in the scrolling, looping designs, nor any patterns for that matter. All he could see was dark blood pooled in places Gor and his men couldn't wipe away.

The dalan were storytellers, it has to be a puzzle...not straightforward, nothing as simple as birth to death. That was stupid, Thorben. Use your eyes, he thought, and looked to the complicated mural carved on the walls all around him. *But it could be anything...*

Thorben cued in on the carving immediately to his right, or the creature perched on top of the rock. Just behind it, on a hill, stood a single, full tree, a blazing sun rising directly behind it. He dropped his gaze to the keys. It was the same tree, duplicated in limb, leaf, and trunk. He looked to the wall again, and scanned around him. A glimmer of light caught his eye, one of the crystals in the rotating mobile overhead catching the firelight. A carving stood just beneath the reflection. He searched the image for several labored moments, his eyes struggling in the gloom, but then he saw it...trapped behind the looping swirls of what he thought must be snow. It was a tree, bare of foliage, what looked like stars and a crescent moon hovering in the sky above.

"Of course," he whispered, scanning to his right and catching sight of the last key image – a budding plant beneath a sky of fluffy clouds and shining sunlight. "The mural is a story, detailing the passing of seasons. Look," he said, pointing to the first. "The plants bud and grow, basking in the sun of spring. Flowers grow in the spring," he said, his eye catching on the second key's ruby marker. "They grow, reveling in the warmth and rain of summer. Forests and fields are green," he continued, looking to the emerald marker of the first key, and then turned to the diamond on the third key. "Plants wither and shed their leaves before the piling snow and ice of winter. Ice is clear, like diamonds."

It all seemed to click together, the gems used to mark each key, with the significance depicted in the mural. Thorben reached for the keys, his hands starting to shake. He turned the middle one first, turning it to the picture of the budding flower, his thoughts turning to the red flowers that grew just outside their home every spring. He turned the first one next, lining the emerald up with the lush tree, and fumbled the last key into place, the dead tree lining up with the diamond.

A heartbeat passed after the final key clicked into place, the slight buzzing of the air next to him fading away. Thorben let out a held breath, as a loud click split the air.

I did it! he thought, and tried to step off the pad. The platform started to shake, the vibrations shooting painfully up into his legs. The buzzing filled the air once again, and the weight intensified, pressing in on him with such force that his back nearly buckled.

"No!" he gasped, clutching frantically to the podium. His insides writhed, as if snakes had crawled inside him. Why didn't it work? It made too much sense not to. *No no no!*

"I don't understand. It made perfect sense," Thorben grumbled, pulling his hand away from the podium to cradle his aching side.

It wasn't just the injuries from Rance's beating that ached now, but his entire body. Thorben could feel it. He was dying.

Chapter Eleven

Dying to Enter

The crypt was killing him...something, a curse, a trap, that the dalan left behind to protect their dead. He couldn't see it, nor could he understand it, but Thorben could feel it, reverberating wickedly in every bone in his body. And it was horrible. He would die here, and his family would never know why, or how.

"I've been a fool. I've taken love for granted, ignored the beauty all around me, and failed to help those in need. Please forgive me," he whispered, his forehead smashed against the podium's cool stone.

Thorben knew he'd erred badle, passing up every opportunity to turn and run from this eventuality. He told himself that he should have known – should have listened to Jez when she warned him in camp. There was a chance he might have been able to lose Gor and Hun in the woods...but what then? Iona knew where he lived, and thus, so would the others.

He started to think about packing up their most treasured belongings and finding a home elsewhere, but shook the thought away. It didn't matter – he'd missed the opportunity to run away. He was a fool.

"You have one chance to see them again," he whispered, pulling his head away from the podium. "Stop being a fool. No one else will pity you."

Thorben swiped at his eyes, unaware that tears had formed. The chamber was blurry for a moment, the flickering light from the braziers cascading in streaks of orange, yellow, red, and blue through the moisture.

Something danced and moved against the wall to his right. He blinked rapidly, clearing away more of the tears, and identified the movement. It was a spot of colorful light, cast against the stone from the crystal mobile hanging overhead. There were dozens of the colorful spots of light all around the circular chamber, but they were just that, reflections.

Thorben craned his neck and considered the strange construct for a moment, the delicate arms of silver metal and suspended crystals turning ever so slowly. Then one of the crystals shimmered, catching the firelight. They weren't all clear, as he first thought.

One of the dangling shards is red. The thought stirred something in his mind, and he looked back to the keys. His gaze caught on the second barrel, and the ruby marker.

No, it can't be, he thought, turning his head painfully back to the mobile. He watched it for a moment, the glimmering structure turning methodically. Clear crystals caught the light, moving into and then back out of firelight, their glimmering reflections splashing across the stone in a dozen places.

"What is it, Thorben? What do you see?" Iona asked, his voice so low he could barely make it out against the buzz.

Thorben couldn't respond, and for a moment he struggled to draw air. Another gem caught some light, glowing in a sudden burst of green. His mind raced, and for several terrifying moments, Thorben searched the keys before him. He choked down a breath, and then another, his gaze moving up to the walls. A tortured heartbeat passed, the pain throbbing into his feet gaining in strength. The weight on his shoulders grew more intense, and his back bowed in response.

I need to figure it out, the answer is right there, he thought, bracing his body against the podium. He only had three chances to get the combination right, but he was also running out of time.

A gust of wind blew in from the broken slab, the burning braziers rippling and surging in response. The shadows danced and leapt, the colorful reflections growing brighter and then dimming in response.

Thorben tried to toss out everything he knew, to start over again at the beginning – that was what he did, figure things out. The answer was there, he could feel it, the crystals were the key, he just had to...

"It's the light...the braziers. There is too much light," he blurted out suddenly, the words leaving his mouth far easier than the breath in that followed.

"What? Light?" Hun asked, stupidly, his eyes wide and unblinking.

"I can't believe I didn't see...it," Thorben yelled, painfully, counting the number of light spots on the walls. There were fifteen glowing spots of light, and five braziers burning. He needed to get it down to three.

"Douse the braziers," he cried, and pushed his weight off the podium. His knees creaked and bent, a sharp pain flaring up his hips and into his back. Hells, his body felt like a boulder. The pressure was crushing him, and he didn't know how much longer he could hold it off.

"But...then it'll be dark in here–" Gor argued, but Thorben cut him off.

"It was never a combination...don't you see," he said, pointing to the mobile hanging over their heads. "The carvings on the walls contain hidden images...the same images depicted on these keys. We have to...turn...them. The mobile...turns, moving like the...sun," Thorben said, but his breath failed him, the words dying in his throat. He remembered the simple pillar of stone just inside the door, a solitary hole bored into its surface.

Iona appeared at his side, his hands hovering as if preparing to prop him up, but he followed his extended torch to the mobile, and then the spots of light reflected on the wall.

"Yes...yes, I see it now, Owl. Quick, douse the braziers," Iona yelled, and moved towards the nearest fire. Thorben managed to hook a hand inside the smaller man's collar and held on, staggering him back.

Iona managed a single step away but jerked back into the podium. He moved to argue, but Thorben pulled him in closer and silenced him with a strangled grunt.

"Torch...pillar...by the door. Small hole," he croaked, leaning against the podium, just managing to hold the torch out. Iona rubbed his neck, but took the torch and looked over his shoulder to the entrance of the chamber.

Thorben took a breath, the air rattling noisily in his chest. He tried to speak, but his body couldn't form the words. He had to hope Iona understood, and quickly.

"I think I understand, Owl." The short man dashed away from the podium, just as Hun dropped a heavy cloak over the nearest brazier. The chamber grew darker, the shadows drawing, and then fell into almost complete darkness as the last fire went dark.

Thorben pushed his body off the podium, a staggering weight pressing his head down. The platform sang beneath his feet, its violent and dark promise pounding into his body. It was the song of his death, and it was growing louder. He managed to turn his head and caught sight of Iona, the man hovering near the doorway. The torch glowed as if suspended in air, and then dropped into the podium's waiting space.

"By the stars, look!" Renlo gasped, pointing overhead. The mobile caught the torch's paltry glow, and the crystals shined to life.

A red gem caught the light, an impossibly bright spot appearing suddenly on the far wall. It moved a hand's width, before sliding right over the carving of the withered, lifeless tree.

Thorben threw his weight forward, and clutched the middle key. He wrenched the barrel around, just managing to match the picture to the ruby. The red gem abruptly shifted out of the light, and for an excruciating moment, the chamber's walls hung in darkness.

Hurry, you cursed thing! he thought, frantically.

Thorben winced and managed a small, gasping breath, the green gem suddenly striking the light. A perfectly round, green orb of light appeared on the wall to his right, and hovered just over a carving of the sun, before revealing the budding plant. It happened so quickly, he almost missed it.

Thorben's fingers curled into his palms as he shifted his weight to the first key. He pried his hand open and wrapped them around the barrel. It clicked once, and then twice, the emerald marker pointing at the correct carving just as the green light disappeared from the wall. He tried to exhale, but only managed to wheeze. The pressure wasn't just crushing him, but strangling the life right out of his body, like massive hands were closing in around him.

Faster, you have to be faster, he thought, desperate to not find out what would happened if he couldn't get the key turned in time. Judging from the amount of blood, it wasn't going to be pleasant. The chamber fell dark, the buzzing noise filling his head. The pressure intensified, his head sagging in response. He lifted his eyes, scanning the darkness.

"Need...just one...more," he croaked as his chin dropped. A white light filled the air. He knew it was the clear gem catching the light, and fumbled for the final key. His balled up fists struck the barrel, arms hooking around the key, but he couldn't seem to control his hands.

*I just...need...to see it, h*e thought, but was already sinking, falling into the pressure. Thorben knew he had to turn the key, that everything depended on it, and yet his body refused. He was out of time.

The stabbing, pulsing energy radiating into his legs shot upwards, through his chest and arms, crumbling him down. He tried to hold onto the key, but it turned and clicked as his arms gave out.

Voices shouted nearby, but they were too late. The death song grew in intensity, coursing throughout him with every raging beat of his heart. He fell into it just as something snaked around his hand.

Denying the pain, Thorben forced his head up. His hand was on the key. Somehow, his fingers were wrapped around it. Iona stood next to him, his hand resting atop Thorben's.

"Together," the small man said, and wrenched on his hand. The key moved, sluggishly, the wood catching and slipping against his palm. Something clicked. Thorben couldn't tell if it was his body breaking...his legs or maybe his back, or the key. His entire world was pain.

Would he feel himself die, or would there just be a flash of light and then...nothing? Thorben hoped that Dennica wouldn't mourn for him long...that she would continue on and try to find happiness. That his children could avoid the pitfalls he'd stumbled into. A tear broke loose from his eye. He hoped that he'd been a good enough father.

Iona's face scrunched up, his palm slick against the smooth wood. Thorben tumbled fully into the pain. He felt heavy, but there was no relief as he'd hoped...no falling away into a dark nothingness. His arm pulled tight as he sunk towards the platform, only Iona's grip on his hand keeping him from falling outright. The platform was death. He could feel it, like a stone mouth waiting to chew him up.

Voices shouted nearby. Something clicked above him, his hand shifting. Another click sounded and Thorben tumbled fully. He felt loose, like flowing water. His elbow struck something hard, his back and head following in jarring fashion.

Thorben's head swam for a minute as he tried to rationalize everything around him. He rolled over, gasping against the pain. But then he sucked down another breath, his mind catching on that strange fact. *I can breathe.* He shifted and moved his legs, a distant grinding noise filling the air. The horrible crawling sensation was gone, a dull ache in his legs, back, and neck taking its place.

A hulking figure ran by in the gloom, a torch burning in their hand. Thorben pushed off the ground and managed to sit. He reached up and touched his face. Was he alive? His head, so blissfully light now, lifted towards the podium. Iona knelt before him, his face scrunched up in fear. The small man leaned forward, his small hands trembling as he helped Thorben to sit.

"You...saved me," Thorben managed.

"That is what friends do," Iona said, refusing to let go. "But it was you, Owl. You figured it out. You saw what the rest of us could not. You saved Jez. I can't...I can't thank you–"

Jez hovered behind her father just as the big men loomed above them.

Thorben turned, running his hands over his legs, and watched as the shiny, seemingly immovable gate started to rise. A haunting glow appeared in the stone all around them, the carvings coming to life. The gate disappeared into the stone archway, the eerie light bursting from the rock, dissipating into the air like a swarm of tiny, orange bugs.

"It's done! We're to be rich!" Gor hooted, smacking his spear haft excitedly against the ground. Hun and Renlo followed suit, jabbing their weapons into the air.

A low noise rumbled abruptly out of the darkness beyond the now open gate, a gust of stale air rippling into the chamber.

Thorben met Iona's gaze, just as the flowing particles of light died away, casting them into near total darkness. Somehow, whether by sheer luck, or his goddess's aid, he'd succeeded, and he wasn't entirely sure that was a good thing.

Chapter Twelve

Tipping Scales

The path forward was open, and it smelled of darkness and things long dead.

Hun circled Thorben and Iona, his crooked nose squeaking with every, stunted breath. He abruptly stopped, eyed the open gateway, smiled a horrible smile, and said, "You two, on your feet! We have a treasure to claim, and you're to lead the way."

Iona jumped to his feet and moved towards Jez, but Hun stepped between them, his anger showing. The girl ducked away from Hun's grasping arms and tripped over Thorben's legs.

"I'm claiming my right to change the deal, as is the guild's way. I think I get to keep the girl by me, from now on," Hun said, and from his tone Thorben thought he just might mean the foreseeable future.

"No! Leave her be, you don't get to touch her. She wasn't part of our deal...stay away!" Iona yelled and shoved Hun back, evidently drawing a similar conclusion. The girl's father jumped forward and punched hard, the unexpected strike catching the mule squarely in the already crooked nose. Hun stumbled a few steps, grunting and spitting. The big man recovered and his hand snapped out in a flash, Iona's head rocking to the side from the blow. Thorben cringed from the smack of skin against skin.

"Father!" Jez cried and lurched forward, trying to reach him, but Thorben managed to hook an arm around her shoulder and hold her back.

"You dare strike a guildsman...you, swine! We own you...you...fool. I'll..." Hun roared and came forward, his face a half-shadowed mask of rage. The mule swung, Iona ducking and staggering back. Hun screamed and lunged forward. The mule swatted again, his fist moving in wide haymakers, before moving to swing with his other hand. He cursed as

Gor stepped in, jabbing the air angrily with the spear. Gor held out the shiny, copper coin.

Hun looked from Gor, to Iona, and Jez, before lifting his yellowed eyes back to the shiny coin. He licked his lips and nodded his head vigorously in response.

What does the coin mean?

"Wait...no!" Thorben yelled as realization dawned. His words felt sluggish as the coin flipped into the air, turning end over end in slow motion. He didn't hear the coin land, he only heard Hun whoop, and a heartbeat later the mule snapped the spear forward. Iona tried to lurch out of the way, but the spear struck home, plunging into the meat of his thigh.

"You animal!" Jez screamed and redoubled her efforts, but Thorben held on with all of his strength. He knew what would happen to the young woman if she interfered.

"His fate's been decided," Gor growled, smashing the coin against his lips before stowing it in a pocket.

Iona cried out, took a graceless step back, and crumpled to the ground, clutching his bleeding leg. Jez wrenched around, a bony elbow driving into Thorben's tender side, and rolled free. The girl scampered on all fours, collapsing onto her father.

Thorben pushed tenderly up to his knees, testing the strength in his legs, before trying to stand. His heart hammered with every movement, coursing blood pounding in his ears. He didn't feel lively, but at least he was alive...for the moment.

He turned to find Renlo hovering behind him, his dark eyes flitting from Gor, to Hun, and back down to Iona. The mule finally looked down and met his eyes. There was pity in his gaze, but also fear, and indecision. Thorben wasn't sure Renlo would hurt them if commanded, but he wasn't entirely sure he would come to their defense either.

"Did you see? He hit me...the swine had the nerve to actually attack me," Hun laughed, as Jez pressed her hands onto the bleeding wound in her father's leg. Iona writhed, his mouth opening and closing wordlessly.

"Aye...and now his blood is tricklin' all over this dusty ground. Too bad he won't live long enough to have learned from his mistake, or reap the treasures that he promised us," Gor said, pulling the coin free and flicking it into the air once again.

"He's served his purpose. He showed us this place, and eventually found the man who could get us in. But now we got the owl," Hun said, and pointed right at Thorben. "We don't need this stuffy little fluffcake anymore...his words drip with snobbery, like his tongue's made o' lace. I'll be damned if I let frilly here lord o're me any longer...'specially since we lined his pockets with so much of our coin. Besides, the pot gets bigger with him gone." The mule accentuated the point by jabbing the air in front of Iona with the bloody spear.

Thorben watched, listening to the mule talk and held his breath, waiting for Reno to step forward and argue the point, willing him to show some understanding or speak reason on their behalf...maybe even some compassion. The smallest of the three mules flexed his arms and then his hands, as if wrestling with a difficult decision. He looked down to Iona and Jez, then, for the first time in a long while, looked to Thorben. He met the big man's gaze, pleas bubbling up from inside, but dying before they reached his lips. Renlo flexed his arms again, and then turned away.

"It's true. Without you here, we got one less person to watch, one less sneak to risk running off with our treasure, and one less percentage to share," Gor said, standing over Iona his eyes frighteningly cold.

Thorben's insides dropped, and he immediately cursed his cowardice.

"We...we had a...deal," Iona stammered, his bloody leg trembling as he tried to sit up.

"Aye, we did. You promised to guide us to a dalan treasure like no other, and in return, we agreed to forgive your debt. You took our coin, knowing fully that it would have to be repaid. An' like I told you before, repayment is in gold or blood."

"You promised to protect me! You told me that I was important to the guild...that..." Iona yelled, but his voice failed, and he slumped over, clutching his leg.

"And you were," Gor said, and knelt down, holding the coin right up to Iona's face. "But you struck a guildsman, interfered with his path. Fate judged you to bleed."

Renlo moved in and pulled Thorben bodily off the ground. He tried to fight back but hadn't regained the strength in his arms and legs yet. Thorben felt like a doll in the man's hands.

"Look on the sunny side of the rock, Iona. Know that your debt will die with you, and you lived by fate's decree...'tis more than life will grace most folk with. The guild will remember you, every time we gaze upon our treasure," Gor said. Hun laughed loudly, a trickle of blood flowing from his crooked nose.

Thorben heaved down a heavy breath, his angry words damming up behind the lump in his throat. He hated himself for it, but he'd never been one for confrontation, especially with men larger and more comfortable with violence. He tried to take solace in the fact that Iona had bloodied him, but it wasn't enough.

"And...and...my daughter?" Iona asked, tears streaming down his cheeks. He tried desperately to grasp Gor's foot, but the big man pulled away.

Renlo forced Thorben forward, toward the open gate. His boots skidded against the stone, but after a few lumbering steps, he managed to move his feet. Iona's voice echoed through the chamber behind him, the man's desperate pleas jabbing into Thorben's guts again and again. Feeling crept back into his legs, and within a few paces, he managed to force his right leg straight and jammed a foot into the ground. Renlo staggered, and for a moment they teetered together.

"We can't leave him here to bleed out. It is not right," Thorben argued, finally managing to squeeze the words out. He tried to wrench around in Renlo's arms, but the man fought him.

"We can, and you should. If you know what is good for you, you'll keep quiet," the guildsman said, his dark eyes cast down.

Thorben hooked his arms free and squirmed with his legs. He didn't have his full strength yet, but it was returning and he managed to get his body turned around. Hun wrestled Jez along behind them – the girl's body thrown over his shoulder like he was grappling a sack of grain. She cried and sobbed, her words devolving into something more animal than human. She banged her fists ineffectually off the brute's back and head, her uneven curtain of dark hair obscuring her face.

What just happened? he thought. *This is wrong, he just saved my life. I can't just let him bleed to death alone and in the dark.* Thorben tried to slide out of Renlo's grip again, managing to free one arm, only to have the mule jerk him back with the other.

"If you let him die...your relics, your treasure, will be worthless!" Thorben yelled, managing to find his voice.

"Whaa?" Renlo asked and abruptly stopped walking, his grip loosening a bit.

Thorben seized his moment and broke out of the man's arms, took a lumbering step towards Gor, almost fell, and just managed to catch his balance.

"Oh yeah? Is that a threat? Are you refusing to do yer part now?" Gor asked, his wide face turning slowly towards Thorben. A glint in the big man's dark eyes sent a shiver up his spine, his already weak knees going spongy. He looked for the big man's coin, dreading the gleam off the small but powerful piece of copper.

Thorben became immediately aware that everyone in the dark chamber was staring at him. Hun's spear leveled toward him, the torchlight glinting off the blood-smeared tip.

You wanted their attention...now be brave, you fool, he thought, and forced in a deep breath. In a fast series of coin flips they'd lost control of the situation, all leverage sliding towards Gor and Hun.

"No...worthless. They'll be less than worthless," Thorben said, the large man taking a slow step in his direction. His thoughts raced, pausing on what he knew, moving quickly over what he'd been able to observe and overhear, and finally to what he didn't. Unfortunately, he didn't know much.

"You can collect every interesting and rare leftover in this crypt, shove them all in a sack and cart them home, but you can't just set up at a market stand and sell them. The Council banned delving and relics long ago. Hells, you'd probably have more luck selling them to a smith for scrap," Thorben said, the argument taking shape in his mind as he spoke.

Gor cleared his throat and rolled his shoulders, the muscles bunching up under his thick, hide jacket. He rubbed the copper coin between his thumb and forefinger. The message was clear. Get to the point.

"The wealthy all seek their own collections of relics and artifacts, but not just that, to build collections grander than those of their society peers. These people understand the risk, and will only buy from brokers and delvers they trust. The Council doesn't punish for owning relics, just obtaining them. The risk is all in the sale, or in a delver's case, the delving."

"So we will find another broker." Gor's response was immediate, and startlingly devoid of emotion.

Thorben swallowed hard, considering his response. To creatures like Gor, a person's life hung on the flip of a coin. The idea made him sick, and he had to tread carefully.

"Yes...if you can find one," Thorben countered, his gaze dropping to Iona. The small man lay on his side, an expanding blood stain darkening his pant leg. His face was slack and turning pale. Thorben was running out of time. He took a tentative step towards Iona, his hands lifted defensively before him. Renlo's boots scraped against the stone behind him, but Gor didn't move.

"The mines are full of men who tried selling relics...most imprisoned for selling fake artifacts to Council agents posing as buyers. Most never even find the real thing, and yet they suffer with the rest. Trust me; I toiled next to many of them, heard their stories, and shared lashes from the same whips. The irony was, most were imprisoned and never actually set foot in a tomb," Thorben said, and pulled his shirtsleeve up and let the torchlight flicker over his brand. "Most had never actually delved."

Gor looked down, the hard lines around his eyes softening just a bit. Emboldened by this small sign, Thorben took a larger step and slid by the hulking guildsman. Iona was only steps away now.

"The best brokers don't just have the ear of the wealthiest patrons, you see. But they do...they know who has coin, and who is most adamantly seeking what. A good broker does far more than that, Gor. A good broker can take a chunk of discarded, rusty metal and give it a story, a legend – say a mask, left in the dust of a single, unmarked tomb. He can take that piece to the right man, spin a tale of a dalan champion struck down at the moment of a tide-turning victory, and in the end parlay for ten...no, a hundredfold what any reasonable man ought pay." Thorben saw the look on the big man's face a heartbeat before it actually formed. He knew the type well enough – the kind that thought peddling illicit goods was as simple as acquiring it and dumping it into someone's hands for a pile of gold. It wasn't determined by the flip of his coin, so the concept was beyond him.

"Hundredfold?" Gor echoed, and Thorben made his move. Grabbing the collar of his jacket, he pulled. The heavy fabric resisted for a moment, but ripped loudly and tore down the length.

"Stop!" Hun growled and moved to flank him, his spear tip leading.

Thorben awkwardly dropped to the ground and pulled the ruined jacket off, then found a worn spot in the fabric and tore it again.

"I told ye to stop!" Hun bellowed, his breath whistling through his crooked, and thanks to Iona, blood-crusted nose.

"Any broker can try to sell your relics. That is true," Thorben said, and looped the length of fabric under the trembling man's thigh, just above the stab wound and pulled it tight. "But what if they can't...?"

Iona grimaced and shifted, just as something hard and sharp came to rest against Thorben's neck. Without looking up, he tore another strip out of the ruined jacked and started to loop it under Iona's leg. He tried to bring the two ends together and tie them, but the spear dug in, breaking his skin and bending him forward.

"I told ye to stop, fool...or I'll bore a hole straight through yer back!" Hun hissed, his stubble-covered lips brushing up against Thorben's ear.

"...or, hells forbidden, you pick the wrong broker and..." Thorben grunted, fighting against the spear's painful pressure. He grasped the second bandage, his hands weaving together and forming a simple knot, and pulled hard. Iona shifted and wheezed, his eyes snapping open wide. An arm curled around his neck and Hun wrenched Thorben back violently.

"I'll bleed you too, then," Hun hissed and shoved him hard. Thorben toppled forward onto Iona, the smaller man's breath rushing out under his weight. Thorben fought and clawed his way free and turned, just as the mule brought the spear to bear. He didn't back away, however. He was tired of shying away from stronger men, from dropping his eyes and conceding arguments. He didn't delude himself. He wasn't honorable, heroic, or even particularly honest, but he was no killer. If the mule was going to wound him, then he would have to do it face to face.

"...or you pick the wrong broker, and instead of gold rushing through your doorway, you have sword carrying men of the Silver Guard kick it down instead. They kill some of you, slap the rest of you in chains, and before you know it, you're battered, branded, and smashing rocks with a pickaxe in a mine somewhere, sleeping on moldy straw and eating rancid porridge. Kill me, and you might get lucky and not find any traps or locked doors ahead of you. Let Iona die and you can whittle that treasure you're expecting down to a commoner's pittance...and spend the measly pile of copper for grisly meat and cheap ale, for that's all it will buy you."

Thorben waited for the blow to fall, the spear point to plunge into his chest and pierce his heart. A single bead of sweat ran down his neck, but then he realized it wasn't sweat, but blood. He didn't care. He'd give more if it meant Hun and his like didn't get to hurt anyone else.

Gor took a measured step towards him, his eyes unreadable in the dancing torchlight. Iona's hand squeezed his arm suddenly, the trembling man's fingers almost as cool as the stone beneath them. His grip felt weak, but he was still alive. That accounted for something. It had to.

"Is this all true, Owl?" Gor asked, his voice breaking the silence, unexpectedly. "Iona told us that you know the treasures we seek better than any other, that you are crafty like a fox, a tinkerer, a watcher, and a problem solver. You were not his first choice as owl, and yet it was you that opened the gate, when none other could. That bit earns my appreciation, but now you tell me that we need him, too, when his death would strengthen your own standing," Gor stopped, and gestured to Iona with a wide palm. "You claim that only he can take our treasures and turn them into gold and silver. How am I to know the truth of it...if you are as crafty as they say? How am I to know that you aren't simply slipping me honey words to save both your lives?"

Thorben swallowed, the lump in his throat finally loosening.

"You have all the leverage here, sir, that is the truth of the matter," Thorben said, glancing quickly to Iona. "You and your men are obviously larger and stronger than we, and have all the weapons. Iona is crippled, and I a branded man, with no wealth, no prospects, and only the promise of tomorrow to guide me. I simply want to return home to see my wife and children."

"And what do we do with ye when your task is done?" Gor asked.

Thorben looked at the large man, his broad forehead casting his small eyes in shadow, like glimmering bits of coal. The question didn't need to be asked, but he understood why the guildsman voiced it. He also understood the unspoken threat. Once he unlocked the crypt's secrets there was nothing stopping them from simply killing him and leaving his body behind.

"I simply want to return home, to hold my wife and children again. To see them grow," Thorben said, understanding the sensitivity of their exchange.

"Return home, with no share?" Gor asked. The big man studied him, his demeanor disturbingly calm.

"No, Thorben. Think of your family...you cannot," Iona said, his voice barely above a whisper. His hand dropped to the broker's leg and gave it a gentle squeeze. He still trembled slightly, but a bit of color returned to his face and his eyes weren't quite so glossy.

"A man able to return home and hold his children again would likely feel rich enough," he said, the words biting at his throat.

A twitch pulled at Gor's face, the coin rolling over in his hand, but then his mouth curved up in a wide smile and he leaned forward and extended an arm. Thorben searched his face for a moment, but reluctantly reached up and accepted. Gor lifted him off the ground, his massive, meaty fingers enveloping his hand up to the wrist. A sick pang spiked in his gut, the sour reality already festering.

"You are as wise as Iona promised, Owl. We have an accord. Iona lives, and we'll make sure you get home safe and sound, as long as you find me my due," the man said, and turned to Renlo and Hun. "The gate is open...let's go find our treasure." The two mules smiled broadly, rubbing their hands together, Hun immediately moving towards the wounded broker.

"Stay away from him!" Jez hissed and pushed between them to protect her father. She hooked Iona's arm over her shoulder and helped him off the ground. The two teetered together, but after a moment, Jez seemed to find her balance.

Thorben flinched forward, his throat tightening as his gaze snapped to the spears hanging at the men's side.

"RAH!" Hun yelled, lurching forward, but burst into laughter as Jez jumped back, her father's weight almost tumbling her to the ground. Gor shared in the laughter, but turned to Thorben, the residual smile not reaching his eyes. A malice lived there, colder than any ice.

"All right, Owl, it's time. You lead the way." The large man held out a torch.

Thorben accepted the light, trying not to meet the man's gaze, and took a surprisingly unsteady step towards the open gate. He gained a bit of strength with each subsequent stride, until he hovered just before the mouth of the dark crypt.

The space before him was dark, a constant, cool breeze blowing against his face. The air smelled odd, an aroma drifting on the currents of air. It was almost sweet one moment, turning sour the next. Thorben searched his memories, but couldn't remember it from any of his other delves. He was about to step foot in a place forgotten by time, a place built up in legend. A shiver raced up his spine as Gor urged him forward, the haft of the spear tapping almost lovingly against his buttocks.

Mani, keep me in your light, Thorben silently prayed, and stepped forward into the realm of the dead.

Chapter Thirteen

A Sea Before Me

The darkness surrounded him, the flickering warmth of his torch seemingly lost in the heavy, damp air. Thorben sucked in a quick breath, spit it out, and gasped again, trying to fight back the panic. He fought to stay calm, but it felt darker and colder than any place he could remember.

"You've stepped into the same darkness before, parted the same shadows. They didn't harm you before, and they won't now. You're just an older man now. It will come back," he whispered, slowly pushing out a captured breath.

Thorben took a step forward and then another. He leaned into the darkness and swiped the torch before him, letting the light reveal the ground. It was smooth stone, the pits and cracks of the cavern behind them now gone.

"Is it always this dark? I can't see...nothing," Gor stammered, his voice rumbling with something Thorben hadn't heard from the large man before – fear.

"Most...yes," he managed in response, then swallowed and took a deep breath. The panic was already subsiding, the crushing weight of the darkness loosening its grip on him. "It is worst at first...your eyes will adjust, just keep breathing and don't stare directly at your torch."

Spend enough time in the dark, and you'll forget what the light of day looks like, he added silently, wishing he could steal their torches and leave them to blunder, alone and hopeless, in the dark.

Thorben moved off to his right, until the light revealed a wall. He ran a hand along the stone, marveling at how smooth it was. In fact, when he leaned in, he realized he couldn't see or feel any chisel marks. *Strange.*

He followed the wall forward until it came to an end, continuing around a corner to the left. A pile of tools lay against the floor, the crate previously supporting them reduced to powdery wood and rusted brackets. His hand hovered in the air over the pile of corroded, time-ravaged implements. The light glimmered off something shiny trapped in the rubble.

Gor was behind him, the light from the big man's torch adding to his own. The mule's hot breath fell over Thorben's neck, the taint of eggs and cabbage burning his nose. He fished the small rock hammer from his belt, the metal still wet from his plunge in the river. He tapped at the pile, the ancient metal fused together long ago. The metal broke apart, and he was able to fish out a small piece. It took another couple of moments, strategically breaking the rubble apart, but finally, Thorben was able to pull a large piece of crumbling strata away. The shiny head of a tool appeared.

"What is it? A bit of treasure?" Gor asked, the excitement tightening his voice. Thorben breathed through his mouth.

"I'm...not sure," he grunted, wiggling it free, but something stuck. He took up his rock hammer and started breaking the rusted metal apart again, until finally, it crumbled and his hand pulled free.

Standing, Thorben lifted the relic up in the light. It was a hammer, the like he had never seen before. It sported a square, flat face and sizable peen on the opposite side. The cheek melded almost seamlessly to a dark-wood handle, a thin vein of silver inlaid down both sides. The tool seemed to vibrate in his hand, the metal ringing as if just struck against hard stone.

Thorben wiped the metal clean on the tattered remains of his jacket, turning it over and inspecting its every surface in the light. How had it survived, when time had reduced every tool around it to scrap? Its metal should have corroded, the wood handle crumbling to dust like the crate that housed it.

"What is that?" Gor asked, reaching in to pull the hammer from his hands.

"A stoneworker's hammer, perhaps," he guessed, although didn't doubt that it would make an effective weapon in the right hands.

Gor hefted the hammer, smacked the head against his palm, and nodded, a smile forming on his face. Thorben noticed a series of symbols etched into the hammer's handle. They seemed to dance in the torchlight. Was it a trick of the fire? Or were they actually moving?

"The first of our treasure...a battle hammer that felled many foes," the big man said, whipping it through the air. "Yes, some wealthy fool will pay handsomely for this." The big man gestured for Jez and Iona to continue, but leaned in as the broker limped past.

"Maybe I have the makings of a broker, too, heh? I can make up stories and lie to rich men. Think of that...by the time we leave this place, we might not need you anymore, Iona," he said, and dropped the amazing tool into his belt.

Thorben stared into the darkness, not letting on that he heard, but his insides broiled.

"Owl, continue, we have bags that need filling!" Gor proclaimed, and gestured him forward with his torch.

Thorben dropped the small rock hammer back to his belt, his eye lingering on the magnificent relic hanging on the big man's belt. Oh, how he longed to pull it free and swing it into his face.

He flexed his hand and moved into the darkness, remembering the lively tingle that pulsed into his fingers when they touched the metal. He couldn't fully rationalize the sensation, but for some reason it felt like the hammer was waiting for something. Was that even possible? *No,* he told himself. It was just a hammer, a piece of metal and wood.

Using his torch, Thorben followed the wall until he came to a small, arched doorway. He passed through into a narrow tunnel, the rock crowding in on all sides. The ground dropped away a dozen paces ahead, a narrow stair leading down and into the gloom.

The air lost a bit of its chill as he descended, but grew heavier, the damp running down the walls around him and dripping off the stone above. He climbed down the stairs for a great while, conscious and alert to the scuffling sounds of those behind him. Iona and Jez made the most noise, the broker dragging his injured leg down every other step.

Thorben wasn't a violent man, but struggled with the urge to push Hun down the stairs, relishing the sound his head would make bouncing off each and every step.

New emotion bubbled forth as he moved down, the stairs seemingly stretching forever. He felt excitement and doubt, but mostly fear. The largest tombs had only ever had three or four chambers, connected by small passages. The path before him was massive and well-constructed, like they were walking into a city.

Thorben stepped off the final step, moving into a wide, dark hollow. Gor and the others filed in behind and around him, Iona's labored breathing a wheezy, painful sound. He turned to find the small man hunched over in Jez's arms. He lifted his head, caught Thorben's gaze, and stood a little taller.

Thorben looked left, and then to his right, the torchlight revealing paths on either side of them, the third continuing straight ahead. Each of the three tunnels extended into darkness.

"A bleedin' maze? I thought the tomb would be small? Iona, you said it would be small?" Hun groused from the back, the guildsman's body framing the opening of the long stair, blocking their path to freedom.

"It is not a maze," Thorben answered, and took a quick step to his left. A small, shadowy pocket appeared in the wall on the side of the passage, the space expertly carved out of the gray stone. A tightly wrapped, skeletal figure lay inside, a delicate shroud pulled over its face. The light revealed something shiny under the wrappings.

"I thought they buried their dead in stone boxes? Uh, what did you call them...caskets?" Gor whispered, leaning over his shoulder, "Let's check this one for jewelry and other precious things." The mule muscled by and reached for the parchment-thin linen covering the body, but Thorben reached out and held him back.

"Wait, no! Don't touch them! We don't touch the dead," he said, immediately letting go of the large man and jumping back.

Gor flinched, his hands going up as if he'd touched something hot. He turned and looked to Thorben, his eyes wide, and not with anger, but alarm. Thorben thought quickly, knowing the big man's shock would quickly turn to anger, and possibly violence. He flashed a look at his hands, ever watchful for his copper coin.

"You're in the realm of the dead now. You mustn't disturb those that rest, lest you anger the lingering spirits. Please...let them stay as they lay."

"Spirits?" Gor stammered, the dark, rotten stumps of his missing teeth making him look like a fall festivus pumpkin in the light.

Thorben nodded animatedly and whispered, "If you are very quiet, sometimes you can hear them, moving, moaning, or calling out for those they left behind. Listen." He pressed a finger to his lips. The big man sucked in a breath and held it, his head swiveling from side to side. Thorben's eyes instinctively dropped to the spear in his hand, and then to the shiny relic stuffed in his belt. He yearned to touch the hammer again. But why? To hold it and feel the lively spark again, or strike Gor down?

Both.

The cavern fell to silence...a stillness unlike any other. The air felt heavy and old, with no hint of the sweet aromas he'd noted above. He could think of no other way to describe it than...dead.

The torches flickered, the dancing flames popping and hissing – gentle, lively sounds that died quickly in the still air. A water droplet suddenly released from above, landing with a soft *plink* against the ground.

Gor's face contorted, the skin around his eyes tightening as he concentrated. Thorben knew what the big man was feeling only too well. When surrounded by the dark, every noise became something significant, no matter how small or far away. Sometimes a person would hear sounds when none existed...driven by imagination and fear. Some delvers never made it more than a dozen paces from the light, while others descended boldly into the darkness, only to be driven slowly mad by the silence. Thorben had seen both enough times to know. The living weren't meant to spend so much time in the company of the dead.

Gor blinked, looked down to Thorben, and opened his mouth to speak just as a strange noise echoed in the distance. The sound bounced off walls, reverberating down the tunnel before them, seemingly seeping out of each and every skeletal corpse. The big man's eyes went wide, his mouth hanging open. Hun leaned closer to one of the walls, turning an ear towards one of the shelves.

It could have been a bat, or a gust of wind from one of the many underground vents. Fortunately for Thorben, Gor didn't know that, and in the cavernous dark, it sounded oddly like muffled whispers. To those uninitiated by the dark, it was the voices of the dead.

"You see? You must leave them as they lay...for all of our wellbeing. You don't want to anger the dead while trespassing on hallowed ground, for once you gain their attention..." Thorben drifted off, letting the tension and doubt build.

"You've...you've seen them? The spirits?" Gor asked, Hun and Renlo crowding in on either side. The big man worked his fingers over and over, the large, copper coin rolling between his knuckles. Thorben felt a little bit of leverage slide his way.

He nodded slowly. "And I pray that you never have to. I've seen delvers scared mute, while others wither away, fading like the dead they disturbed. Do you see how they wrapped the bodies?" Thorben asked, passing his torch closer to the skeletal remains.

Gor nodded and leaned in, his mouth falling open.

"They wrap them in special anointed cloth to ensure the spirits can't settle back into the body...for if they do, they can become trapped and vengeful. Best not to linger, do not call out to the dead here, and like I said, never disturb them," he said, adding to his story before rubbing the goose bumps popping up on his cold arms. Gor crowded in a little closer behind him, his dark eyes flitting more eagerly between shadows.

Thorben turned and led the group back to the hub, his confidence growing with each passing moment. He turned to take the middle of the three paths, Gor not only staying close behind him, but also walking on his tiptoes. He'd effectively put some fear into the man, and silently thanked his luck, and more realistically, the late nights spent around their fireplace telling scary tales. It had been a tradition for him and his boys since their early thaws, even though in more recent seasons, Dennah had proven to possess the most devilish imagination of the group. In truth, he borrowed very heavily from her most recent story about a spirit that lived in a tree and lured travelers from the nearby road to their doom. He would have to borrow more from his children's stories if he wanted to keep Gor and his mates from getting too confident.

I only need to plant the seed and let the dark do the rest, he thought.

The center passage was lined with carved-out hollows three high, each space filled with a carefully wrapped body. He'd never seen the dalan treat bodies so, but didn't want to admit as much to the others. Then again, in all of his delves, he'd rarely actually seen remains, just stone sarcophaguses, metal urns, and the occasional open-air burial.

Thorben paused for a moment, his eye catching on one of the burial hollows to his right. The wrapping had broken open, the thin fabric now clinging to the dark, damp stone. He stopped and took it in, one fact registering above all others. The figure was short, a child's height from head to toe. The realization struck him hard.

“These aren’t dalan. I think these are dwarves?” he snorted, stepping closer. The torch hovered in, the light revealing the shrunken, skeletal body in greater detail. It was covered in finely tailored linen, the fabric shining with what looked like metal thread. Armor hung over the figure’s ribcage, the enameled metal glimmering red and black. A helm sat atop the small skeleton’s head, a crease in the bone extending from above the left eye diagonally across its face, ultimately splitting the jaw in two. A deep gouge appeared in the bones of the figure’s chest beneath.

Thorben shivered as he imagined the weapon and violence needed to rend bone in such a manner. It was undoubtedly the wound that killed the warrior, and had surely been a bloody, horrible sight to see.

“Dwarves? I thought this was a dalan crypt?” Gor asked, his eyes dropping to the body. They went wide suddenly, and he jumped back. ”Wait! The…wrappings…does that mean?” The large man gestured towards the body with his torch as if he expected it to start moving at any moment.

“Don’t get too close. Best not to take any chances,” Thorben said, and gestured to the group to move back and continue along the path.

“If we cannot disturb the bones, how do we find relics?” Renlo asked, falling in step next to him. Thorben considered the question, his gaze sweeping back and forth to both sides of the passage. The stone angled down with each step, the space growing in size and height. The shelves carved into the walls grew in frequency – where there once were three, there were four, and five, until they lay a dozen high. The torchlight continued to reveal more.

“I have…I’ve,” he murmured, trying to respond, but ultimately failing. It wasn’t a complicated affair. He would break into the tomb, look around, and took what looked interesting. But this…this didn’t feel like a tomb. Not like any he’d seen before. There were hundreds – no thousands of bodies. No. This was a mass grave. He was standing in the largest grave he'd ever seen, and couldn't stop wondering if he would join them.

"I need to know," Thorben whispered as his torch sputtered and started to go out. He leaned into Renlo and pulled a fresh fire stick from the guildsman's pack, lighting it from the old one. "How do I live through this? How do I make it home to my wife and children?"

Renlo met his gaze as the new torch fizzled and surged to life, the bright light revealing the glimmer of armor under more of the bodies around them. Thorben tried not to notice, tried not to look at all the death, but there were so many of them and they all started to look like him. The shadowy pockets of ancient remains came alive in his mind, moving and shifting, the bones crackling and popping.

Stop it! They are dead. You are alive. Your family is alive. You will make it home to them! You will journey to Klydesborough and watch Paul takes his tests. You will see him become a river watchman.

"You want to leave here alive?" Renlo asked, his dark eyes flitting to the dark walls and their skeletal inhabitants. "Give him his treasure. Give him what he wants. Fill his bags, but also build him up. He is strong and feared for good reason, but beneath it all, he believes in the fates. Things either have value or not, they are good or bad, they live or die. There is no in between. Prove to him that you have value and he will make sure you walk out of here."

"But what if there..." he started to ask, but bit off the words. Renlo's head half-turned, waiting for him to finish the thought, but Thorben couldn't spit it out. He knew, anyway. If he couldn't find Gor his treasure, he wouldn't have value.

Laid to rest here with hundreds...no, thousands. Another fool joining an army of the dead.

He continued forth quietly, the ceiling suddenly rising up as their path led them into a massive cavern. He cursed involuntarily and stumbled as someone ran into his back.

"Mother's milk," Gor stammered.

The path led ahead and down, the darkness broken only by a host of small shafts of light shining in from above. The darkness prevailed, but the permeating glow revealed a cavern spanning like a valley, stretching at least a league in every direction. Their path continued on, intersecting with dozens of others, creating a curving, branching maze of walls, each path seemingly hollowed and lined with the dead.

"Impossible," he breathed.

"There's so many," someone whispered, and Thorben turned to find Iona standing beside him, Jez still wedged under one arm. "Have you ever...have you ever...?"

Thorben shook his head, understanding the question even if Iona couldn't voice it.

"You've heard the stories of the Great War...?" Thorben asked, suddenly. Iona nodded, Gor murmuring quietly on his other side.

"Bloody and grim – armor, flesh, and soil alike rent and aflame. The lands of dwarvish kings, their dalan allies aside them, tumbling into the abyss of war, to clash blade with blade against a dark and terrible foe...generations of soldier, artisan, and commoner ferried from life in the setting of a few, lonely suns. A land, oh a land, tainted by the spilled blood and magic of its people, left for the wild gods to heal. I do step foot in this place willingly, but aware of its loss...the cost of blood so long ago paid, but this home I must make for the path behind me is closed," someone said behind him.

Thorben turned to find Renlo standing alone in the passage, his eyes unfocused. A dying torch hung limply at his side.

"Beautiful words. Are you a poet?" Jez asked.

Renlo shook his head, his wide, stubbly face and close-set eyes giving him a brutish, wild look. He pulled a torch out of his bag, lit it, and dropped the sputtering one to the ground.

"They aren't me words...they are from an old tome me father owned. It was his treasure. The only thing he said 'had any value in this world of lords and gold'. He read me that passage o're and o're every moonrise before bed. He'd say, 'see me boy, there is a king a man can be proud of. One day we'll have a leader like that again. That king will come, and they'll fix this broken world of ours," he said, and Thorben swore he saw a tear roll down his cheek.

"So you're saying all of these dwarves died in a war?" Gor cut in, pulling Thorben around by his shirtsleeve.

"The story fits," he replied, weighing his response. "They say it was a battle that covered this land from border to border in death, that the conflict watered the ground with the blood of an entire generation of dwarves. It is a tale told at fireside pubs in every corner of Denoril. They say it was the reason that the dalan left these lands."

"Every tale has to start somewhere," Gor rumbled, and turned to survey the valley below. He turned back, his torch hovering between them, the light catching his profound cheekbones and casting his eyes in dark shadow. "There is enough dwarven armor in here to outfit a thousand small men. But this many dwarves died...fighting alongside dalan. That means dalan died, too. That also means there are some of them buried here...somewhere, waiting for us to find them. Right?" The big man enveloped Thorben's shoulder with a wide palm, his hand clamping down like a smith's vise. It wasn't a loving or even reassuring embrace. It was a reminder.

"This place is unlike any crypt I have ever delved," Thorben answered honestly, a stab of fear accompanying his words. "But if they are here, I think I can find them."

Gor nodded and slowly pushed him down the path. Thorben locked eyes with Renlo, the short man's face expressionless and stoic once again. But then, ever so subtly, the mule nodded.

Thorben turned and set off at a fast walk, the sea of dead spanning beneath him.

Chapter Fourteen
The Makers' Shanty

The path ran straight and true, curving steadily down into the valley. Thorben tried to keep a tally in the back of his mind, but there were simply too many dead, the walls now looming a dozen high with shelved remains. After a time, he gave up, wondering if there were enough people in all of the boroughs to fill the hollowed out walls. Hells, were there enough people in the whole of Denoril?

Death and dust. They were all like me once – sons, daughters, fathers, and mothers.

The further they traveled into the valley, the more it changed. The walls on either side went from smooth, featureless stone, to almost polished marble, curling, flowery carvings decorating the flat surfaces, while detailed beasts and winged figures appeared like effigies from the upper reaches. A break in the path appeared, the intersection of pathways affording them a view down another dark route. An immense statue sat in the middle of the intersection, forcing them to skirt around it.

Thorben's torchlight revealed a group of lifelike stone figures, huddled close to the ground, their armor and stature eerily similar to those laid to rest around them. A larger figure – a woman, sprawled above them, her flowing gown morphing into a pair of enormous, feathered wings. She sheltered the group of weary soldiers, her embrace almost motherly.

Although she was more animal than woman, Thorben recognized something in the likeness. It took him a few moments to rationalize it, but then it fell into place. It was her face. The graceful but pronounced nose, the slight brow and large eyes. It was the same face he gazed upon every time he paid tribute to his goddess at the temple in Yarborough.

"My Goddess, my light. Show me a *good* path," he whispered and reached up to place a hand on the statue's bird-like foot. His gaze dropped and caught on something hanging from a hook in the stone. "Look," he said, gesturing towards the small satchel with his torch.

"Offerings?" Gor asked, as Hun crowded around, the hunger for wealth and treasure gleaming in his eyes. Thorben reached in and tried to pry the small bag open, to glimpse inside, but the strap broke on contact. The satchel fell to the ground, crumbling to dust.

"It appears..." he muttered and dropped down, gently pushing the ruined bits around. The bag's contents materialized out of the dust. But it wasn't the shine of coin or the sparkle of gems as he'd hoped, but small bones. He held his hand out above the scattered bones, the truth quickly and painfully evident. "They're fingers."

"Mother's milk. You're telling me they cut off their fingers and left them as...offerings?" Gor asked, his face surprisingly bright. The big man moved quickly around him and scooped up the next closest satchel, and crushed it in his palm. The dust plumed and drifted to the ground, and when he opened his fingers again, the torchlight revealed the same, stubby bones.

Iona dropped to the ground, his daughter immediately fussing over him. The broker pushed her away several times, their conversation urgent and hushed. Finally, the girl seemed to win out, and huddled over his wounded leg. Thorben wanted to help, but hovered nearby, unsure whether she would want or need his help. Gor made his way around the base of the statue, and when he reappeared on the other side his arms and pants were covered in dust.

"They were all full of fingers! How 'bout that? What would a god have need with a bunch of severed fingers?" the big man laughed, and clapped his hands together, the dust pluming.

Thorben watched the big man, but glanced back to the ground, the bones scattered in a powdery mess on the stone. It sickened him that he'd broken open the offering, but that he'd also not stopped Gor from destroying the rest.

"They were craftsmen, artisans, and stoneworkers. Is there anything folk like that value more than their hands?" he asked.

"They're just dust now, and no good to anyone. Dead fingers don't amount to gold in my pocket. Let's be on our way. My due, now that has value to someone. To me," Gor said, eyeing Thorben indirectly.

Thorben rushed forward to help Iona off the ground, only to see him push off and stand on his own. Gor sniggered, and shooed them both forward with the point of his spear.

"I'm all right, Owl...but thank you for your concern," the broker said, favoring his injured leg before straightening. He took a step forward, and leaned into Thorben unexpectedly. "Keep your eyes open...watch for our moment. Watch for it, Thorben. They have eyes all over the boroughs. They're probably watching your home at this very moment. We need to be smart."

"But your leg...I can help you," Thorben said, looking back down to Jez, who still sat on the ground. He looked up to meet the broker's gaze. His cheeks didn't look quite so hollow, or his eyes sunken. Even a splash of color had returned to his cheeks.

"Watch for it," he whispered again, and then moved past.

Jez grunted and struggled to her feet, Hun pulling Thorben away when he moved to help her stand. The girl looked exhausted, her mouth pulled tight as she gasped for breath.

"Ain't gonna be finding our treasure helping girls off the ground, Owl...on with ya. You lead, now!" Hun grunted, and pushed him forward. Thorben set off down the path, the broker's words tumbling awkwardly in his head.

"Watch for our moment," he mouthed, troubling over their meaning. Did Iona intend for them to fight back...or to escape? Thorben considered the flaws in either possibility. They had no weapons, and one of their numbers was lame. Gor looked strong enough to fight all three of them off at once, and if they ran, how far would they get?

The darkness lifted ever so slightly as they reached the bottom, the narrow beams of light splashing against the stone in bright pools. The light diffused from there, the dark, damp air greedily clinging to shadow. He reached the bottom of the valley, the pathway opening up into a wide square.

Thorben didn't find more bodies, however, but what looked like a village of no more than a dozen small buildings. He passed the first stone structure, the building roughly mortared together with unevenly shaped dark stone. The small collection of structures looked oddly like the shantytowns he'd seen outside the mines in Darimar, where poor laborers and servants lived – the unfortunates that kept prisoners like him fed and alive, if barely. He leaned in tentatively to find the ancient wood door hanging halfway open.

"Wait!" Gor growled, and pulled him back, "let me check it out."

The mule stooped and kicked, his foot punching clean through the door, the wood crumbling almost on contact. He staggered, smacking his forehead on the low doorway.

Cursing, Gor pirouetted and dropped his spear as he fell. The weapon landed with a loud *clang,* the metal blade slapping the stone hard. Thorben's eyes flashed from the spear, to Gor, and finally to Iona. The broker's eyes dropped to the spear, as if to say *pick it up...use it.*

Watch for our moment.

Thorben was closest. He took a half step forward, his hand extending for the weapon, but froze. Hun stood between Jez, her father and Gor. Indecision held him in place, his gaze suddenly flitting to the sword hanging casually from the mule's waist. Thorben wasn't a fighter, and would be no more at home with a spear in his hand than a fish would be wearing boots. Could he pick up the spear and bring it to bear before Hun pulled his sword? He carried ample hate for the man, but could he kill him – cut him...bleed him? Nothing was stopping the guildsman from pulling his blade and cutting Jez and Iona down before Thorben could close the distance.

Gor shook his head and cursed loudly, the big man pushing up to a knee. Thorben hastily pulled his hand to his body and turned away from the weapon, immediately cursing himself for inaction. Relief flooded into him a heartbeat later, however, as Renlo appeared from the other side of the building. He'd been behind him the whole time. Watching. Waiting. If he'd picked up the spear and tried to use it, the man's spear would have found his back before he took a single step forward.

"D'ya see that? Bout bashed in me brains," Gor said, scooping the spear off the ground and shaking his head. He turned towards Thorben, a large goose egg already forming on his forehead, while a small trickle of blood ran down his right temple.

"At least we know there ain't nobody about. If there t'was, that racket definitely would have brought them forth," Hun bellowed, his harsh laugh ending in a phlegmy cough. The commotion echoed all throughout the wide cavern, bouncing distantly, before returning as if from an entirely different group of fools.

Gor swiped a palm across his face, clearing off the blood, and punched Hun. The shorter guildsman hit him back, the two men grunting and laughing.

The big man turned back a moment later, the laughter dying almost as fast as it started. He leaned on the spear, wiping the blood on his pants, and gestured to Thorben, and then the door.

"Owl...this is your part. See if there are any of those precious relics inside. Renlo, you're smallish, go in with him."

Thorben moved for the door, the dark-haired mule moving in behind him. He stooped and pulled himself through the doorway, the door now a pile of papery debris at his feet.

The building looked even smaller on the inside, the black stone and lack of windows creating a dark, claustrophobic space. Once inside, Thorben was able to stand, the low ceiling just barely clearing his head. He moved the torch from left to right, stepping over what looked like it had once been a chair.

Renlo grunted and wheezed, struggling to pull his broad shoulders and deep chest through the door. He staggered through a moment later and fell against the far wall.

"Wait...I need to make sure nothing is gonna-" the mule said, pushing off the wall.

"It's of no need, Renlo," Thorben said, interrupting him and waving the torch out in the middle of the space. "I don't think these dweorg have any fight left in them...not for a long time, from the looks of it."

"Dweorg?" Renlo muttered, and moved in beside him, adding his own torchlight to the space.

Four small bunks filled the rest of the small structure, their posts and beams so small he could have almost mistaken them as his children's beds. They weren't empty either; a short, yet stoutly constructed figure lay in each.

"My people live in the boroughs now, but we moved there from the lakes...driven away by the tyrant King Djaron. My grandfather was a trader and a lumberman. He traded regularly with the dwarves of Braakdel. They called themselves 'the dweorg' which means 'understone' in their tongue. My family has referred to them thus ever since," Thorben said, the times sitting at his grandfather's feet and listening to stories immediately coming back.

The dwarves lay preserved in position as if they had all just laid down for a sleep. Dust coated blankets covered them from toe to neck, the woven fabric inlaid with colorful threads, forming interwoven patterns. Long, white, stringy bears clung to their skulls; a heavy nightcap still snuggly in place.

Thorben hovered between the beds, afraid that if he stepped too heavily, or accidentally bumped them they would crumple to dust, just as the door. A table sat against the far wall, stone bowls strewn about - any food left within them long ago rotten or eaten by vermin. A pair of blunted chisels sat next to a ruined platter, a heavy hammer resting next to it.

"You best check 'em. Like I said, relics are what he wants and if ye want to return home, ye best give him what he wants," Renlo said, clearing his throat.

Ducking down, Thorben checked under the small beds, under the table, and in a small cabinet on the far wall. Finding nothing, he moved back to the beds and hovered over the dead dweorg.

"Please forgive me," he whispered, peeling the ancient blankets back from the first dwarf. The small figure wore a heavy nightshirt. The fabric was stained and covered in holes, draped over the boney remains like old winter snow.

Thorben moved from one bed to the next, and so on, checking each with as much care and respect as possible. They wore no jewelry, and their pockets held nothing of value.

"There is nothing here...they appeared to die as paupers..." he said, but glanced back to the first dweorg. There was something wrong with the small figure's hands that he hadn't noticed before. Thorben turned to the others, and then Renlo.

"They don't have any thumbs."

"They what?" Renlo asked, taking a half step forward.

"Look at their hands," Thorben directed, "their thumbs, they have all been cut away." The mule leaned in, holding his torch close, but pulled away, his mouth opening in a shocked and horrified grimace. It was evident now - the missing digit, the surrounding bone marred and gouged as if by a blade.

"Now we know where the offerings came from," Renlo said, after the silence stretched between them.

Gor waited for him outside, his expectant smile fading as his eyes dropped to Thorben's empty hands. The mule shooed him back out to the lane, guiding him to the next closest building as if he was an unruly goat.

It went on for a while. Thorben and Renlo squeezed their way into the small buildings, only to find eerily similar scenes - ancient-looking dweorg craftsmen, sprawled out on their beds as if death came for them while they slept, their hands mangled. They found moldering hammers, blunted chisels, and decomposing dishes, but no valuables.

Thorben pulled his body free of another building, his back sore from having to stoop over. Gor met him immediately, his hot breath falling on his face.

"Ain't nothing inside worth taking? I can't fathom it...there has ta be something...some relic with 'em...coins, jewelry...a damned hammer!"

Thorben shook his head, truly sobered. He felt like he understood a little more of this place's story, and it wasn't what he'd expected.

"These dweorg. They built this place...laid all these dead to rest. Or maybe they didn't lay all of them to rest...maybe they are the sons, or grandsons of the stoneworkers that first opened this tomb. What I mean to say is, they were the last ones to work here...perhaps spending their entire lives tending to the dead and honoring them proper to their kinds' beliefs. Then, they sealed the entrances, and died. The only thing they left behind was their blunted tools, their worn out bodies, and knife-mangled hands. It's a tragic story...one that cuts like a blade in the telling. All of the death and loss, the horrific side of war we've only spun in story up till now. Think of what we could learn from this place...what the Denil scholars could learn."

Gor's mouth drew tight as he listened, and Thorben knew why. He'd expected a treasure room filled with piles of gold and silver, just like in the popular legends, not a somber tomb of fallen dwarf soldiers and their selfless caretakers. It wasn't what Iona had promised.

"Monks and scribes are welcome, after I get..." and the guildsman lifted an empty bag, shaking it to accentuate its emptiness. Thorben understood the expectation. He nodded, and set off towards the only remaining unsearched building.

Thorben stopped outside the last building, this structure the smallest of the lot. The almost sheer wall of the valley sat not a dozen paces beyond them, the shaped stone jutting up into the darkness above. A twist of anxiety hit his guts as he turned to consider the basin. What would Gor do if this building didn't yield any potential treasure? Would he demand that they continue looking, or was this the end of his road? Would he be content with ruined hammers, blunted chisels, and severed dweorg thumbs? They were valuable to him, for their story, the dedication, care, and love, but they weren't the kind of relics wealthy men paid for.

Watch for our moment, Iona's words bubbled up into his thoughts once again, and he couldn't help but think it had already passed. Renlo silently passed by, and they considered the solemn structure together. Thorben hadn't seized his moment, and so far hadn't given Gor what he wanted most.

Please...just let me see my family again!

The entrance to this building was closed, unlike the others, its door banded with iron, not the typically rickety and rotted portal. Renlo sucked in a breath and came forward, driving his boot into the door. His foot struck with a surprisingly solid *thud,* the large man staggering back from the unexpected resistance. The guildsman gathered up his bulk and came forward again, kicking the door with a loud grunt. Again he staggered back.

"What's this?" Gor asked, and pulled Renlo out of the way. The big man roared and surged in, driving his heavy boot in with a vicious kick.

The collision resounded like a mighty drum, the sound echoing from inside the structure and off the valley behind them. The mule raged and kicked again and again, the door taking his abuse without a creak or groan.

Thorben shied away, Gor's rising fury a terrifying sight. He jumped back when the big man fell back from another failed attempt, but he wasn't snarling, or grimacing…but smiling.

"Owl…you see this? The best treasure can be found behind the stoutest of doors, heh?" he asked, chest heaving from the effort. "We just need to…just need to break this down. Can you smell it on the air? There is treasure in there!"

Caught off guard by the man's question, it took Thorben a moment to understand. Hun leaned in stupidly and sniffed the air, his nose squeaking loudly.

"Truly! I can smells it, too!" Hun said, and smacked him forward with his spear haft.

Thorben pulled the small rock hammer from his belt and slowly approached the door. He ran his hand along the stone, inspecting the frame with his torch. The rock felt cool, the mortared joints tight and precise. He tapped against the stone in a dozen places – the rock felt hard, just like the gate at the entrance. A closer look revealed a rune etched at the very top of the doorway. He found another, the small engravings blending in with the stone's porous surface.

"Perhaps we can leverage the door open," Thorben said, afraid to share his finding with the others. He didn't want to consider that there might be another set of keys somewhere, with a magical, soul-crushing podium waiting for him.

Gor came forward and stuck the spear into the space between door and frame, where Thorben indicated. The weapon bent, the handle groaning from the strain. Gor pulled it free and jammed it back in, this time finding better purchase between stone and wood. The wood groaned again, the handle bending severely. Thorben jumped back just as Gor staggered to the side, the oak shaft splintering loudly.

Straightening slowly, Gor lifted the two broken halves of his spear, and then promptly threw them into the darkness. The mule stood deathly still for a moment, his shoulders bobbing in time with his gasping breath, and then he exploded into motion. Gor kicked the door, again and again, before throwing his fists into the wood, flesh and bone smacking against wood with sickly *cracks* and *snaps.*

Thorben slowly gravitated towards Iona and Jez. Even Renlo and Hun appeared visibly shaken by the big man's outburst. He reached the broker and his daughter just as Gor pulled back from the door, and reached for the sword on his belt. The big man broke the blade free but stopped. His head dropped.

He'll turn the blade on us!

The mule released his grip on the sword suddenly and wrenched the gleaming hammer free instead. Thorben reached for Jez, desperate to push her towards the exit, to make her run and save herself. He saw the hammer snap back and swing forward.

We need to run...now! Thorben thought, confident the man's wrath would turn their way. But before he could move, a bright flash and loud *crack* filled the air, a wave of heat and sound knocking him to a knee. Dust and debris pelted his face and arms.

He coughed and shielded his eyes, the concussive noise echoing into the distant corners of the valley. Thorben wiped his face, and braved a glance after a moment, to find the air before him filled with a haze of dust and, he sniffed, smoke. Jez and Iona lay on the ground next to him, the girl coughing and rubbing her eyes.

"What...what was that?" Hun stammered. The guildsman hovered somewhere before Thorben, swaying on wobbly knees, but remained upright nonetheless.

Pushing off the ground, Thorben reached out and first helped Jez, and then Iona to stand. They moved through the dusty haze together, Hun and Renlo just ahead of them.

My Goddess, did he set off a trap of some sort? he wondered, and moved forward cautiously, silently hoping they would find Gor's body, broken and bleeding on the ground.

Gor materialized out of the dust, the hulking man very much alive, standing before the small structure, the gleaming hammer still in hand. Thorben pushed around Renlo, his eyes playing tricks on him in the dust-tainted air. He tried to step closer, but his boot struck a chunk of stone and sent it rattling away.

Thorben's toe throbbed, but he swallowed the pain and lifted his torch and inched in. Gor's hammer strike hadn't simply knocked open the door. No. It had shattered half the rocky doorway, tumbling part of the wall in. The doorframe looked as if it had been struck by a battering ram.

"Truly a relic! This ain't no normal hammer," Gor mumbled, and turned away from the building. His face was covered with dust, a line of tears running down each cheek. "Would it...do that if I hit a person with it?" the big man asked, suddenly, lifting the shiny hammer up in the torchlight.

Thorben jumped back, a horrible and haunting grin pulling the big man's mouth tight. He looked from the ruined wall, to Gor's face, and back to Iona. For their sake, he hoped they never found out.

"Alright, Owl, in with ya," Renlo muttered and pulled him forward.

"Wait...I," he argued, but strength won out, and he was guided to the building. Thorben shoved his torch through the jagged hole in the building first, then lifted his leg through and twisted the rest of his body inside. It was a tight fit, and he silently thanked the kids' voracious appetites. Too many second portions and he likely would never fit.

He stood and looked around, while Renlo scraped and grunted, wedging his too-large frame into the gap. The inside of the structure was dark and dusty, the floating particles drifting like snow. There were no beds like the other buildings, from what he could see in the limited light. He turned the torch from side to side, holding his breath as the torch started to lose life.

Several low tables sat against the wall to his right, the wide surfaces covered in rusted pickaxes and moldering rolls of parchment. Thorben picked his way forward through the rubble, his torchlight revealing the back of the space. Renlo grunted, huffing and wheezing as he fought to push his bulk through the gap.

An ancient chair appeared to Thorben's left, the long-dead remains of a dwarf still perched upon it. He approached, his eyes roaming over the dweorg's silken robes, elaborately designed scarfs, and bauble-laden hat. The stone floor ended just beyond the chair, dark soil and red vines sloping down into a wide hole. He leaned over the space, but the light from the dying torch failed to pierce the shadow.

He turned back to the dweorg, desperate to see as much as possible before Renlo managed to squeeze inside and resume his over watch. He leaned in, holding the torch as close to the strange dweorg figure as he dared. The light illuminated even more than before, glinting off metal-capped teeth, as well as what looked like gem-studded rivets driven into the small figure's skull. Ripples of color flowed out from the strange, metal ornamentation, as if dyed by some strange magic.

Is it the touch of sorcery? he silently wondered, remembering his grandfather's stories. It was commonly known that the short folk decorated their bodies with metal; in similar fashion to the wealthy women in Ban Turin, New Dilith, or Laniel, piercing their ears and noses with rings and gems. This looked different, however, and he wondered if magical crafts were involved.

The torchlight sparkled off something green inside the dweorg's skeletal body, the glint shining through the thin garments. He quickly glanced back to check on Renlo, and spun back, his fingers working to pull aside the confusing tangle of braided necklaces and metal chains. Thorben eased the bauble-covered necklaces out of the way, the smock's simple clasp disintegrating in his fingers, just as Renlo finally squeezed through the hole and fell, cursing, to the ground.

Panicking, he eased the delicate fabric open, almost knocking the skeletal dwarf's skull from its neck in the process. He cringed, reaching down and beneath the ribcage, his fingers groping in the dark, hoping there weren't any skittering vermin hiding inside. Something small and hard moved under his hand and rolled. Thorben flinched, and squeezed it between his thumb and forefinger, and pulled back, the body tilting in the seat.

Gambling on its worth, Thorben opened his palm, the light revealing a worn ring, inset with a single, square cut emerald. Torchlight approached, so he hastily stuffed it into his pocket, took a quick step to his right, and crouched down next to the hole in the ground.

"I could have gotten stuck for good. Why did you not help me?" Renlo groused, walking and breathing heavily.

"Huh?" Thorben asked, "Oh, well I thought you wouldn't want someone pulling and grabbing on you like that. I know I wouldn't." He immediately turned back to the seated dweorg and stood.

"Well, ye could have at least held my torch. I almost got stuck in that damned hole..." Renlo muttered, but Thorben interrupted him.

"Just look here," he said, gesturing back to the dwarf. "Look at his garments...at his necklaces. This dweorg must have been someone of great import. Perhaps a shaman or chieftain...maybe even a sorcerer. He is covered in relics! Hells, he is a relic...just look at the veins of color in the bone, the gem studs decorating his body! Oh, how those must have hurt! But think about it, you could put him on display, just as he sits. Just think of how much a wealthy, merchant lord would pay for the remains of such a dweorg. This is it! This is what he wants...this is his treasure. And look," he added, catching sight of a knife on the table not two paces away. "This knife cut the fingers from the others. There is your story!"

Death and dust, Thorben thought, disgusted by his own excitement. He was encouraging someone to steal the poor dweorg's body, to sell, and have displayed. But he had to keep Gor and his fellows happy. In Renlo's words, he had to 'give him what he wanted'."

The guildsman leaned in to look, but Thorben had already moved away, holding his torch down close to the ground. He patted his trousers, feeling a pang of anxiety from the ring's presence there. Would they know he took it? Would they see it?

Calm down, you fool, he thought, quickly, and forced his hand out to his side. They would only know if he told them, or continued to act the fool.

"Were it like this when you found it?" Renlo asked. "It looks like someone rumpled him up a bit?" The anxiety spiked again, and Thorben knew he had to think fast. He didn't know what the men would do if they thought he was holding back on them, or worse, stealing what they believed was *their* treasure.

"Of course...I mean, he, or they have been dead for so long. What would keep them from falling into a pile of bones by now?" he stammered, half-standing. Renlo muttered something Thorben couldn't hear, but continued to hover near the body.

"Gor! Come look!" Renlo suddenly shouted.

Damn...hells!

"Wait...over here! Where does this lead?" he said, excitedly gesturing towards the hole in the ground, desperate to pull the attention away from the dweorg's body.

Thorben leaned in and swept his torch over the space after Renlo reluctantly pulled away from the remains and stepped up next to him. Renlo pulled a fresh torch from his bag and lit it. Thorben accepted the new torch and hastily tossed the old one down the hole. The stick struck, bounced, and rolled, the light almost dying before it came to rest. When the fire rekindled, Thorben cursed, all thoughts of the dweorg shaman gone.

"Goddess, cleanse me with light," he muttered, and dipped his head apologetically, silently apologizing for his blasphemy. Renlo didn't respond. He just looked to Thorben, his eyes dark and unreadable, and then slowly looked back down into the hole, at the widening passage, and the dark, stone doors.

Chapter Fifteen

Seeing Ghosts

Thorben considered the dark tunnel, and then the ancient dwarf, just as the door flew off its hinges. Gor's massive shadow squeezed through the ruined doorway and into the small building.

Before Renlo could stop him, Thorben took a step down the steep slope, and then another, his boots sliding uncomfortably against the thick ivy. He reached the bottom of the steep slope at a run, his side and legs aching with every step.

I will sleep for a dozen moons if I get out of this alive, he thought, and cradled his side. *Not even the boys, or Dennah's screaming will wake me. I will never complain about lumps in our mattress again.*

The strange, dark ivy rustled under his feet as he set off slowly down the passage. The doors loomed just ahead, their surface shining with veins of gold, silver, and blue.

Something...a buzzing tickled his hip and Thorben instinctively brushed at his clothes. Images of large, chitinous bugs popped into his mind, their bodies fat and grotesque, their legs too numerous to count. They were there in every cave and tomb, waiting in the dark, scuttling from shadow to shadow in search of anything to eat. In his experience, size didn't deter them.

He patted his shirt, his trousers, and then waved the torch in a circle. If one of the tiny beasts had been on him, it had evidently skittered away. *Good riddance.* Shivering from the thought, Thorben moved towards the door.

The stone portals weren't just smooth, but appeared flawless, like undisturbed lake water in the early morn. His eyes crawled over the stone, hiccupping on a shape etched into the massive slabs. Thorben had to move to the side, testing different angles with the torch, but the glare subsided, and he couldn't suppress a wide grin.

"This is it!" he yelled, a jubilant and almost child-like spike of excitement bubbling up inside. For a rare moment, he forgot about the danger, Gor's indifference to life and death, the pile of dead delvers stacked by the entrance, and Hun's murderous raid on the innocent travelers.

He heard the others sliding down the slope behind him, tromping on the strange vines, the light from their torches magnifying his own. The buzzing tickled his hip again, and he swatted at the spot. He smashed it with a fist for good measure.

"The dwarf on the chair, Renlo says it is a relic–" Gor said, tromping up behind him.

"Do you see it? Tell me you see it!" Thorben interrupted, moving right up to the glossy stone.

"Yes, Owl. It is magnificent," Iona said, the broker appearing right next to him, Jez at his side. The carving of the eye was massive, extending into the body of both doors, the star-shaped pupil embossed with what looked like gold. Lightning bolts extended out the top, glowing a subtle and eerie blue in the light. He pulled the torch away, and the stone pulsed for a moment, the color remaining before going dark once again.

"You did it, Owl! You found it...our treasure. The eye marks it, just like the entrance. It is just beyond this door, I can feel it. Now, open it. Let's open the door!" Gor said, and rushed past him, throwing his bulk against the stone slabs. The big man grunted and strained, his musk filling the air. Hun rushed forward and threw his weight against the door as well, but the doors would not move.

"Maybe we need more lev..." Thorben started to say, but a flicker of light reflected off the doors, catching his eye. "Wait! Did you see that?"

It didn't look like a torch, but a streak of hazy green light. He turned and almost bumped right into Renlo, the heat from the mule's torch hot on his face.

Thorben flinched and pushed past, the guildsman grumbling as he tried to shuffle out of the way. By the time Thorben's eyes readjusted to the darkness, the source of the light was gone – if it'd been there in the first place. He stood in the ankle-high vines, peering into the darkness, watching and waiting.

"There!" Thorben yelled, and pointed, just as the light appeared again, streaking from one side of the tunnel to the other. He dashed forward, his hips protesting, but made a handful of steps before the glow disappeared into the stone.

"What is it, Thorben?" Iona asked, limping up behind him.

"I, uh..." he stammered, searching the darkness. The fact that he used his name was not lost on him. There was a slight tremble to the broker's voice. He could feel it from all of them – equal parts alarm and fear.

"Didn't you see it? There was a light..." he said, frustration mounting, but the tingle hit him again, buzzing against his hip. This time it stung, almost burning against his skin, just as the glow emerged from the stone and hovered in the shadows not ten paces to his left.

"We didn't see anything," Iona responded, alarm obvious in his voice. The flicker of light split the darkness, moved, disappeared, and then reappeared even closer.

"No! I see it again," Thorben yelled, and pointed right at the spot. The buzzing, crawling sensation increased, and he pounded the spot with a fist. He couldn't tear his eyes away from the light to check, but there was something there, biting him.

"We don't see anything," Jez gasped, coming forward and placing a hand on Thorben's arm. He pulled away and spun.

"How can you not see it? It is greenish light, like fireflies floating right there, in the open," he yelled, pointing directly at the spots of light, but blinked hard. The light was gone again. Thorben turned to find the entire group looking at him, their eyes wide.

"Is it the spirits?" Hun asked, turning from the door.

"Don't listen to him. Hun, push! Renlo, come, lend us your strength!" Gor said, quietly gesturing him forward. "Owl...instead of chasing shadows, why don't you figure out a way to open these doors! My treasure awaits me," Gor said, eyeing him sideways, before throwing his weight against the slabs of stone.

Growling, Thorben turned in a circle, casting his torch about. He searched both walls of the tunnel, carefully working his all the way back to the entrance, and then back down the other way. He searched from the arched ceiling to the ground slowly, the black ivy hiding nothing, and everything at the same time. He tried to pull it off the wall for a better look, but the plant was affixed with a terrible strength.

He turned back to the group, his rising anxiety interrupted by another stab of pain in his hip. Thorben brushed his trousers, rubbed the spot, and spun in a circle, trying to catch sight of the ghostly light. He staggered as the pain bit deep and crouched down, rubbing the spot.

Hells, what is biting me? he thought, his frustration bubbling over. A spot of flesh just over his hip throbbed and burned, but there was nothing there. He held the torch in close, the flames almost licking his shirt, and pulled his trousers back. His skin shone pale in the firelight. He saw hair, a few freckles, but that was it.

Gor and his guildsmen strained and grunted, but the massive stone doors didn't open. They turned on him as one, their expectation and frustration written plainly on their faces. *Open the door, clever man.*

How am I supposed to know what to do? There are no signs...no pedestals, no pull chains, no levers. It is dark as night in here and they just expect me to...know. Hells, most doors simply pushed open. I need time to explore – time to figure this place out, Thorben thought, and cast the torch about. But he couldn't focus on the search for a means to open the door, not when the strange light could appear at any moment, and the pain wouldn't relent.

The tunnel felt both familiar and completely unlike any place he'd ever delved before. What if the door was barred from the other side? It was not unheard of for an appointed slave to stay behind and bar the entrance, only to slowly wither away and die, joining the dead they were selected to protect.

He took a weighted step back towards the group, his mind spinning through a host of possibilities, each new one more improbable than the last – a pile of dwarves stacked up on the other side, their hands removed, or a cave-in. Perhaps the tunnel collapsed, as ancient places so often did.

Thorben hovered in the middle of the tunnel for a moment, only open air spanning between him and his escape, his family. Desperation tightened his throat, making breath hard to draw. He could turn and run. He could probably even make it out or lose the mules in the twisting paths of dweorg dead above. Then he looked to Iona and Jez, and his heart sunk. They would die.

The broker's words hit him again. *They have eyes all over the boroughs. They're probably watching your home at this very moment.*

Stifling a curse, Thorben moved back towards Gor and the others. The sting bit into his hip with every step forward, and he dug a knuckle into the spot. *My family is okay. Nothing happened to them, and nothing will,* he thought, willing away the other, darker possibilities. He would make it home to them. He would keep them safe. They would keep their hands, and their lives.

Dennica, Paul, Henrick, Tymon, Darro, Reginald, Kenrick, and Dennah, he thought, rattling off their names in his head. They were why he was still alive, and they were why he would continue to stay that way. *To see them again.*

"Can you open the blasted thing or not?" Gor asked, his tone clipped and impatient.

Thorben wanted to retort, to tell him to open it himself, but bit back the words as he caught a hint of copper gleam in his hand. He shook his head as he approached Hun, and lurched, the pain biting into his hip so hard his leg almost gave out. His eyes started to water from the pain, the haunting light suddenly appearing amidst the group. It was larger now, closer – an indistinct cloud of greenish light.

It was right there in front of them, and they couldn't see it.

"Be gone, spirit!" he growled and moved forward, suddenly, swinging with the torch. It was teasing him. That was it, mocking his failure.

"A spirit? Is it near me? Get it away," Gor cried out in alarm, swatting at the air.

Iona pushed Jez to the side, just narrowly missing the fire from Thorben's torch. It passed through only air, his grip failing as a horrible pain ripped into his leg. He staggered hard into the cold, stone doors. The light was there in front of him, in the stone. The damned light.

Thorben cried out and pushed, his back and legs protesting. He shoved as hard as he could, the pain flaring in his hip like a red-hot poker driving slowly into his flesh.

"Why did he say that? Did he really see a spirit? Where is it?" Gor stammered.

"Owl, are you all right?" Iona asked, closer than the others.

People bunched up around him. He could feel them, their hands groping, their voices whispering, but all he could focus on was the door and the light. Maybe it was the magic of the keys, working to finally finish him off. No. It was the light, whatever the light was. He was sure of it.

Thorben smacked his head against the stone and pushed again, his arms and shoulders shaking with the effort. The pain bit again and he smacked the spot. His fingers slipped into his pocket, something hard and surprisingly warm brushing against his fingertips.

The ring, he thought, just as it moved, slipping around his middle finger of its own accord. The metal band wiggled up the finger before he could pull free, a lively jolt stabbing into his hand and shooting up his arm. The stone door vibrated suddenly, coming to life under his palm. He tried to push away, but the slab shuddered, and swung inward.

"Arrgh," Thorben gasped, trying to move his feet to compensate, but the ivy snared his boots, and he tumbled forward. He landed hard, the strange, dark ivy wet and scratchy against his face. And...it smelled. He gasped down another breath. Sweet...almost sickly-sweet dew coated his face from the leaves, the pungent smell overriding all others.

Thorben wrenched his hand free from his pocket and pushed off the ground, scrambling back to safety. The massive doors swung into the darkness, a gust of old air crawling over him. It carried that same, sweet smell. It turned his stomach, filling his thoughts with rotten things–overripe fruit, spoiled cream, and dead animals.

He shook his head, clearing away the cobwebs of mania that sent him into a frenzy, and swiped his face across a shirtsleeve, the torn and tattered remains of his jacket tearing further. A small, green glow stabbed through the darkness ahead of him. He waved his hand, the light moving along with it. The ring was warm, pulsing gently against his finger, the square emerald glowing with a gentle, inner light. The pain in his hip receded, leaving only a warm echo of discomfort, and the dull ache in his ribs and leg.

"Mother's milk! How...I...what was that?!" Gor stammered as the others moved tentatively behind and above him. The big man scooped his torch out of the ivy and straightened, the glow splitting the dark. "I'll be," the big man breathed, "I don't know how, but you did it, Owl! Just as Iona said...just as you've done up till now! How did you do it? Was there a hidden switch or lever?"

"It was a..." Thorben started and flinched, hastily pushing up to his knee and smothering the ring's glow with his free hand. What would he tell them? What should he tell them? An image of the dead dweorg's shanty flashed into his head, and their mangled, missing fingers. That would be him if Gor found the ring, and he would be alive when they cut it off.

Someone grabbed him under the arms before he could muster a story and lifted him off the ground. Thorben felt the ring pulse against his finger a heartbeat before the dark space ahead came alive. Metal ground against metal, light blossoming in the heart of the deepest shadows.

Thorben reacted, throwing his hands up to cover his face as the light intensified, a rumble like thunder shaking the ground beneath his knees. The others howled, and he felt someone fall down near him, the ivy shaking from their weight.

Pulling his hands down and shrinking away, Thorben squinted against the glare, his eyes watering. Was it an attack? He pushed back up to his knees and then shakily to his feet, his imagination manifesting monsters hiding in the bright light, blades or claws ready to cut him down. A manic swipe of his sleeve cleared away some of the tears and the chamber came into focus.

Looking around, Thorben found the others still on the ground. Jez and Iona were pressed together, their faces down and eyes closed tight. Gor half-stood just a few paces away, his massive palms covering half of his head. He spotted his torch, lost when he swung at the strange specter, now forgotten a few paces away. The stick smoldered, the fire smothered by the foul smelling and sticky dew covering the ivy.

Thorben looked down. The ring still sat snuggly on his finger, the gem, although not as bright, pulsed green. He hastily tried to pull it off, but the band was tight. In fact, he couldn't even turn it in place. He dug his fingernails under the band and wrenched on it as hard as he could, but it was stuck fast.

"Death...and!" he grunted and wrenched on the ring, his knuckles popping from the force, "dust". No matter how hard he pulled, the ring refused to move.

"That light...my eyes!" Gor muttered, and staggered away from the wall. The big man swiped at his face, and then the air before him, clawing at it like an animal. The big man seemed to gather his senses a moment later, and opened his eyes. He squinted, his mouth pulling up into an uncharacteristic smile.

"You did it, Owl. You did it!" Renlo said, coming up behind him and clapping his arm.

"Clever as a fox, remember, Iona? That's what you said before we let you leave to gather him up. Remember? Like we told you, this was your last chance, so you'd better make it count. And you said 'If anyone can get us into that vault, it's Thorben Paulson'," Gor said, lifting his voice into a falsetto as he did a very poor imitation of the broker's voice.

Stuffing his hand back into his pocket, Thorben looked from the big man to the chamber, the sudden praise making him feel more than a little awkward, especially considering the company. The light surged one final time, before dimming to a comfortable glow, allowing him to open his eyes comfortably.

Odd, metal lanterns hung from the walls. Shaped like massive insects, their swollen abdomens glowed like bright balls of fire. As he watched, one of the lanterns moved, its metal carapace sliding noisily open, just before its abdomen glowed to life.

So, that was the strange noise, he thought.

"It's...it's magnificent," Hun howled, "Let us plunder everything of worth from this place! Think of the gold...the gold! We'll be rich men. Rich!" The guildsman set off down the passage slowly, head swiveling from side to side, taking it all in.

"I never thought it possible, Owl. Time after time we trekked to that place and watched them fail to figure out the secret of the three keys – those damned things, and that damned gate. I wanted to smash them and crush that gate, but...I thought we would never get to see inside, let alone this place!" Gor said, stepping his way.

If Thorben didn't know any better, he'd swear the big man was genuinely appreciative. Fortunately, he knew the truth. He'd seen the dried blood and piles of bodies...of men just like him. They probably had wife and children, just like him. Hells, he almost joined them.

"You've proven your value, Owl!" Gor continued, pointing at him with the copper coin and looking off into space. "I think I might have to give you a small reward after all. Now come along, let us claim our treasure."

Our treasure, Thorben thought sarcastically, rubbing the ring's smooth band with his thumb. Thorben watched the big man move away, very aware that Renlo remained just off to the side.

"Did I not tell you?" Renlo said, after a moment, "he gets what he wants, and you get yours." The mule moved around him and towards the tall, lean statues lining both sides of the passage ahead. Despite his muscular build and taller than average height, they towered over him.

Thorben walked lightly forward and stopped by the first statue, his fingers sticking together. He involuntarily reached down to wipe them clean on his trousers, but they were sticky, too. A quick glance showed that his hands were covered in what looked like reddish sap, the same sticky mess covering his pants and boots. It wasn't dew on the ivy after all.

"Why do you follow him? You recited Alrik's passage with great care. You could be a lyric, or a playwright," Thorben said, looking from the statue to Gor, the river guildsman moving just ahead of them.

The chamber's bright light glistened off the dark leaves covering the ground, the ivy's blood-red stem and dark foliage wet with the sticky fluid. Thorben rubbed his fingers together. It looked oddly like blood.

Death and Dust. The plants look and smell like death down here.

"A lyric," Renlo laughed and scratched his face. "Only in my fancies! But life ain't about to allow someone like me to do that. My family's been fisherfolk for generations. My grandad was, like his father afore him. Then my da afore me, and I, and so on. Ain't a way to make much coin, but the guild looks after its own, and Gor is the guild. I give him my loyalty and the taxmen leaves me be. Without Gor and the guild, there is no respect. It's simple like that."

Thorben thought on his words, chewing on the reality of it all. In truth, he didn't blame the man. If someone had offered him the same protection just a few sunsets prior, he'd likely have considered it. Hells, who was he kidding? He probably would have agreed on the spot.

Drifting off in thought, Thorben's gaze followed the ivy up the legs of the nearest statue. The figure was tall, easily a head and a half again his height. The ivy continued its climb up past the waist, the intrusive plant apparently growing into the stone itself. The effigy's head was larger than Thorben thought normal, an elongated jaw and nose contorting the carved features. A quick glance to the next statue confirmed it. Each was different, exaggerated and horrific in its own way.

Renlo moved on ahead and disappeared around one of the statues. Jez drifted to his left, her arms wrapped protectively around her body. One of the monstrous stone totems loomed above, making her look so horribly small. Like a child. A pang stabbed into his middle, and he thought of his own daughter.

Iona stepped up next to him and stopped, taking the chamber in with a low whistle. He leaned to take the weight off his injured leg, and wiped his pale, sweaty face on a sleeve.

"I thought you had gone mad back there."

"I don't belong in places like this anymore," Thorben said, and tried to pull the tattered jacket closed in the front, but the ripped garment swung open again.

"I hope you can understand..." Iona started.

"A man should do what is needed to keep his loved ones safe. It is why I am here, after all. To say otherwise would feel a betrayal," Thorben replied, and promptly continued, leaving the small man behind.

"I just mean to say...I am indebted to you now, several times over. I pulled you into this scheme, lied to you...when you were well away from this life. And then you saved me, when most men wouldn't have. They could have killed you, Thorben. Hells, I thought they were going to. Men who interfere with the River Guild disappear all the time."

"I couldn't just stand by and watch..." Thorben admitted, unsure how to put the experience or his thoughts into words. He was angry with the man...angrier than he'd ever been, but they had history. He didn't know Iona had a family, let alone a daughter. In reality, it came down to that. Thorben looked at Iona and saw himself, and saw Dennah, not Jez.

He ran his thumb over the ring in his pocket, and considered showing it to Iona, but though better of it and casually slid it back into his pocket.

"Like you said...we need to watch out for one another, and wait for our moment." He turned away from the broker and hoped that the ring's light didn't shine through the fabric of his pants. Iona nodded, before turning back to the chamber, his face haggard and still a bit pale. Renlo meandered a short distance ahead, but seemed unwilling to go too far.

The dark ivy crawled halfway up the walls and statues, branching off and hanging like tree limbs in the air. The narrow space looked oddly forest-like. With the odd lanterns and ivy-covered figures around them, Thorben could almost forget they were so far underground.

"This place doesn't look like anything delvers have described before. What have we stumbled upon?"

"I've never seen anything like it...older and stranger," Thorben said, his fears only growing more profound. He continued slowly down the passage, examining and cataloguing everything in his mind. It was miraculous and terrifying all at the same time.

"Whatever this place is, my plan is the same. I give them what they want...fill their pockets with relics and gold and make them rich men. If I do that, they'll let you and Jez go free, and me back to my family. It's my hope, and what keeps my feet moving forward," Thorben said,

The broker considered him for a moment, and then looked back to his daughter, who stood a dozen paces away. Jez hovered beneath one of the strange statues, her arms tucked in tight. She looked small and fragile beneath the stone monster, like a frightened animal about to be consumed.

"Don't let him fool you, old friend," Iona said, suddenly, leaning in close, "Gor may smile and praise you now that you've gotten him here, but he cannot be trusted. He is an animal – a barbaric and violent killer only concerned with the guild's interests and elevating his standing. If given the chance..."

Renlo cleared his throat and Iona abruptly pulled away.

"Stop yer whispering," the guildsman grumbled, "I *can hear you."*

Iona nodded and limped on ahead, giving a particularly gruesome statue a wide berth. The beast was wide and strong, with a horrific set of small arms sprouting from its chest. Spiny ears jutted out of its long head, its splayed jaws filled with far too many sharp teeth.

"I've found something! Come...come quick!" one of the men yelled from ahead.

Thorben and Iona moved forward, Jez waiting and following in their wake. Gor and Hun talked ahead, their voices echoing loudly. Maybe they spotted the strange floating lights. Perhaps then they would believe him.

They passed underneath the statues, the stone denizens' seemingly hollow eyes following him with each step forward. A creeping, crawling sensation worked its way up Thorben's back, and he knew that it wasn't bugs this time.

The passage curved down ever so slightly, the ivy covering the ground thinning out. He searched the shadows warily, his growing desire to turn and run almost stronger than his curiosity. And yet it was his will to survive, to see his family again that kept him moving forward.

The vines grew in size, branching together, until the strange, red plant was as large around as his forearm. They passed into a round chamber, a dozen massive doorways leading off into different directions. Thorben spotted Gor and Renlo immediately, their torches glowing warmly straight ahead. He paused, considering each of the dark portals, hesitant to put so much unknown to his back.

Iona urged him forward, and together they approached the closest doorway, the arch of the immense portal carved in ornate fashion. It was a woman, her flowing garments and feather-covered limbs wrapping around the entirety of the wall. They stopped just short of the opening, the woman's legs coming down on either side of them. Thorben didn't find it as perverse as the fertility statues they erected in the springtime, but it was close.

He knew she was just a statue, but she'd been carved in such amazing detail that he half expected her to move, or speak. Hells, in different light he thought most would mistake her for a giant, working diligently to keep the mountain of stone from crashing down. The ambient light revealed similar statues carved into the other doorways, different but the same. All beautiful figures wrapped around and into the stone.

Gor, Renlo, and Hun stood a few paces back from the doorway, their eyes locked on the adjacent space. He skirted around them and passed between the massive, carved woman's legs, his shadow disappearing as he stepped into the chamber beyond. He gazed out over a wide cavern, odd pillars forming a ring at its gloomy center. Fallen leaves covered the ground at his feet, creating a plush layer under his boots.

Where did the leaves come from?

It wasn't the columns, the leaves, or even the woman carved into the doorway that had garnered the mules' attention, but something just visible through the ring of dark columns.

It was a single, gray sarcophagus.

"This is it!" Thorben whispered, and turned back to the others, a shiver coursing up his back.

Jez ran through the doorway for a better view, just as a strange, animal howl echoed through the tunnels behind them. A heartbeat later another sound followed, not unlike the scrabbling of claws against stone.

Gor and Hun turned as one to track the noise, their spears held ready. Thorben moved back, pulling Jez behind him. He caught a flash of green from the ring on his finger, just as something shifted above them, dust and rock raining in a powdery cloud. Thorben impulsively looked up and caught a face full of grit. He coughed and sputtered, just as a massive form fell from above.

"Look out!" Jez yelled, and pulled him. They tumbled together, sprawling amongst the leaves, a deafening crash washing over him.

"What...was that?" Thorben mumbled, wiping leaves off his face and pushing up to his knees.

He looked to the doorway, to see if the others were all right. But they weren't there...no, the open doorway wasn't there. The statue stood before them, her posture tall and majestic.

Thorben stood and helped Jez to her feet, blinking frantically to clear away the tears and dust. They slowly backed away from the statue...where the arched doorway had stood just a moment before.

"Where did they go?" Jez asked, her dark eyes flitting from the stone to Thorben.

"I don't know." He reached out and tentatively touched the statue and the wall. It was cold, and damp, just like the stone next to it.

"Father!? Father?!" the girl screamed, rushing forth and pounding on the statue's legs. "Where did they go? Where did they go?" Jez screamed until her voice broke, and then fell to her knees, gasping for breath.

Thorben spun on the spot, his gaze drifting over the circle of columns, the distant sarcophagus, and then back to the statue. He tried to block out the sound of the Jez's sobs while ignoring his own panic at the same time, but his heart pounded like an overbearingly loud drum in his chest.

His hands shook as he searched up the statue's legs, moved sideways across what had been the open doorway, down to the ground, and moved back across, rifling through the thick layer of leaves. But there was nothing.

"Hells," he spat, struggling to even identify the statue's mortared joints in the poor light. "It's impossible!"

Thorben muttered quietly to himself, tapping the stone with his hammer before jumping back and viewing the wall from a distance.

"I knew it...I knew it...I knew this would happen," Jez moaned, her shoulders bobbing and cheeks wet with tears.

The arch was in fact gone, as if the statue had come to life and pulled the wall closed behind it. *Don't even think it. That is impossible...it's impossible,* he thought. Thorben grasped the ring and tugged before dropping down next to Jez.

"Hello! Can you hear me? Are you all right?" Thorben screamed, and then smashed his ear up to the wall, listening for a reply. He couldn't hear anything, save his own loud breathing.

"You knew what? What did you know, Jez?" he asked, turning back to the girl, his gaze nervously flitting up to the stone burial.

"I told him...I told him that there was nothing waiting for him in here but death, but he refused to listen. He wouldn't...he wouldn't. I wanted to run away...I told him we should run away and find my brother."

"You have a brother?"

Jez nodded, sniffling. "Yes, he's just a boy. Just five winter thaws old."

"What about your mother...his, mother?" Thorben asked.

"She ran off, almost a season ago...took the thief's share of dad's money with her, and Sam. She took my brother and we don't know where she is," Jez said, wiping her nose and eyes.

"Jez, is your brother safe?"

The girl coughed, and shrugged her shoulders, a pair of glassine tears breaking loose from her dark eyes. "Mother was good to us, but she had fits...would fall to the ground and shake, and sometimes lose control of her body completely. She would look and act strange afterwards, talk and act as someone else. She would always come back to us after a while though, but it got worse, right before she left."

It all clicked together in Thorben's mind...the dark, hollow look in Iona's eyes, his protective behavior of Jez. He'd likely gone to the River Guild and asked for their help in locating his runaway wife and child. With his wealth stolen, he would have had only promises to offer as payment.

I wish he would have just told me. I could have...would have helped him, Thorben thought, dropping a reassuring hand on Jez's shoulder.

"One thing at a time. First...let's find a way out of here, and then we will locate your father. Maybe we can..." he said, but faltered. He couldn't stomach the thought of making false promises. Not now.

"How?" Jez asked, lifting a hand toward the statue. "Ivy that bleeds, statues of monsters, a sea of dead dwarves, and a doorway just turned into a wall...and the statue? I don't understand what happened."

"This place isn't like any other tomb, that much is clear," Thorben said, admitting it for the first time out loud. A chill crept up his back as he said it, but shook it off. "The best thing we can do is move forward, and just maybe, our path will become clear."

Jez accepted his hand and stood. She wiped her face, tucked her dark hair behind her ears, and rolled up the sleeves of her heavy shirt. Thorben nodded, and she responded with a crooked, but guarded smile.

It's better than a snarky comment, he thought.

They turned, facing the wide chamber together. Thorben moved to step forward, a subtle light amidst the columns catching his eye. He hiccupped mid-step and almost fell. Jez cast him a sidelong glance, her raised eyebrow framing the simple question.

"Did you trip?"

Thorben shook his head, searching her face.

She can't see it. But why?

He turned back to the sarcophagus straight ahead, and the ghostly, pulsing light hovering above it.

Chapter Sixteen

Face to Face

"It is a sarcophagus...or a burial casket..." Thorben said, unable to tear his eyes away from the glowing light – it was strangely man shaped, he could tell that much, even from a distance. Not a flicker of light or a blur of motion, but an eerie, glowing, figure. Plain as day.

Flail me if I'm seeing things, Mani! Is it real, or are my eyes playing tricks on me? Mani, tell me I'm not going mad! Mani tell me I'm not seeing the dead! He'd tried to scare Gor and the others with tales of spirits, but now...

"Not just any burial! Perhaps it is as my father said. This is *the* dalan burial – the *one* folks have whispered about since before the first delvers. Let's get closer and see what treasures it holds, then we can give Gor what he wants and be away from here!" Jez breathed next to him, interrupting his dark thoughts. The girl pulled on his arm, but Thorben refused to move.

Thorben pulled his eyes away from the glowing figure, the stone sarcophagus, and the dark columns surrounding it just long enough to look at the girl. His fear faltered for a moment and he marveled at how much she looked and sounded like her father. How had he not seen it before?

"Yes...I know, but don't you see the...?" he asked, the fear returning as soon as he pointed towards the glowing specter.

"See the what? Is it the...the lights again? Do you see them? Tell me, because I don't see anything," Jez said, and stopped pulling on his arm. The girl shrunk back, but didn't hide behind him.

Thorben shifted his feet to back away, but paused. There was no archway anymore, just a wall of solid stone. The only way was forward.

"Look carefully...on top of the casket. What do you see?" he asked, pointing straight ahead, desperate to hear that someone besides him could see it.

"I see a stone box...what probably holds some ancient, withered dead person, and hopefully the shiny trinkets these men want so they leave us alone!" she said, leaning forward and studying the chamber. "But that is all. Now tell me what you see, please. And don't just tell me stories to scare me...I'm young, yes, but I'm not some stupid girl."

Damn...damn! He'd desperately hoped that she could see it, too. He shook his head, his gaze flitting from her brown eyes to the distant burial.

"Let us get a bit closer, then maybe I will see it, too," Jez said when he couldn't respond and pulled him forward.

Thorben moved his feet reluctantly, boots catching and snagging on the vines under the leaves. He looked down, freed his boot from the tangle, and lifted his head back up, not fully suppressing his surprise. The strange, glowing figure was gone. He reached up and rubbed his eyes and looked again.

"No...it can't be. I don't understand," he gasped, ripping his hand away from Jez and turning in a frantic circle, searching the dim chamber for the glowing figure. It could be anywhere, appear anywhere at any moment.

"What is it? You're scaring me!" Jez cried, stepping away from him.

Thorben thought for a moment, but decided that honesty was the best course, and that it might help alleviate his own fear if someone else knew. He was tired of suffering in silence.

"Back in the entrance chamber, by the doors, I started to see lights...like fireflies, in the darkness. And then, just a few moments ago I saw a glowing...person atop that burial straight ahead. Not just a blur of light, but an honest to goddess glowing person, and it all started when I found this," he said, and pulled his hand free of his pocket.

Jez's eyes locked on the ring, the sparkling emerald glowing gently.

"Whoa! Where did you find that?" she asked, pulling his hand closer for a better look. The gem in the ring pulsed, the green light bathing Jez's face.

"Be careful," he said. The girl nearly pulled him over, her tug far stronger than he expected from someone so slight of frame.

"I found it *in* the dead dweorg, the one sitting in the chair at the mouth of the tunnel. I took it for my..." Thorben said, but faltered, struggling with how much he should tell her. "At first I took it, thinking of my family. You see, it is small and easily hidden. I could probably find someone to buy it on my own, for far less than your father, mind you, but what little coin I could get might feed my family this winter."

"I don't blame you for that, especially after what happened back in the entrance chamber. You saved father's life, and Gor...he had no right to swindle you like that. You're the only reason we got in here, and to take away your share..." Jez said, shaking her head. And yet, her gaze did not leave the ring.

Thorben nodded, but interjected, desperate to unburden himself of the rest of the strange story. "It was in my pocket when we came to the tomb doors. I felt something stabbing, biting my leg, and thought it a crawler bug at first. That's when I started seeing the lights."

"You were acting–" Jez breathed.

"Crazy, I imagine," Thorben chuckled, uncomfortably. "I put my hand into my pocket, when I pushed on the door. The ring..."

"What..." she asked, but stopped mid-word, her eyes dropping back down to his hand.

"It slid onto my finger...of its own accord, and now I cannot get it off."

Jez's mouth scrunched up, cheeks, eyebrows, and forehead following suit. She held her hand out, and reluctantly, Thorben offered his. The girl turned his hand this way and that, her own looking child-like in comparison. She gave the ring an exploratory tug, then a little harder, before trying to turn and twist it free. "You're right. It is not for coming off!"

Thorben nodded, pulling his hand back in and giving the ring a small pull.

"In? You said you found it *in* the dead dwarf?"

He nodded again. Goddess, he hadn't even blown or wiped it off before sticking it into his pocket. The idea made his skin crawl.

"He was just a skeleton, so I just had to reach in and pick it up."

"But why was it *in* a dead dwarf?" Jez asked, and reached down to wipe her hands on her pants.

He lifted his hand up and inspected the ring, the metal pulsing gently against his skin in response. "I guess I never actually thought about that," he said, and proceeded to give the ring another tug.

"You're wearing a ring that glows, that you found inside the hollowed out body of a dead dwarf, and now you're seeing strange things...lights, ghosts," Jez said, and took a half step back.

Thorben nodded, suddenly very aware of how bizarre it all sounded. He silently cursed the decision to follow Iona, but also the impulse to pick the damned ring up and stick it in his pocket.

"It sounds like magic to me, and something Gor would very much like to have. It is the kind of relic that might convince him to let us go, to let my father go and forgive his debt," she said, looking up from his hand to meet his gaze, "and you can't get it off."

Thorben nodded solemnly, watching the girl carefully. He grasped her meaning, even if she didn't intend it as a threat. Thorben understood the stigma of magic well enough, too, almost as well as he understood loyalties. They were both often dark in nature, and prone to shift when convenient. The ring could carry a curse, its magic killing him at that very moment, but if Jez decided to leverage her knowledge of the ring against him, Gor and Hun would likely kill him first.

I should have picked it up and put it in a bag, tied it up, and stowed it someplace safe right away, he thought. *No, I never should have picked it up at all!*

"Please...don't tell the others. At least not right away. Give me some time to figure out how to get it off," he said, and quietly stuffed the hand back into his pocket. Jez's gaze followed his hand, and then slowly lifted back up to his eyes. Finally, after an oppressively long moment, she nodded. He knew that she was weighing her options – whether the magical ring could buy her and her father's safety, or whether she should betray him, if and when that moment came. He didn't entirely blame her.

I have to convince her that is not in her best interest, he thought. For if Gor discovered the truth, the big man wouldn't be denied simply because it was stuck in place. He would carve Thorben like a ham – cut off his finger, his hand, or his whole damn arm, if that's what it took.

Thorben swallowed and started forward, the lump returning to his throat. He watched Jez, quietly, and hoped that he could trust the girl. She seemed a nice sort, but Thorben had seen enough of people to know they acted out of need. They weren't blood, and if it came down to him or her father, he knew which way she would lean.

Death and dust.

They moved slowly through the leaves, the mist and shifting light playing tricks on his eyes. One of the columns creaked and groaned as they approached, and then another.

Are they...moving? he wondered, the movement catching his eye. His thoughts instantly shifted away from Jez and the ring on his finger as a branch appeared out of the mist overhead, swaying gently as if in a breeze. He spotted another branch, and then another, an entire twisted and gnarly canopy materializing out of the gloom.

They are trees? How is that possible?

"Wait...are those...trees?" Jez asked, as if reading his thoughts.

"They don't look like any tree I have ever seen," Thorben replied, moving carefully under and around the lowest, swaying branch.

He moved closer to the eerie trees but froze, the air changing around him. It was cold and painfully damp, as if he'd stepped into a gust blowing off a wintry lake. He looked to Jez, pulling his gaze away from the strange trees, and the casket, visible just beyond. The girl returned his look, her entire body shaking visibly.

Turning back to the casket, Thorben shivered, rubbed his arms, and resumed. The light from the strange lanterns trickled down out of the trees, but their branches left long, shifting shadows. The constantly moving shade and curling, drifting fog played tricks on his eyes. The ground appeared to move, drifting back and forth, undulating like ocean waves.

Thorben had to look away as his stomach turned uncomfortably. His gaze caught on the burial. He saw no sign of the strange, glowing figure, but immediately started to doubt. Had it been a trick of the light and fog?

Mani, watch over me, he silently prayed.

Thorben passed between two of the trees. Their bark was red and glistened in the low light, rivulets of thick sap running down and dripping off long, pale thorns. He exhaled into cupped hands, rubbing them together to fight the chill. The ring pulsed against his skin, the metal a small bit of warmth. He gave it an exploratory tug, confirmed it was still stuck firmly in place, and turned sideways to give the barbs a wider berth.

"Death and dust..." he muttered, "what kind of tree grows underground?" There was no sun, no rain...nothing to feed such plants. It felt wholly unnatural. Thorben eyed the clearing ahead, planting his foot with every step, prepared to kick off and run at the first sign of danger.

The sarcophagus sat another dozen paces ahead, the mist growing thicker around the stone box. The air became heavier – the cold settling on his skin like a sodden and icy blanket. He grabbed the tattered remnants of his jacket and pulled them tighter around his body, his boot snagging on something in the mist. Thorben stumbled forward, corrected, and found sure footing once again.

"What is it? What did you find?" Jez asked, ducking down next to him, her teeth chattering together.

Thorben carefully swept the leaves away, moving carefully as to not disturb what lay underneath. He didn't find a trip line as expected, but a ropey vine jutting up and out of the ground.

"It's a vine of some sort," he grunted, struggling to pry his foot away from the strange growth, but the greasy vegetation had snarled and tangled up almost all the way around his ankle. "I just caught my foot...how did...it get so twisted...about?" he grunted, breaking the plant and finally pulling free. Thorben lifted it into the light. It wasn't a vine at all, but a root of some kind. The twisted, fibrous shoot pulled tight and seemed to squirm in his hand.

Releasing his grip, Thorben jumped back to his feet, the root disappearing into the fog. He swore he felt it move in his hand.

"It's just a plant, right? It's not a snake or something?" he asked. But the girl shrugged, teeth still chattering together. It was dark, foggy, and they were both hungry and cold. Nothing seemed certain any more.

Thorben kicked at the leaves, unwilling to get any closer than absolutely necessary. He followed the bulbous roots to the casket, where they disappeared back into the thick leaves.

A sea of dead dweorg, a glowing stomach ring, bleeding trees, and now moving roots...death and dust, what kind of place have I led us to?

The stone burial shone gray in the subtle light, the side nearest him covered in intricate carvings. He circled slowly to get a better look but stepped into a patch of painfully cold air, and gasped.

"H...e...l...l...s!" His breath escaped in a foggy cloud, turning to icy crystals right before his face. The air bit at his exposed skin and he suddenly longed for his torch. Even that small bit of fire would have felt nice, but it was gone...lost to the ivy in the other chamber.

"Why...is it so...cold?" Jez asked, the skin around her eyes and lips turning dark. Thorben shook his head, sucked in a breath, the air making his teeth hurt, and spit it back out again.

"This isn't right...we should...go."

He shook her off, "we find something to take with us first. If we find Gor again and have nothing to offer, things will go badly. If I can find...something...extraordinary...then your father is...all the better for it." He couldn't possibly hope that she would forget about the ring, but maybe...just maybe, she wouldn't mention it if he found something better.

"No burden," he mumbled, kicking the leaves again, revealing more of the nasty roots. The plants wound all the way around the stone base, like gnarly red and brown snakes, looping in and out of the fog. They made his skin crawl.

Thorben leaned in closer, his eyes struggling to pick out small details in the gloom and fog. Jez knelt down next to him, sucked in a shaky breath, and blew hard, scattering the thick, bubbling mist. The branching, crawling roots reappeared just under the foggy cover, worming their way into the stone itself.

He followed the strange vegetation up the side of the casket, tracing it to the lid, where they spread like stringy fingers, bound to and corkscrewing clean through the stone.

Thorben slid his hands under the stone lid and lifted. The heavy rock shifted, a crackling noise filling the air, like hemp rope stretching but refusing to break. He hesitated and ran a finger around the gap between base and lid, confirming what his eyes couldn't see in the gloom and fog. The odd-looking plant had grown all the way around the box, the looping, crisscrossing flora effectively sealing the box closed.

*Strange, it looks too perfect to be by chance – how? Why would it do that? It's grown all the way around the lid, and perfectly at that, almost as if...*he thought, and instinctively reached out, hooking a finger under one of the stringing roots, just beneath where it disappeared into a crack in the lid.

Jez appeared on the other side of the sarcophagus, her eyes wide, and shook her head. "Wait!" she said.

Thorben hesitated, lifting his finger just enough to stretch the plant taught.

"Look at the way it is growing," she said, her teeth chattering loudly. "Doesn't it look like...well...the plant is trying to keep it shut?"

"Trying to keep it shut?" he asked, laughing nervously at the thought. "That would mean the plant is capable of reason, and that cannot be the case. Plants don't think, they just...grow. Perhaps it is just drawn to the stone...like the ivy that climbs the bluffs of Darimar or the River Watch tower on the fork of the Snake River. They're just plants...they do what they do," Thorben said, as if talking to one of his children. Jez, however, didn't look entirely convinced. She rubbed her arms and backed away, eyes sweeping the clearing.

*It doesn't feel right, but I have to, child. I need to find Gor a truly remarkable relic, something that will win us all favor, so we can all walk out of here alive. Maybe...*he thought, desperately clinging to hope, *with a little something in my pocket with which to feed my family.*

Thorben curled his finger back under the root and pulled. The greasy wood stretched from the pressure, but resisted. He looped another finger in the gap between stone and wood, braced his other hand on the sarcophagus for leverage, and pulled with all of his strength. Crackling, snapping, and finally popping, the root gave way. The fibers broke, the reddish sap spattering large droplets over the stone.

"See...it is just a plant," he said, drawing her gaze back to the stone. *A strange, grotesque, and horrifically smelling plant,* he added silently, and motioned her forward.

"Let's break these and see what is inside...for your father. We'll take what we can carry and leave straight away to find the others," he said to Jez. The girl stepped forward tentatively, her arms not pulling away from her body.

"This is the way we keep father safe...keep us all safe," Jez said quietly, as if talking herself up to the task.

Thorben quickly moved to the next strand, Jez finally unwrapping and moving in to help. He hoped desperately that he was right...nothing had gone as he'd expected so far, the last thing he needed was more surprises.

Jez hooked a finger into one of the roots and started to pull, her arms shaking visibly with the effort. Thorben took hold on a thicker stem, a violent tug breaking the root and tearing away a bit of stone in the process. He moved on to the next, rubbing the strange, sickly sap between his fingers. There was something about the plant - beyond its greasy, stringy texture and foul odor. It was the way it pulled apart. It reminded him more of cutting tendons and sinew when butchering a kill, than snapping wood.

The sickly sweet smell intensified as the next root broke. Jez finally managed to snap one, almost falling back in the process. Thorben reached for the last root on his side, his fingers now completely coated with the stinking fluid. He pried the root up, the wood snapping free from the stone. One full side of the rectangular box was now free from the brambles, its sap running like dark blood down the gray stone.

Thorben hooked his fingers under the lip and gave it an exploratory tug. The slab broke free from the base, bits of dust and rock rattling into the leafy groundcover. Something stretched, refusing to let the slab come free.

"What's the matter?" Jez asked.

"In some burials, the lids were mortared into place. That isn't the case here, but there is something...something we can't see holding the lid in place. I just need a moment to look," he said, trying to wipe the sticky mess on his pants.

Jez broke another root, nodding quietly, visibly cold and uncomfortable. Thorben followed suit, snapping a few small strands in quick order before his hands crawled over something far larger. He ducked down next to the sarcophagus, the painfully cold mist bubbling and drifting up over his knees and thighs.

The shadows were heaviest on this side of the burial, the ring of trees scattering the haunting, orange light in a confusing dance of light and dark. Thorben discovered a thick, coiling bramble growing out of the mist, the greasy wood creeping up the side before disappearing through a surprisingly clean hole in the stone. It didn't feel broken or chipped, but smooth and purposeful, as if it had been carefully drilled through the rock.

"The plant is growing through a hole in the side of the...box. I think...maybe it has grown up and onto the bottom of the slab," he grunted, his hands scrabbling over the dark stone.

Thorben followed a dozen smaller stems growing off the main root, the offshoots all curling up and worming their way into the stone lid. He tried to wedge his fingers between the large root and the stone, but it was too strongly affixed. The smaller branches were tighter yet, affording him no leverage to pull.

Shaking and teeth chattering, Thorben reached for the rock hammer on his belt, but stopped and cursed his forgetfulness. *You really have slipped, Thorben,* he thought and pulled open the flap to his bag, and fished out the small knife.

"You're taking so long, and it's not getting any warmer in here. Let me try and lift it. I'm stronger than I look."

He heard the girl wrenching on the solid piece of stone, granite grating against granite as the slab shifted ever so slightly. Thorben wedged the knife between the stone and the first small root, the blade sliding easily through the stringy fiber. He ran the knife down the stone, cutting the remaining smaller stems in a single, strong swipe.

"Hold on for one moment, I am going to cut the large root. Then we will try it again," he said, as Jez stopped trying to shift the stone. She settled somewhere over his shoulder, watching, grumbling quietly.

No, Thorben, he thought, answering his own unasked question. He'd never had to work so hard to break into a sarcophagus before. Hells, some were already crumbling open when he found them. Thorben tried not to think about why this one was so different, but more troubling, why the disagreeable plant had grown all over and into the crypt.

The knife bit into the thick root, the blade cutting easily through the greasy bark, but stopped, the meat of the stem evidently much harder than its exterior. He sawed at it for a moment, the blood-like sap seeping out and around the blade.

"It's too tough," he grunted, putting all of his weight on the blade.

"Let me try..."

Thorben pulled the knife away, turned it flat, and wedged it between the root and the stone. The blade slid in with little resistance and he pried up, the wood popping, and with great satisfaction, starting to tear away from the stone. He jammed the knife in again, closer to the hole, and managed to pry the entire length of plant away.

Jez moved in and took a hold on the plant, and together they pulled. A quick tug broke the plant free from the ground, the long, looping strand lifting into view from the mist. Thorben braced his foot against the sarcophagus and pulled hard. The plant resisted, but he could feel it tearing loose inside…from something.

"It's so greasy, I can't get a good hold," Jez said, pulling anyway.

Thorben found a hold closer to the stone and they gave another great pull, his shoulders and side protesting. The plant snapped and creaked before unexpectedly tearing loose. They fell back, Thorben's boot snagging and sending him tumbling to the ground. The thick mist enveloped him like icy water, but he managed to plant his feet and stand quickly, the thick root still in hand.

"I got it!" he cried victoriously, shaking the troublesome plant in the air.

"Finally! Let's see if there is anything worth taking, so we can go find father," Jez said, running back to the sarcophagus, and immediately putting her weight to the slab.

"What is that?" Thorben whispered, his gaze dropping to the end of the dangling root. It branched into dozens of smaller, fingerlike growths, large clumps of something dry and stringy hanging at their ends, trapped and snarled in the bramble.

"Is that leather…clothing maybe?" He pulled it closer to his face, but cringed. Long strands of wispy, white hair stuck out of the leathery clumps, pulpy chunks of desiccated muscle and fat clinging to the underside.

"I think it's…skin." Why would the plant grow into someone's flesh?

"We've almost got…it. Are you going…to…help me? It's so…heavy," Jez grunted, her mouth screwing as she wrenched and shoved, fighting to move the massive stone.

Thorben moved to drop the greasy plant just as it contracted violently in his hand, shriveling on itself. An eerie, green fog erupted out of the greasy bark, fizzling into the air as the root dried-up.

"Hells," he grunted and let go, the green mist filling the air around him. The strange fog rippled into a dense cloud, pooling around his right hand and the pulsing, green gem in his ring.

"I think...I've almost got it." He heard Jez, heard the stone grinding, sliding, slowing working its way free, but couldn't see anything beyond the green cloud. Couldn't she see it? Couldn't she smell it?

Panicking, Thorben jumped to the side, flicking his hands to clear away the fog. It burned his eyes, the overpowering odor of overly ripe fruit filling his nostrils. A flash of bright green light caught in his vision, the gem in the ring blazing to life. The strange, stinking fog swirled violently around his arm, his hand, and then abruptly disappeared into the glowing stone.

"What...what was that?" he said, coughing and sputtering.

"What was what?" Jez grunted, but her back was turned as she leveraged against the stone slab. "There...it's moving. I got it!"

Thorben saw the girl tip forward as the sarcophagus's lid broke free and slid a handbreadth. He managed a single step in her direction, before the ring on his finger started to vibrate. The metal grew incredibly hot against his skin, just as a bright flash seared his eyes.

"Goddess," Thorben gasped and fell away from the burial, the sudden flash washing the dark chamber away, leaving a sea of brightly colored spots in its place.

Jez cried out and he heard something fall to the ground, the dry bed of leaves crunching under the weight. There was something else there, too – a ringing, humming sound like struck metal.

"So...cold...c-c-cold. I can't see. P-p-pushed me...w-w-why did you push me?" Jez sputtered, her words barely intelligible.

Thorben rubbed his eyes, cursed, and blinked rapidly. He felt the girl at his feet and blindly bent over and helped her to stand, lifting her out of the frigid mist. Jez fought him, her body shaking as she pushed away.

"It wasn't me, girl. It wasn't me," he whispered, his vision starting to return. The bright blobs of light faded, a dark circling closing in around them, the chamber's misty gloom materializing slowly.

Jez silently met his gaze, and together they turned back to the sarcophagus.

Chapter Seventeen
Reflections of Life

"Mani flail me!" Thorben cursed, Jez's cold hands latching painfully onto his arms. Tears filled his eyes, making his vision horribly blurry, but he could see well enough to identify the bright blob on top of the sarcophagus.

He blinked and swiped a sleeve across his face. Still a bright, blurry blob. He blinked and swiped again. Less blurry. Then he saw it proper. It wasn't just a ball of light, an indistinct cloud, or a floating, firefly-sized orb. It was a short, glowing man standing atop the stone box, his back turned to him.

Not again, he thought.

"W-w-who...w-w-what is that?" Jez muttered, shoving her body into him, pushing them both back. Thorben grabbed her arms, stilling her, and then lifted a shaking hand and pointed at the glowing figure.

Jez nodded, her hands clamping around his wrists, her nails biting into his skin. The short, ghostly figure lifted his hands and arms, as if the sight of his own appendages was a surprise. He patted his chest, and then his short, but incredibly powerful-looking legs.

"Not natural...not at all," Thorben breathed, just as something moved inside the stone box. It was a quiet noise – a shuffling, creaking, shifting, like a loose floorboard or his wife's old rocking chair on an exceptionally cold day. The glowing figure looked down, as if drawn to the sound.

"Is there something moving in...there?" Jez moaned, and tried to tear free from his hold and run.

The ghostly figure lifted his bare feet, noticing the sarcophagus for the first time. His dark, hollow eyes scanned the stone box, crawling over the broken strands of root, to Thorben's knife sitting on the corner. He didn't remember setting it down, or Jez taking it. Then the ghostly dwarf lifted his face, and looked directly at them.

"No! It's looking right at me...let me go!" Jez yelled, and twisted violently, her fingernails digging deep gouges into his flesh. The girl broke free, Thorben stumbling out of the way.

The ghost studied him for a moment, his mouth screwing up under his bushy beard, but turned back to the sarcophagus when something scraped against the inside of the stone box – something dry and hard, taping and scratching against the underside of the stone lid.

"This is...impossible. Mani, tell me this is impossible," Thorben mumbled, finally managing to blink and move his feet. The dweorg's head snapped back around, his face seemingly clarifying with each passing heartbeat. His eyebrows grew, long eyelashes sprouting as shining eyes appeared out of the hollow pits. The mass of beard straightened, the unruly tufts pulling together as large, shiny rings appeared. Several decorative studs appeared on his left cheek, glimmering gems affixed to their ends.

Thorben shook his head, trying to deny the truth of it, but the dwarf jumped down off the sarcophagus, his feet landing in the misty leaves without a sound. His form continued to change, defining shape and clarity, silken shirt and robes appearing over his naked form, bauble-laden necklaces and scarves encircling his neck. The dweorg lifted his hands, his mouth opening as if trying to speak, but couldn't seem to find voice. Thorben could smell him, too, the smell of ripe fruit growing stronger by the moment.

He took a halting step back, his mind screaming at him to run, but his legs refused. He wasn't just seeing a gods' honest spirit, a dead dwarf no less, but the dwarf he found seated in the chair by the entrance to the crypt. He was sure of it. It had to be.

The dwarf tried to speak again, a haunting, eerie noise filling the air. Thorben managed another step back, a strangled cry building in his chest. The dweorg took a step towards him and looked down, his eyes falling on Thorben's hand, and the ring. The square gem glowed with a healthy light, pulsing in time with the jeweled studs adorning the ghost's face.

The dwarf opened his mouth in a mournful cry, the sound broken and distant. He pointed a single finger at Thorben's hand and spun, gesturing back towards the sarcophagus. Somewhere beneath the strange, haunting cry, he thought he heard the scrabbling *scritch scratch scritch* of fingernails scraping against stone.

"No, no, no," he muttered, and finally broke free from fear's snare. He lurched back, stumbled on the covered roots in his haste, caught his balance and turned, moving away from the casket. A horrible shiver ran up his back as he turned away from the dweorg, but couldn't bear to stop.

"Just run...just run and don't look. Never look," he whispered, the cold mist obscuring the ground at his feet.

Jez ran somewhere ahead. He could hear her moving, hear her frantic, almost strangled cries, but couldn't see her. Thorben barreled haphazardly through the ring of thorny trees, almost impaling himself on the barbs in the process. The spines snagged his jacket and arms instead, tearing the remnant of his already tattered garment off in the process.

Free of the trees, Thorben picked up speed. He ran, stumbled, caught his balance and continued. The back of the cavern appeared, a lantern throwing the natural cave wall into deep relief. Thorben turned, despite every ounce of his resolve telling him not to. The dweorg was there, moving silently through the trees, his legs from the knee down simply melting into the thick mist.

"Leave me be! Be gone, spirit," he yelled, and surprisingly, it stopped. Thorben turned to find Jez standing just ahead, slumped over and heaving for breath. She spotted him, straightened, look past him, and frantically motioned for him to hurry.

"Hurry. It's behind you," she cried out. "Hurry."

Thorben pumped his legs, his side aching, and stumbled up to Jez. She stood in the mouth to what looked like a side chamber, thick stalactites hanging from the ceiling in the opening, reaching like teeth down to chest-level.

"I t-t-thought you were just trying to scare Gor and the others. I thought you were just going to scare us! Why didn't you tell me?" Jez cried as he approached, her face bleached of almost all color.

"It was the...the. I didn't...I was just telling a story," Thorben stammered, trying to find the words.

He stopped and sputtered, heaving to catch his breath. The chamber curved back around to their left before them, the gently sloping wall leading right back to the distant statue, the door still frustratingly closed behind her.

"What will it do to us? Oh, gods, what will it do?" Jez ducked around him, her eyes going wider, what remained of her color draining away.

She saw it. Jez actually saw it and not just a spot of floating light in the air, or a reflection on a wall. She saw the dweorg's spirit. A little while ago that would have been the most wonderful revelation. At least he would have known that he wasn't crazy, but now...

He turned and found the dweorg still moving toward them, but not quickly. Hells, the short, glowing figure was walking along casually, as if out for a stroll.

"I don't know what it will do to us. I don't know if it can." Thorben turned back to the girl, frantically picking through the piles of useless information in his mind. Nothing seemed to help...he'd never actually seen a spirit before, not in all his many delves.

"Come along then. Please. I hear something in this cavern..."

"Hear what?" he asked, grasping her arms and pulling her firmly aside. Thorben turned his head at the mouth of the cave, listening to the darkness. There was something there, but it wasn't what he'd feared. It wasn't the skittering, scratching in the sarcophagus. It was a gentle rush of air, like a gentle river breeze, with something else...something quiet just beyond audibility. There weren't any lanterns visible in the cave. It was dark. No, frighteningly dark.

"It's better than standing here..." he said, but Jez stiffened next to him.

"Thorben!" she croaked, and violently ripped at his arm, tugging him towards the dark cave. He staggered forward and turned. The dweorg was standing just a few paces away, practically right on top of them. The ghostly figure lifted an arm and pointed back towards the sarcophagus, his mouth falling open. It wasn't words, but a wail – a horrible, bone-chilling cry. The ring buzzed against his finger, the metal growing hot.

How? There is no way it could have covered the distance...not that fast.

Jez pulled him again. He moved to follow her into the cave, struggling to tear his gaze away from the specter. His foot caught, and he tripped, stumbling forward. He turned, catching sight of Jez ducking into the darkness, a jagged stalactite hanging between them. He felt his face hit the stone, an explosion of color washing over his vision, and then everything went black.

* * * *

Bang – crack. Crack – bang. Somewhere nearby, a hammer struck a chisel. Thorben felt his gut tighten at the sound. It was strange, he could feel it, the revulsion, but couldn't see his own body.

Bang – bang. Bang – crack. Boom. A flicker of light blossomed to life not far ahead, the darkness parting like a thick curtain.

The light grew stronger, a foul smell filling his nose. Thorben straightened and coughed, throwing his hands out to either side. He caught both sides of the claustrophobic tunnel and pushed, struggling and straining, fighting against an almost instantaneous stab of panic.

It was the Council's mine. The same damn mine, the tunnels crowding in around him, their weeping stone and stinking tunnels a burden he'd never forget. He was back. How was he back? His arms gave out, and he fell to his knees, the porous stone jagged and unforgiving.

Thorben lifted his right arm, the sleeve of his filthy, tattered shirt falling down past his elbow. That damn shirt. The only one he'd been able to wear for six long thaws. Pink, angry flesh appeared in the tunnel's dim light, his brand so fresh it almost glowed.

"No...no...no," he moaned and slapped his hands over his face. How was this possible? How...?

Bang – crack. The stone shook as men pounded with hammer and chisel, extracting ore from the rock, smashing chisel and flesh in equal measure. The smell grew closer, more intimate. It wasn't just the unwashed bodies and sweat, but the sour pang of fear and despair, mixed with rock dust and blood. *The smell is death.*

His stomach rumbled hollowly. It was a hunger unlike any other, a bottomless need that tainted every thought and movement. It was a hunger that followed a man the rest of his life – a hunger more intense and intimate than any pleasure he had, or ever would, experience.

A man howled somewhere ahead, his cries of pain and anguish reverberating off the close walls. Thorben willed him to be silent. Noise only brought on the guards, and their lashes bit deep, regularly flaying flesh from bone. His pain was their pleasure.

He pulled his hands away and glanced down at his other arm. He numbly picked at a scar on his forearm, remembering the whip's sting clearly enough.

"I don't under...stand," Thorben muttered, a sob working its way up from his belly. "How am I...here? Did I just dream it all? Is my family just a dream? Was none of it real?"

The thought gripped him with a crippling wave of despair, the stinking stone reaching up to grab him. Tears ran freely, covering his cheeks and falling to the stone. Thorben pushed himself up and wiped his face. He heard it. He definitely heard it.

"H-h-hello!" he croaked weakly. Damn his voice. Damn him for sounding so weak.

Thorben crawled to his feet and ambled forward. The mine tunnel curved to his right, a man coming into view, his back and shoulders heavily stooped, his body splayed out, legs and arms twisted in painful looking knots. His back was to Thorben, the skin pocked and scarred from disease and the whip.

"Ugghh." The scratchy voice echoed out of the tunnel ahead, the prone man shifting slightly.

He tried to crawl around the prone man, but there wasn't room in the tight tunnel. If the guards showed up while he was trying to help him, they were just as likely to flay Thorben as well. He looked up and down the tunnel, struggling to remember the layout, and then turned just as the elderly prisoner moaned softly, the words muffled and unintelligible. His ribs showed with every wheezing breath.

"What? I can't hear you," he whispered. The old man mumbled again, but like before, he could not make out the words.

Thorben cursed and crouched down, carefully untangling the old man's legs, vigilantly avoiding the open sores. Snotty corruption seeped out of the boils, leaving bloody trails across his pale flesh. Pocks killed more men in the mines than starvation or guards, and Thorben was eager to stay clear. He hooked a hand around one shoulder and rolled him over, while lifting to help him to sit. The old man's head rolled around, his thick, white beard gathered up in a single tie, bits of food and rock still trapped in the unkempt mess.

"Zoocah Meaguel," Thorben whispered, remembering the old man's name. He was a particularly withered old crone, even when he first arrived at the mines in Darimar. He'd spent so much time under the ground that his healthy, sun-kissed Ishmandi skin was paler than even Thorben's, his black hair white as freshly fallen snow. The mines hadn't just broken him, but consumed him, body and soul.

But Zoocah died the thaw before I was released. I remember it plain as day. A tunnel collapsed and the rock crushed his legs. He lay in that dark tunnel, moaning and crying for help, but beyond our reach for days before finally passing.

"Nooaahhh. Muuuusssttah, nooot..." the old man moaned, his mouth stretching wide, his scabby, black tongue jabbing at the air. Thorben tried to pull away, but the old man's hands clamped onto his arms, his grip impossibly strong for someone who looked so fragile.

"Let me go!" Thorben tried to break free, but the old man's fingers dug in, crushing his arms. He teetered for a moment and then staggered forward.

Zoocah twisted Thorben's right hand closer, the air shimmering around the old man's face. The middle finger on his hand started to burn, right before a green flash split the gloom. A silver ring appeared on his finger, almost melting out of thin air.

Zoocah started to shake beneath him, his face scrunching up and contorting, his arms and hands shrinking and widening. Thorben watched in horror as the pocked, diseased and broken old man shifted into someone else entirely. A heartbeat later, a much shorter figure writhed beneath him, bauble-laden necklaces and gemmed facial studs sparkling in the dim light.

The tunnel faded quickly, the rock shifting and vibrating, the dripping limestone bleeding color until a more porous, gray stone surrounded them. The air became colder around him – stuffier, closer, and older.

"Ee gristuda. Ee gunta reesa!" the dweorg growled, but flinched at the sound of his own voice.

Thorben flinched, too, as the short figure abruptly lurched upwards, pushing him off the ground. He tried to push away and run, but the dwarf moved in the same direction at the same time. They bounced off one another, tried to push free and only managed to tangle up their arms and legs.

They spun, staggered, and wrestled, both grunting and cursing in their own tongues. The tunnel dissolved again, and they broke apart, staggering away. Thorben caught his balance and turned, taking in a much larger space.

"Papa. No!" It was a girl's voice, distant and small. He spun, the dwarf almost perfectly copying his movement. They were in a round chamber, wood scaffolding built up all around the walls. A thick section of wood platform was constructed in the middle, three gleaming metal rods sticking out of a hole in the ground.

"No, papa, please come home. I don't want you to stay. Please come home...please, please, please," the girl shouted. Thorben spotted a dwarf woman in a flowing red and gold dress standing by a short, wide doorway. She struggled, her arms hooked around a young girl who fought to break free. The dweorg from the tunnel appeared next to him, taking several steps forward as the little girl finally broke free. She ran straight into his arms, her small hands clasping desperately at his wispy robe.

The woman appeared, pulling her back, but the girl lifted a necklace free and held it out. The dweorg dropped to a knee and allowed her to drop it over his head. She kissed his cheek and then disappeared, her voice echoing distantly.

"Lynheid...me little girl. Me little girl! It can't be. Ee was... Ee was locked away for so long... Ee never thought ee would see ye again, except in me dreams." The dweorg pulled the necklace free from the others, a number of shiny, horse-shaped charms catching the light. He closed his eyes and whispered her name over again and again.

Thorben watched the dwarf open his eyes and stumble forward, searching the darkness for the girl. He spun back as loud grunting voices sounded behind him. He watched a troop of stout, strong-legged dweorg carry a slab of rock into the chamber, carefully line a hole in its base, and drop it over top of the shiny rods sticking out of the ground.

It cannot be, Thorben thought, starting to put the pieces together. Another group of dwarves carried a pedestal into the chamber, three barrel-shaped wooden keys gleaming in the light.

"Lynheid!" the dweorg cried, holding the necklace to his face, but the air around them grew dark, heavier yet. A host of dwarves pounded and chiseled, hollowing out the gray stone, while others carted away pushcarts full of rubble and debris. Thorben could smell them and feel the fragments of stone against his skin as hammer smashed against rock.

Thorben turned, cursing quietly as a line of shrouded bodies appeared on the ground, stretching as far up the tunnel as he could see. Dweorg craftsman gently laid them into wall hollows, the rest pounding and shaping the stone with a speed and determination he'd never seen before. Carts rolled down the underground path, adding to the queue of dead faster than the workers could lay them to rest.

They moved down the tunnel, Thorben unaware that his legs or feet were moving, and yet they moved nonetheless. The tunnel widened, sloping down, the walls growing and branching off, the numbers of hollows increasing substantially, bodies filling them, appearing as if from thin air.

They reached the bottom of the valley, the small buildings rising up around them. Thorben watched the craftsmen lovingly lay their fellows into new hollows beside their warrior brethren. The stoneworkers barely numbered a dozen now, haggard and stooped, broken by time and their labors. They looked older, weathered, and worn down, their beards grayed with age. If they stood still long enough, he had difficulty telling them apart from the stone, as if they were slowly returning to the rock.

They left the maker's shantytown behind, the strange black doors appearing ahead. The space felt different than he remembered – brighter, the air not yet tainted by so much death.

The dwarves hunched close to the archways of a dozen identical rooms, tapping lightly with hammers, fingers, and palms against the stone. The air filled with their voices, quiet at first, but growing in unison. Thorben watched as the rock started to move – sharp edges, hard lines, and porous surfaces flowing into graceful curves.

The dweorg stumbled forward, ignoring his stooped counterparts as the magnificent statues slowly appeared out of the rock. A number of tall figures appeared from the darkness behind them, their long, lean bodies so out of place amongst the short and powerfully built dwarves. A woman walked at the head of their procession, her white-blond hair pulled into a tight, elaborate braid. She wore a flowing blue dress, the hem lined with a number of long, brightly covered feathers. And yet it was her eyes that Thorben found so mesmerizing. They were large and colorless, like eerie mirrors.

She is dalan. Mani alive, she has to be. They are dalan.

"Hullo, Matrona," the dwarves said, their voices seemingly echoing out of the stone. The tall woman bowed lightly and her mouth moved, but he couldn't hear her words. They were in the round chamber then, the worn-down dwarves dropping a stone box into place.

The dalan, tall and almost noiseless in movement, approached, a withered body held lovingly between them. They lowered the figure into the sarcophagus, a mass of tangled, branching roots woven into and around its flesh. The dalan came forward in turn, depositing fantastic relics and treasures into the box – a shining helm, a mirror lined with gems, and a short dagger set in a gleaming, black scabbard.

He recognized the horrible plant, its greasy chutes already working its way out from the hole in the side of the stone box, smaller shoots growing and worming their way up and over the lid.

"Let them rest for evermore, evermore and onto the end of time," the dalan said in unison.

The dweorg bowed their heads, their skin pale and heavily wrinkled, and their hair wispy and colorless tufts.

"Keepers of the dead...may the honored find rest here, and may your ancestors honor your sacrifice. Let us hope that the blood shed by those in this place be the last this land has to suffer. May Gruteo himself welcome you at the gates of the Forgefather, and allow you to rest, once and for all," the tall, magnificent dalan woman said, but her people were leaving, fading into the misty darkness.

"Seal the door. Seal away our dead. Destroy it when your work is done. You must destroy it," the dalan's voice echoed distantly. A heavy grating noise filled the air, and Thorben turned in time to see the remaining dweorg slide a heavy slab into place over the crypt.

Thorben was standing in the maze next, the hollows of dweorg dead rising up all around him. A grim-faced dwarf sat at a small table, a knife clutched tightly in one hand, and a pitcher in the other. The stooped, broken craftsmen formed a line before the table. One old man shuffled up, dropped his battered hammer into a bucket, took a gulp from the pitcher, and dropped his hands onto the table. The seated dwarf dropped the knife down quickly, rocked it forward and then back, severing the workman's thumb.

Thorben grimaced and covered his mouth as the dwarf promptly sawed through the other workman's thumb, scooped the two severed fingers into a little bag, and handed them to him.

"So the dead may rest. Blood to dust," the dwarf behind the table said.

"Blood to dust," the workman echoed, wrapping a bandage around his left hand and then awkwardly shambled away. Thorben watched the old dwarf carry the bag to the base of the massive statue, the goddess looming high overhead, and dropped the offering onto a hook in the stone.

He watched the small troop come forward, one by one, without argument or anger, without sniffle or tear, and allow the dwarf to mangle their hands – a craftsman's truest and most valuable tool.

The old dwarves shuffled off, one by one, retiring to their small, dark homes, where they crawled into bed, and closed their eyes. The old dweorg with the clinking mass of trinkets around his neck rubbed the horse-charm necklace between his gnarled middle and pointer fingers. He walked beneath the strange monstrous statues, the plants sprouting from the stone sarcophagi already rooting beyond their chambers, sprouting like trees, branching over the walls and ground like ivy. A heavy mist seeped from the plant, drifting along the ground and flowing off the vines on the walls.

The dweorg lifted his left hand into the air, the gem set in his ring glowing brightly. Thorben felt the band on his own finger hum in response. The strange, insect-shaped lanterns in the antechamber immediately went dark, their metal carapaces sliding shut. The massive, black doors swung in noiselessly, closing with a resounding *boom,* sealing the crypts shut.

The old dweorg limped up the tunnel, pain and exhaustion crying out from every movement. Alone now, except for Thorben, whom he didn't seem to see or hear, he slumped into a chair at the tunnel mouth, pulled the ring from his finger, and slapped it onto the table. Gnarled, mangled hands scrabbled for a hammer, lifting it awkwardly without thumbs, and hoisted it up high.

"What are you doing?" Thorben asked, but his voice felt muted and dead. The withered old figure gave no indication he heard or could see him. He could feel it – the dwarf's longing and despair, his loneliness like a shadow that followed the worn-down man's every move. The ring was a key, and not just to the crypts, but the whole underground. He could feel it, somehow, someway, the power living in the stone connecting them on a level too deep to understand.

The dweorg sniffled, baring his teeth as tears flooded his eyes. He exhaled violently and brought the hammer down, the blunted face smacking hard against the pitted table. He sobbed a name quietly, and then threw the hammer, the tool rattling loudly somewhere in the dark structure.

"Lynheid, my girl. What has happened to you? To your mother, me love? Ee can't...ee can't see you anymore. What of Granjmor, and the rest? Did ye find a suitor, continue our line? Ee will die and never know...just die here, alone, amongst the dust and bones," the dweorg cried, scooping the ring off the table. He held it up before squinting, tear-filled eyes, and then choking down sobs, stuffed it into his mouth and swallowed.

"No, not alone. Ee will not die down here." The short, weathered old dwarf swiped at his tear-stained face, and then slapped the table with surprising vigor. He nodded his head, and pushed off to stand, a determined glint shining in his tired eyes.

A pain stabbed into Thorben's hand as a green light flared from inside the dweorg's body, shining out through his thin garments and wispy robes. The old man rocked backwards and fell into the chair, his feet flopping wildly against the ground, mangled hands clutching desperately at his throat.

Thorben crumbled to his knees, the ring wedged onto his middle finger growing both hotter and heavier. He ripped and twisted, fighting in vain to pull it fee. The dweorg flopped again, a green light burning from his eyes, nose, and mouth, and then he went horribly rigid.

The ring pulsed and then some force...some invisible entity lifted his hand above his head. Thorben cried out and tried to pull it back down, but something unbelievably strong held it in place. He was jerked upright, and then he was standing in the darkness, a horrible, throbbing pain reverberating in his head.

Thorben gasped and opened his eyes. His hand hung out before him, four glowing fingers intertwined with his, the jeweled ring burning brightly between them. He pulled free, the glowing dweorg staggering back at the same time. His fingers...his hand...the spirit, he could feel him, as if he were flesh and blood, just like him.

He fell back against a wall as everything started to spin, the pain burning more keenly behind his eyes, and his stomach lurched viscously. Thorben reached up instinctively and found an angry, painful knot on his forehead just above his right eye. He pressed his eyes shut until everything stopped spinning, and slowly opened them again, first looking to his right and then left. The cavern was dark and he couldn't immediately identify where he was, or how he'd gotten there.

Where is Jez? Where am I?

"Who are ye?"

Thorben stiffened at the sound, and turned to find the glowing dweorg standing just a few, short paces away, his dark eyes locked on him.

Chapter Eighteen
Connected

"W-w-who am I?" Thorben sputtered, his heart beating like a runaway horse in his chest. In response, the dweorg nodded, crossing his thick, short arms over his chest.

"My n-n-name is, well, I'm Thorben."

"What are ye? Some sort of vision, an apparition, or maybe a projection? Why are you haunting me?" the dwarf asked.

"Do you mean a 'spirit'?" *Did he say "haunting me"?*

Again the dweorg nodded, turning his head to look around the dark space. Thorben's confusion deepened and he rubbed the aching spot on his head. Had he died...no, was he dead? He felt real enough. The pain throbbing in his head definitely felt real enough.

"No. Last I checked, I am still alive," he said, pushing away from the wall and using his feet to feel his way along in the darkness. His answer seemed to confuse the dweorg, who looked around the chamber again, took a step in one direction, and promptly turned back around.

"I can hear you, but I don't know who you are. I just sat down for a minute's rest, to think about my...and I think I fell asleep. I thought about...them. And how I missed...her. Beyond that, I'm having a hard time...can't seem to straighten my, recollections..." the dweorg trailed off, and Thorben watched as he lifted the horse-charm necklace away from the others and brushed it against his cheek.

Thorben considered him for a moment - he could hear him, but more, he could understand him. And yet, the dweorg didn't seem to remember much beyond sitting down at the table. Was there something Thorben was missing? The vision, or memory, whatever it was, felt so real...vivid. Hells, he'd touched him. He couldn't explain it...their hands had been connected when he'd roused from the strange vision, as if they were joined by the ring. A thought stabbed into Thorben's mind, but the pain made things foggy. It was a name. Yes, a girl's name.

"You said her name...'Lynheid'. Is that your...your daughter?"

The dwarf stiffened, his eyes immediately narrowing. "How do you know that name? Who told you about her?"

So he couldn't see me in the vision.

"I heard you...I mean, I saw her when you," Thorben sputtered, and pushed back against the wall as the dweorg ran at him, covering the distance between them in just a few, silent steps. Now that he was close, Thorben could see that the dweorg didn't look like the broken old man in the vision anymore, nor did he move like it, for that matter. He looked younger, more vital.

"Who told ye that name? Answer me."

Thorben searched the ghostly dwarf's face, trying to read his dark eyes but failed to grasp the best response. How does one respond to a ghost...dwarf?

"I heard you say her name," Thorben finally said, deciding on a shade of the truth.

"Heard me say it? How is that possible...I ne'er seen you before in me life. I don't know how you know about my Lynheid, but you best bite yer tongue. I'm not sure how much you know about understone folk, but we're a protective lot, and that little one, she's precious to me."

"I'm telling you the truth. I heard you say her name. Honestly, on Mani's grace...I would never hurt a child."

"Again, I ain't never seen ya, so have it your way, stranger. Just know that I'll find out eventually, and if you mean her ill, you'll have me and my hammer to deal with."

Thorben nodded and dropped his hands, having not realized that he'd lifted them defensively.

"How in the Forgefather's anvil did you get in here, stranger? You're a longlegger, but not dalan kind. Who are you and what business do you have here? This place was sealed, hallowed...I know, as I sealed it myself, so speak quickly."

"We found this place, and..." he started to say, but stopped. He couldn't say it, not after all that he'd seen, all that the old dweorg and his people had sacrificed. How could he tell him that they'd broken in to defile the sacred place and plunder its wealth? "I came upon this," he said, finally, and held his hand up, exposing the ring.

Part of Thorben hoped that the old dweorg would simply be able to pull it free, rid him of the burden. Then he could find Jez and Iona and leave the place behind. He'd never delve again...spend his time finding some other way to pay his way and support his family. *Death and dust,* he'd never even think about delving again.

"Gunta strike you down! Where did you find that? That...that ring was mine...entrusted to only me," the dweorg cried. He lifted a mangled hand and pointed a stubby finger at Thorben's hand. The short man spun, patted his robes, jingled his bauble-laden necklaces, and then lifted both hands up to his face.

"I didn't steal it, honest. Like I said, I found it."

The dweorg blew a loud raspberry and snorted. "You stole that. Ha! More likely that the stone becomes clouds and clouds stone, and Gunta turns the world upside down. That ring was mine...mine to hold. Mine alone! My burden, it is the...key, and it never leaves my person." The dweorg seemed to swell with anger, his stubby pointer finger tapping accusingly into Thorben's chest.

"I, well...I mean I found it," Thorben started to say, but stopped, not entirely sure how to continue now that he'd brought it up. What would happen if he told the spirit the truth about where he found it? Would something horrible happen? Thorben's thoughts spiraled down into

Dennah and his boys' ghost stories, the ever darker and nastier endings only coming alive in his imagination.

"Give it back, you thief!" The dweorg's hand snapped out in a flash and wrapped around his wrist, thick fingers locking around the ring. He yanked Thorben down and pulled, his strength staggering. He felt the sharp pull on his finger, the knuckle popping in response, but the metal band would not slide free. Instead, the metal grew hot, the gem pulsing with a sudden and very bright surge of light.

"Let go of it! You must give it back to me. You don't understand what it...you don't understand why..." the dweorg wrestled with his hand, stammering, his cheeks puffing out animatedly.

"I can't...get...it...off," Thorben growled and managed to wrestle free.

"You listen to me, long legs. I don't know how you got in here, but you do not belong. This place is for the dead, and the dead alone. I'll give you this one chance. Hand over what you stole, and go. Or I'll..I'll."

"I just told you, I can't get it off. I found it in you...inside your corpse, in the chair, outside the black doors," Thorben said, smashing his back up against the wall and preparing to fight him off again.

The dweorg cocked his head to the side and immediately went quiet. He looked at the ring, his eyes slowly crawling up Thorben's dirty and tattered clothes until their eyes met.

"You took it from...my...what? Now you're telling me jests," the short man laughed, his baubles jingling. "Did the forge barons send ye? Do ye carry a message, a scroll perhaps? Who put you up to this? You don't look like dwarf folk, but ye certainly sound like one. They sent ye, didn't they? Ye found me sleeping and just lifted it, that's it. I just laid down mine head, and you took the ring as a little jest. Now we've had a wee chuckle, and bellies are rosy, but you must hand it over."

"Forge barons? No, no one sent me. And what do you mean, I sound like dwarf folk?"

"What do ya mean, what do I mean? Plain enough. Yer speaking to me, aren't ya? Your grasp of the khuzdul tongue is good, too, almost as good as dweorg-born, although your accent is odd. Yer lips aren't quite strong enough for it."

Khuzdul? And then it hit him. His grandfather spoke of the dweorg of the lakes speaking in their old tongue, "stone speak", as he called it, because the words felt like "stones rattling around in one's mouth". The dweorg merchants in Braakdell would only barter in khuzdul. His grandfather never ceased to complain about it, but over the course of his many thaws bartering picked up a goodly portion of the language. He regularly complained about Thorben's grandmother in the tongue, and she was never the wiser.

"Listen, I didn't find you sleeping. I guess I don't know how to...say it. I found you, your remains...your skeleton, on that chair. This ring," he said, lifting up the hand, "was inside your body. I reached in and pulled it out. You were...are dead, for a good long time, I reckon."

"Now that is not a funny jest...telling folk they're dead, long legs," the dweorg grunted, and promptly set off towards the back of the cavern.

"Wait, where are you going?"

"To show you that you're just a jesting fool and prove you wrong. Then, I'll take back my ring and remove you promptly from this place. Come with me."

"I...I don't think that is a good idea," Thorben called out, and fumbled his way through the darkness to follow. Had Jez gone this far into the darkness by herself? She surely wouldn't have gone back – not to the burial chamber, with the freezing mist and the closed archway.

No...she went forward. There was no way out back there...she knew that.

"And you think stumbling upon a sleeping dwarf and stealing from him *is* a good idea?"

Thorben considered the dwarf for a minute, sorting through the memories from the vision. Could he really not remember? Was any of it even real, for that matter?

"No, but please. You must listen to me. I want to leave this place...eagerly, actually, and as soon as is possible to get back to my family, but there are others here with me. I need to find Jez. She is a young woman, and her father. They are in danger," Thorben said, his insides clenching up. The chamber led into a small, dark passage, the ground uneven beneath his feet.

The dweorg walked just ahead, his glowing form casting the otherwise lightless passage in a dim, green light. He skipped ahead, falling into step behind the small figure, his pace surprisingly fast considering his short legs.

"How can you see where you are going? It is so dark in here."

"You haven't the eyes of an understoner," the dweorg laughed, his voice ringing against the stone. "And you are right, Thorben long-legs. This is a dangerous place, and the living have no business here."

Thorben sucked in a breath but couldn't immediately reply. The dweorg wasn't wrong. In fact, Thorben agreed wholeheartedly. He wished that he'd never agreed to accompany Iona. Oh, how things would be different.

"Might I at least know your name? I feel a bit odd not knowing what to call you." *A bit odd doesn't cover half of it. I'm following the spirit of a dead dwarf that may just be trapped in a ring that I was stupid enough to put in my damned pocket, through an ancient crypt full of thousands of dead warrior dweorg, thumb-less stoneworkers, crypt keepers, bleeding, stinking vines, freezing mist, and statues that move. Not to mention a disgraced, destitute illegal goods broker carting his young daughter into the dangerous wilds, all to satisfy a debt to a murderous gang of river guildsmen after his wife ran off with his fortune and son.*

"I will have to redefine what 'odd' truly is if I make it out of here alive," Thorben muttered.

"Myrddin. Me name is Myrddin Luck Hammer, First Stonesinger to the late king Gruteo Brave Hammer."

"For what it's worth, it is nice to meet you, Myrddin," Thorben said, struggling to keep pace. The last thing he wanted was to be left alone in the dark passageway by himself, as the dwarf seemed to be the only source of light.

They followed the passage around another bend, the walls opening outward, an incredibly low, rumbling sound filling the air. Thorben felt and tasted the water on the air before he saw it. A massive shelf hung high up on the opposite wall, a wide, dark sheet of water spilling into a chasm just beyond his feet. The waterfall disappeared into the black, hitting bottom somewhere far below.

The path past the chasm was narrow – barely a pace wide at the base of the wall, the stone dripping wet and covered in spongy moss. Myrddin continued forward, his stout legs and small feet carrying him quickly along the treacherous path.

"Is there...another way...through?" Thorben shouted, trying to be heard above the spilling water.

Myrddin stopped on the narrow path, turned back, shook his head, waved him forward, and continued across. Thorben scooted his feet forward, the toes of his boots hovering just over the drop off. His gaze dropped to the wide cavern, the darkness yawning hungrily before him.

"I...d-d-don't think I can do this," he stammered and pulled back from the edge. Myrddin was already most of the way across and didn't seem to hear him. Thorben's heart started to hammer in his chest, his hands and knees already shaking.

He glanced to his left, where Myrddin's fading light was leaving heavy shadows on the narrow path, and then back to his right, and the winding, branching tunnel that would lead him back to the burial chamber, only if he didn't wander off in the wrong direction and get lost. The darkness was already closing in, swallowing the mouth of the tunnel and creeping his way.

He was back at the river again, the dark, seemingly bottomless water spanning before him. Misty water droplets sprayed on his face, spattering into his eyes and mouth. He didn't have a spear at his back this time, but the darkness felt just as dangerous.

It's just water, you coward. It's just damned water...a really dark, deep hole in the ground. There was no way for him to know how far the pit dropped, or what was waiting for him at the bottom - a lake or underground river, or jagged unforgiving rocks.

Before he could stop himself, Thorben slid his back against the wet stone and took a single, shaking step along the narrow path. The moss was squelchy, shifting and squirming uncomfortably under his boots.

He shuffled sideways, working hard to keep his eyes up and away from the falling water, but more, the sprawling darkness. His left boot slid forward half a pace before connecting with solid stone.

One step at a time. One step at a time, he thought, sucking in a quick breath and trying to force his heart to slow. Myrddin reached the other side of the walkway and entered the tunnel, his light dropping dramatically. The waterfall almost instantly plunged into darkness, the sound of crashing water surrounding him.

"Wait...no, wait! I cannot see. Come back!" Thorben shouted, the cursed lump forming in his throat. The darkness deepened, the sound and drenching water crushing down around him.

Myrddin said something, his laugh just breaking through the waterfall's din, but he was still moving away. Thorben panicked, sidestepped, and tried to take another quick step but his boot landed and promptly slid forward. His balance shifted as his foot slipped off the ledge. He fell straight down and dropped his left hand, his butt and palm hitting the wet ledge at the same time.

Thorben snapped his head back, banging it painfully on the stone, stars bursting forth in the darkness. His butt slid forward, but he managed to scoot his back against the stone. He hovered there for a terrifying moment, one leg hanging off in the open air, the other bent at an odd angle to the side, while his rear and left hand sank and slid deeper into the soft, cold moss.

"Well...this is...awkward," he grunted and laughed. It wasn't funny at all. In fact, besides his plunge into the river he'd never been more scared in his life.

The spraying water drenched his face, choking his nose and mouth, peppering his clothes. He turned his head to suck in a breath, but could feel his left hand sinking and sliding, the water soaking in around the broken, mashed moss, turning the matter underneath to mud.

His butt slid and he moved his left hand for a better hold. His right hip and knee screamed in protest, the weight and angle all wrong for a man of his age. Thorben tried to push up to stand, but his hand slipped. He would need both hands, but his balance was tenuous and he dared not pull the other away from the wall.

"This is it, Thorben," he muttered, choking back equal parts water and desperate sob. He forced his eyes open against the stinging water, his left arm shaking from the strain. He could just give up, tip forward and fall into the darkness. Give up.

"Earls and their tax collectors, merchants and their hired muscle, relic brokers and their daughters..." he grunted, trying to push himself up on the ledge again, his hand almost sliding out from under him this time. Even the ground worked against him. Of course, it did.

Thorben shook his head, trying to keep some of the water from running down into his eyes. He had to keep moving, find a way to get back onto his feet, otherwise...

"Come on...Thorben!" he said, urging himself on, but the chunk of moss broke free under his hand and slid into the darkness. He felt it move, felt it fall away. There was no more light. No more hope.

"...hungry children, hungry hedge rats, greedy guildsmen, ghostly dwarves, walls that move, underground pits and waterfalls...what next? Mani, what next? I'm not sure I can take more. My family? I'm not sure they can take more. I'm cold...I'm tired and hungry. It's just too much, and I don't see a way out of here. No exit...not when the darkness conspires against me! Am I to become a ghost, too?" he muttered, spitting out a mouthful of cold water. Everything was darker than dark now...devoid of warmth and hope. It was death and release, an end to all the battles.

He slid his left hand and found better purchase, locked his elbow, and pushed. His right foot slipped as he pushed off, but managed to get his butt off the soggy moss. His hand slid, only a frantic grab for another hold stopping him from tumbling into the darkness.

Why are you still fighting? Why are you still moving forward? It is hopeless. Hopeless.

Thorben staggered against the rocky wall, the simple act of not falling into the void taking seemingly every muscle in his body. He was tired, beat up, and hungry.

"You're not supposed to give up...you're not. You have kids who need you," a distant voice echoed in his mind.

Thorben swallowed hard. Yes, the boys, all strength and youth, and fire. They would likely give him many grandchildren. Dennah - he wanted to see her grow into a woman, but...they were so very far away, beyond the underground city of the dead and the thick, stone walls. Beyond the dark pit and choking water. Beyond it all.

"You have a wife and a home."

He sucked in a breath and coughed, the drenching spray of water hitting him squarely in the face now. He wouldn't fall to his death, but drown, sitting there on a slimy, moss-covered walkway, one ass cheek hanging in a moldy breeze.

"But for how long will any of it be ours - the home, the wife, the children? Will Dennica stick by me when things get worse? If it all went away? Men like Lamtrop will see to that," he lamented.

Thorben shrugged, slipped, and pushed himself up. *Do they even need me?* The thought of Dennica and the kids threatened to send him pitching right into the darkness. Without him, his wife could remarry, perhaps to an honest man who made a real wage and could provide for her. His boys were almost men. They would make a life for themselves with or without him. He wanted...no, needed to see them, but it was a selfish need. All of it was selfish...*his* need.

"Dennah has her mother, she doesn't need me," Thorben muttered, giving voice to the dark thoughts ringing inside.

Stop sulking, Dennica's voice suddenly rang out in his thoughts. She'd sent him away while the Council's tax collectors pillaged their cellar. He'd been sitting in the corner, staring daggers at the men, loathing them, himself, and every bad turn his brand had ever brought him.

"I don't sulk-" he sputtered, but knew in his heart that he was. And worse, he was trying to give in.

Death and dust, this is all my life has been, backed up against a wall with only horrible options in front of me. There is...can be no better.

"Thorben, is that you?" someone shouted suddenly.

He started at the voice, his hand sliding off the path. His weight shifted, and he slipped forward, right off the narrow ledge.

"No no no!" he cried out, scrabbling against the wet stone. Thorben threw his left arm out and wedged his forearm into place on the ledge, just managing to spin his body towards the wall as his right boot slid free.

He slung around, slapping his right elbow onto the ledge before his weight carried him down, his body now dangling into the sprawling darkness.

"Thorben is that you?" Jez called from the darkness on the other side of the ravine.

Thorben hauled his body up and tried to kick his right boot onto the ledge, but the ache in his side flared. He grunted through the pain, his weight swinging back beneath him, but found a small foothold and took the burden off his arms. It wouldn't help for long.

"Jez!" he yelled, struggling to find the air.

"Oh my gods. I thought you were dead...back there...when you hit your head. You just lay there, so still, and not breathing. I'm so glad you're...I'm sorry for leaving you. So sorry. Please forgive..."

"No...I'm alive...for the moment," he grunted, trying to kick his leg up onto the ledge again and failing.

"I made it across all right, just don't look down. I can't see you, but follow my voice. It's a narrow path, but straight."

"I...slipped and can't get...back up."

"Stay right there. I'll crawl out and help–" Jez said, but Thorben cut her off.

"No! The ledge is too narrow." He slipped, sagged down the wall, and fumbled, scrabbling against the wet stone for a better footing. "I don't think I am going to...make it. Just go and find your father. Get him to safety, so you can find your brother."

"No!" Jez yelled immediately, her voice echoing against the dark chasm behind him. "I'm coming out there. I can't just leave you here."

"Jez...I can't get back onto the ledge, and I don't know how much longer I can just hang here." Thorben felt the fear of his death fading away. Hells, this had been his life up to now, barely hanging on, waiting for one more slip to send him plummeting down into the dark nothing. Part of him longed for it.

"Fight. Try again. You can't just give up."

"I…can't…" he mumbled, knowing that she couldn't hear him.

"Your girl needs you," Jez yelled, her words stabbing into him.

Thorben slipped again, his elbows and forearms sliding towards the edge, his sides and shoulders threatening to give out. How did she know that he'd just been thinking about Dennah? How did she know that she needed him?

"Come on. Fight! Please! I know your daughter needs you to come home to her. Look at me, my father is the only reason why I'm here. I know he isn't the most honest of men, but he's *my* father, and I also know that he loves me and would do anything for me. My mother is, well, was, a nasty, greedy little woman. She worried more about what our neighbors and their betters were doing…what they wore, ate, where they went than my brother or me. She loved money more than us, too. But *he* was there when she wasn't. After she left and took everything, I still had him. He taught me things that I never would have learned from her, and you are no different. You're just like him, and if I need him, then your daughter *needs* you! Trust me. They all *need* you more than you know! Look how far you have gotten us! My father would be dead right now if it weren't for you. They need you…we need you. Please."

Thorben stared down the dark wall where he figured Jez stood, her face appearing in his mind. He figured that she had her hands on her hips, and her eyes squinted in that typical half-frown. He wanted to believe her, but…his doubt rose up like a black wave again, filling him bodily. *Or, if you'd stayed home, they might have found a way free from Gor. You came of your own selfish need for wealth and security, and likely killed them in the process.*

Thorben slumped under the weight, the muscles in his shoulders spasming painfully. His head drooped forward against the stone as he fought to suck in another breath, the strain making his chest and throat impossibly tight. He couldn't remember ever feeling emptier – not on the wagon, bound and shackled on the way to stand before the magistrate for sentencing, or even in the mines, when his stomach shrunk, his back ached, and his hands and feet bled from the labor. It had all led up to this, for thaws beyond count, the weight bowing his back and slowly smashing him into the ground.

"Hey! Did you hear me? Come on, please answer me," Jez yelled, her voice biting into him like a lash.

He blinked, let his weight rest on his foot for a moment, and sucked in another breath.

"It's hard not to...you're screaming," he yelled.

"Good...because I'm coming out there."

"No," he growled, coughing and sputtering on the water. "You have to go."

"You can't tell me no. I'm coming out there. Either I can help, or we'll fall together. You didn't give up on my father, and I'm not gonna give up on you. If your daughter was here, and she was in my shoes, would she give up on my father?"

Thorben tried to swallow down the guilt, the girl's staunch refusal to let him simply give up more than a little sobering. Her mention of Dennah stabbed into him deeper. No, Dennah wouldn't let anyone slide slowly to their death. Even at seven winter thaws she would try to help...foolishly, and dangerously, but she would help.

Jez refused to give up on him, after her own mother walked away, stealing her little brother and tearing her life, her world, in half. Was that what Dennah would become? Was he doing what her mother did? Did they all need him more than he realized?

"Please no! I don't want you to get hurt...let me try again," he yelled, and sucked in a deep breath. He set his jaw, pulled in his gut, and clenched his fists.

Thorben had given up, even if he was too cowardly to admit it. He'd given up after being released from the mines, letting men look down on him and talk down to him because of his brand. They spit on him, swindled him, paid him a fraction of what they'd pay less-talented men for inferior work, and he never stuck up for himself. He turned the other cheek, and struggled through it all in silence.

"Can you manage it? I can lean out and help you up if you get close enough," Jez called.

"I think," he grunted, pulling his body up with his arms, but his boot slid free of its small perch. Thorben slumped back down, the weight almost pulling his arms off the mossy ledge, but he refused to despair. He was tired of feeling sorry for himself, eating the crap everyone and everything seemed to give him. If he was going to fall to his death, at least he could do it fighting.

"I c-c-can't get back up on the ledge, b-b-but am going to try to crawl my way towards you." Before the girl could respond, Thorben lifted his right arm and walked it out to his right and lifted his foot off the small shelf of stone. His entire weight immediately sagged onto his arms, shoulders, and back, his aching side and stomach shaking and quivering with the effort.

"You carried logs with father and pa out of the timber for a whole season as a child...chipped bark, sawed beams, and hoisted them into place. If you can do that, then you can do this," he whispered, sputtering and coughing as more water spattered his head and ran down his face.

A muscle tweaked in his back, but Thorben pushed through it, hugging his chest to the wet stone and walking his weight sideways with his arms. His elbows sunk into the moss, but the spongy cover held.

He moved slowly, painfully, half an arm length at a time, his boots scrabbling, catching, and sliding against the wet stone. His shoulders tired, then his sides and stomach, the muscles in his back burning from the strain, but he refused to stop.

Thorben wheezed, something catching in his side. He fought against it – the pain, the tremors, the fatigue, the water, and the darkness. He hadn't died in the mines, or any of the arduous days since. He'd been right there at Dennica's side when she bore seven healthy, screaming babes. None of that killed him, and neither would this. But damn, it hurt. He just wanted to rest for a moment, let the weight off his arms and shoulders, catch his breath, even for just a moment.

"Don't you quit on them, Thorben. If life isn't going to give you anything, then take it. You are...going...to...see Paul pass his...trials," he hissed, clenching his jaw so tight it ached. "Hold...little pebble...again." He walked his arms forward again, and then again, but his hands had gone numb, and then his forearms.

Thorben forced in a breath and moved his arms but couldn't feel them anymore, almost every muscle shaking in unison. He moved beyond the ache, the fatigue, and the numbness, every reach feeling like it would be his last. His body begged him to give up the fight and simply relax, to fall into the black and the promise of whatever Mani had planned for him next.

No! I want to see my family again, he thought, lifting his numb right arm and slapping it along the ledge. It was a small thing, but he just wanted to sit at the dining table again, listening to his children, the hectic, chaotic mix of stories and squabbles...the chatter he'd come to secretly love more than anything else.

"Just a few...more...it...has to...be," he wheezed, but felt his arms sliding, his body giving in.

"Thorben," Jez gasped, her voice sounding out of the darkness right next to him. "I can see you...I can see you. I can almost reach..."

He felt something brush against his right shoulder.

"Just a little further...you can do it!" she said.

Thorben grunted and fought, but couldn't feel his arms. He hoped and prayed they were moving, but couldn't know for sure. Something slapped his shoulder again, and then his back, cold fingers hooking inside his soaked shirt collar.

Jez wrenched and pulled on him, the contact with another person – someone who cared – helping more than anything else. His numb elbow smacked hard into stone.

"You made it. My gods, I didn't think you were–"

"Help me up first...not out of...woods yet," Thorben growled, struggling to gain any lift and pull himself free.

Jez leaned over him, her hands crawling under his armpits. She grunted and strained, heaving on him with abandon. Thorben kicked and flailed against the stone, managed to lift himself up a little, and then a little more.

Jez yelled, her mouth right next to his ear. He felt her arms wrap around him in a hug, and then they were sprawling back to the stone. Thorben rolled to the side, his arms shaking at his side, but managed to push away from the edge. He gasped, laughing and crying, his emotions closer to the surface than ever before.

"I'm so sorry. I shouldn't have left you. I almost killed you! I'm horrible...I'm a horrible person," Jez said, crouching in the darkness next to him. She tentatively touched his shoulder, but shied away.

Thorben awkwardly pushed himself up to sit, his arms still shaking, but feeling quickly returning. He reached out and caught the girl's arm before she could walk away and pulled her into a hug.

"Thank you. Thank you," he muttered over and over, still trying to catch his breath. "Thank you for not giving up on me."

"I...I..." Jez squeezed him back and sniffled loudly.

"You saved me," he whispered. She had, and in more ways than she probably realized.

Chapter Nineteen
Crawling Forth

Thorben and Jez walked together down the dark passage, the noise from the waterfall receding behind them. They followed a gentle curve in the passage, a light ahead casting the stone in a warm glow.

The passage turned to the right, leading off into the darkness, another leg running straight ahead and through another stalactite-covered opening, and a well-lit space beyond. Thorben allowed Jez to go first, carefully picking his way through the low-hanging rock formations. He kept a hand on the closest stalactite, and once on the other side, reached up and rubbed the goose egg on his forehead.

Thorben pulled up his right sleeve. Chunks of moss and dirt covered the pale skin of his forearm, barely concealing dark bruises and several cuts and scrapes. He rolled up the other sleeve and found the same.

"Does it hurt?" Jez asked.

"If not for you, these would be the least of my concerns," Thorben said, his voice low and scratchy.

They turned together and looked out over a wide, circular chamber. A familiar ring-shaped formation of trees stood straight ahead, a dense layer of fog drifting aimlessly around a stone sarcophagus in the very center.

"I don't understand. Did we just go in a big circle..." he said, struggling for a moment, but then spotted the distant archway. The statue was different – a man with spiky hair and a multitude of strong-looking arms – he could see that much from where he was standing, and more importantly, the doorway was open.

"This chamber is different. We can get out!" Jez said, and immediately started forward.

Thorben followed, his gaze sweeping back down and catching on a solitary, glowing figure standing a stone's throw from the sarcophagus.

Myrddin didn't look up when he approached, the dweorg's attention remaining locked on the burial.

"You just left me back there. I almost died," Thorben said.

Wha...?" Jez asked. She'd taken a wider path across the chamber, willfully putting as much distance between herself and the stone box as possible.

"Yer still here, ain't ya?" Myrddin asked, not looking away from the sarcophagus. He mumbled more, but he couldn't hear what he said.

Thorben shivered, the cold mist making his wet clothes and damp skin feel even heavier. He braved the trees and approached the dweorg.

"What did you say? I didn't hear," Jez said, approaching from behind.

"Is this why ye are here? You and this girl," Myrddin asked, pointing back over his shoulder to Jez, without looking.

"Is what...?" Thorben's question died in his throat as he followed the dweorg's gaze to the stone burial. The stringy roots were torn away from the sides, the sticky red sap spattered all across the carved stone. The heavy lid was turned off at an angle, allowing someone just enough room to reach inside.

"Is this why you are here? To desecrate the remains me and mine laid to rest, to interrupt their sacred slumber and steal from the dead?" Myrddin growled, spinning on him.

Thorben staggered back, but the dwarf turned to Jez, his dark eyes lidded, his teeth showing in an angry snarl. Iona's daughter looked from Thorben, to the crypt, and back, her gaze cutting right through the dweorg.

"How about you, girl? Are you here to claim the dead's wealth as your own? There isn't a fouler kind of thief in all the world...isn't a less honorable coward."

"So, Gor and the others were more successful than we were," Jez said, "do you think he got what he wanted? Will let us go now...let us all go home?"

"Girl...did you hear me? I'm speaking to you...directly, to yer face. Tis disrespectful...shameful...spiteful," Myrddin sputtered, his anger growing. Thorben could see it, and feel it. His figure glowed more brightly, matching the grimace on his face. The ring pulsed in time with his voice, the metal growing warm once again.

"You should never ignore a dwarf. Once our temper is up, it will stay up for a good long while...ages, like the stone itself! I was to walk you out of this place, but now...now I'm thinking about locking ye up in chains in the darkest space I can find and throwing away the key," Myrddin stomped right up to Jez, the green glow from his body lowlighting the dark circles around her eyes.

"She's not ignoring you, good dweorg," Thorben said, as calmly as possible.

Myrddin turned on him in a heartbeat and pounded his fists against his thighs, the mass of bauble-laden necklaces jingling loudly. Jez turned his way, too, her mouth opening in a silent, confused, and unanswered question.

"She cannot see you, Myrddin. It is like I told you, and honestly, you are dead."

"Who can't see who? Thorben, what are you talking about? Who is 'Myrddin'?"

"She can see me...she's just playing a wretched jest...like you were before. I know it. You fool longleggers and your jest, thinking everything is funny. Well, jesting about someone being dead ain't funny," Myrddin argued and turned on Jez again.

"As you can probably gather by now, this place isn't like any of the other crypts I've delved before. When I hit my head back there, I opened my eyes, and well, I was back in the Council's mine again. I don't know if I was dreaming, but it felt real enough. There was a man there. He was injured and I tried to help him. I remembered him from my time in chains. He died of pocks," Thorben said, and rolled up his sleeves far enough for her to see the finger-shaped bruises on his upper arms. "He grabbed onto me, and as soon as he touched me his body started to change. He became the dweorg...the dead one I saw at the casket–"

"Stop saying that! I ain't dead, fool longlegger. I just laid down me head for a bit, and then...then..." Myrddin interrupted, but stammered and staggered back a few steps.

"When I came to, I could see him, the dweorg...sorry, dwarf that we found up at the crypt's entrance, the one in the chair. I can see him, as plain as a warm sun shining overhead. He is standing right there," Thorben said, pointing at the ghostly dwarf.

"Why can't I see him? Is he touching me...oh gods, is he going to hurt us?" Jez recoiled, jumping back and spinning on the spot.

"I just...I just...laid down me head," Myrddin stammered, his dark eyes locked on his hands.

"I don't think he wants to hurt us...although I don't want to guess whether he can or not. I can tell you that he is not happy that we are here, or," Thorben silently pointed to the sarcophagus, and his breath caught. A subtle green light shone out of the partially opened burial, wispy trails of mist bubbling up and into the air, curling around the stone lid like grasping fingers.

"What...what do you think it wants with us? Does it just want us to leave?" she asked. Myrddin looked up from his hands, seemingly breaking free from his trance. He finally seemed to notice the green light pulsing brighter from within the sarcophagus.

"No. They mustn't rise," he muttered. "You fools...what have you done? They must stay sealed. Must! They told me...many times...told me, the dalan must stay sealed away. 'Tend the sorrow trees until they're grown, to lock away our evil natures'. Tend them...tend them, we did," Myrddin said.

"What does that mean, Myrddin? Lock away their evil natures?" Thorben asked, taking a step back. A strange noise echoed out of the box - a snapping, scratching sound, as if someone was dragging their fingernails against the underside of the stone lid.

"What is that sound? Oh gods, is there something in...there? I want to leave...Thorben, can we get out of here? I'm scared...none of this makes any sense," Jez said, her eyes sweeping over the dark trees after breaking free from the tomb.

The lid of the sarcophagus rocked to the side, stone grating and dust scattering loudly into the leafy groundcover. Thorben gestured to Jez, motioning for her to move away, to get out of the chamber.

"Gruteo's hammer, get ye gone, or you'll join the dead down here," Myrddin growled, and moved forward to push Jez towards the exit. The dwarf's extended hands passed right through the girl's midsection. The unexpected lack of resistance sent Myrddin right through her, stumbling, and to the ground behind her. He straightened, looked at his hands, and back to the girl, his eyes wide in shock.

"Eh," Jez cried and twisted around, flailing her arms as if she'd suddenly walked through a cobweb. "W-w-what was that? S-s-so cold!"

Something dark curled up and wrapped around the sarcophagus lid, the stone slab shaking again. Thorben swallowed and his breath caught. *Mani flail me...they're fingers.* He staggered back, grabbed Jez's hand, and yanked her around, setting off at a desperate run.

Thorben ducked through the thorny trees, careful to not pull Jez into them by accident. They ran towards the arch leading out into the dark hub chamber, his eyes gravitating up to the massive statue framing the entrance. Dust rained down, and he swore the stone figure started to move. A tingle bit into his finger under the ring, and his whole hand seemed to hum.

No...don't you dare. You stay open, damn you! he thought, frantically, pulling Jez hard and kicking into a faster run. His boot snapped on a vine, tripping him, but the plant broke and he managed to keep stride. They charged under the arch and stomped heavily out into the hub.

"Thorben, what is happening," Jez gasped, pulling on his arm, her hands trembling violently. "I-I-I..."

He turned back towards the chamber, just as the stone lid of the sarcophagus slid free and tumbled to the ground, a cloud of mist and leaves pluming around it. A dark shape slowly appeared from inside the box, half-standing and half-crawling, its movements jerky and wholly unnatural. Myrddin sat on the ground not ten paces away, his face in his hands.

Thorben jerked back as Jez pulled him towards one of the other archways. He had to do something. Could he help the dweorg? He was a ghost...did he need help? The dark shape crawled spider-like out of the box, the sight of it almost loosening Thorben's bladder entirely.

"It's coming this way," he muttered, as the dark figure dipped forward and moved towards them, its body practically disappearing into the layer of cold mist.

Thorben watched the dark figure moving towards them in the mist, a silent wish filling his thoughts. He wished for something to come between them, to block the horror away, to make them safe.

"...find my father!" Jez pleaded, but he couldn't catch all that she said.

The ring pulsed a little brighter, the metal growing warm against his skin just as something moved above them in the darkness. He swiveled up to track it as Jez wrenched him away. The statue shifted, the elegant, almost beautiful man's face rotating his way, the smooth, featureless eyes turning towards him.

Thorben's guts twisted about, a horrible shiver running up his back. He pushed to run as the massive statue came to life, multiple arms twisting and straightening, its unnaturally long legs breaking free in a shower of dust and rock. And then with a crash, the statue straightened, pulling its arms together and slamming the archway shut.

Chapter Twenty
The Neverdead

Thorben and Jez ran from archway to archway, stopping only long enough to scan the chambers inside for Gor and the others. He stopped, turned, counted, and continued. Twelve chambers, two archways closed.

They found Iona and the others in the last chamber, the guildsman standing around the sarcophagus. Jez ran forward, stumbling and crying, into her father's arms.

"Jez...Thorben, thank Mani, thank every god old and forgotten, we thought you lost," Iona gasped, throwing his arms around his daughter.

"We have to leave...now," Thorben said, looking from Iona, to Gor, and chancing a glance back to the archway. He felt a prickling from the ring - a subtle vibration that echoed deep inside. It had been there the whole time, he was just too preoccupied and distracted to notice or listen. It was the crypt - the stone, the strange sorrow trees, the black vines...all of it - buzzing or singing as if it were alive, and somehow the ring connected him to all of it, and Myrddin.

"Aye, we'll leave after we finish...and look, Owl," Gor said, hoisting a bag into the air, metal trinkets and artifacts clattering together inside. The big man's hands and sleeves were covered in thick, goopy sap. "These boxes are full of fantastic left-behinds - daggers, circlets, clasps, and even a hairbrush. We found it, and didn't even need your help. Iona assured us that they will fetch a king's ransom with his buyers."

Thorben looked from the big man's face, his rotten teeth and ruddy cheeks, to his slightly yellowed eyes, back down to the sarcophagus, its lid pulled off at an angle. Shriveled shoots and broken brambles curled off to the side, a stream of green mist bubbling into the air and flowing back into the open crypt.

Can't they see it? Can't they see any of it? he wondered, as a noise echoed out of the hub behind him.

It is coming, whatever it is. You need to move, you fool!

"It's not safe…these burials…these plants. They were sealed for a reason and we've disturbed them, they will…" he said, growling in frustration and turning back to the hub, a tickle running up his back. Something was there, moving, he could feel it.

"Is this more of your spirits talk?" Gor asked, looking to Hun and laughing. "You spooked me good back there in the darkness, surrounded by all them dead dwarves…with yer talk about angering the spirits. I tell ya, we looked in these boxes, and you know what we found?"

Thorben moved to argue and reached for Iona to pull him back towards the exit, but Gor spoke first.

"We found the treasure that Iona promised us, and some shriveled up, dead people. They are just dead…long dead by the looks of 'em, and we ain't seen no spirits or any of the other stuff you tried filling our heads with. There is nothing, Owl, no spirits, no ghosts, or things that crawl out of the dark corners. You were just telling us stories."

Renlo shifted uncomfortably off to the side, his dark eyes flitting up to the chamber exit. Did he know? Could he hear something? Thorben met his gaze, but the mule quickly looked away.

"I don't know how you closed that door back there, but it was mighty tricky of ya. I'm guessing that was your plan all along, clever man, to get us down here, and find some way to trap us, maybe even kill us. Heh? I'm believing that he was never going to help us find our treasure, right, Hun? I'm thinking that the owl here wanted the spoils for himself," the big man said, turning to his smaller counterpart.

Hun sniggered, nodding, and tapped his spearhead against the sarcophagus. *Tap tap tap.*

"That is absurd. I–"

"A branded man, struggling to pay his way to the taxman…a desperate man," Gor interrupted, "Iona told me, right after you about smashed us in that door stunt back there. Told us everything, when he thought you and his girl were dead."

Thorben looked to Iona, the small man still favoring his wounded leg. He looked away, refusing to meet his gaze, a series of fresh bruises and scrapes now marring his cheeks and chin.

"I don't hate you for it," Gor said, accepting the spear from Hun. The smaller guildsman rested his elbows on the sarcophagus and licked his lips, before turning to Thorben, a horribly smug smile firmly in place.

"We're all here for our own ends – Iona because his wife ran off with his gold, his daughter because he wasn't man enough to keep his woman satisfied, and you are here because you are desperate, broken," Gor said, and stepped out from behind the sarcophagus. Hun chuckled, leaning forward on his palms as if readying for a spectacle. The green glow flickered out of the dark box, the strange mist flowing in and around Hun before disappearing inside. The guildsman couldn't see it. How could he not see it?

Thorben knew what was coming next, and took a step to his right and back, moving away from Iona and his daughter. He took a look at the ground around him, trying to find the best footing, but couldn't see anything in the damned foggy leaves. His hand wove into his bag, searching, groping for his rock hammer. It wasn't much compared to a spear, but it was better than nothing.

"You impressed me back there in the entrance chamber when you figured out the trick with those three keys, but I'm starting to think even that was one of your tricks. Iona has use to us, value, but he's got no trust left with the guild. His daughter will stay with us until he sells our relics, to ensure he fulfills his duties as needed. We got what we came here for, that is what is important. Iona will sing our song, and if he doesn't, well, then his daughter will suffer for it," Gor said, shifting his gaze to Iona and shaking his head, the shiny copper coin now gleaming between his fingers. "If his daughter isn't enough incentive, then we'll track down his runaway wife and son. We'll kill her, but a son...now I think we can agree that a son is a special kind of leverage to a man like Iona. "

Thorben looked to the broker, the man's dark eyes stabbing daggers into Gor. Jez stood next to him, her dark eyes filled with doubt and fear. How had he allowed himself to get wrapped up with such people, to delve, and desecrate things better left to rest?

"And you...you're no owl, Thorben. You're a fox, and any fisherman worth his silt knows you never suffer a fox to live, lest he will run off with your catch." The big man tossed the bag of relics to Hun, who set it down on the crypt and leaned in to watch.

"I don't want your relics. I don't want anything from you," he said, and watched the big man's thumb snap up, the coin flicking into the air, shining as it fell back into his big palm. He knew there was nothing he could say that would dissuade Gor now, nor did he really want to. He was tired of cowering, bending, and scraping, tired of being a prisoner to fear. No, he was fed up with being told that he had no value...less than any other, by men no better, or worse, than he.

Gor opened his palm to look at the coin. Thorben heard something in the chamber to his back – a crawling, scraping sound. The guildsman smirked. "A Thatcher's bundle, sorry clever man."

"Not better than a Ram's head? I thought it was the other way around? Chance is fare, balanced. It's the same every time – honest, fair, and unbiased, unlike you," Thorben said, returning the big man's gaze. He pulled the rock hammer out and held it behind his leg. The green light glowed more brightly out of the crypt, shifting and pulsing, as if something was moving. The strange mist surrounded Hun's upper body, flowing rapidly into the box.

Renlo moved around to his left, sidestepping slowly, quietly to block him in, but Thorben caught the movement in his peripheral vision.

Damn! Be ready.

Gor laughed loudly, his rotten teeth appearing as his mouth pulled into a self-satisfied smile. "Oh, Owl, the fates have already decreed that you are going to die down here. They did before you ever set foot in this place. I was just allowing them the chance to choose how. It is me. I am blessed with your death."

Thorben swallowed, the lump absent from his throat now, the hesitation and doubt, gone. He brought the hammer out as soon as the big man flinched forward, lifting it above his shoulder to strike.

"Argh...what?" a startled shout rang out, stone grating loudly against stone as Gor stabbed straight for his midsection.

Thorben jumped to the side, swinging the small hammer hard diagonally across his body. The big man's thrust missed, but he quickly reset his feet, preparing for another attack.

Hun cried out again, and Thorben turned in time to see the crypt's stone lid upend wildly before falling back and cracking in half. Hun tipped headfirst into the box as Gor snarled, jabbing the spear again. He narrowly missed the skewering blade, and pointed. The large guildsman sneered, but readied the spear and set his feet.

"Your man!" Thorben pointed and yelled, finally managing to form the words.

The big man reluctantly turned, Renlo already moving towards the sarcophagus. Iona and Jez huddled together and shied away as Gor wheeled about, his voice booming in an unintelligible string of curses and commands.

Thorben watched as Gor joined Renlo at the burial, hooked an arm around the struggling man's legs, and wrenched him free. Hun flopped over the lip of the stone box, thrashing and flailing onto the misty ground.

The two men picked their counterpart off the ground, only to jump back as he flailed around, clutching his neck in one hand and tearing his sword free with other.

"Did you fall in?" Gor asked, halfheartedly laughing.

"Rah! No I didn't...fall in," Hun snarled, stomping his feet. He clomped in a circle, his face twisted and red. Thorben watched him pull his hand away. A round, bloody wound marred his neck, the flesh broken and torn beneath his scruffy stubble. Dark blood dribbled, soaking into the collar of his thick shirt. "Something grabbed me, and...and...bit me."

"Something? Bit you?" Gor echoed, his voice rising into a bark of a laugh.

Thorben retreated several steps and looked sideways to Iona and gestured towards the archway. The broker's eyes, wide and unblinking, flitted from him to Hun in rapid succession.

"You fell in. We saw you," Gor said, lifting the spear and slapping it against the edge of the stone box. "You probably put too much weight on the lid in just the right spot and it shifted." The big man turned back to Thorben and managed a single step towards him before a horrible, agonized keen split the air. The raspy, breathless cry echoed off stone and mist, seemingly filling the chamber around him. Thorben's skin prickled from the sound.

A black, desiccated hand appeared on the lip of the sarcophagus, and then a forearm, and shoulder. A mangled, withered form slumped over the edge and tumbled into the mist. Thorben saw it, but the guildsmen were too busy arguing.

Jez turned and screamed as the shrunken figure stood, appearing out of the mist like a silent, melting shadow. Thorben almost dropped the hammer, his hands twitching and shaking. The horror straightened, its skin as dark as mossy tree bark, shriveled and cracked, pulled tight over desiccated muscles and knobby bones. It lifted its arms out to the side, dry skin cracking and flexing, and tilted its head back, the round, lipless mouth pulling open to reveal brown, time-ravaged teeth. The undead creature wailed, its voice ruined and broken.

"W-w-what is that thing?" Gor stammered, pointing at the emaciated figure with the tip of the spear.

Another cry echoed out of the archway behind Thorben, and then another, and another. A silence stretched between heartbeats, until a host of horrific shrieks seemingly filled the space.

"That's what bit me. It must be..." Hun snarled, gesturing to his bleeding neck.

"Leave it, Hun. Let's be gone from here," Gor argued. He reached for his shorter counterpart, but before he could grasp him Hun lunged forward. The guildsman drove his sword deep into the creature's midsection. The blade broke easily through withered flesh and muscle, audibly striking bone and knocking the ghastly figure to the ground. Thorben turned to Iona, the broker holding Jez in a smothering embrace.

He grabbed him by the upper arm and jerked him back towards the archway. Iona staggered and finally managed to tear his gaze away from the horror, as it smoothly ambled off the ground again.

"Hun, let's go!" Gor snapped, hooking his counterpart by the arm and wrenching him around.

"Argh...no," Hun snarled and spat, fighting and kicking.

"Go...while we still can," Thorben hissed into Iona's ear. The broker managed a nod, his eyes wide and mouth pulled tight.

"I ran it through twice. Why isn't it staying down?" he heard Hun ask, as the two men continued to argue. Thorben heard blades stabbing into flesh over and over, metal swinging, cutting and smacking against bone and sinew.

They turned and made it several paces towards the exit, a large form darting out to block them. Renlo held his spear out to block the exit, his eyes nervously flicking between Thorben and over his shoulder to Gor and Hun.

"This...none of this is what we expected. The dead...they're rising...somehow. Please, let us just go. This isn't about treasures anymore. We just want to live. Me, my daughter, and Thorben, we just want to live. We're not fighters," Iona said, speaking before Thorben.

The guildsman twisted to look past them, blinking rapidly, his hands clenching and unclenching around the spear shaft. He coughed, started to speak, seemed to choke on the words, and backed them up with a threatening jab of the spear. Thorben could see it in Renlo's eyes – the bewilderment, the shock and horror, but mostly, the fear.

"Please, Renlo, I know you don't want to hurt us. We don't want to cause you or the guild any trouble. Iona just wants to get his daughter to safety, and I would very much like to hold my wife and children again. None of us have to die down here," Thorben said, stepping forward until the spear tip came to rest against his sternum. He met the man's dark eyes and refused to look away or back down. He trusted that deep down inside Renlo there was a decent man, a man eager to be like the king in the verse he recited for them earlier in the crypts.

"But Gor..." Renlo swallowed his words and looked back to his large counterpart, just as Hun chopped his sword down, severing the ambling horror's left arm at the shoulder.

He suddenly pulled the spear back and nervously nodded for them to go. Thorben pulled Jez and Iona by but stopped, as a pair of shadows moved through the arch, shambling slowly their way. They were too late.

How...how are the dead moving? Death and dust, I should have been faster. We should have gotten out of here by now!

A desiccated figure appeared from the distant chamber, colliding with the first two corpses and knocking them to the ground. It ran towards Renlo, its limbs and joints snapping and popping, each and every movement a disjointed and horrific mockery. The tattered remains of a white dress hung over its shoulders, withered, shrunken breasts and long wispy hair the only indicators that it had once been female. A long scar marred her face, the flesh under it hanging in a torn flap, exposing yellowed bone and stringy tendons beneath.

Thorben grabbed Renlo and pulled him around, the big man grunting and cursing in surprise. The female corpse wailed and staggered stiffly, clawing at the air where the guildsman had just stood, before tumbling in an ungainly sprawl in the mist.

"There are more!" Thorben cried, as the two in the archway regained their feet and approached. They groaned and clicked, their exposed teeth gnashing the air. Renlo whirled about and caught the first with the spear, the creature giving no indication it felt the bladed tip pierce its body. The big man ripped the spear free, the corpse staggering to the side while its counterpart shuffled in around it.

"Thorben!" Iona yelled as the female lurched off the ground and came at Jez, its teeth and joints creaking and popping loudly. He jumped forward and swung the hammer, catching the creature in the left shoulder. The impact swung her around, the withered flesh cracking and tearing.

"They're dreygur...like in the old stories. They have to be...the dead that refuse to rest, but it's impossible," Thorben gasped, but struggled to believe his own words. Those stories were old...they were just lore. Or were they?

"Iona, get back. Renlo, I need your help," he yelled, swinging at the dreygur again and missing. A form moved in before the corpse could lunge again, a sword blade erupting through her chest and driving her forward and to the ground.

Hun dropped a heavy boot onto the corpse' back and stabbed the sword down again and again, punching half a dozen holes in the leathery skin. Gor stomped up, breathing hard and drove his spear hard into the dreygur at Hun's feet, splitting the skull and pinning it to the ground.

"Go," Thorben shouted, pushing Iona back towards the arch. Renlo and Hun jumped in front of them, stabbing and pushing another of the withered creatures back, its wail like a frigid, north wind.

They passed through the arch and into the hub. A hand clamped onto Thorben's arm before he could follow and spun him around. Gor's ashen face leaned in, his eyes wide.

"What is this, Owl?"

"I tried to tell you," Thorben growled and ripped his arm away, taking a large step back and lifting the hammer threateningly. "Back there, at the crypt, I tried to tell you but you wouldn't listen. We saw it in the other crypt, after the archway almost smashed us to death. They're dreygur, just like in the old stories. The plants, the roots and trees growing on the crypts...I believe they were planted there for a reason...maybe to keep them from rising somehow. I don't know why or how, it's all so...well, none of it makes sense. They're dalan...they're magical. Maybe a part of them never really dies. All of this is beyond me."

Thorben refused to shrink under the man's glare, and lifted the hammer to strike when he shifted.

Gor smiled. "Dreygur? The dead...returned? What do you mean, 'part of them never really dies'?"

"You saw it yourself. I can't explain it...I've never seen anything like it, in any crypt on any other delve. The tales about the dreygur are old, back to Fanfir and ancient burial rites, but so are the dalan. They are just supposed to be stories, but think about it. We know the dalan are shapeshifters, beings of incredible power, grace, and magic. Where does that magic go when they die? Priests believe our soul escapes our bodies after our passing, and is either taken to the black lake of sorrow, and then the underworld, while a select few are chosen and taken to J'ohaven's hall. What if the dalan's magic remains in their bodies, after everything that makes them mortal leave? What if it is that magic that makes the dreygur live beyond death?"

Gor watched him, his forehead scrunching up.

"That is why you're here, I guess, because you are crafty enough to ask all of those questions. I'm not like you, Thorben," Gor said, surprisingly using his name. "I'm the hand of the fates, the guild's muscle. I hurt people that need hurting, kill those that need killed, and collect that which needs gathered. Right now, they're in our way, so I kill."

And stab me in the back as soon as I turn, Thorben thought.

"Only a fool refuses to ask questions."

"I like this new you, Owl. It's like you found your stones, but the fates have already..."

"The fates be damned, Gor, and you along with them. I'm getting Iona and his daughter to safety. Everything else can wait," Thorben interrupted and turned, pushing the broker and his daughter toward the exit.

Renlo led them into the tunnel to the crypt's entrance chamber, Hun right behind him, the bag of relics clinking and rattling at this belt. He followed quickly, the ivy rustling quietly underfoot. The light from the next passage grew brighter as they followed the gradual curve, but Renlo planted a foot and stopped. Hun ran into his back, nearly skewering him with the sword.

"What the..." he groused, as Renlo swiped him with an elbow.

Thorben stepped cautiously out around the two men and swept the adjacent chamber with a quick glance. Renlo had stopped for good reason, as a small group of dreygur ambled slowly away from them, moving in a rather unmotivated fashion towards the crypt doors and the maker's shanty beyond. The massive, ghastly statues loomed on either side of the shambling horrors.

"Seven of them," Renlo whispered, leaning towards Hun.

"We push through them, quick-like. You saw them back there, they ain't fast or strong. Then there's nothing between us and the exit and we walk in the sun again," Hun hissed back, his nose squeaking quietly.

Thorben watched the horrible, withered creatures hobble through the ivy and counted. *Seven,* he thought, the hammer's handle growing clammy against his palm. *One in the first crypt, another in the room beyond the waterfall, and the guild took down three. That's five. Twelve sarcophaguses, twelve dreygur.* He just had to trust in the guildsman to get them through the creatures, and then he could figure out a way to get Iona and Jez to safety beyond that. Perhaps he could negotiate a new deal with Gor, if the big man didn't kill him outright for his blasphemy about the fates.

Renlo and Hun kicked off and ran forward, the two men reaching the first dreygur together. Hun spun it around with a thrust of his sword, Renlo cutting in right after and driving his spear deep into its chest. The dreygur moaned, bits of dust pluming from its mouth and nose. Thorben managed forward as Hun cut down violently, striking the creature in the chest and knocking it off its feet.

The two guildsmen stepped over the body, moving as a team to take on the next. Thorben pulled Jez and Iona along, giving the fallen, emaciated corpse a wide birth. It shook, clicking and moaning, but didn't get up.

Hun and Renlo took down two more dreygur in short order, their group working methodically through the crowd of staggering undead. Hope blossomed in Thorben's chest as the two guildsmen cut down another, Jez and Iona picking their way carefully through the scattered bodies. The remaining three dreygur turned, groaning and clicking strangely.

"We're almost through. Push," Gor yelled, stomping up behind him.

Renlo readied his spear and moved to strike just as another loud cry rang out from the passage behind them. Thorben turned in time to see one of the dreygur amble out of the tunnel behind them, a piece of its head hanging off, a severed arm clutched loosely in its remaining hand. The female in the tattered white dress appeared next, a hole punched through the leathery skin covering her skull. The other dreygur ambled in right behind it, their bodies chopped apart and broken from the guild's weapons.

"They're nothing to be scared of. I've seen children put up more of a fight," Hun laughed and turned, chopping at a horribly thin dreygur. Its eyes and mouth hung open like dark, bottomless pits, its long, jagged fingernails ripping at the air. Hun missed with his first strike, but cut back in a follow-up, the blade bouncing dully off the emaciated corpse's arm. He kicked the dreygur, staggering it, and moved forward, cutting at its thin neck. The guildsman jerked awkwardly, the sword missing the mark. A dark form surged forth from the ivy, boney, disfigured fingers clutching greedily around his right leg.

"Look out!" Thorben yelled, as the dreygur bit into Hun's leg.

"Argh," the guildsman yelled, twisting about and cutting down at the creature. The blade bounced off spine and ribs, but the dreygur only pulled tighter to his leg.

Thorben jumped in to help, but something moved in the ivy between them, the motion barely registering in his peripheral vision. He spotted the dreygur moving in the bushy undergrowth, and then spotted another one.

"In the ivy," he gasped, jumping back just as the creature lurched into view, swiping for his legs.

Renlo skewered a dreygur, pushing the creature back just as Hun stomped the corpse free from his leg. The dreygur tumbled into the ivy, blood covering its shriveled lips and nose. It opened and closed its mouth, bits of the guildsman's skin stuck between its teeth. Its body started to shake violently.

Thorben sucked in a breath and turned to Gor, but the big man's back was turned, his spear jabbing ferociously at a group of dreygur pushing in from the tunnel.

"Fire blasted hells, it took a chunk out of my leg. The damned thing tried to eat me," Hun snarled and turned, just as the horribly thin dreygur fell over him, the withered flesh of its upper arm hanging loose.

The corpses appeared in their midst, rising out of the ivy, hands clasping and teeth snapping. Thorben smashed the closest in the face with his hammer, the strike knocking its head aside and breaking the jaw loose on one side.

Hun's sword cut deep into the thin dreygur's chest, but the creature pushed right through, its hands finding purchase on his arms and pulling it closer, sliding its body hilt-deep onto the blade.

Jez pulled free of her father and ducked right under the arms of one dreygur, falling to her knees as another lurched towards her. Iona hobbled back out of the way, jumping behind the largest of the statues – the six-limbed beast, to avoid the shambling, snapping corpse.

Renlo kicked a dreygur, knocking it onto its back, the withered corpse's claw-like fingernails tearing off the left sleeve of his heavy jacket. He ducked forward to help Hun, jamming his spear clean through the emaciated dreygur, but it ignored the strike and pitched forward, biting into the guildsman's meaty arm. Renlo released his grip on the spear and leaned in, tearing the shriveled figure off Hun and throwing it bodily against the wall.

The dreygur hit, grunted, and screeched, Hun's sword and Renlo's spear now sticking out of its body like a macabre pincushion. Thorben picked Jez up off the ground, yanking her around and swinging his hammer at the same time. He missed, and pushed Jez up onto a half wall between statues, jumping up to join her just as three dreygur fell forward, clawing at his legs.

Thorben pulled Jez behind the statue and around the other side, his heart thundering painfully in his chest. They ran out from the other side just as the dreygur impaled on Renlo's spear screamed. Jez ran into his back as he stopped moving, and together they watched the emaciated figure shake and dance. It screamed again, the noise sending a cold shiver running throughout Thorben's body. It wasn't a dry, crackling moan anymore. It wasn't a dead sound.

The ambling dreygur turned as one, shuffling on unsteady feet as the impaled corpse reached down and pulled the spear free. It moaned, fumbling with withered hands, pulling the guildsman's sword from its body a fingerbreadth at a time, until the blade tumbled into the ivy.

Thorben wanted to run, to pull Jez to safety, but couldn't seem to move his legs. The dreygur that bit Hun's leg was moving behind the guildsman, its body shaking and changing, the withered and desiccated flesh crawling and moving. It coiled and jumped, landing on the big man's back with almost no noise.

"Hun!" Gor bellowed, but the previously impaled dreygur screamed again, the alarmingly human sounding noise filling the cavern and drowning the big man out.

Hun spun, trying to wrestle the creature off his back as it snapped down again and again, biting his neck and the side of his face, teeth breaking and tearing away skin. Renlo ran forward to help, but the thin dreygur burst forward and slammed into him, the impact sending the considerably larger guildsman sprawling back in the ivy.

Thorben watched in horror as the corpses converged on Hun, the stout, muscular man spinning, kicking, and punching, flailing out into the walkway between statues before collapsing under their combined weight. Teeth and nails dug and tore clothing, ripping through and into meaty flesh. Hun screeched and cried, his voice quickly dying in a wet, raspy gargle.

You...need...to...move! he thought, and finally managed to move his feet. Jez sobbed, crying, her body shaking as she watched the mass of undead creatures tear Hun apart, his blood and ripped flesh spattering their bodies.

He pulled the girl forward, but she resisted, and then suddenly broke free. Thorben staggered after her, but refused to leave the safety of the statue's shadow. He watched Jez jump down, stay low, and disappear behind the next statue down the line. A heartbeat later she reappeared, her father limping next to her. Together they moved back around the statues, and hugging the far, right wall, cleared the mass of feeding dreygur.

Renlo stood just inside the massive, black doors, his haunted gaze stuck on the ground. He didn't move, didn't even seem to draw breath, until Thorben drew near.

"It...it...knocked me right off my feet. H-h-how? There wasn't anything to it, no weight. I couldn't get there...I couldn't help him," Renlo said, his eyes not moving.

"It wasn't your fault. There is nothing you can do for him now. Come on, let's go." Thorben hooked the big man's arm and tried to pull him around to the door, but he wouldn't move. Hells, he felt as solid as a chunk of granite.

Jez pulled on his arm and they moved into the doorway, a massive, presence abruptly sliding between them, knocking Renlo to the side and looming above Thorben. Gor's fetid breath fell on his face, the hulking man breaking Jez's hold on his hand and swinging him around.

"Where are you going, Owl?" he growled, pushing Thorben to his knees. The big man stood over him, a glassy, crazed look haunting his eyes. "You're not leaving yet...not yet," he said, shaking the shiny, copper coin in the air right in front of his face, "Hun had the bag. Hun had my treasure."

Thorben swallowed and half-turned, his gaze quickly sweeping over the walkway between rows of statues. The toes of Hun's boots poked out of the thick, black ivy, the rest of his body covered in grasping, writhing bodies. He could hear claws tearing, teeth biting and tearing into muscle, sinew, and bone. A sick, twisting sensation pulled at his stomach, a sour taste creeping up his throat a moment later.

Gor waved the shiny coin in the air again, then flipped it and slapped it against his hand. "Hun is gone, as the fates decided. His death was to our benefit. We go and claim our treasure." The big man stomped around him and carefully scooped the spear and sword out of the ivy, his gaze never leaving the feeding dreygur.

"We attack while they are feeding and distracted. If we all fight together, we will drive them back, claim my relics, and then we will leave and seal them inside." The big man held the sword out, blood-smeared handle first.

Thorben stood, edging away from the weapon, and moved to put Gor between him and the throng. Gor turned, watching him, and lifted the spear towards Iona.

Behind the guildsman, a dreygur fell away from Hun's grisly remains. It rolled in the ivy before standing smoothly, clicking, croaking, and twitching. Its body changed right before his eyes, the wrinkled, desiccated flesh bubbling and smoothing, shrunken, decomposing muscle growing and filling out. The dreygur hopped away from them, moving towards one of the larger, more horrific statues. Its body snapped and popped, bones shifting and rearranging. The creature's neck snapped sideways, and then popped back up, as if bending on a joint.

"As you say, they are 'your' relics," Thorben said, and pushed off his knees and edged around the big man. Iona and Jez were already moving away, through the large doors and into the dark tunnel, watching the sword held between them. He gestured for them to go, to move faster, and to get to safety. His skin crawled and itched, his legs twitching...he needed to run. Run fast.

Gor looked back to Hun's body once, and Thorben moved quickly, taking advantage of the distraction to duck through the doorway. He made it under the arch before a meaty hand wrapped around his neck and wrenched him around.

Thorben was looking down the dark passage and the slope leading up to Myrddin's hut one moment, and at the big man's rotten teeth in the next. Gor pushed him up against the wall and pressed the sword sidelong against his chest.

"Take it and do as I say!" the guildsman snarled, the blade's sharp edge resting against Thorben's throat.

"No." More of the dreygur were moving away from Hun's masticated body, his entrails pulled out and looped over the dark ivy. He could smell the man's blood on the air, hear the creatures moving, the snapping and popping of their bones, but also a strange, chirping noise. It sounded eerily like birds.

"Take it in your hand, or in your guts. I'll bleed you and feed you to those things, use you as bait...meat to get my treasure." Gor reached down and grabbed his hand, fumbling the handle into his palm. The gem in the ring pulsed green, the light illuminating the side of Thorben's face.

"What's this?" Gor stammered, twisting his hand around and looking at the ring.

Thorben shook his head and tried to pull away.

"You found this in here, didn't you? I would have seen it before. It's...it's...part of my treasure."

Thorben tried to pull away, but the big man slid his fingers over the ring and tried to wrench it off.

"Death and dust," Thorben cursed as his knuckle popped, his finger almost pulling off with the pressure. He managed to close his hand and push away, the big man staggering back a step.

"Like I said earlier, I get your death. I'll pull it off your dead body," Gor snarled and tapped his shiny coin against his lips. The big man flipped the sword around, letting the blade roll lengthwise over his hand, before deftly snatching it by the handle. He dropped his right foot, pulled the sword back, and smiled.

Thorben cringed, waiting for the blade to cut, but refused to look away. He'd lived as a coward, dammit; he would at least die on his feet, with some dignity.

Gor's sword twitched forward, just as an arm hooked inside his elbow. The big man's eyes went wide, just as Renlo dropped his hip and swung him around. Gor pirouetted, half-spinning and half-tumbling across the passage, before crashing loudly into the wall on the other side.

The big man roared, tapped the sword against the wall, and came back at him. Renlo jumped between them, throwing a shoulder into the bigger man's midsection. They careened off to the side, a mass of muscle, wrenching arms, and swinging knees.

Thorben took several loping steps up the passage but turned. The commotion had attracted attention. The dreygur were hopping about, slowly moving their way, their bodies all shifting and changing, their joints snapping and bending to angles unnatural for any man or woman. They were coming.

Gor pushed Renlo back and came at Thorben, murder written plainly on his face, but the smaller guildsman swung in hard, catching him in the chin and knocking him sideways.

Renlo looked back, met his gaze, and mouthed, "Go!"

"Come with me," Thorben said, gesturing him desperately down the hall.

Renlo's small, dark eyes met his, his mouth and forehead scrunched up in a severe frown. He shook his head and pointed towards the exit. "Go, now!" he yelled, and turned back just as Gor's massive frame bowled him over.

Thorben smacked the small hammer against his thigh, took a halting step forward, and cursed. The dreygur were in the passage, tentatively watching the two men fight. The closest cocked its head to one side, and then the other, its eyes now large and dark, its neck long and grotesquely slender. Then it leapt onto Gor's back, its mouth wide, exposing jagged, sharp and broken teeth.

"Thorben...go," Renlo yelled, and knocked the beast free, another jumping in to take its place. Gor pushed up to his feet, and swung his sword in a violent arc, catching the closest dreygur across the chest, the blade hitting Renlo in the process.

Thorben turned and ran.

Chapter Twenty-One
Ascent from Hell

Thorben hit the slope leading out of the passage at a full sprint, the change in grade buckling his knees and sending him sprawling face-first into the ivy. He kicked, clawed, and pulled his way forward. His face was numb, the sticky dew now covering his lips, nose and mouth.

He surged over the top edge, his frantic momentum almost carrying him right into the far wall. Thorben straightened, gasping for breath, and found Myrddin standing just a few paces away, his outline pulsing with a gentle glow. He approached to find the dweorg standing over the seated remains, the bauble-laden necklaces glimmering in the ghostly light.

Myrddin spoke without looking up, his hand reaching out and passing through the necklaces, as if trying to lift them free.

"I remember now, Thorben long legs. I remember all of it – cuttin' my workers' hands, watching them die, and then sitting right here and waiting for mine own end. I-I-I remember dying. I do. I remember walking this place for a long time after...for so long I started to forget, then it was all fog and darkness. Until you, that is. That was me that opened the crypt doors, somehow. And later, the arch. I could hear you...your thoughts, wishing for safety and a barrier between ye and the violent men. The magic goes deeper here, I can feel it now."

"I can't stay...Myrddin. They...well, the dead. They are alive...they killed Hun, probably Gor and Renlo, too. They ate him. They're coming. I have to get out of here," Thorben said, and loped forward into a run.

"Wait...please," the dweorg called, his voice softer and, somehow, more distant. "I am bound to this place, and to that ring. I remember now. The dalan gave it to us, its magic like a key to seal this place once their dead were laid to rest. I fell into despair at the end, and didn't want to destroy it like they told me to do. I wanted to see my Lynheid again and knew it was my key to get out. I swallowed it, thinking to hide it till later, but the ring's magic. It trapped me..."

The sound of scuffle echoed from the passage mouth, louder and closer than before. A blade sang, splitting flesh, a pained, horrible cry ringing out a heartbeat later.

"Myrddin, I'm sorry. I have to get out of here. I don't want to die. I want to see my children again," Thorben said, a pang of guilt stabbing into his insides.

"I know. Please...carry something for me. You've already got the ring, but please, I'm not for knowing if I can leave here. If...when...well, if you make it past the gate. I know I can go that far, and I know I can seal the gate again to give you a chance. But I'm beggin' ye, take the tokens from my Lynheid with ye. Take them to Braakdell, so she knows that her pa loved her more than anything, and always will."

Thorben swallowed, looked to the shack door, back to the passage entrance, but made for the chair instead. The dweorg pointed desperately at the skeleton's neck, and the mass of tangled necklaces.

"The horse charm. The horse charm," Myrddin whispered.

Thorben fumbled awkwardly with the clinking mass, his fingers shaking and breath catching, but he couldn't make out any individual shape. He pulled them closer, but the shack was dark, save for Myrddin's greenish glow.

The dweorg said something just as Thorben lifted the mass as one and pulled it free of the skeleton's head and wispy hair. He lifted it over his head and dropped it around his neck, quickly moving to leave.

"Wait...wait," Myrddin said, "and just inside the shirt. Something else. Please."

Thorben ran back, glancing to the slope leading down to the passage and the distant crypt. The ivy was moving. Something was coming out of the hole!

He reached down into the thin garment, the fabric crumbling almost on contact. His fingers brushed against ribs and then hit something solid. Thorben ripped it free, knocking Myrddin's skeleton from the chair, the bones rattling noisily to the ground.

Turning, Thorben sprinted for the door just as something appeared from the hole. He caught a glimpse of pale flesh, splattered with dark blood, the green glow catching on glassy, wide eyes.

His boots slid on the fine dust and debris of the shattered doorway. He stumbled only once and jumped out through the hole in the wall, and into the open, fresh air of the maker's shanty.

Thorben sprinted between buildings, the wide chamber and open air a blissful reprieve from the claustrophobic tunnels of the dalan crypt. He followed the curving road out of the dwarven village, stuffing the token from Myrddin's corpse into his bag. Jez and Iona appeared on the path ahead, the girl laboring to help her father forward.

"He'll not make it moving like that," Myrddin said, his glowing form appearing at Thorben's side. He easily matched the pace, his short legs and large boots moving with no sound.

The tunnel stretched ahead and up, the grade for their ascent far steeper than he remembered on the way down. Then again, he wasn't running for his life from flesh eating corpses and murderous guildsman.

His legs were already growing heavy and his lungs burning from the exertion. He approached Iona and Jez, the two passing from the fading cavern's light into the narrowed tunnel, the ceiling sloping down and draping them in shadow. The two were there one moment and gone the next.

"Myrddin, it's so dark, can you..." Thorben said, huffing to catch his breath.

The dweorg nodded and waved his hand. Braziers on either side of the walkway sparked to life, warm, yellow flame filling the shiny bowls all the way into the distance. The light splashed up the walls, flickering off the dwarven skeletons and their armor gleaming, revealing the cavern ceiling far overhead. The space was larger and more elaborate than he ever would have guessed. The walls weren't rough stone as he'd previously thought, but murals, carved on every available flat surface.

Thorben slumped against his knees and looked back down the road. Something tumbled out the door of the furthest building, several following close behind. He stood straighter as more followed, spilling out of the small structure. He counted five, six, no eight, at least, moving fast and low to the ground, like animals.

Run.

They scaled the side of the buildings, moving onto the roofs, running up the stone with frightening ease, moving with speed Thorben never thought possible. The dreygur, if that was what they still were, scattered between the buildings, disappearing and reappearing in flashes, streaking and moving together like a pack of hunting wolves.

Run.

A lone figure stumbled from the building after the others, noticeably larger – a man, wide-bodied and muscular. He could see that much, even in the dim light. *Is it Renlo? Did he survive?* The man's shirt and hair were dark. It looked like...Thorben squinted against the gloom, his confidence growing by the heartbeat.

"It's Renlo...he made it out. He is coming!" Thorben shouted back up to Iona and Jez.

The big man ran through the buildings, limping, falling, and getting back up. He moved onto the path, running directly towards him, his gait irregular, every other stride shorter and quicker.

Come on! Faster, he silently urged the guildsman on, and took off towards him to help.

"He's of blood, for blood. Ye best away, and quick about it," Myrddin said, matching his gaze down the path.

A strangled, angry bellow echoed up the path, as if in response to the dwarf's words, the sound both animal and human at the same time. The man ran up the path and passed by a set of burning braziers. The light glinted off something metal and shiny in his hand – a bloody sword. Thorben skidded to a halt. The light...his hair. They weren't black at all. Renlo had short, messy dark hair and a dark blue stitched shirt. This man, he was covered in...it was blood, covering him almost from head to toe.

"Death and dust," Thorben cursed, his voice going weak.

Gor used the long spear like a cane, smashing the haft into the ground to propel his bulk forward. His gasping, unintelligible words finally snapped Thorben out of his daze. He turned, pushing into a stiff-legged run up the path.

"Ye cannot fight him...he's too strong. You'll have to outrun him to gate. If ye can, then I'll seal it behind ye," Myrddin said, matching his pace, and showing no sign of strain either.

"Thank...you...for that," he sputtered irritably, the enormity of the "if" more than he wanted to wrestle with.

Thorben clutched to a cramp in his side and gulped down air, pumping his legs and arms as fast as they would go. The distance shrunk between him and the broker, the path beyond a seemingly never-ending slope up and away. Jez turned as he approached, Thorben staggering into them and wrenching the smaller man's arm over his shoulder.

"We have to...go...faster," he gasped and wrenched them both forward.

They hobbled, stumbled, and ran up the path, Iona bouncing awkwardly between them. Jez grunted and strained, but Iona's breathing became labored – a horrible, strangled wheeze. The smaller man barely had the strength to hold his head up.

"I...can't...do it...anymore," Iona gasped, slumping heavily between them.

"You have to." Thorben clenched his jaw and redirected them to the right, Jez almost falling under her father's weight. The girl turned as they limped through an intersection and cried out. He could hear Gor moving up the path somewhere behind them, his massive frame and boots sounding more like a rampaging monster than a man. Then the *tap tap tap* of the spear haft sounded and Thorben pulled Iona forward a little faster. The image of the bladed spear filled his head, the sharp tri-bladed tip stabbing into Iona's leg. That would be his belly, or chest.

Myrddin moved next to him, more shiny braziers bursting to life as soon as the dweorg got close. The side passage led into a wide, long chamber, broken up by row after row of chest-high walls.

They pushed past the first several rows, Iona's boots moving but doing little to help them along. Thorben pulled them off to the left and down a row. Narrow shelves had been chiseled into the short wall, perfectly preserved flowers, knickknacks, and offerings covering the flat surface.

"The walls of tears," Myrddin whispered, looking around sadly. "An entire generation of my people, those of them left alive, came through here to bid their loved ones fair journey to the afterforge."

He managed to drag Iona a little further; Jez slumped down on his other side, now barely able to pull her own weight along. They came to the end of the wall, another cutting off to the right and moving perpendicular. Thorben staggered a few paces in and let Iona slump to the ground, the broker crumpling into a pile and clutching to his wounded leg. Collapsing next to Iona, Thorben pulled Jez down and pushed her against the wall, smashing a finger against his lips as a boot scraped loudly against stone not far away.

Iona bit his lip, wheezing quietly as he tried to catch his breath. His face was pale, pinched, and horribly drawn. Thorben looked down to find his injured leg quivering violently, the ragged bandage wet with fresh blood.

"Owl...I know you're in here, Owl?" Gor hissed, his voice filling the space like a swarm of angry snakes, the sound bouncing eerily off the half-walls.

"I know...I know...I know...Owl...Owl...Owl," the echoes bounced off stone for several moments.

Thorben sucked in a quiet breath, but even that sounded impossibly loud in the still air. He moved sideways, putting a hand on Jez's shoulder to calm her, and dropped to his hands and knees, managing only a single, crawling step. The mass of necklaces shifted, jingling, the brassy metal and innumerable charms clinking and jingling together. He froze and cursed under his breath.

"Owl...why are you hiding? Are you afraid? Are you? Does a branded man feel fear? Is he hardened for it? Or does it make him weak and timid?" Gor's boots tromped somewhere nearby, the spear tapping loudly against the stone. Thorben bent down, wiped his forehead on the tattered sleeve of his shirt, and drew in a deep, quiet breath. He pressed the necklaces to his chest and slowly lifted his head, his legs shaking and burning as he hovered just beneath the lip of the wall.

Mani, help me get clear of this and I will dedicate the rest of my life to helping everyone, as you teach. I will raise my children in your light, be selfless, and give to those less fortunate.

Tap...Tap, the spear rapped against stone again and Gor laughed, a low, phlegmy sound.

Thorben peaked up and over the wall. The guildsman was barely a dozen paces away, moving slowly down one of the adjacent rows, his large head swiveling away from him. His shirt was ripped and torn, jagged, meaty wounds visible all over his shoulders, arms, and neck. But there was too much blood for it all to be his. It couldn't be, or he would be dead.

Is it Renlo's blood? Or from the... Thorben shook free from those thoughts, another wave of guilt and grief threatening to wash up. He didn't want to consider that Gor killed Renlo...and all because the guildsman tried to save him. He didn't feel worthy of that kind of sacrifice.

"You are hiding because you are a coward," Gor spat, his breathing loud, ragged, and wet. There was something about his voice that sent a chill down Thorben's back. Something he couldn't immediately identify.

"You're also a fool. Do you hear them? Do you? They're coming for all of us. They'll tear us apart, one by one. They'll feed on us."

The big man turned, a horrible wound coming into view on the side of his head. The skin on the left side of his scalp was torn, leaving his ear to hang slightly off-kilter. The light struck his eyes and Thorben instinctively ducked, the necklaces jingling once again.

"Ha ha ha," Gor laughed crazily, and Thorben heard him turn.

"Ferret...fisher...weasel, and you," the big man snarled, the smack of the spear abruptly stopping. "All are slinking, slippery, thieving vermin. You took that ring when I wasn't looking. Did Renlo know? Did he see? Did he give it to you? He was guild...my brother."

Thorben listened, but without the tapping spear he couldn't tell where the man was. He couldn't seem to hear his boots, or his breathing, either. Had he gone?

Thorben held his breath and listened. A droplet of water plinked not far away, and another sound, perhaps a breath of wind, moaned. Then he heard something moving behind him, or it could have been in any other direction. Every sound echoed, reverberating off the short walls, making it impossible to tell.

He heard it again. It was soft, like the *patter patter* of bare feet against stone. Thorben turned, the scrape of his soles and the rustle of his pants grating against his nerves. He took Jez gently by the arm and pulled her forward, urging her to move. The girl crawled forward, stooped over, her hair falling like a dark, tangled curtain over her face. Thorben moved to Iona next, but couldn't crawl with half the grace or stealth as the girl.

"Come come, we need to move. Quick and quiet," Thorben whispered and helped Iona off the ground. The broker grimaced and fought, tears filling his eyes and running down his cheeks. His boot scraped the ground, but managed to limp along after his daughter.

"Oh, they're close now, Owl. I can't wait for you to see them up close, like I did. They're horrible...twisted, brutal, and wonderful. I killed one, you know. Slit it from belly button to neck, and then hacked its head clean off, and still its body writhed and moved, as if trying to find its missing piece. I survived because I cut Renlo. I cut him deep, and those things tore into him. As soon as they had his blood, his flesh, they didn't care much about me. That's how I got out of there. They're ravenous. But it was you, Owl, you killed him. Not me."

"We just need to get out of here...get far enough away from him and we can make a run for it," he whispered, trying to encourage Iona forward, but the broker was struggling to even crawl, his wounded leg dragging like a dead tree limb behind him.

Myrddin moved above him then, the dweorg's hollow, dark eyes scanning the space.

"He'll not outrun them. I don't think you will, either, Thorben long legs. I see them. They move like no beast I've ever seen before – swift as a gust of wind and quiet as a shadow. They are death."

Iona gasped and collapsed, his body smacking the stone, blood dribbling from the bandage on his leg and dripping onto the floor.

"I hear you," Gor hissed. A flurry sounded not far away, and Thorben turned just as the big man scuffled and landed hard, his upper body leaning over the wall behind them. Gor's head turned, down the row, his glassy eyes locking onto him. "There you are...Owl!"

Thorben's chest tightened and he sprawled back onto Iona, the broker writhing and fighting to push him off. Gor's face was horrible - blood smeared, dirty, and covered with oozing lacerations, his eyes wide and bloodshot. His mouth cracked in a wide smile, half of his teeth missing or rotten.

"Mani flail me," Thorben cursed and rolled free. He pushed up, wrenched Iona from the ground and shoved the man behind him. His hand dove into his bag, his small knife jabbing under one of his fingernails. Thorben cursed and pulled the knife free, fumbling for his rock hammer, but the tool had fallen from his belt.

Jez and Iona smashed into his back as they edged away from Gor, the large man kicking over the half-wall. His bulk knocked a number of offerings to the ground, his boots landing and smashing them to dust.

"Your blood will flow now, and when they're feasting on your corpses, I'll stroll out of here." Gor leveled the spear at him, the blood-covered sword held tight in his other hand.

Thorben lifted the knife between them. It felt small, so horribly inadequate. Movement flitted off to his right, and then left. He turned to track it but there was nothing there. Another shadow moved to his left, and this time Thorben caught sight of pale, streaking flesh and wispy hair.

"Iona...they're..."

"All around us," Jez said, her voice strained. Thorben whipped around in a circle, almost cutting Iona in the process. Dark forms jumped in and out of the shadows between fires, making almost no noise. But then they were all around them, perched on the half-walls like massive, fleshy, disfigured vultures.

The dreygur looked even less like people now. The closest beast leaned forward on its stone perch, its jagged fingernails scraping against the rock. Its head twitched to the side, the knobby bones in its neck popping and shifting, before swinging out and lengthening. The macabre face lifted high in the air, its wide, dark eyes horrible and unblinking. The creature opened its mouth, exposing twisted, jagged teeth, and issued a most peculiar noise. It chirped, its thin, black tongue flicking against the air.

The air filled with a chorus in response. Iona moved, and the closest creature shifted, sniffing at the air and edging along the wall.

"You see, Owl? Aren't they magnificent?" Gor asked, moving slowly towards him. Thorben watched the dreygur move in, disappearing between shadows, closing in around the big man. Their bodies were still changing, shifting and morphing. Wispy hair fell away, boney ridges appearing under its skin. The closest dreygur clicked loudly and leaned forward, the shriveled nose falling off its face, the desiccated flesh dissolving to dust before hitting the ground. The flesh surrounding the nasal passage shifted and flowed, growing into something that looked far more beast.

Jez shifted, moving back, but none of the creatures seemed to notice. Thorben looked down to Iona's leg and the fresh trickle of dark blood. He looked back up to Gor. The man was bleeding from a dozen wounds, not to mention the gore that wasn't his own. The creatures attacked Hun, whose nose had been bleeding.

"They smell the blood. They're tracking the blood," Thorben whispered, realizing the truth of it. Both men practically rank of blood and sweat. An idea formed in his mind, and he lifted the small knife to his wrist. "Iona, when I give you the word, take Jez and run."

Mani, take me quickly, he prayed silently, but a hand snapped out and wrenched the knife free from his hand. Iona held Thorben back, his other hand reaching down to pull the ragged bandage from his leg.

"No."

"Take Jez, Thorben. Keep her safe," The broker said, lifting the small knife before him. Blood dribbled out from the wound on his leg, soaking into the stained fabric and spattering the ground.

"Father...no!" Jez cried and tried to push past, but Thorben held her back.

"I have so much to answer for, all those men. Their deaths are my burden. They are on my conscience. Jez, I hope that someday you can forgive me. But, please, find your brother. Find him, and keep him safe. Do it for me!"

Iona turned and moved towards Gor, the tattered bandage falling to the ground. The dreygur moved in eagerly, chirping and clicking, their circle tightening as the two men drew closer together. Thorben pushed Jez back at the same time, hoping beyond hope that one of the beasts wasn't directly behind them.

"What do you think you're doing? Now you want to be in control?" Gor growled, glancing to either side at the approaching dreygur.

"I was never in control, Gor, and that was the problem. I never should have come to you and your guild when Priscilla ran off. I should have been a man and found her myself."

"That is because you're weak."

"Men like you will always need men like us, because you've got no stones. It's up to strong men like me to..."

"My wife never listened to me, never took me seriously. Just like you. She tried to control me, just like you. She took everything from me and ran. You put coin in my hand and lorded the debt over my head. You held me at sword point and made me trick all of those delvers...made me watch them die. Enough, Gor. I have control now! I say when it ends." Iona reached up and ran the blade across his forearm. Fresh blood appeared, dripping onto the stone. The dreygur started to chirp and click more loudly, their heads popping up, their tongues lashing and tasting the air.

"Stop doing that!" Gor growled, swiveling the spear around towards the nearest creature. The beast turned its head down to consider the spear but did not back away. Its dark eyes swiveled from the shiny blade up to the man's blood-spattered and scratched face. Calculating. Emotionless. Ravenous.

"I have the control now. Do you hear me? I am strong," Iona said and lumbered forward.

Gor snarled and pulled the spear around, catching Iona in the stomach, but the smaller man didn't stop moving his legs. He pushed, grunting and crying, clawing towards the bigger man until the spear tip pushed through his back. The guildsman staggered, releasing his grip on the spear handle and lifted the sword to strike, but Iona fell against him. The broker's hand swung in again and again, plunging Thorben's short knife into Gor's chest, arms, and neck. The blade slapped hard, steel punching through the big man's heavy jacket and shirt, sliding deep into skin and muscle.

Blood ran and spurted, the two men falling back in a heap.

"Run, Owl! Run...run...run," Iona howled, his hand driving the knife into Gor's chest. The dreygur swarmed in, their pale, twisted bodies propelling them forward with an inhumanly silent grace.

Jez punched and kicked, clawing to push by, to run to her father's aid but Thorben wrapped his arms around her thin frame and lifted her free of the ground. He carried her away, despite the pain in his own body, pushed forward by a singular purpose – to survive.

He carried Jez down the path between short walls, dropping her feet to the ground when a twinge bit into his back. Myrddin stood in a dark shadow, glowing against the darkness. He held his arm up and pointed to their left. Thorben pulled Jez around, the girl weeping openly.

"We have to go back…we have to help him," she moaned, her lip trembling.

Thorben urgently moved her along in silence, lacking the words to argue, or even console her. They ran back along the new path. Myrddin appeared again, motioning them right this time as he navigated them through the maze of half-walls. Thorben pulled Jez around another corner, just as Iona screamed out behind them. No, it wasn't just a scream. The man said his name.

Jez planted her feet, jerking him to a halting stop. He turned, to see Iona's face appear momentarily through the throng of churning, pale and frantic bodies. The broker's arm snapped out, lobbing something dark into the air.

"I'm sorry," Jez's father mouthed and promptly disappeared back into the throng. Gor bellowed and threw one of the creatures against a wall, but he too disappeared under the mass of churning, clawing, and biting monsters.

Jez pushed Thorben aside and sprinted forward.

"No, come back," he yelled, but the girl deftly caught the bag before it hit the ground, planted a foot, and turned. She sprinted by him, stuffing the bag of relics into his hands, before running towards their path to freedom. He followed, tying the bag to his belt and passing Myrddin, who promptly disappeared and reappeared further up the ascending path, his glowing figure a distant, glowing beacon.

Thorben ran, stumbling forward on aching legs. His heart hammered and he gasped for breath, but refused to stop. Jez easily outpaced him, the young woman moving up the slope with all the speed and grace he lacked.

Thorben watched Jez disappear into darkness ahead, and tromped heavy-footed after her. He finally reached the spot where she had vanished, the brazier's light shining off the bottom few steps of the steep stairwell. He lifted his foot onto the first stair and then the next. A scream rang out somewhere in the massive chamber behind him, the sound bouncing and echoing off the walls of corpses.

Thorben sucked in a breath, forced it out, and gasped in another. He looked up the steep stair, Jez ahead somewhere in the impenetrable gloom. Then he turned, despite every fiber of his being begging him to move forward and up.

The road spanned behind him and down, before opening up on the wider chamber far below, the maker's shanty a distant cluster of small buildings. The brazier's warm light pushed the darkness away, but pooled in the skeleton-filled hollows, only the amber and gold armor left to glint and shine.

The braziers in the distant shantytown started to go out, the buildings slipping quickly into darkness. In the span of a few heartbeats the darkness swallowed the buildings and crept up the steep road, moving like a surging beast straight towards him.

Thorben turned and pushed up the stairs, his hands crawling out to either side to find the walls. He fumbled up half-a-dozen stairs one at a time – the risers short and obviously designed for dwarf legs – before taking two, and then three at a time.

The darkness closed in, the small amount of light flickering in from the passage behind dwindling with every step forward. Then it was gone. Thorben fumbled up the steps, his numb and tired legs jerking ungainly in the act, his boots missing steps as frequently as he found them.

"It's just darkness. It is just darkness. It cannot hurt you. They won't come. They won't come," he mumbled, but his reassurance didn't help. In the quiet between loud breaths Thorben could hear Jez somewhere ahead, her boots scraping against the stone, her gasping, desperate noises amplified in the tight space.

A light appeared ahead and above – not a torch, but faintly green. It was Myrddin, the ghostly dweorg waiting for him at the very top of the stairs. He was waving, encouraging him forward. Thorben staggered up another chunk of steps but had to look down, the distant light making the climb even more cumbersome.

A noise echoed from the stairs behind him, and he tried to ignore it, dedicating all of his focus to finding the next step and hauling his body forward. But it was there, audible even over the ringing in his ears and his raging heartbeat. The beasts wouldn't come for him. They were preoccupied...busy.

You're meat, and predators won't pass on an opportunity to feed. Of course they are coming for you.

Scritch scratch...scritch scratch.

"It's nothing...it's nothing. Just move faster. You're almost there. Just move faster."

The numbness crept up into his thighs and hips, the act of climbing beyond tiresome, beyond the familiar burn of fatigue. He refused to stop. *Find a step – push. Find a step – push.*

Myrddin grew closer, the dweorg's hand sweeping violently through the air, as if Thorben was caught in a current and he was trying to pull him along. The dwarf's light just made the darkness around him feel deeper, the distance between them emptier – a void his body refused to cross.

"Yer almost out. Faster. Faster," Myrddin called, his ghostly voice not echoing in the space.

Thorben fell forward and clawed his way up step by step, but he couldn't tell how many steps lay between him and the exit. The passage was featureless and black between him and the glowing dwarf, a terrified, animal part of his brain telling him that he would melt into the stone, the darkness, at any moment.

The scratching grew louder behind him, closer. He hobbled up two more steps as something brushed against the back of his left leg.

No! Thorben jumped, failing to swallow down a terrified cry.

Scritch scratch. Scritch scratch.

He kicked, the exhausted muscles barely flipping his foot forward and onto the next step. He hauled himself up, pushing against the stone walls, moving for the next step as something clamped around his left ankle.

"Myrddin!" Thorben cried out as he tipped forward, almost kissing the stone. He kicked free, his boot connecting with something solid. A grunt followed and the pressure released on his leg. He clawed forward, managing another step, then two. Myrddin was there, a dozen paces away, his greenish glow bathing the steps between them in a faint light.

"Fight! Climb! I can't pull you out. I've awakened the gate and am ready to close it, but I can't help you, too. I haven't the strength for both. Hurry!"

Claws bit into the back of his leg and he flopped, missing the next step. His shins banged against the hard stone, his balance tipping and sliding back. Thorben fell down several steps, kicking to no avail. He rolled over, strong, clammy hands crawling up his legs, pulling him down...down and into the darkness.

"No! No! No!" he fought, the bag of relics flopping at his belt and rattling against the stone. The horror appeared, pallid, gray flesh gleaming in the dim light, blood and pulpy meat spattered over its face, mouth gnashing, exposing jagged, yellow teeth and a black, flicking tongue. Its eyes shone black and unblinking as it clawed at him, pulling at his arms and snapping, fighting to pull his neck to its mouth.

"No," he fought and pushed, hooking the creature under the jaw with a hand, struggling with all of his strength to hold the gnashing teeth at bay. The dreygur's neck shifted and popped, elongating in his grasp, the head creeping closer, its mouth snapping snapping snapping. He grunted and kicked, pushing the beast back a little, but another of the creatures clawed at his feet, another beyond that fighting to pull itself over top of the others. They were a snarling, clicking, slathering mass, filling the tight stairwell, fighting each other to tear him apart, to devour him.

Thorben slapped his bag, but his knife was gone. Iona had taken it. His arm started to shake, the dreygur's weight increasing as the other beasts crawled atop it, pushing its snapping teeth closer to his neck.

His hand fumbled over the bag of relics, the flap popping open all on its own. He jammed his fingers inside, hoping desperately that something, anything could help. Metal clinked and rattled together, and he felt something soft, like leather, but then his fingers brushed against something smooth and cool. It vibrated, humming with untold destructive potential.

Thorben wrapped his fingers around it and pulled, relics rattled onto the stone as the hammer pulled free. Its glossy metal shone even in Myrddin's distant glow, its handle vibrating, quietly begging him to bring it to bear.

Trapped in such close proximity, Thorben swung the hammer up into the dreygur's face. The creature snapped back, but tipped forward once again, snapping and snarling with even more fervor.

Thorben hit it again and again, but he couldn't generate any swing or power. His mind filled with the memory of Gor's destructive display in the shantytown – the noise, dust, and debris – the unimaginable violence needed to tear through solid rock.

They're dwarves...their tools would be for working the rock. His arm started to give out, just as Thorben flipped the hammer around and swung it against the opposite wall.

He registered the impact, a bright flash burning in his vision. The exploding stone pushed him violently against the wall, smoke choking him, dust and grit filling his eyes. His head rang, and he tried to speak, felt his mouth moving, but couldn't hear the words. It was another few moments before he made sense of anything.

Thorben rolled over, coughing silently. He crawled up a step, fighting to regain control of his senses. Everything was white, but a black ring developed on the edges, slowly, painfully closing in. He could see again, but barely, and turned down the descending stair. A fist-sized chunk of the passage to his left was gone, dust and debris still falling from the hole.

A mass of twisted, tangled bodies churned just down from him, their pale flesh pocked with dozens of bleeding wounds, shards of fragmented rock still lodged in place.

Thorben untangled his limbs and pushed towards the light, Myrddin's arms waving at him, his lips moving. He understood what he wanted, even if he couldn't hear his words.

The dweorg was a dozen paces away, and then closer. Thorben turned as the dreygur untangled and came forward. He shielded his face and swung the hammer down into the ground. The head hit a smooth stair, the hammer ringing against his palm. He felt the ground shake, the dust and shattered pieces of rock hitting his shins and arms, but managed to protect his eyes this time.

Thorben shoved his body up another step, and then another, coughing and sputtering. The ringing in his ears started to subside, the beasts' shrieks and cries rising up in a bone-chilling chorus. The first hammer blow had wounded them, stunned them even, but they were still coming. They would never stop coming.

He managed to get his feet under him and kicked upwards. He could see the stairs now, Myrddin's light bathing the top of the stairwell with his glow.

Step – push.

He was just paces away, his hands scrabbling against the smooth stone, clawing and searching for a hold...anything he could use to pull himself the rest of the way.

Step – push.

He was trapped in a nightmare, his legs refusing to move him, to propel him away from the horror, but this wasn't a dream. Thorben clawed at the air just as the dwarf jumped back. His hand hit something solid – warm and soft. Jez was there, in the opening, both hands wrapped around his. She pulled and he moved, the last length of stairs passing beneath, no floating, beneath him.

The world seemed to tip forward and his balance shifted, Thorben almost falling over the last step. They were moving, running, bouncing off hard walls, an impossibly bright light just ahead. He shielded his eyes but Jez wouldn't let him stop. She pulled on his arm, wrenching him through a wide archway.

Thorben caught sight of Myrddin straight ahead, the dweorg standing at the podium, his hands hovering over the three keys, the wooden barrels glowing warmly. He looked back to find the shiny gate descending, thick metal bars dropping over the dark passage, but it was moving slow. Pale things moving beyond the gate, and Thorben pushed to his feet, holding the hammer ready.

"They're coming. Faster! Faster!" he yelled, although he could barely hear his own voice. He screamed it again and again, falling back. The monsters were coming, but they staggered and clawed at something. Still, the door was closing too slowly. They would slip through. They would get out.

Thorben half turned. It was the light from the broken door. It was painful to him. To them it must have been excruciating. He crossed the distance in a few painful steps and swung the hammer. The first strike vibrated up his arm, a small crack forming along the remaining door. The stone was beyond solid – imbued with some form of magic.

He swung the hammer again and again, using his whole body in every strike. Finally, the slab shook and fell away, a deluge of blinding light spilling over him.

Thorben spun, holding an arm up to shield his eyes. The sunlight hit the gleaming gate, but he squinted through the glare. The dreygur were there – blurry, pale figures shrieking and jumping around, writhing like butter in a hot skillet, but then they were gone, streaking back into the dark. He dropped to his knees, letting the hammer fall to the ground and watched the gate crash against the ground.

Chapter Twenty-Two

Reborn to the Sun

Thorben sat in the sun for what felt like days, the warmth on his skin the most wonderful thing he'd ever felt. His eyes eventually adjusted to the bright light streaming through the widened door, the entrance chamber dimming, while the cursed passage beyond the gate slipped into inky shadows.

He found Jez collapsed on the ground not far away, her back turned to the gate. She opened her eyes and caught his gaze, but didn't speak. A moment later she turned away, and stared at the open door. She sniffed, making an obvious effort to hide her tears, but Thorben pretended not to notice. She'd earned them, and so much more.

They stayed there until the sun grew dim, the shadows in the chamber lengthening dramatically. Thorben stretched his legs, cursing the pain, and despite his desire to stay on the ground and rest, he stood. He went outside and gathered some wood and kindling, the river providing a wealth of dried flotsam washed up from higher tides.

Thorben built a fire in the middle of the chamber and pulled his bag open. He lit the fire with his broken flint and steel, and sat down to rifle through everything else. Jez appeared quietly at the fireside, neither speaking nor appearing with any fanfare. He let her sit in silence, understanding all too well the grief she was struggling to process. Nothing he could say would bring her father back, so there was nothing for him to say.

He drew out his change of clothes, the shirt and trousers rumpled but mostly dry. Thorben pulled his tattered shirt off and tossed it onto the fire, before pulling on the cleaner one. He reached back in the bag, found something slender shoved in the corner, and pulled it out.

"It was hers...my Lynheid's. She gave it to me that day...the last one, when her ma took her away for the last time," Myrddin said. The dweorg sat next to him, his short legs crossed together, the tip of his beard resting in his lap.

Thorben held the brush up in the firelight. It was silver and highly polished, although heavily worn in spots. An intricate pattern adorned the back - a beautiful, spiraling flower. He turned it sideways, appreciating the magnificent craftsmanship.

"I crafted that with my own two hands...smelted the silver, carved the casting, and sang the metal into shape. It was one of the few things her ma let me give her. A Stonesinger's duty is to their people, you see. We weren't banned from having families, but it was discouraged. Our life was one of sacrifice and service. I weren't much of a father, because of it, weren't never around to be one. When I was, I was distracted...always thought that I would have time to give the child what she needed later. We were at war, after all. I thought I would have time to be a father after the fighting stopped, but then it did, and more responsibilities came. And more. And then more. I kept putting her off until there was no more time. Then she was gone." Myrddin gazed at the fire, his voice even hollower than usual.

"I will go to Braakdell and deliver these, as you've asked," Thorben said, lifting the necklace away from his chest.

"Hmm?" Jez asked, lifting her head groggily off the ground.

"I was just, well..." he said, but handed the brush over for her to see. She accepted it, her dark eyes roaming over the shiny metal, but then looked up, and cursed.

Myrddin looked from Thorben, to the girl, and back. "Can she see me now?"

"I-I-I can hear you, too," Jez stammered. Her eyes flitted to the brush and back across the fire, to the glowing dwarf.

"Jez, this is Myrddin. Myrddin, this is Jez."

"Hello, it is nice to meet you, finally," Jez said, and the dweorg nodded his head in response, his bushy beard split in an uncharacteristic smile.

Jez turned to Thorben and said, "I thought you were, well..."

"Crazy," Thorben finished for her, and she nodded.

They talked quietly together for a long while after that, Jez and Thorben chewing on strips of salted meat and hard, stale bread. They refused to look at the gate as they talked, for more than once he swore he saw the firelight glimmer off an eye in the darkness or a pale streak of darting skin. He didn't hear anything moving, but now that he'd experienced the dreygur terror in the deep dark, he knew better.

The night passed quietly, Thorben fighting sleep and the dreams he knew would come. He peeled his body off the stone at the first sign of dawn, scooped the magnificent hammer up and stowed it securely in his bag. Gor's relic bag flopped around on his belt as he turned towards Jez. He'd forgotten all about it.

Thorben lifted the leather satchel, his hand passing clean through the opening in the top to a hole torn in the bottom. Every valuable the three guildsmen had found was gone, scattered on the dark stair, locked firmly behind the stout gate, and guarded by hungry terrors. The emptiness inside him deepened. He would leave empty handed.

At least I have my life, he thought, and for the first time looked to his left, and the pile of dead men. Iona had lured them there under the same pretenses as him, or similar enough – wealth, acclaim, the forgiveness of a debt, or maybe the removal of a brand – and they all died for it. He looked over to Jez, her dark eyes searching his face for a moment before she too looked over to the dead men.

The girl watched him silently as he worked to pull the dead men off the pile and drag them outside. She followed, her arms crossed defensively over her chest, and stood out of the way as he went back inside and, one by one, pulled the delvers outside, through the short maze, and lay them on the sandy riverbank.

"It doesn't feel right leaving them in there, jumbled together...not when we made it out," Thorben said, straightening after depositing the last man in the line. He brushed his hands off, Jez taking a tentative step forward.

"W-w-what are you to do with them?"

He looked over the men for a moment, and although he knew what he wanted to do, he struggled with how to say it. In the end, he decided on honesty.

"I don't have a shovel to bury them, proper, but we can honor them in the old tradition of my wife's people, back when Yarborough was built around the King's Way Bridge. 'We came from the waters and in death, are returned', as they used to say. Her mother, grandmother, and great-grandmother would give their passed loved ones to the river, believing the current would carry their spirits to the afterlife," he explained.

Thorben pulled the first man down to the water's edge. "Mani, take this man into your keeping and cleanse him in your waters," he said, quietly, and pushed him into the current. He watched the dead man bob beneath the surface for a moment, the swift current pulling him down river before he reappeared, floating like a piece of driftwood.

Thorben returned to the next man in line and found Jez waiting. He stooped over and started to pull him along, only to have Jez join in and help. They stood above him at the water's edge – a balding fellow a few thaws older than Thorben – reciting a brief prayer, and gave him to the water, too.

Jez caught him by the arm as he turned back to the others, the girl's eyes large and wet with tears.

"Are they...are they why he did it? Why he..." she couldn't say it, and Thorben couldn't blame her. She'd watched her father die. No, she watched her father give his life so she could live. He knew that she was thinking about that very thing, trying to rationalize it, and like he, struggling with the guilt and inadequacy it left in its wake.

"A good father will do almost anything to keep his children safe," Thorben said, finally, the words resonating deep inside. Jez sniffled and wiped at her face.

"Your father might not have been perfect, but he was here for you and your brother. There is honor in that...a nobility, of accepting one's flaws, but more so in trying to rise above them to provide a better, safer life." He was talking about Iona, but Thorben realized that he was talking about himself, too. He'd been thinking about it since the previous night, when Myrddin told him the sad tale of his daughter. Yes, he had to return home with empty pockets and nothing to show for his time, but he got to go home. That, in itself, felt like a small treasure, although he wasn't sure Dennica would completely agree. He'd taken what little coin they had, and had nothing to show for it.

Thorben knew he had much to answer for, and even more to work towards. He would work twice, no, three times harder to earn a wage for his family – chop firewood, barter, and labor to keep them fed and safe, but he would do it...and without complaint.

"I miss him," Jez said, sniffling. Thorben wrapped an arm around her shoulder and pulled her close.

"I know," he said, patting her back as her tears finally flowed. She cried for a long time, falling into violent fits where she could barely breathe, only to relax and almost fall to the ground, her voice weak and trembling.

Thorben held her through it all, patting her back and smoothing her hair. His own tears flowed, despite his best efforts to hold them back. He mourned Iona and Renlo, despite their parts in the whole ordeal. He'd struggled through enough of life's harsh realities to understand how easy it was to start down the wrong path, each bend and fork in the road leading you further from where you wanted to go or who you wanted to be.

He was alive, but felt diminished for it, the two men's sacrifices dimming the sun and lengthening the shadows. Thorben decided that he would honor them, in his way. He wasn't sure what that was yet, but knew it would come to him in time.

After Jez's tears finished, she helped him pull the rest of the dead men to the river. Thorben silently searched them with his eyes before giving them to the water. Some quiet part of him hoped for a sparkle of gold or silver, a necklace or gem-encrusted ring...anything he could barter for coin on his way back through the boroughs, but it appeared Gor and the others had picked them over already.

They got to the last man – the youngest by far, his brown hair short and unruly, his cheeks peppered with pock scars, freckles, and blood. His eyes were open, light brown, empty and staring, but hazy.

"I must reconcile with ye," Myrddin said suddenly, Thorben jumping from the sudden noise. The dwarf appeared from behind a river tree, its narrow trunk bent out over the water.

Jez looked to him, but then pulled the brush out of her belt, and turned to consider the dweorg.

"I cursed you down there, when ye tried to open that crypt. I said, and felt, much anger towards ye. I even started to hope that you wouldn't make it out of there. Then I saw that beast of a man. He would have killed you all."

"Yes, he would have," Thorben nodded, and looked up. The dwarf's eyes were different, and it took him a moment to register why. They weren't just dark, hollow holes anymore, but eyes, light and brimming with emotion. Myrddin looked to Jez for a moment before continuing.

"You carried forth my Lynheid's necklace," the ancient dwarf said, Thorben involuntarily reaching up and touching the mass of charms and necklaces. "But now I see you tending to these poor souls, where almost any other folk would have left them back in that chamber to rot. You honor them, like I did to my dead long ago. You've earned the respect of this old Stonesinger."

"It just seems like the decent thing to do, after everything that happened."

Thorben bent down to move the last man into the river. His threadbare, worn shirt pulled up, exposing his pale belly. The top of a small bag stuck out from the waistband of his pants, the leather drawstring catching the light.

His fingers twitched towards the coin purse, but looked to Jez, then Myrddin. He flinched, pulling his hand back, waiting for the harsh glare, the admonishment. There was no hulking, sword-toting brute behind him this time, only a dark, gurgling river. Pulling relics from the tomb of long-dead folk at spear point was one thing, but lifting the coin purse from dead men felt wrong.

"What are you waiting for? Take it!" Jez said.

"It feels wrong...especially after everything we just went through."

"He can't spend that coin in the afterlife, and the fish in the river definitely don't need it. You need the money...for your family," Jez said and reached down, pulling the coin purse free. She shook it and held it out.

Thorben looked away from her for a minute, but caught Myrddin's gaze. The dwarf nodded his head towards the offered sack.

"You didn't kill that man. You don't even know who he is. If his coin can feed your family and keep your children warm, then I don't know a man, god, or dwarf who would condemn you for taking it."

Thorben hesitantly reached out and took the purse, immediately surprised by its heft. He squeezed it, and slowly loosened the drawstring. The morning sun slipped into the bag, glimmering off copper and silver. Thorben tipped it over into his palm and let the coins spill out. A fair share of copper coins, strikingly similar to Gor's, fell out first, followed by a mass of silver. Thorben shook the bag to dislodge the rest, only to see a small pile of gleaming gold fall onto the top of the pile.

There was more coin in that purse than Thorben had ever had at one time, truth be told - more than the taxman had taken for the past four thaws combined.

Thorben numbly dumped the coin back into the sack and securely tied it to his belt. He cleared his throat, and managed to croak out a short prayer. Then they eased the last delver into the water and silently watched him float away.

They collected what little they could salvage after that and departed, deciding to follow the riverbank south, instead of braving the deep river crossing and dangerous climb to the north. Jez led and they spent the morning and early afternoon navigating around rocky banks and narrow sandbars. They camped for the night in a recessed cove. They managed to catch a fish and start a fire, all with some thread from his old shirt, a broken wire from the handle of his ruined rock hammer, and some salted meat.

They ate quietly and settled in for the night, an unanswered question hanging between them. Jez didn't appear to know how to ask it, and he wasn't in any mood to hurry her.

Thorben lay propped against a mossy log, the river bubbling and gurgling away nearby. He watched the sky long after Jez fell asleep, the moon and stars hanging peacefully in the inky black. He dropped his gaze and watched the girl for a while, troubling over what he could do for her.

He awoke at sunrise, but thankfully didn't remember any of his dreams. They spent the next morning following the river, the rocky bluffs eventually giving way to narrower slopes and several branching tributaries. Thorben led them across a narrow spot, the water still making him nervous, but not so much that he lost his wits.

A quick climb brought them out of the river valley, where they immediately stumbled onto a camped group of soldiers. Thorben stopped, and for a moment considered dropping back down the slope, but then realized how guilty that would make him look.

He gave Jez's arm a reassuring squeeze and guided them forward, putting on the most welcoming smile he could summon. He glanced to the east and noticed another small camp on the other side of the river. Soldiers walked up the ridge above the river valley as well, tromping north. Had he not seen them? Or were they just lucky?

They were a dozen paces away from the camp before a soldier looked up from the fire. Thorben threw him a friendly wave, Jez following his lead. The young man jumped up from his seat, armor and scabbard rattling loudly.

"You, stop right there!"

"Yes, sir," Thorben said, fighting to keep his smile in place.

"What were you doing down there? This river is off limits by the Council's decree."

Several other soldiers took notice and walked over, standing just behind the first man.

"Off limits?" Thorben asked, trying hard to look confused.

"Signs are posted. Only a blind man could miss 'em."

"Well, my apologies. My, uh, well, my young niece and I were passing through on our way to see some relatives to the east. We came upon the river to the south, had worked up a hunger with our walking, and I decided to try my hand at catching something to eat." Thorben held up the thread and crude hook. "I didn't have much luck, I'll tell you that much," he said, laughing. "Instead of tromping back down through the swampy land, we found this nice little hill and came out here. Just a little stop and back on the road."

"They look like a couple lakers, heh? Grimy lakers," one of the other soldiers said, elbowing the man next to him.

"Fishing, eh?" the young man asked, his eyes crawling up from Thorben's boots. The other soldiers shuffled in a little closer.

He realized how bad he must look – dirty, battered, exhausted. A quick glance to Jez confirmed that she looked no better. They looked like vagabonds. Certain bloodlines splintered off many thaws before, fracturing families between the lakes of Karnell and the Boroughs. Thorben knew that some families still carried bad blood over the division.

"Council's edict says no one is allowed near the blood mound burials. This river valley leads right by it. Are you telling me you don't know that?"

Thorben shook his head and turned to look back up the river valley, even more soldiers taking notice and starting to move their way. His hands grew clammy, the dwarven hammer a touch heavier in his bag. He reached down and subconsciously fumbled with his sleeve, pulling it down well past his branded wrist.

"Edict also says that trespassers are to be taken and questioned. Repeat offenders are jailed."

Thorben knew he would be in trouble if they decided to search him and found the brand. Once that happened he would be guilty in their eyes.

"Why don't you just come with us, our captain will want to ask you some questions," the young man said, and reached to lead him forward.

Thorben's gaze caught on an emblem embossed on the man's black armor – a fearsome fish holding cross spears in its mouth.

"Wait, are you boys with the River Watch?"

The young man stopped and nodded.

"My oldest son is set to take his trials soon in Klydesborough. He's wanted to be a river watchman since he was knee-high," Thorben said, proudly, a genuine smile taking shape. His insides warmed at the thought of Paul.

"I did my own trials there, too. Tell him to be mindful of the water trial. Proctor Barnhardt gives the young men who suck up to him the best canoes."

"...the water trial means slag. Does he have his own bow for the archery trial? The bows they give out are crap," another of the young men said, chiming in loudly.

"I remember. My bow string broke on my second to last arrow...lowered my score by two points."

"The trial of knowledge is the hardest," a third young man chimed in, "tell him to keep his wits in his head and his britches dry. That's the key. They'll drill him on every bit of knowledge that seems needed, but it's not the answers they're after, but in how he responds."

The young soldier nodded in agreement and turned back to Thorben. "So you're from the Boroughs then?"

"Born and bred in Yarborough. My wife's family has lived there since the King's Way Bridge still stood. We've booted hills dirt in our blood."

The young men went silent, although Thorben swore they looked more at ease. They quietly ushered them forward through the camp, moving through a small field, and finally to a narrow, well-used road. A sign pointed off to the right, towards Braakdell and the lakes, and another to the left, to home. They paused on the roadside as a patrol passed by. A tent stood on the other side of the road, the black fabric richly embroidered with the River Watch fish and spears. It was a tent fit for a commander, a man of station.

Thorben's belly flopped over as the young men pulled them out into the roadway. The young soldier stopped halfway across, the others circling around them. He looked to each of them in turn, confusion turning to panic.

"If your son has booted hills dirt in his blood, he'll pass those trials for sure. But just in case, give him my luck, and tell him Proctor Barnhardt is a sucker for sweets, especially maple candies. Now go on, and be careful, the roads are dangerous lately," the young soldier said, and nodded his head down the road.

"Thank you. Maple candies," Thorben said, reaching out and clasping the young man's hand.

They turned and made off down the road, but stopped when the young soldier called after them.

"And tell your son to be mindful of a posting in Pinehall, eh. The women there have an eye for River Watchmen, and more than a few brothers have come home to surprise family with a woman and child in tow."

"Wise advice," Thorben called back and waved.

"How did you know how to..." Jez asked after they'd walked a fair distance down the road.

"When the young man called us 'lakers' I knew. There were some families that broke apart many, many thaws ago. Some settled in the boroughs and others in the lakes. It's a river folk and lake folk thing, I guess. One doesn't always like the other. As soon as he called us that I hoped that they would warm to us if they knew we were from the hills. It helps that Paul is preparing for his trials. The River Watch is a brotherhood, after all."

They made good time on the roadway, hard-packed dirt allowing for faster walking. Myrddin appeared and disappeared regularly, but his stays grew shorter and shorter, until the ghostly dweorg vanished right in the middle of a conversation. It was odd, too, as he could tell the dwarf wasn't necessarily aware of the gaps in time. Thorben tried to hide his alarm when Myrddin would disappear or randomly pop in. Jez watched him suspiciously, but he could only shake his head.

He could feel the magic in the ring, the power binding him to the dwarf, losing its strength. The band wasn't quite so tightly bound to his finger. In fact, he could wiggle it back and forth.

A crossroads appeared that evening, signaling a turn north or south. Yarborough was just a decent walk north. It would be late and dark, but he would finally be home.

They'd barely started on the northern path before Jez cleared her throat, her gaze stuck on the ground at her feet.

"About what my father said...what he asked, and well, where I am supposed to go. Did you mean it, when you said that you would help find my brother, that you would help us?"

Thorben took a deep breath. He'd been preparing for this question since they left the crypt.

"Yes, I meant what I said," he said, still struggling with what that actually meant. He'd been pulled into this entire ordeal because of his struggles, and was about to willingly take on more responsibility, more mouths to feed. "You can stay with us. My wife will take a bit of convincing, but leave that to me."

"And my brother? He isn't safe with her," Jez said, her dark eyes locked on him.

Thorben nodded, taking note that the girl wouldn't even refer to her mother by name.

What kind of mother could affect a child so? Dennica is going to kill me.

They both grew tired and stopped after sundown, and thanks to a bright, full moon decided to walk the rest of the way in the dark. The house was dark and quiet when he turned down the lane. Thorben stood on the edge of the gardens, apprehensive to approach his own home. He felt awkward, after leaving the way he did – in the middle of the night.

Thorben let Jez in through the kitchens, an old fire burned down to coals in the oven. The house was dark, quiet, a beam creaking gently somewhere in the next room. He made up a bed for Jez in the sitting room before the fireplace and retreated to kitchen, where he lit a single candle and sat down to think.

Chapter Twenty-Three

Broken but Whole

Thorben sat at Dennica's chopping table for the better part of the night, watching the candle burn and considering what he would tell his wife, but also, how. He chewed over it again and again, fighting between the notion of telling a lie, and unburdening his own conscience and telling the truth, and then accepting whatever hell his wife threw his way.

Whatever it is, I will deserve it, he thought.

The wind whistled and rattled through the trees outside, a mouse scurried somewhere beneath a floorboard, and the house breathed and shifted, creaking and groaning in familiar ways. And yet, it felt unfamiliar at the same time.

Whether he was willing to admit it, the crypt changed him. He felt uncomfortable with the darkness, the subtle sounds that filled the quiet moments. Everything beyond the flickering candle flame was danger, the shadows hiding dangers his eyes could not see, but his mind knew were there. Thorben fought sleep for fear of that darkness, but also because he knew his dreams would find him eventually.

His eyes drooped and his head became heavy in his hands, but a gentle, green light suddenly filled the dark corners. Thorben turned to find Myrddin standing next to the small table, the dwarf looking out of place amongst the tall furniture.

"I feel it now," the dweorg said, a subtle wrinkle pulling at his mouth. His beard twitched and he stepped up to the table.

"Feel? What do you feel?"

"I am slipping...back to the ring's emptiness. I didn't notice it before, but now...now I remember it from the long-ago time. The magic in that ring is strong, but no power can last forever. I don't ken how much longer I'll be able to come to ye."

"Is it where you were before I found the ring?"

Myrddin shrugged, licking his lips. The jeweled studs in his face glimmered briefly, like twinkling stars in a night sky. "How am I to ken for sure? I remember wandering the tombs for a time, swallowing that infernal ring, and laying my head down. Then I was awake again, and I was with you."

Myrddin's form shimmered for a heartbeat, his glow losing a bit of its luster.

"What do I need to do?" Thorben asked.

"I don't ken, Thorben long legs. I was a Stonesinger me whole life. That ring is dalan crafted, its magic strange and unknown to me. I have to go back to the dark place now. I'm not sure how much longer I can keep coming back. Please, promise me again that you'll take my Lynheid's gift to Braakdell. I need to hear you say it again, before I go back there, before I start losing myself again."

There was sadness in the dweorg's eyes, and Thorben felt it keenly. He could only imagine the short man's pain – of being separated from his child, and locked in a prison of darkness and death, the fading memory of loved ones as the only solace.

"I promise, Myrddin. I will take it there myself. And I will take this with me, so you can see her for yourself," he replied and pointed to the gently glowing ring on his finger.

"Thank you..." the dwarf responded, but faded away before he could finish.

Pre-dawn warmed the sky not long after, the earliest light shining in through the small kitchen window. Thorben opened up the top half of the door, cool, early morning breeze and bird song washing over him. He stood there for a long while, relishing in the sweet-smelling air and the calming sounds as the world woke up around him. It all felt and sounded so alive, a stark and welcome contrast to everything he'd lived through recently.

"So you trek off in the dead of night, like some man with a shame, leaving only a note. I think you run off on me and your children, only to wake gods' only know how many sunrises later to find you shadowing the kitchen door...looking like, well, a man thinking about running right back out that door," Dennica said, her voice sleepy but sharp.

Her words cut into him, and Thorben accepted the sting. He deserved every...single...one, and so much more.

Thorben turned to find his wife standing in the doorway, her hair a tangled mess and her heavily worn nightgown rumpled. She looked him over and stepped forward, a hand sliding up to her mouth.

"Here, please sit. I will make you some tea and then we will talk," Thorben said, and gently guided her over to sit down. She didn't argue and watched as he made a fire and hung the kettle. He set the tea to steep, finally setting a steaming mug in front of her on the table.

Dennica picked up the mug, blew on it for a moment, and took a sip. She reached up to tuck a few strands of hair out of the way, and took a deep breath.

"I didn't accompany a caravan south to Ogre Springs. I was approached by someone the day I went to Lamtrop's, a man from my past, who made me an offer only a fool would accept. I left in the night because I knew you would talk me out of it." Thorben took a breath, allowing his wife an opportunity to soak it in and respond.

Dennica reached up and rubbed her left eye, glanced out the door, and slowly sipped her tea. She didn't slam the cup down, smack the table, or start yelling.

"And the girl slumbering away on the floor in the other room?" she asked, her voice a bit unsteady.

She was mad, Thorben could tell that much. He took a healthy drink of his tea and proceeded to tell her everything, every detail, small and large. He didn't gloss anything over, or lie. The truth was hard in the retelling, like slowly spitting out rotten bits of his insides. When he finished, Dennica finished her tea, wiped her mouth on a sleeve and scratched her left eye again.

"Coin isn't all our family needs..."

"It wasn't just coin, my love," Thorben said, "Iona told me that he knew a cleric, powerfully gifted in the healing arts, and if I delved for him this one time, he would have her remove my brand. This was my chance to wash this shame away, and finally, be the good and honest man that you deserve." He felt tears welling up, the shame bubbling forth.

A tear appeared in Dennica's eyes, and she shook, fighting visibly to hold them back. "Damn you, Thorben Paulson. How many times have I got to tell you that it doesn't matter to us? That scar on your wrist isn't who you are to us. You've been a good husband to me, and raised seven honest children. We've done all that together, and we can continue to do it together..."

"It's not, though. The children don't know about my brand. I've kept it covered all this time, but can't keep it from everyone out there. They know, and to them, this," he said, and ripped the shirtsleeve up, "is all I am, and all I will ever be."

Dennica swallowed hard and put her fingers to her lips.

"This was my risk...my chance to wipe my slate clear, and maybe for once, make it so we didn't have to scrape along for everything. Maybe for once, we could sit back and prosper."

"Why could you not tell me at least...be stubborn and insist on going, but at least tell me? I'm your wife and deserve at least that."

"Because I am a coward and a fool."

"Aye, you're a fool, a daft fool, but you are no coward, Thorben. Yes, you've made bad decisions, and you've paid for them time and again. But you're one of the bravest men I know...if not thick in the head."

"Pa!" a scream sounded from just beyond the doorway. Dennah appeared, streaking into the kitchen and about knocking him over.

The girl squeezed him tight, her hands and legs hooked clear around his body. The pressure hurt, but Thorben didn't fight or push her away. He squeezed her right back, pulling her close so he could kiss her cheek.

"Where'd you go, pa? Where'd you go?"

"I...went on a little trip. I'll tell you all about it later, Pebble."

"Hey, pa, you want me to help you chop firewood later?"

"Sure, Pebble. We'll chop a whole load together."

"I'm gonna go wake up the boys and tell 'em pa is home. I'm gonna jump on 'em," Dennah said, flashed Dennica an excited smile, and ran out of the room.

"And what of the girl?" Dennica asked.

"We'll be taking her in for a while. Her father, Iona...he's the reason why I made it out. He asked me to look after the girl, right before..."

"Another belly to fill. Thorben, we don't have enough food to fill our mouths. How will we make it through the winter?"

He reached across the table and pulled her hand out, dropping the bulging coin sack into her palm before she could pull away. Dennica met his gaze, squeezed the bag, tested its weight, and then reached down and slowly pulled it open.

"Mani's mercy! There's..."

"Enough to stock our cellar and pantry for the winter, buy Paul a new bow and take him to Klydesborough for his trials, and buy planting seed for next season."

"A new dress," Dennica said.

Thorben looked at her for a moment.

"There are three things I need from you before I'll even consider forgiving you for all of this. First, you get down on your knee right here in this kitchen, before me, and before your beloved goddess, and promise me that you will never run off like that again – that you will not keep me in the dark." She eyed him expectantly, her mouth pulling tight.

Thorben pushed away from the table and dropped painfully to a knee.

"I swear to you that I will trust in you, and share all things."

"Good, because if you do, I won't let you back into this house. Next, I want you to tell the children the truth. Tell them about your brand."

Thorben winced, the demand slapping across him like a hot lash. It was the thing he'd feared more than anything, save for death, his entire adult life. He wasn't sure if he could stomach the looks in their eyes, discovering that he was a wretch, a tainted man.

"I..."

"No!" Dennica scolded, cutting him off. "You have let that damned scar rule your life the entire time we've been wed. Tis your shame, husband. You cover it, loath, and fear it. Stop giving it power over you. Tell your family the truth. They'll still love you, and just maybe, you can stop hating yourself for a change."

Thorben looked down to his arm. He couldn't see the brand, but he could feel it as keenly as if a shackle and weight were clamped in its place. He swallowed and looked up, his wife's eye half-lidded and sharp, her head cocked at an angle.

It made his stomach knot up to admit it, but she was right. Thorben slowly stood, and nodded his head.

"Good, and third, I want a new dress."

"That sounds perfectly reasonable," he said.

"Good. If you can make good on those three things, I'll consider forgiving you. But for now, go wash up for breakfast. You stink. And you best decide what you want to tell our young ones about that young woman who's sleeping in the other room."

Thorben left and retreated to their room upstairs, where he slowly washed, favoring every nick and cut, scrape and bruise. The smell of cooking eggs drifted up from downstairs, a pain in his belly driving him to move faster. He pulled on some clean clothes and went back downstairs.

Kenrick, Reginald, Darro, Tymon, Henrick, and Paul all sat around the table, talking animatedly. He patted each on the shoulder as he moved around behind them.

Dennah sat in front of the door to the boys' small washroom, her attention fixed on the handle.

"What is Dennah doing?" he asked, walking into the kitchen.

"I sent that poor girl..."

"Jez," Thorben said.

"I sent her in there with a change of Darro's clothes, some water and soap. Dennah is beside herself that there is another girl in the house right now."

"I pity her when she comes out," Thorben said, and they shared a quiet laugh. It didn't last long, but it was a start. He knew it would take time to win her favor back. He would always have her love, fortunately, but her trust would take work.

They sat down and ate then, Jez squeezing in on the end between Dennica and Kenrick. Dennah sat across the table, watching eagerly. They ate – the clatter of dishes and silverware, tankards, and the boisterous conversation one of the most beautiful things he'd ever heard. Thorben savored it, eating slowly, listening and watching. Plates started to clear and the boys grew restless. Dennica gave him a look, and he knew it was time.

"Everyone, I have a few things I would like to say," he said, standing up and smacking his tankard against the table.

The conversations died away, Dennah and all six boys turning his way. Jez seemed to understand what would happen next and seemed to shrink in her chair.

"Everyone this is Jez..."

"Jezebel. I'm Jezebel," she said, suddenly.

Thorben smiled. "Jezebel is going to be staying with us. Her father and I were...close when we were younger. Unfortunately, he passed recently, so she is going to live with us. Jez...ebel," he stuttered, correcting himself. "This is Dennah, Paul, Darro, Reginald, Tymon, Henrick, Kenrick, and my wife, Dennica. Everyone welcome her to our home, please."

The room filled with noise as they all spoke at once, welcoming and shouting greetings across the table. Dennah slapped her palms down and hopped in her seat, barely containing her enthusiasm.

"There is something else I need to tell you," he said, and paused, rearranging his fork and knife next to his plate, allowing him a few extra moments to consider what he would say. And before he could lose his confidence, Thorben pulled his sleeve up and held it up for everyone to see. He told them all about his arrest for delving, his stay at the Council's prison mine, and what the brand meant. He didn't want to cry, but a single tear found its way down his cheek. One became two, and then more.

Thorben tried not to look at them all, at their eyes. He didn't want to see the disappointment, the disgust that he saw in everyone else. It was natural.

The room went quiet after he'd finished, but he refused to sit. He wanted to stand before them and accept any punishment, any anger they felt the need to throw his way. He was done hiding his brand. The silence stretched out for another couple long moments, and he reached up to wipe the tears away.

Paul pushed his chair back and stood, the other boys following suit. He watched them, terrified that they would leave in silence...that they would reject him. He could handle shouting and screaming, but the idea of angry silence and disappointment was unbearable.

The boys moved around the table, Paul reaching him first. His eldest didn't walk by, however. He wrapped his arms around him and pulled him into a suffocating hug.

"That brand isn't who you are, father. It is not who you are to us," Paul said, as the other boys crowded in, wrapping their arms around him.

"You're a good man, father. Always have been, always will be," Kenrick said, the other boys echoing similar sentiments.

Thorben squeezed them all in, his tears flowing and breath catching in his throat. They were crying, too, all of them. Dennah dove into their midst, pulling away arms and burrowing until she was at his legs. She hugged him and cried. He wasn't sure if she understood why, or if she was crying because everyone else was, but that didn't matter.

* * * *

Thorben spent the next moon cycle working his hands to the bone, helping Dennah chop firewood, rooting out the burrowing hedge rats, and restocking their cellar. He struggled sleeping at night, but found a single burning candle helped.

Dennica awoke often and asked him if anything was wrong, but he struggled telling her the real reason why he couldn't sleep. The dreygur haunted his dreams, the visions of pale, mottled flesh, torn bodies, and red blood not so easily banished from memory.

Thorben also found himself hovering before the windows, watching the lengthening shadows between trees. They celebrated Paul's name day with a raucous party, a goodly population of Yarborough's youths filling their yard to help his eldest celebrate. He noticed Kenrick and Jez spending more time together, the quiet young woman and his middle son taking long walks together, or climbing the old oak across the way to sit in the shade.

Dennah haunted the older girl's footsteps. He walked into the sitting room the night before they were to leave for Paul's trials and discovered the two girls whispering before the fire, taking turns playing with each other's hair. He stood in the doorway for a long while and watched, laughing quietly to himself.

They set out on wagons the next morning, carting the whole family through the boroughs. They stopped in Laneborough to buy treats. Thorben took Paul to a sweet shop and helped him pick out a gift to give his proctor. He pointed out the maple candies, and purchased a few extra for the ride back.

Klydesborough was a mass of street vendors, performers, and criers. They visited a fletcher's shop and purchased Paul a new bow and forearm guard. His eldest hugged him and cried a little when the fletcher strung the bow for him. Thorben cried a little, too. He wasn't ashamed of it anymore. It felt good to let his emotions show.

Thorben sat next to Dennica on the back of the Bear Claw River that afternoon, surrounded by his family. They watched Paul paddle quickly against the current. His canoe looked just a little more stable, glided just a little faster than the other young men. Thorben unwrapped a maple candy and handed it to his wife, chuckling quietly.

They cheered Paul on at the archery field, and then waited nervously outside the River Watch boathouse as he sat before the proctors for his trial of knowledge. Thorben fidgeted with the ring, noting that he could turn it all the way around now. Would it come off if he pulled on it? And if it did, what would happen to Myrddin?

"I did it! I did it!" Paul yelled, emerging through the door a short while later. His brothers crowded around, congratulating him. Thorben approached when they had all finished.

"Congratulations, son," he said, shaking his hand. "What next?"

"Training. They'll take us all the way down the Snake...all the way to the Crystal Waters. I won't know what my posting will be until I'm sworn in as a brother. I'm hoping for something close to home, but we'll see."

Thorben chatted with Paul for a while, both surprised and impressed with how grown up he sounded. His little boy, their first born, was a man. They treated Paul to a last meal, a fish boil on the beach, and all hugged him goodbye before he reported to the boat master to begin his training.

Dennica held a smile while he walked away, but broke into tears as soon as he was out of sight. He hugged her, and together they walked to the docks, Dennah, Jez, and the boys walking behind.

"Are you sure you have to do this now? Winter is so close. What happens to you if you get to Madus and a cold spell moves in?"

"Yes, I'm sure. And, no, I'll get there and back just fine. We haven't even had a frost yet. This is something I need to do now, or I feel I may never get the chance."

Dennica nodded, sniffled a bit, and wiped her eyes. He was being honest and open, just as she'd asked. She didn't necessarily like that he was leaving already, but she seemed to understand why.

Once at the docks, Thorben checked with the dock master about ships heading toward the lakes. The old man, salt-colored whiskers hanging down both sides of his mouth, pointed him to a slip several spaces down. They walked up to the large riverboat, its long oars stowed on deck and sticking straight up into the air.

"Hello?" Thorben called.

"Hello to you, sir," a gray-haired man called back, his head popping over the side rail of the pilothouse.

"The dock master said you were heading down river, towards the lakes. If that is the case, I would like to book passage for two."

"Aye. We're taking on cargo tonight and setting off at morning tide. I have a small cabin if you don't mind sharing."

"I think that sounds quite agreeable," Thorben said, and shook the seasoned captain's hand. He fished money out of his coin purse and dropped it in the man's hand.

"Welcome aboard the Kingfisher, sir. I'm Captain Tovy. Load up any time before tomorrow morning. Feel free to stay aboard tonight. If not, just make sure you're here before sun up morrow."

Thorben walked Dennica and the children back to the wagons, hugging each before loading them up onto the wagons.

"I won't be gone long," Thorben said, bending over to kiss his wife on the cheek.

"That's good, because I don't want my bed to get cold," she replied, throwing him a half wink. He watched the wagons rumble down the roadway, refusing to move from the spot until long after they'd disappeared around the last bend.

"Are you ready?" he turned and asked Jezebel.

"I think so. Are you?"

He nodded, and together they walked back to the docks, the city glowing to life as nighttime fell.

They walked down the dock and approached the Kingfisher. Thorben reached down and adjusted the ring on his finger. He looked up to find a ghostly dwarf standing on the prow of the ship, his gaze locked down the dark river.

About the Author

Aaron started his academic career in criminal justice, but eventually connected his life-long love of literature with his passion for writing. After finishing his debut novel, Within, he attended and graduated from Southern New Hampshire University with and Undergraduate degree in English and Creative Writing, with focus on Fiction. He released his first novel as *The Winter of Swords,* and is excited to release the next two volumes in the overthrown series, *Before the Crow,* and *A March of Woe,* in 2019. Aaron is also releasing *The Delving,* an all-new supplementary novel, helping to build the lore and world showcased in his six part fantasy series.

Besides writing, Aaron is constantly searching for a portal to Middle Earth, working to keep his two daughters from taking over the world, and supports his wife's desire to vacation in Skyrim. Check out his website www.aaronbunce.com for information on current books, series, as well as news on upcoming releases.